RULES OF JUSTICE

RULES OF JUSTICE

EXCEPTIONAL S. BEAUFONT™ BOOK 8

SARAH NOFFKE

MICHAEL ANDERLE

DISRUPTIVE IMAGINATION

Copyright © 2020 LMBPN Publishing
Cover by Mihaela Voicu http://www.mihaelavoicu.com/
Cover copyright © LMBPN Publishing
A Michael Anderle Production

LMBPN Publishing
PMB 196, 2540 South Maryland Pkwy
Las Vegas, NV 89109

First US Edition, August 2020
Version 1.01 June 2021
eBook ISBN: 978-1-64971-130-4
Print ISBN: 978-1-64971-131-1

THE RULES OF JUSTICE TEAM

Thanks to the JIT Readers

Angel LaVey
Dave Hicks
Deb Mader
Diane L. Smith
Dorothy Lloyd
Heidi Bauer
Jackey Hankard-Brodie
Kerry Mortimer
Paul Westman
Peter Manis
Veronica Stephan-Miller

If we've missed anyone, please let us know!

Editor
The Skyhunter Editing Team

For my first reader, Juergen.

— Sarah

To Family, Friends and
Those Who Love
to Read.
May We All Enjoy Grace
to Live the Life We Are
Called.

— Michael

CHAPTER ONE

The target skipped and sang down the cobbled road known as Roya Lane like an idiot rather than the grown man he was. King Rudolfus Sweetwater was notorious for being brainless, but watching him from the shadows, Nevin Gooseman saw firsthand how much of an imbecile he was.

Abducting him shouldn't be hard. Once Nevin had him in custody, then the dimwit would lead them to the Great Library, according to Lorenzo Rosario, a Councilor for the House of Fourteen. Lorenzo was a longtime resource who often gave Nevin the inside scoop on private matters.

Currently, the Great Library was closed, but someone like King Rudolfus could gain entry. Nevin needed that if he was going to find a spell to remove the shield on the evil dragons. Then his military forces could take the beasts down, once and for all.

No good came from allowing such awful creatures to prowl the Earth. The Dragon Elite was entirely too powerful. The mortal world didn't need to be governed by a magical organization. Even as a magician, Nevin knew that. The magical world was policed by the House of Fourteen. The mortal one should be governed by its own—with the exception of Nevin, who could oversee matters from public office.

Until Nevin could remove the shield from the evil dragons, he'd have to rely on other methods for discrediting the Dragon Elite. Several things were already in the works and would be such a blow to their reputation, Nevin was certain there would be no recovery for the dragonriders. Once the world saw how dangerous and lethal dragons were to mortals, they'd be begging him to get rid of the new population. His military forces were prepared to do just that.

Currently, the goons he'd hired to grab King Rudolfus were hiding on the other side of the Crying Cat Bakery, waiting for the fae to cross their path. He was so much in his own world, this wasn't going to be hard. If Nevin hadn't preferred not to get his hands dirty, he could have just done it himself, but he wasn't the muscle. He was always the brains, the instigator.

King Rudolfus was almost to the narrow alleyway that ran along the shabby bakery run by two looney women. Nevin didn't understand how such establishments were able to survive with their strange, eccentric style and disregard for orderly practices.

It was rumored the bakers used illegal magical ingredients and indulged in other questionable activities. However, because they were associated with the Dragon Elite and people like King Rudolf, they got away with their crimes, which angered Nevin to no end. Once he had time, he'd go after the bakery. Things in his jurisdiction were run *his* way, and everything was under his authority.

When the fae crossed the stretch of darkness by the alleyway, a pair of strong hands reached out and grabbed him. One covered King Rudolf's mouth, and another went around his chest, restraining his arms.

There would be no fighting the giant Nevin had hired. He was so much bigger and stronger than the puny fae.

Still, King Rudolfus put up a fight, and a muffled scream echoed in the deserted alleyway as he kicked and tried to resist. The giant picked King Rudolfus up and held him against his chest, squeezing him so tightly that Nevin spied his face flush red.

"Don't kill him," Nevin muttered into his earpiece, knowing the giant could hear him.

The barbarian nodded at once and let up on King Rudolf. The giant backed into the darkness of the alleyway where an illegal portal had been created that emptied straight into Nevin's secret headquarters. It was there he'd have the fae interrogated and find out how to get into the Great Library, and anything else of use the king might know. Nevin wasn't holding out much hope there would be a lot of useful information. It was unlikely King Rudolfus knew much of anything, but if he got them into the Great Library, that would be enough.

Breathing a sigh of relief, Nevin strode casually for the alleyway, intent on following the giant through the portal. He ducked into the dark passage just as the door to the Crying Cat Bakery swung open. A woman with short hair and a ruthless expression poked her head out.

"Rudolf?" she barked, looking back and forth as Nevin watched from the shadows, his back cemented against the brick wall. "Where is that damn man? Always late."

She shook her head and pursed her lips. "I could have sworn I heard that crazy-ass man singing."

"I told you that you were losing your mind and hearing things again," another woman called from inside.

"No, I believe I heard you plain and clear when you said you robbed the sundry shop the other day," the first woman said, still looking to the cobbled street like King Rudolfus Sweetwater was hiding somewhere and about to jump out and yell "Boo!"

"See, that's what I'm saying," the woman inside the bakery argued. "You're not hearing things right. I said that I wear a robe on Sunday."

"Really? Then why did I find a whole box of beef jerky and cigarettes in your sock drawer?"

"Because you're a snooper," the woman answered. "Stay out of my stuff, or I'll start lacing your food with hallucinogens."

"Again?" the woman in the doorway asked, quite seriously. "I'm not sure I mind that so much. The year you did that was really memorable. I made lots of friends and backpacked all over the world."

A laugh echoed from the bakery. "You never even left our basement."

The woman gave the alleyway one last look before abandoning her search. "Let me help you cut that dough. Remember it needs to be really dark in here. Let's turn off all the lights. The faster you do it, the better."

Nevin shook his head at the absurdity of the two women as the door to the bakery shut. He really couldn't understand how businesses like that were allowed to remain open. They wouldn't be much longer. First, he had to plan the demise of the Dragon Elite. That was already going as planned with King Rudolfus in his custody.

Smiling with satisfaction, Nevin Gooseman stepped through the portal to his secret headquarters, excited to start the next phase of his plan.

CHAPTER TWO

Ainsley cleared her throat and shook her head. "No, let's try this again." She stuck her hands on her hips, giving Trin Currante a stern expression.

Looking up at the tall cathedral style ceilings in the dining room of the Castle in the Gullington, Ainsley sang, "The rafters look quite nice today, Castle."

The cyborg, who was also the newly appointed housekeeper for the Castle, let out a long breath that was marked by electronic noises. Her training hadn't been going as expected…well, as she'd expected. "The rafters look nice," she said.

The shapeshifter, who had traded her usual brown burlap dress for a yellow silk gown that hung off her shoulders, sighed. Ainsley didn't look much like a housekeeper anymore. With the return of her memory, she'd taken on her former role as a diplomat for the Elfin Council. They were amazed to have her back and were waiting for her to be cured so she could leave the Gullington safely.

"No, you've got to really mean it, or the Castle will know your heart isn't in it," Ainsley scolded.

Trin, who looked like her usual self in all black clothes and covered in bits of metal, wires, and gears, grunted with frustration. "I just don't get it. I figured as a housekeeper for the Castle that I'd sweep and mop and whatnot."

Ainsley laughed a high-pitched sound that made both Sophia and Wilder flinch. "Oh, you thought wrong. This isn't like a normal castle, and it requires a lot more work than if it were. You might dust a bit here and there, and you'll cook from time to time. If you're doing the job right, then the Castle takes care of most of the work for you. Your job is mostly to make it feel good. It's about caring for its soul."

Trin shot Sophia a look that said, "What in the hell have you gotten me into?"

She slid down in her seat at the dining table, avoiding the cyborg's gaze.

"I still don't understand." Trin returned her attention to Ainsley. "The Castle is Quiet, the groundskeeper, right? Why can't I just say nice things to him?"

Evan laughed from his place at the table next to Wilder. "I tried doing that mate, and it only makes the grumpy gnome madder than hell. He's a very strange little guy. Total masochist from everything I can tell."

Ainsley shook her head, ignoring the dragonrider. "Quiet is the Gullington, but the Castle is a very specific part of him. It's like you doing crunches to strengthen your arms. It just doesn't work. So, if you want to do the job right, you focus on the Castle. Focusing on Quiet is the wrong approach."

"That was a good analogy," Wilder complimented, narrowing his gaze at the phone that Sophia had gotten for him. Watching the two-hundred-year-old dragonrider learn how to use modern technology was even more fun than watching Evan. Although the devices were intuitive, for the ancient, out-of-date riders, it was taking a lot of getting used to.

"I don't have to do crunches to maintain my six-pack abs," Evan boasted.

"Must be nice," Trin muttered, looking overwhelmed.

"Yeah, but for all his learning, he can't fix stupid," Ainsley teased, trotting off for the kitchen.

Trin didn't seem to know whether she should laugh or not, although Wilder nearly doubled over.

Evan patted the dining room table in front of Sophia. "Where's that cure for Ainsley? I want that woman out of here as soon as possible."

Sophia sighed, feeling the sadness that had been building lately at the thought of Ainsley leaving the Gullington for good. "It's not ready yet. It should be soonish."

Evan leaned back, folding his hands behind his head and propping his boots up on the dining room table with a dreamy expression. "Then, I can finally live my life without restriction."

Ainsley strode through from the kitchen, carrying a large tray of roasted chicken and vegetables. She narrowed her eyes at Evan and used magic to cause the back legs of the chair to slip out, making him topple over backward.

Wilder howled with laughter as the shapeshifter laid the food onto the table. With a curt nod, Ainsley glanced at Trin. "Evan is not to put his feet on the table under any circumstances." She pointed at NO10JO, the cyborg dog stationed on the other side of the threshold. He was busy giving them looks of longing from the entryway. "That mutt isn't to enter my dining room...I mean, well, the Castle's dining room. Those are the rules, and they will be followed even when I'm gone. Is that understood?"

Sophia was impressed at the authority Ainsley displayed. It had shown up with her memories and made the eccentric housekeeper seem like so much more than she already was.

"Yes, I understand," Trin answered, seeming eager to please even if she'd been thrown into something she hadn't quite bargained for. When Sophia recruited her to be the housekeeper, to replace Ainsley when she left, she hadn't really elaborated on what that would mean or described how strange the job would be.

Evan seethed with anger as he pulled himself up from the floor and righted the chair. "That was a nasty little stunt. When did you start retaliating?"

Ainsley shot him her own rude stare. "Since I realized that you're just a lowly jerk who has no right to disobey my authority." She swung around and strode back in the direction of the kitchen.

Evan folded his arms and scowled. "Can you believe the nerve of that one?"

"She's a five-hundred-year-old shapeshifter who holds one of the highest positions in the Elfin Council," Sophia argued. "What I can't believe is she hasn't done worse to you."

"I liked her better when she was a housekeeper without any hobbies," Evan complained.

Since Ainsley had recovered her memories, the Castle had been full of music. She played multiple instruments like the violin, piano, and cello. She was also skilled in many forms of dance, spoke several languages, and was proficient in archery and swordsmanship. Sophia knew why Hiker had fallen in love with her all those centuries before. She was a catch, and yet, he'd let her go.

"Speaking of hobbies," Ainsley said, coming back through the swinging door like she'd been a part of the conversation all along. She placed a bowl of freshly baked rolls on the dining room table. "Evan is not to play football in the corridor because he breaks stuff, and it angers the Castle."

Trin nodded, looking at the quickly growing spread on the table. It was making Sophia's stomach grumble. She hoped the others would be along soon so they could eat.

"Evan is not allowed to breathe either," he sang, impersonating Ainsley's Irish accent. "That angers the Castle. The Castle doesn't like it when Evan moves, thinks or pretty much exists."

Ainsley batted her green eyes at him. "And here I thought you didn't know the truth."

Mahkah and Quiet entered the dining room. Both gave the table of delicious smelling food strange looks.

"You're wondering what Ainsley is up to serving us real food, aren't you?" Wilder asked, sensing their apprehension.

Mahkah gave a polite smile while Quiet muttered something, taking his usual seat and tucking a napkin into his shirt collar. He picked up a fork and a knife and looked ready to dig in.

"I've always served you real food," Ainsley argued. "Since I don't have any ill will toward Hiker, I've decided to serve him and you something you want."

That was the most astonishing news Sophia had heard. She had found the elf incredibly impressive since learning about her past and many talents. Her ability to get over the fact that she and Hiker had once been in love and he'd broken her heart was rather remarkable.

Ainsley was headed back for the kitchen when Hiker and Mama Jamba entered. The leader of the Dragon Elite was obviously stunned by the spread in front of them, whereas Mother Nature seemed annoyed.

"Don't worry," Ainsley sang, carrying a tray of pancakes as she swept through the door once more. "I've got your favorite." She laid the plate in front of the short woman with large silver hair, earning her an endearing smile from Mama Jamba.

"Why thank you, dear Ainsley," the southern debutant said sweetly.

The elf nodded and stepped back beside Trin. "Mama Jamba loves a short stack for breakfast, lunch, and dinner. The Castle knows how she likes them, but you've got to put in the orders."

Trin scratched her head full of wire-like hair. "I don't understand. So you don't cook? Not really? You put in orders?"

"I do both," Ainsley stated. "It depends on the Castle. You'll figure it out." She laughed. "Then things will change. They always do. There are no two same days in this place."

Quiet mumbled something.

Ainsley nodded at him. "I was just thinking the same thing."

"What?" Trin asked, looking between the pair. "What did he say? What were you thinking? I'm missing something."

"Get used to it," Evan muttered, watching as Hiker carved the chicken.

"It's quite easy to understand Quiet," Ainsley argued. "You'll figure it out in time."

Trin didn't appear as confident.

"Also," Ainsley continued. "The guys aren't allowed in the pantry since they don't know how to clean up after themselves."

"What about her?" Evan asked, pointing an accusatory finger at Sophia.

"Oh, S. Beaufont can do as she pleases," Ainsley said, curtseying in Sophia's direction. "She makes her bed every morning and doesn't leave dirty clothes all over the floor."

Evan shot her a scathing look. "The Castle just loves her. Pink Princess can do no wrong. Before long, Hiker will be putting her on a pedestal where we all have to look up to her and bow to her undeniable grace."

Sophia gave Hiker a nervous expression, wondering when he would announce she'd be taking on a leadership role. He cleared his throat and made a minute head shake. The timing wasn't right for that just yet. Sophia was relieved and impressed at how well they communicated nonverbally. For as much of a pain in the ass as the Viking was with his stubbornness, Sophia actually got him.

"The only way we can ever look up to her is if she's on a pedestal," Wilder said with a laugh.

She pretended to be offended. "Keep it up, and I'll lock your phone so you can't get back into it."

Hiker narrowed his eyes at the pair. "Again, I don't want phones at the table. I have allowed them against my better judgment, but there must be rules."

Wilder nodded at once, slipping the device into his pocket. "Of course, sir. My apologies."

"Trin, are you going to join us?" Sophia asked, watching the cyborg stand uncomfortably.

She looked as though she'd swallowed one of the many bolts that comprised her. "I-I didn't think the housekeeper—"

"Oh, don't be absurd," Ainsley interrupted, buzzing in and laying a bountiful green salad on the table. "The housekeeper is part of this merry bunch. The Dragon Elite won't be as successful without you, so learn to join in on things. It's more fun that way too." She slid elegantly into a seat and nodded to the chair beside her. The long dining room table that ran the length of the hall wasn't full. With one more person occupying its many chairs, it was starting to feel like it could one day be filled with dragonriders and staff.

Trin took the seat and forced a smile.

"Very good," Hiker said, looking down the table. "Ainsley is right. Everyone here is a part of the Dragon Elite, serving our mission in their own unique way. We must never lose sight of that."

He lifted his goblet and appeared, much like Ainsley, like a new version of himself. "Now, I say we toast our newest member and all the possibilities ahead."

In unison, they all lifted their goblets and clinked the glasses, muttering "Cheers."

When Sophia had taken a sip, she noticed the tiniest bit of regret in Hiker Wallace's eyes. He might be relieved that Ainsley was okay with things, but there was something still lying across his heart and marking his eyes with stress. She hoped to help him if he'd allow it.

CHAPTER THREE

Mama Jamba wasn't in her usual place in Hiker's office when Sophia and Wilder came in one minute early for the meeting the leader of the Dragon Elite had called. Instead of being perched on the sofa with her feet curled under her, Mother Nature was leaning over the Elite globe, her brow furrowed as she studied it, humming the song *California Girls* by the Beach Boys.

Evan rammed into Sophia's shoulder as he strode past her and plopped onto the couch in Mama Jamba's usual spot.

"Watch it mate," Wilder said, a warning in his voice to the other dragonrider.

Evan scoffed at him. "Pink Princess likes it. This is our sibling rivalry thing, so don't interfere."

Sophia shook her head at Wilder, dispelling his protectiveness. "It's fine. Evan thinks that being mean to people is the way to endear himself to them. He wonders why he doesn't have any friends."

"Come here, boy." Evan patted the couch and NO10JO, who had been in the form of an ottoman, shapeshifted back into his form as a cyborg dog and jumped onto the sofa. "I have friends. Look who loves me so much he made himself into a footrest, anticipating my needs." He let the dog lick him on the chin and smiled.

"The one creature who loves you and they reduce themselves to being your footstool," Wilder said, shaking his head. "Yes, please teach me your ways, Evan. You obviously have this relationship stuff down."

He shook his head. "Well, at least I didn't hook up with the first girl to enter the Castle in five hundred years."

Wilder winked at Sophia. "Really? Because I call that capitalizing on a good opportunity, especially since she's the best girl on this planet."

Hiker, who had been busy sorting through papers on his desk, glanced up. "Are you lot quite done yet because I'd like to begin."

"Mahkah isn't here," Mama Jamba remarked absentmindedly, rotating the Elite globe. She appeared to be searching for something.

"Hey, Mama Jamba," Evan began. "Not that I'm trying to do your job or anything, but why is it that you're looking at a globe of this planet when you created it? Do you really need a map?"

She glanced up in obvious irritation. "I know what I'm doing."

"Which is?" Hiker asked, a hint of skepticism in his voice.

Mama Jamba arched an eyebrow at him and smiled. "You'll find out."

"I can't wait," he said dryly.

"So, Mama Jamba," Evan sang. "Is there a place that you regret having created, like Florida or Yemen?"

She scowled at him. "Yemen is a perfectly lovely place. And no, just like all my creatures on this beautiful planet, they all serve a purpose and are perfect in their imperfections."

"Well put," Sophia mused.

"Except for flies," Mama Jamba added after a moment of reflection. "They are nasty little beasts I really shouldn't have created. It was a Monday, what can I say."

"Good, you're here," Hiker said as Mahkah entered his office, looking rushed.

"Sorry, sir," he replied, bowing slightly. "I was working with the dragonettes. They are becoming quite demanding."

Hiker nodded. "There is only one of you and many more of them."

"It's true, but I can handle it." Mahkah didn't sound so sure.

"I'm happy to lend a hand," Sophia offered.

Evan coughed, and it sounded very much like, "Suck up."

She narrowed her eyes at him.

Before she could volley her own insult at her "little brother," Hiker broke in. "That's actually a good idea and brings me to our first order of business."

"Sophia is now in charge of shoveling all the dragonette poop littering the Expanse," Evan guessed. "Great idea, sir. She's closest to the ground, so that makes a lot of sense."

Hiker shook his head and directed his attention to Sophia. "No, I've decided that as we grow, we'll need more leadership."

Mama Jamba glanced up from the Elite globe, giving Hiker an encouraging smile.

He cleared his throat. "I will remain the main authority over the Dragon Elite. However, I've elected that my second in command, who will mostly handle directives when in the field, will be Sophia."

Evan's mouth popped open as he exclaimed, "Whhhhhat?!"

Wilder pressed a hand on to Sophia's shoulder. "Nice."

Mahkah nodded appreciatively at her.

"Do you need to lie down, sir?" Evan asked, indicating the couch where he was sitting with NO10JO. "You're obviously not well."

"He's perfectly healthy," Mama Jamba argued.

"That I am," Hiker stated. "Sophia has displayed natural leadership skills that make her the right choice. I haven't and probably won't always like her challenging me, but Mama has gotten me to see that this will help with balance. I don't need someone who follows my lead blindly, but rather looks at it from a fresh perspective. I think we can all agree that you all are much too similar to me to do that since we've spent many decades together."

"Many, many decades." Evan sighed, sounding weary.

"Furthermore," Hiker continued. "This leadership is in line with our goal of balance. It makes sense to have the new and the old. The feminine and the masculine."

"The sassy and the stern," Evan chimed in.

Hiker let out a breath. "Like I said, I'll be your main leader, but in the field, I'll have you defer to Sophia. Wilder and Evan already have phones and can communicate with her. And we've..." He gave her an uncertain look before continuing. "Yes, we've decided that Mahkah should have one too."

"Yes, sir," Mahkah replied obediently.

"I think this makes a ton of sense," Wilder said, looking at Sophia proudly. "You automatically take the role of leader during missions."

"Thanks," she said coyly.

"That's because she's a bossy know-it-all," Evan declared.

"Who can eat your lunch now if she wants to," Mama Jamba stated before glancing at Sophia. "But you won't, and that's why you're the right choice. Well, one of the many reasons, anyway."

Hiker cleared his throat. "Yes, I trust Sophia to be fair and just in her role as a leader."

Wilder smiled at her. "You'll be good. You're a lot like Adam."

The mention of the dead dragonrider's name, who had once been Hiker's best friend, made him stiffen, grief obvious on his face. "I guess she is. Sophia definitely challenges me much like him."

"And she's willing to take risks," Mahkah agreed. "Calculated ones, though."

"And she has that beard, just like good old Adam," Evan teased.

This seemed to soften Hiker up a bit. He smirked. "Anyway, as I was saying, it would be good if you, Sophia, assisted Mahkah. It's volunteering like that which makes you a good choice. Leadership definitely isn't a glamourous role. Not if you're doing it right."

"So does this mean that when you're not around, what she says goes?" Evan asked.

"It means that but I plan to be here fulltime," Hiker told him. "It will just be good to have someone to defer to, but this is mostly in anticipation of new riders joining us, which could be very soon or many years from now. I want to be prepared."

"It will be nice once we have some new faces around here," Evan said, continuing to pat the dog.

Wilder scoffed at him. "Thanks a lot. It's been nice sharing the

Castle with you for the last hundred years, only to get tossed aside when you have the opportunity to make new friends."

Evan nodded. "Yeah, out with the old and in with the new. Hope we get more female riders. I could use a good—"

"It's better if you don't finish that sentence," Hiker interrupted.

"Snogging," Evan said, finishing his thought anyway.

Hiker batted his eyelashes with annoyance. "Anyway, since the demon dragonettes are protected, we need to switch our efforts to fixing mortal's perceptions of them while also tracking them down. I don't know where they could be or what sort of trouble they could be making for us." He scratched his head. "Unfortunately, I don't know where to start with looking for them since most of our efforts before didn't work."

"I think I can help with that," Mama Jamba said, her attention still on the Elite globe.

Hiker appeared as though he'd just been slapped in the face. His mouth dropped open and his eyes widened. "Now it's my turn to ask if you're feeling all right."

She shook her head, rotating the large orb in its ornate stand. "I'm fine, son. I'm not going to point you in the direction of each of the demon dragonettes, but I'll offer a solution."

"You can't make them appear there, then?" Hiker asked, indicating the Elite globe.

Mama Jamba shook her head. "I could, but that's not how it works. Only those who choose to be a part of the Dragon Elite show up here, and those demon dragonettes leaving mean they don't want to be associated with us."

"Yeah, I get that, but even if they don't want to be a part of the Dragon Elite, it would still be good to know where they are," Hiker reasoned. "They could be causing a lot more trouble for us while we try to manage our reputation after the nonsense that Nevin Gooseman has been spreading. I just need to be able to get control over things."

"I can take the lead on that, sir," Evan chimed in.

Sophia coughed, and it sounded very much like, "Suck up."

Hiker drew in a breath. "Actually, I thought Soph—"

"I have a mission for her," Mama Jamba interrupted.

"You do?" Hiker questioned. "That's what you're going to help us with?"

Mother Nature nodded. "Yes, if you, Sophia, go and get me a certain ingredient, then I can use that to show you where the dragonettes are. It won't be exact, but it will give you enough."

Hiker shook his head. "I'm just not used to having your willing help on things. This will take some getting used to."

"You shouldn't get used to it," Mama Jamba told him. "Remember, finding the dragonettes isn't the same as bringing them back. You can't force a dragon to do anything. Really, you should never force anyone, but especially not a dragon."

"I just need to know where they are. Then we can keep an eye on them and ensure that even if they are protected with the shielding spell, they aren't causing trouble. Not to mention that magicians and other magical creatures can still see them, and I worry how much influence this Nevin Gooseman has."

"What do you need me to do?" Sophia asked, looking at Mama Jamba.

Pressing her finger to the Elite globe, Mother Nature smiled. The area glowed brightly for a moment before dimming once more. "You should go to Sherwood Forest in England and forage for mushrooms."

"Glamourous!" Evan exclaimed.

Ignoring him, Sophia squinted at the old woman. "What kind of mushrooms?"

Mama Jamba shrugged. "I'm not sure. Get them all."

Sophia lowered her chin. "All of them?"

Mother Nature nodded. "Yes, I've created a nice breeding ground for the types of mushrooms I need for the tracking spell, but it usually works too well. It will create all sorts of different varieties and do lovely and bizarre things to other plants and animals."

"Bizarre?" Sophia questioned.

"There will be man-eating squirrels now," Wilder joked.

Sophia didn't think he was wrong. "Okay, Sherwood Forest. To get mushrooms. All of them."

"Oh, look at our new illustrious leader, Little Pink Riding Hood." Evan was enjoying this too much.

"You are going to Yemen, Evan," Hiker said, changing the subject.

"Say what?" he complained at once. "Why?"

"Because there's a dispute over land, and I want you to intervene," Hiker explained. "It's more important than ever that we be the adjudicators the world needs. It's needed and it will help with world views."

"Yemen..." Evan growled.

"At least it's not Florida," Wilder teased.

"Wilder, I'll need you on the goodwill tour," Hiker continued. "The world needs to see us as brave and dependable and god-like."

"Then why are you sending him, sir, and not me?" Evan questioned.

"Because they don't need to see us as clowns," Wilder shot back.

Evan stood and NO10JO joined him. "That's fine. I'll go do the tough work while you flash a toothy grin and wink at mortals."

"You bring me back a souvenir from Yemen, you lucky dog," Wilder joked.

Apparently thinking he was talking to him, NO10JO turned back into an ottoman, obviously nervous he was being sent on a case.

Hiker looked at them, his patience obviously waning. However, when his eyes drifted to the ottoman dog, he hid a smile. "All right. You all have your orders. Get out there and make me proud. Or at least, make it so I don't want to kill you when you return."

CHAPTER FOUR

W*here in Sherwood Forest?* Lunis asked, giving Sophia a speculative glare. He swished his tail back and forth as they stood on the Expanse, creating a gentle wind. He was like a cat and wagged his tail when angry, irritated, or excited.

Getting away from the Gullington would be good for the blue dragon because the dragonettes, even the angel ones, were grating on his nerves. He had the privilege and "curse" of watching after the young dragons. Mahkah thought he was the best suited for it, being closer in age to them, but Lunis hadn't found the responsibility to be that much of an honor.

"Mama Jamba didn't say where in Sherwood Forest the mushrooms could be found," Sophia answered, watching as angel dragonettes leaped over unhatched eggs, playing leapfrog.

It's over one thousand acres of overgrown forest, Lunis stated dryly.

"So, we should leave early."

What kind of mushrooms and how many?

"All of the kinds of mushrooms, apparently," Sophia answered. "And all of them."

Lunis batted his eyes at her, not appearing amused. *This is sounding better by the moment.*

"Want to stay here and mind the dragonettes?" Sophia teased.

Not on your life.

Sophia laughed. "What about your life?"

Lunis lowered his head and gave her an annoyed expression. *Make me hang out with these rug rats any longer, and I'll probably end myself.*

"They can't be all that bad," Sophia reasoned.

They are all teething and guess what they like to gnaw on? Lunis asked.

"Your bad jokes?" she questioned.

They don't get my jokes, he retorted. *And no, my tail. My scales. My horns. My everything.*

"Sounds like they love nanny Lunis," Sophia teased.

He glared at her. *If killing you didn't end me, I might consider it at this point.*

She threw up her hands. "Your hostility is palpable. Let's get out of here and get your attention on a dangerous mission that will no doubt be a convoluted series of tasks and offer way more than we bargained for."

To Sophia's surprise, Lunis grinned. It was a strange expression for a dragon to wear unless they were him, and he got away with such weird behavior. Most dragons didn't smile and had serious expressions. Lunis was nothing like most.

You really know the way to my heart, he responded as Mahkah strode up, one of the dragonettes perched on his shoulder like a very strange bird.

There's something different about you, Mahkah, Lunis joked. *Did you get a haircut?*

Mahkah, who wasn't good at jokes and hadn't cut his long hair in many decades, glanced over his back at his long black braid. "No, but maybe I've gotten a bit more sun lately, working with the angel dragonettes."

Sophia laughed. "I think he's referring to the growth you have on your shoulder."

Looking up at the creature, which was about the size of a barn owl, Mahkah smiled mildly. "Oh, this one has taken a liking to me," he replied, giving the lavender dragonette an affectionate expression.

"Is that typical when you've already magnetized to a dragon?" Sophia asked, not having found much on that subject in *The Complete History of Dragonriders.*

He frowned. "I don't think so, but not much is typical about the new generation of dragons, which Lunis is evidence of."

Sophia looked at her dragon proudly. "Yeah, he's not your typical dragon."

Mahkah stared out at the Expanse where dragons were frolicking and playing in very un-dragonlike fashion. "The new generation seems to be taking after our famed Lunis. They are more light-hearted than the dragons we once knew, the ones I grew up with. They are playful. That's why I elected Lunis to watch after them. I hope that's all right." He gave the blue dragon a questioning expression.

Let's put it this way, Lunis began, *you're not getting anything for Christmas.*

Not having gotten the joke, Mahkah nodded.

"Well, I appreciate it," the old dragonrider said. "The other dragons aren't as well suited for this job, being from different generations and all."

Sophia, as with Wilder, often forgot how old Mahkah was, being the second oldest dragonrider at the Gullington, right after Hiker. He had been around and witnessed the behavior of many dragons, making him the resident expert on caring for the magical creatures.

"A dragon won't magnetize to more than one rider, right?" Sophia asked, looking at the little dragon who was nibbling on Mahkah's hair as though it were hay.

He didn't seem to mind. "I don't think so. It wouldn't work in a technical sense. I don't suspect the new generation will magnetize for a while. Lunis did before hatching, but that's rare. Well, actually, it's the only one I know of. Just like you."

Sophia blushed, always feeling a strange bit of pride about being the first and only female dragonrider. She didn't know if one day she'd be joined by other women or how long she'd be the only female among the "guys." It didn't matter to her either way, but as a new leader for the Dragon Elite, she did want some diversity. She looked forward to other riders joining them. That was the reason she'd been elected—in the hope there would be more riders to manage one day... hopefully soon.

"What do you need help with?" Sophia asked, remembering she'd volunteered.

"Honestly, I'm still studying what the new generation needs most," Mahkah answered. "They are a handful, but different than Coral, Simi, Bell, and Tala. They needed more physical maintenance, and these tend to want more emotional support."

Very much like the rider who spawned them, Lunis observed.

That made sense to Sophia. The first one-thousand dragon eggs had been spawned by the first male rider. She'd spawned the second set—the last remaining dragon eggs.

"I think," Mahkah began thoughtfully, "if Mama Jamba has given you a mission to find ingredients that will help track down the demon dragons, it would be the best use of your attention. I'm terribly worried about what could be happening to them. They are wild and in a world that doesn't understand them. We might not be able to control them, but at least if we can find them, we can keep an eye on the dragonettes. Although I'd prefer Lunis' help, he should go along with you, obviously."

Sophia agreed with a nod. "So, you want us to set off for Sherwood Forest right away then?"

He nodded. "The sooner, the better. I fear tracking them down will be a process. I'm grateful Mama Jamba is assisting in the matter."

"Yes, I think it speaks to the severity of the situation," Sophia agreed, realizing it had to be important if Mother Nature was helping.

Lunis gave her a meaningful expression. "Grab some sandwiches, and let's get on the road."

Sophia laughed, always enjoying the light nature of her dragon. She was glad she was born to this generation, although she secretly wondered if they were different because of who she was.

CHAPTER FIVE

The excitement Lunis felt leaving the Gullington was palpable as Sophia rode with him over the Barrier. The wind tore through her hair, whistling a tune like it was excited too.

Lunis, like Sophia, was always eager to soar into the skies, whether they be blue, gray, or dark. The air was where they both felt most alive. That was never truer than as they sped for Sherwood Forest, away from the Expanse and, more importantly for Lunis—away from the dragonettes.

Mahkah was right to assign Lunis to oversee the small dragons. He wouldn't stifle their spirits like the older, more rigid dragons. They were about customs and doing things as they had always been done, whereas Lunis held an extra room inside his head that was full of possibilities. The new generation had that too. Sophia, as well as Mahkah, didn't want those rooms locked. However, at the end of the day, Lunis was a dragon meant to soar and battle and explore, not a nanny. It was best for him to get out, leaving the charge of caring for the young dragons to Mahkah for the time being.

Where should we land? Lunis asked in Sophia's head. It was a beautiful thing shared between practiced rider and dragon, making them one. Her inclination made him veer right. Her slightest hesitations made him slow. The reins remained in her hands, but they were mostly useless since all steering was done purely by her thoughts.

She mused for a moment, considering their options. It was like randomly picking a spot on a rotating globe. Sherwood Forest from the sky looked all the same. Green, green, green. Punctuated every so often by patches of lighter shades of green.

Although Sophia had loved to play roulette with world globes when she was little, that seemed like haphazardly leaving a little too much to chance.

What about over there? she responded, indicating the area to the east.

Because your GPS tells you that's where a Starbucks is located, he joked.

She laughed. *No, because there's a stream and where there is water, there are mushrooms.*

This is a British forest though, he argued. *There will be moisture every-where. I'm guessing this place is jam-packed with mushrooms. I hope you didn't have plans for Christmas because we'll be spending it here, foraging.*

Sophia shook her head. *Mama Jamba wouldn't have sent us here for something so extensive.*

But she wants all of the mushrooms, he complained. He wasn't really complaining, rather sounding excitedly challenged.

There has to be a trick or something, Sophia reasoned, looking at the luscious forest.

To her surprise, Lunis sighed. *Maybe, sometimes, our job is just to collect mushrooms.* He sped toward the babbling brook in the distance and then added—*all of them.*

Our mission is to protect the dragonettes, she stated with confidence. *That has to happen sooner rather than later and especially before Christmas. My reasoning says to land by the water. Then we will explore from there, letting our intuition guide us.*

She felt Lunis smile underneath her. Although she couldn't see his face or his ancient eyes, she could feel the grin—such was the beautiful connection between the two, dragon and rider. His expressions etched themselves on her heart and vice versa.

Don't ever lose that part of yourself, Sophia.

She peeled back, holding the reins, more for comfort than necessity. *What? What part of myself?*

The part that keeps you faithful, he answered. *You might be brave. You might be smart. No one will argue that you're damn easy on the eyes, but the very best part of you is that you believe there's always a way.*

Well, okay, she said, blushing for many reasons.

That's the reason you're successful so often, he continued. *You believe. You hold onto hope.*

Sophia lowered herself because she felt a fondness for her dragon and the need to be close to him and also because they were coming in for the landing.

If I learned anything about hope, it's because of you, Lun. I was born very much alone, in a busy family, with few friends in the world until you came along.

He shook his head, and she spied it from her place low on his back. *That's not the way the story goes. Sophia Beaufont could have had any friend she wanted, but she stayed to herself, saving her energy for the ones who would be not just companions to her, but the best ones for her.*

Oh? she asked, pretending this part of their history was new to her.

Yes, and that is the day I felt your presence and knew I wanted no other, he went on. *One day you'll come to terms with the truth.*

Which is? she asked with sincere curiosity.

That you know how to draw the ones you want to you, he answered. *You don't put out a pot of honey for bees, like most.*

I think you're overthinking things, she said, bracing herself as the winds intensified as they descended. Lunis' wings flapped, compensating for the rush of wind whisking through the old trees.

I don't think I am, he argued. *You, Sophia, fly fish, looking for a specific variety. That's how you found me. And Wilder and so many others. You don't settle. Which is why we always feel like the winners when you pick us.*

Sophia didn't know what to say to these words from her dragon, so she didn't say anything as he landed on the soft meadow that sparkled with possibilities.

CHAPTER SIX

Everything was too quiet as Sophia got down off Lunis upon reaching the clearing between the trees and creek. The trees, full of leaves, didn't move when she gazed at them like they were having a strange staring contest. To her surprise, the brook she could have sworn had been rustling from the air was still and quiet.

Sophia tensed, sensing that something was awry. Not wrong, but definitely not right.

"What do you suppose?" she asked Lunis, knowing he'd fill in the gaps.

There's snipes hiding in these parts that have quieted the forest, he joked.

She gave him an annoyed expression. "You've already tried to get me to go snipe hunting. It won't work."

The dragon, who reached up well above her head, shrugged. *If you don't want to find small, cuddly creatures buried in the ground, that's your call.*

"They don't exist," she seethed. "That's just a prank that older siblings tell younger ones to keep them occupied and give themselves entertainment."

Maybe, he reasoned. *Only one way to tell. Do you want me to retrieve your bat and sack so you can find out for yourself?*

Snipe hunting, Sophia had learned, was a cruel joke that people played on naive children, telling them to go into the middle of the woods to find fictional creatures by pounding the ground with a bat while waiting patiently and quietly with a burlap sack. After hours or days, depending on the child, they gave up, realizing they'd been duped. Lunis had tried to play the prank on Sophia and Wilder, but a quick search on Snopes.com had extinguished his trick.

"I don't think there are snipes here," she said, chewing on the words as she strode carefully for the creek. "But something is hiding, I believe."

Like, it all went quiet when we landed, Lunis agreed.

"Yeah," she replied, feeling very much like Dorothy when her house fell on the yellow brick road. She tensed suddenly, waiting for all the munchkins to spill out and start singing. Sophia wasn't sure if that would be a welcome surprise or a jarring one.

"Why is it the creek isn't making any noise, although it's moving?" she said to Lunis in a whisper over her shoulder, her eyes on the babbling water.

His eyes were on the leaves of the trees, which should have been whistling with sounds but were quiet. *I'm going to go with magic, Bob, for two hundred.*

"This isn't a game show," Sophia laughed.

My entire life is a game show, he reasoned.

Sherwood Forest was quite possibly one of the most beautiful places Sophia had seen, and that was saying a lot. Maybe it was because she preferred trees and organic mounds of moss-covered earth over architecture and human innovation. For whatever reason, the place was mesmerizing with its many trees growing on top of trees. Wizard beards—that were long strands of green moss—hung from the branches, swaying in the silent wind and dew droplets clung to leaves before sliding down and landing in the blades of grass. On an ordinary day, under ordinary circumstances, this would have been a playland. As it was, a mystery was definitely unfolding. One that Sophia and Lunis would no doubt have to solve before they got the bounty they were seeking.

Sophia knelt by the creek, straining to listen for the sound of the water gurgling past her. It was absent even when she was close by.

Do you know what lives under toadstools? Lunis asked, quite randomly.

Sophia rose, arching an eyebrow at him. "Toads?"

He shook his head. *Don't be absurd.*

"Indulge me then," she said, feeling tenser by the moment. The forest was hiding secrets from her.

If my memory is correct—

"Meaning the collective consciousness of the dragons," she interrupted.

Yeah, whatever, he dismissed her at once. *It would be the keepers of the most ancient forests.*

Sophia scrunched up her brow, not following her dragon, although she could often see the collective consciousness of the dragons, thanks to the chi of the dragon. She just wanted to be granted exclusive access like Lunis. "I don't know what you mean."

He snickered. *They are sneaky little creatures, which is why most never see them.*

"Are you going to indulge me?" she asked, her irritation about being kept in the dark growing.

Stop looking with your adult eyes and start looking with your child ones, he insisted.

Sophia stuck her hands on her armored hips and scowled. "I expect that sort of stuff from Mae Ling and Mama Jamba and Father Time, but not you, Lun!"

There was a scampering of noise under the leaves on the ground in the distance that caught Sophia's attention. She jerked around at the same moment it settled, giving her no clue about what caused it.

Giving the area a tentative glance, she cautiously turned to face Lunis. "What's going on, and what do you mean?"

He scampered forward. *I get it,* he said. *I didn't at first, but once we got here, I did. I understood what Mama Jamba meant and why she gave us such a bold task.*

"Are you going to explain?" Sophia asked, continuing to give him a rude stare.

If you'll wipe that expression off your face, maybe, he replied.

Sophia pretended to plaster a pleasant grin on her face. "Please, School Master. Do educate me."

He batted his eyes at her. *Remember when you were a child...all those minutes ago.*

Her fake expression evaporated, once more replaced with a scowl like an adult waiting in line for coffee. "It's not like that."

Yes, I know, he said dismissively. *It's important for this exercise. When you're a child, you see what there can be. You see possibilities. It's why mortal children see fairies when their parents don't. They see ghosts the adults dismiss. They see a world full of things that exist, but no one believes them. You see, they don't understand the concept that you have to see to believe, but rather they fall into the mindset that you believe it to see it.*

Sophia gasped, remembering what he was talking about from her own childhood. "Therefore, they only need to see it to believe it."

Exactly! Lunis exclaimed.

Sophia blinked at the brook and forest and the meadow, thinking that magically something would appear. When it didn't, she frowned at Lunis. "What am I missing?"

Too much whimsy, he explained. *Stop using the logical part of your brain and start just looking at things as they are. It's not a tree and creek and sky. It's a wonderland that you construct just by letting it unfold in your imagination.*

Sophia shook her head at him. "You sounded too much like a hippie just now."

He nodded. *I thought so too, but the reasoning is sound. Just try it. No confounds. No judgments. Just the way you were when you were a kid and waiting for the world to expose itself, instead of using your preset knowledge to define it.*

Sophia nodded, recognizing the genius in this method. "Okay. I'll try."

She stared at the different areas, not trying to focus on them, but rather the opposite. Instead of seeing a brook the way it was, she tried to let it be what it wanted to be. Instead of seeing the meadow and expecting to see stumps and pebbles, she allowed it to surprise her with its arrangement. When Sophia looked into the forest, she didn't use her past constructs to tell her it would be full of trees with branches and moss-covered ground, but instead just opened her mind to an infinite world of possibilities.

What she saw when her eyes focused was beyond a child's dream. It was a pure and absolute fairytale, the things of whimsical dreams.

CHAPTER SEVEN

Twigs were no longer twigs. Leaves didn't just lay strewn across the forest ground. The bark of the trees wasn't just littering the floor. Those things were true, but around all, another story was being told. One Sophia had never seen before, until that moment. She never wanted to see the world any other way as the noise of the forest came alive.

Scurrying across the forest floor were little one or two-inch beings made of leaves and twigs and other bits of the forest, playing and frolicking. They also seemed to be working, moving things in different directions.

It reminded Sophia of a scene out of *Tinker Bell* where the fairies employed flower petals to engineer parts of wagons, and walnuts to be gears in pulley systems. The forest was suddenly awake with productivity while also full of the whimsy of the process. It was alive with fun. It was almost as though the creatures were singing while they were working, but they weren't. They were quiet, and yet she could finally hear the sounds of the forest.

It was different than she had expected. It wasn't the usual swishing of branches overhead or the creek rustling but rather a sound that was almost like music. Sophia instantly liked it and bent her head closer to the earth to listen, wanting to hear it in its most pure form rather than employ her heightened senses.

"It's amazing," she said to Lunis after a moment.

It's been there all along, he remarked. *Just imagine what else is out there in the world that we don't see just because we have been conditioned not to?*

She shook her head, not wanting to think of the possibilities. It was sort of discouraging, although it too carried a world of potential —literally.

"So they can help us," Sophia said, wondering if she could talk to the tiny creatures who seemed not to even notice her as she lowered down to the forest floor, careful to not step on them. To her amazement, they moved out of her path instinctively, not coming close to her hands and feet as she got onto all fours by the stream.

I think they have helped us many times, Lunis mused. *It makes sense they've always been in the background doing something of significance.*

Sophia nodded, feeling a new sense of astonishment, which was rare for a magician raised at the House of Fourteen, which was actually the House of Seven, recruited by the Dragon Elite and the first female dragonrider in history. Even she had things that could surprise her. The world, Mama Jamba's planet, was full of surprises.

"So, what do we do?" Sophia asked, feeling strange hunched on the ground with a large dragon perched overhead.

Try the novel idea of asking, he suggested.

Sophia nodded and cleared her throat. "Yeah. Okay."

It didn't feel like the logical approach, but when she searched her brain, there didn't appear any other really viable ones. She decided to try the straight forward one.

"Hey....um...forest creatures..." she began, feeling lame. "I was wondering if you could help me? I'm looking to gather mushrooms."

Like they hadn't heard her, which would have been impossible since she was a giant on broadcast above them, the creatures continued to move about, some of them loading up wagons with tiny twigs and others playing a game that looked like hopscotch.

Sophia glanced at Lunis with an expression that said, "What the hell, now?"

He shrugged. *Did you bring a donut?*

"Did I bring a donut?" Sophia repeated with irritation. "That's your response? Like I need to bait the little creatures."

He shook his head. *Nah. I'm just hungry. Those guys will come around. Just keep talking. So about the donut? My tum-tum is rum-rumbling.*

"You're ridiculous." Sophia stood, brushing off her pants. "You think they can help me?"

They are in charge of the forest, he reasoned. *I think that if anyone can, it would be them.*

Sophia nodded, noticing how the forest was a kaleidoscopic array of greens. It was weird. In most forests, there was an abundance of green, but here it was overwhelming. So much so, it took Sophia a moment to realize that it wasn't right.

"Why aren't there any flowers?" Sophia asked, scratching her head.

Lunis tilted his head to the side. *Not the season?* he supplied.

She shook her head. "No, there should be flowers. Or something besides just ferns and leaves. Even the dirt…"

Sophia trailed away, noticing now how even between seeing the strange forest creatures made of dirt and nuts and leaves and twigs, there were no other colors. It was as if they had all been stolen from the forest. Even the stream was absent of color, not reflecting the blue sky above.

Before Sophia could ponder a moment longer, a howling that pierced her soul cut through the air.

"There it is," she whispered, unknowingly having expected the approaching danger.

The twig creatures and their friends made of leaves and other bits of the forest scurried away, disappearing at once. Not because she didn't believe this time. They disappeared out of fear, and Sophia knew that by instinct. She knew something else that was more important than anything else she'd learned that day.

She had to end whatever was creating the noise—whatever was taking the color from the forest—scaring those who owned it.

CHAPTER EIGHT

"**D**oes anyone want to take a guess at what that could be?" Sophia asked, finding Lunis and herself suddenly alone in the forest, although moments prior they'd been surrounded by newfound friends.

Traveling salesmen? he postulated.

Sophia shook her head. "They are usually annoying. This is downright bone-chilling," she said after another ear-piercing howl.

For a moment, she wondered if it was a werewolf but remembered her sister, Liv, had conquered the lore on them, reverting the packs back to their natural order. So that didn't make sense unless things had gotten out of hand again in Romania.

She considered other options, but they were too numerous and overwhelming. She turned to Lunis. "What the hell?"

We fly off now and find a Krispy Kreme and return when conditions are more favorable, he suggested.

Sophia dismissed him with a shake of her head. "No, whatever is causing that ruckus is what's causing the absence of color in the forest. We have to help the...whatever they are."

Let's call them twig-people, he suggested.

Sophia nodded. "Yes, we have to help the twig-people. I still contend there should be flowers and weeds and other things besides trees and ferns. Something is responsible for the reason there's no flowers or varieties here."

Like mushrooms, Lunis offered.

Sophia threw up a finger. "Exactly. Like mushrooms."

Another howl cut across the air, this time closer, bringing with it a certain threat.

So we kill the mysterious source of the howling, and then what? Lunis asked, sounding casual.

"Then we see," Sophia replied. "First, we have to figure out what's causing it and why it's so impossible to kill."

She pulled her sword from its sheath and turned to face the wall of the forest where the noise was drawing closer.

Why do you think it's impossible to kill? Lunis asked tentatively.

Sophia narrowed her eyes as the branches began to stir. "Because otherwise, the twig-people would have gotten rid of it, rather than let it take control of their domain."

CHAPTER NINE

Sophia hadn't expected to see a dog spill through the branches and leaves, and what tore through and halted twenty yards away wasn't like any canine she'd ever laid eyes on.

Wow, that mutt is ugly, Lunis remarked under his breath.

The creature was definitely of the magical variety. Sophia could feel that much about the dog-like animal. She also knew it was dangerous by the way it bared its jagged teeth at them and narrowed its black eyes. Lunis was right. It was one ugly dog with strange spikes running down its spine, mangy short brown hair covering its huge body and oversized claws protruding from its paws. The dog's face was all wrong with an oversized snout, and tiny ripped up ears. It was about the size of a bear and appeared about as hungry as one at it eyed her and the dragon.

"I don't think offending the puppy is a good idea," Sophia said, her sword already in her hands.

I don't think Ugly speaks English, Lunis remarked, taking a protective stance. Even though they obviously had the advantage since the dragon was so large, that didn't make Sophia extra confident. There was something about this creature she thought shouldn't be underestimated.

For some reason, that sparked something in Sophia's memory from Bermuda Lauren's book, *Magical Creatures*. "That's a Chupacabra."

She wasn't sure how she knew that, but the description fit. If she was correct, then the sword would do them no good. No wonder the twig creatures had not been able to defeat the animal trespassing in their forest. Chupacabras were nearly impossible to kill with magic or weapons.

Which means we're screwed, Lunis muttered, watching the animal as it stalked back and forth, growling low in its throat and keeping its soulless eyes on them.

Lunis wasn't being pessimistic, Sophia knew from her studies. The monsters, which were known for sucking the blood of goats and other livestock, were nearly impossible to kill. Fire only made them stronger. It was apparently impossible to pierce their skin with a sword. They repelled magical attacks. That left them with no real options as far as Sophia could tell.

"Well, we can't run," Sophia reasoned, her gaze trained on the beast. "It's taking over the forest and destroying the twig people's home."

How did it get here anyway? Lunis mused.

She shook her head. "I don't know. They are supposed to be in South America, right?"

He nodded. *He's definitely a lost dog.*

"As long as he's here," Sophia continued, "finding the mushrooms will be impossible. Nothing seems to grow here with him hanging around."

Yeah, just the trees remain now, Lunis added.

Sophia thought hard, trying to remember everything she'd read in *Magical Creatures* about the Chupacabra. Their lifestyle of drinking animal's blood made them immortal like vampires, and much like those monsters, they were fast when they wanted to be. Presently, Ugly didn't appear to want to expend the energy. He was lumbering back and forth, drool seeping from his growling mouth.

"Light," Sophia whispered to Lunis. "I remember something about how bright light was the only thing known to weaken a Chupacabra."

He glanced up. *Which is why he's made a home under the dark canopy of Sherwood Forest.*

Sophia nodded, remembering how her eyes had to adjust to the shadowy forest when they first arrived. She remembered now that Bermuda had said the Chupacabra mostly came out at night due to their weakness connected to light. Ranchers that wanted to protect their livestock used floodlights to deter the predators, but they were very crafty and often disabled the lamps.

When she sheathed her sword, the rabid dog paused, seeming to know she was about to do something. In a flash, he disappeared, moving faster than any creature Sophia had ever witnessed. Sophia spun around, feeling a brush of wind as Ugly darted behind them. Protectively, Lunis turned, his tail curling around Sophia, creating a barrier.

The trees swayed violently, but there was no sign of the monster.

"Where did Ugly go?" Sophia asked from the corner of her mouth.

Lunis' eyes swept the area rapidly. *He's on the move.*

Sophia knew that was the most accurate thing Lunis could say. The beast was darting around in front of them, weaving in and around the trees, so fast it was impossible to get her sights on him.

Lunis' head jerked to the side as Ugly drew in close. He chomped, his teeth making noise.

The dog had brushed up next to him, nipping at his scales. Although it was unlikely he could penetrate dragon hide, Sophia didn't want to chance it.

She held up her hand and from her palm, a beam of bright light radiated out. Waving it in horizontal motions, she heard the animal retreat, but not for long. A second later and she felt something at her back. She spun to see the Chupacabra flee back into the bush.

"He's too fast," she stated, waving her hand of bright light.

Yeah, and he knows how to avoid the light, Lunis agreed.

She knew what he meant. Only briefly had she caught sight of

Ugly as he ran, his head down and gaze directed away from the beam of light.

"Well, we know what its weakness is, but how are we going to use it to get rid of him?" Sophia asked.

We have to employ another strategy, Lunis explained, whipping around as Ugly sped around them again, his teeth making biting sounds as he passed.

"Which is?" Sophia asked.

Light will kill him, Lunis muttered, scooting Sophia in so he was closer to her as the beast got more daring, biting at them as he moved by in a blur. *However, we have to draw him out and slow him down.*

"How do we do that?" Sophia asked, her heart drumming with fear. She'd always been scared of dogs, not having been around the animals growing up and hearing they were always wild at heart, even the tamed ones.

Invite a dog's greatest enemy to the fight, Lunis said victoriously.

CHAPTER TEN

"A cat?" Sophia questioned at once.

Well, yeah, Lunis stated. *Can you summon one?*

The only cat Sophia knew was Plato, and he wasn't really a normal cat. He was a lynx, but also so much more. If she were Liv, then she could summon Plato, and he'd magically appear. However, she wasn't her sister and didn't know how to find the lynx on a whim. Summoning another cat was beyond her.

"I don't think I can," she mumbled, tensing as Ugly dared to get even closer than before with the last pass.

Lunis' tail thumped on the ground, making it shake, but that didn't seem to deter the rabid dog much. He howled with evil delight as he retreated back into the woods.

"I can't summon a cat," Sophia began. "But, I might be able to improvise." She gave her dragon a sideways look, a meaningful expression in her eyes. He caught it and peeled back suddenly.

No, he protested at once. *Actually, let me put it this way. Hell no.*

"It could work though," she argued, realizing he'd read her mind and knew her idea.

Neck tattoos can work, but that doesn't mean anyone should get them, he argued.

Sophia shook her head. "Here I was, thinking of getting one for my next birthday."

Ugly sped back, and Sophia shone her palm at him as he was leaping, his teeth bared and claws going for her throat. He darted away at once. It was close, and he was getting bolder. It was only a matter of time before he got clear in to attack her.

"We're running out of time," she argued, giving Lunis a begging look.

He shook his head. *I can hold him off.* Waving his tail continuously, he created a defensive measure that would keep the Chupacabra back for a little while. *Why don't you try an illusion of a cat?*

Sophia grimaced. "I don't think that will work. He needs something tangible. Something he can smell. That's a powerful sense for a dog."

Steam issued from the dragon's nostrils when he sighed. *There has to be another way.*

"There isn't, Lun."

Lowering his chin, he gave her a resigned expression. *You're sure you can do it?*

"I think so," she answered. "I've never tried, but I'm excellent with disguises."

This isn't like putting a hat on someone, he argued.

Sophia yelped with pain when the Chupacabra's teeth grazed the back of her arms as he leapt past her. She clapped her hand to the laceration, which hurt much more than she would have expected. The creature's bite had to be full of poison.

Lunis' eyes widened with concern. *Are you okay?*

She nodded. "Yeah, but he's had a taste of blood..."

Sophia didn't have to finish the sentence for them both to know what that meant. Its howl was full of hunger. Then Ugly was moving around them even faster, with an excitement that was palpable.

Lunis seemed resigned as he nodded. *Fine. Let's do it. Make me into a cat.*

CHAPTER ELEVEN

The magic it would cost to disguise a dragon into a house cat would be considerable, and would almost deplete Sophia. If it worked, then it would be worth it. All she needed was just enough magic to create the beam of light once more, and she could end the evil dog, and bring peace to Sherwood Forest once again.

"Okay, are you ready?" Sophia asked, focusing her attention on Lunis even though she knew this made her vulnerable to an attack by Ugly. Lunis had her back, though. Literally. He was wrapped all around her, protecting her as she readied the disguising spell.

Yeah, but if this doesn't reverse, then I'm going to eat you, he threatened.

"It's a disguising spell, not a neck tattoo," she stated.

He nodded. *Thank goodness. I don't have time for such bad life decisions.*

"Also, how are you going to eat me when you're so little?" she questioned.

Lunis flashed her a wicked grin. *One bite at a time.*

Sophia wanted to laugh but knew she needed to concentrate. It was going to be the most complicated disguising spell she'd ever done. She thought Lunis was right, and it was the only way to draw the Chupacabra out. Right now, he was playing with them and taunting them, streaking by and nipping at Lunis and her. However, Ugly needed to meet his match, and everyone knew that dogs hated no one more than cats and vice versa.

"Okay, are you ready?" Sophia asked, daring to squeeze her eyes shut.

She felt Lunis nod in her head. *Do it.*

Opening her eyes, she lifted her hand, trying to stay focused as he defended her with his tail as Ugly darted past them. His mouth chomped like a crocodile hunting flies in the swamp.

Muttering the disguising spell, Sophia prepared to watch the transformation happen immediately. Lunis didn't shift. He didn't shrink. He didn't even grow a set of whiskers.

Her energy depleted, and Sophia was afraid she'd wasted all her magic. Then the features on her dragon slowly started to shift, and her chest tightened with hope. The change was so gradual that if she didn't know what she was looking for, she would have missed it entirely.

Sophia reached into her cloak for the emergency stash of chocolate she kept for such occasions, feeling more tired than she had been in recent history. It was difficult to pull the wrapper off, and it demanded all her focus.

That's why when she took a bite and her vision cleared, she was surprised by the sight before her. Her dragon was gone, replaced by one of the cutest things she'd ever set eyes upon.

CHAPTER TWELVE

G et that look off your face said the tiny kitten sitting where the massive dragon had been before.

Without Lunis surrounding her, Sophia realized she was vulnerable. She whipped around and noticed the clearing was quiet. A rustling shook the branches in the distance, but there was no sign of the dog.

Figuring he was peeking through the leaves and trying to determine what happened to the large dragon that had been perched over her, Sophia chanced a look at the blue and green kitten.

His long fur was blue like the color of his scales with little markings of green along his face, body, and tail. The bright Puss in Boot eyes he regarded her with nearly sent Sophia into cute overload, a condition many who watch cat videos on YouTube suffer from.

"What look?" Sophia dared to ask, realizing she regarded the dragon slash cat with dreamy eyes.

You're looking at me like you want to put a big red bow on me and stick me in your handbag, Lunis muttered, looking down at his dainty paws with disgust. He was the cutest thing Sophia had ever laid eyes on with his huge eyes and tiny little tail. When he wagged it, the force looked like it would take him off his short legs.

"If I had a bow and a handbag, you know what would be happening," Sophia warned.

He shook his head. *This better work or that monster is going to gobble me up in one bite.*

Sophia tensed, remembering the severity of the moment. She gulped and gathered herself. "It will work," she said, trying to sound confident. "Strategy over brute force, right? That's the best approach."

Lunis gave her a doubtful expression. *If squashing the mutt had been an option, I would have preferred that to this.* He lifted a paw and held it in the air, eyeing it like it was nuclear waste.

Sophia heard the bushes rustle behind them. She tensed, realizing she was blocking the view of the kitten. She couldn't hold the disguising spell for long, so time was important. Balling up her fist to hide the light beam spell she was about to create, Sophia gave Lunis a tentative expression.

For all his complaints and doubts, the adorable kitten-dragon nodded curtly. It was go time. Either this worked or they were going to have to rely on plan B, which as far as Sophia could tell, involved running like hell.

CHAPTER THIRTEEN

At Sophia's back, Ugly sniffed the air, then let out a low growl that sounded like tires rolling over gravel. She knew having her back to the beast was a risky move, but they were turning the tables. She believed his curiosity over what he could smell on the other side of her outweighed his desire for blood—if only momentarily. That's all they needed to take advantage.

Sweat dripped down Sophia's brow, although it was cool in Sherwood Forest with a gentle breeze making the leaves dance overhead. She gave Lunis one last cautious look as she heard the beast take a step closer. Ugly wasn't moving like before, sprinting past them. As she had intended, they had done something to make him pause. They had given him something he hadn't expected and hopefully hadn't planned for. The key to taking advantage in most dangerous situations was to introduce something unexpected. The surprise may not last for long, but it only took a moment to distract an opponent and take the upper hand.

Lunis blinked at her, his eyelashes long, and his eyes sparkling with cuteness. Sophia pushed away the urge to cuddle him and stepped to the side, showing Ugly what was on the other side of her.

The massive beast stiffened all over when Sophia spied him as she turned to face the creature. The muscles under Ugly's patchy fur tensed. He froze, his chin low and his eyes on the kitten only a few yards away.

Lunis was standing straight, his back arched slightly, and his fluffy tail doubled its size. The hair on his back was sticking straight up, and he looked like a cat about to pounce. Even with his small size, the kitten was a formidable force—as were most cats when standing off with their common enemy, the dog.

Sophia held her breath, her eyes skipping between the Chupacabra and Lunis. They were having a staring contest, and it wasn't going to last long. She started the light beam spell in her closed palms, finding it more difficult than before due to her magical reserves being low. She could do it, she told herself.

Her fingers began to warm, but she kept them tightly shut, pressing them into her palms until the spell was complete. Any light would scare Ugly away. What she needed was something stronger than before. She couldn't leave anything to chance. Sophia needed the brightest light she could conjure. Something as bright as the sun that would send the Chupacabra back to the hell it crawled out of.

CHAPTER FOURTEEN

The spell wasn't complete when Ugly raced across the clearing, straight for Lunis the kitten.

Sophia nearly bit her tongue, but she didn't move otherwise. Neither did Lunis. He held his ground, rising up with his back high in the air.

The Chupacabra halted when his nose was inches from Lunis. His head was low, and his black eyes merely slits, whereas the fluffy kitten had his head held high and eyes wide—no fear present on his face.

If Lunis had run, then Ugly would have chased. That much was obvious. The old chase game had been going on for centuries between dogs and cats.

As it was, the lurking beast didn't seem to know what to do with the tiny kitten who refused to back down from the fight that was building in intensity. Ugly's tail was stiff as a board, as were all of the muscles in its body. It appeared to hardly be breathing as it glared down at the kitten.

Lunis, Sophia knew, was running out of options. He could hold the beast off for only another moment. Then the chase would begin, and that's when things would get complicated and dangerous.

Sophia needed to end the Chupacabra before that happened. Lunis wouldn't survive a chase. Ugly was much too fast. The light in her palm wasn't bright enough. She knew that purely based on instinct. For this to work, the beam of light would need to be so bright that neither she nor Lunis could see it. Only light that was too much for their eyes would have the effect they needed to finish off the mutt.

Come on, Sophia urged in her mind. She wasn't connected telepathically with Lunis—having to devote all her attention to the disguising and light beam spell. However, she knew he was about to take off. She could feel it, and the idea terrified her. All Ugly would have to do was leap forward and grab the kitten up by his teeth and wring him out. Then there would be no more kitten, and the spell would be over, along with their chances of defeating the Chupacabra.

The rabid dog couldn't kill Lunis in this form because he'd just revert back to his dragon body. However, the irony wasn't lost on Sophia that they'd chosen a really vulnerable form to put Lunis into when facing the most dangerous dog she'd ever laid eyes on. She almost smiled to herself, enjoying the irony, but her attention was stolen as the tiny kitten picked up his back leg, telegraphing his next move.

The chase they wanted to avoid was about to start, and they had no choice. Sophia had to just hope that Lunis got enough of a head start because the light beam spell wasn't ready yet.

She needed at least another minute. Taking in a sip of air, she hoped Lunis lasted that long as the kitten tore off to the right.

The chase had begun.

CHAPTER FIFTEEN

Apparently, Ugly hadn't expected the tiny kitten to take off because he tensed as Lunis streaked across the forest ground, making progress in the opposite direction.

The Chupacabra recovered quickly though and took off at once, an ear-splitting howl ripping from his mouth as he bounded after the kitten. Lunis' little legs worked fast to carry him over the leafy ground. He had to bound high into the air to clear the thick roots that covered the dirt.

Sophia was grateful to see he'd employed a speed spell to compensate for his smaller strides. If he hadn't, then he never would have made it to the large gnarly tree before Ugly reached him. In a fluid movement, Lunis clawed his way up the trunk, not stopping until he was on one of the higher branches, looking down at the massive dog.

Ugly had nearly gotten Lunis as they sped across the forest, his jaw snapping as he bounded after the tiny animal. Thankfully his attempts to eat on the run slowed him down slightly, giving Lunis the advantage he needed.

Now the huge dog perched at the base of the large tree, his paws resting halfway up the moss-covered bark and his tail wagging angrily behind him.

Lunis too, was waving his puffy tail, a hiss radiating from his mouth. It was a strange noise to hear coming from her dragon, but it elicited the right response from Ugly. He howled loudly, madder than hell and more importantly, completely distracted. They had the Chupacabra exactly where they wanted him. Now Sophia just needed to finish the light beam spell.

Ten more seconds, she thought, daring to look down at her hand where the light was now spilling over her fingers.

Ugly's head jerked to the side as he barked, sounding more like a real dog than the demon he was. To Sophia's surprise, he backed up a few paces, his eyes starting to glow with hostility.

Sophia nearly yelled out when the Chupacabra bounded forward again and threw his massive paws and body into the tree trunk. To her astonishment, his weight and force were nearly enough to shake Lunis out of the tree. Sophia spied real fear on the kitten's face as he clung to the branch for dear life with his sharp claws. Falling out of the tree would ruin everything and would put Lunis in serious danger.

Ugly backed up again, encouraged by his near success with the last attempt. Like a bull about to charge, he scraped his paw against the dirt, pulling up small roots.

The look Lunis flashed Sophia spoke volumes. He couldn't withstand another assault. This one would be bigger. It would knock him out of the tree. Their chance was now.

Glaring down at her hand, Sophia let out a breath. She didn't know if the light beam would be enough to end the Chupacabra, but they were officially out of options.

CHAPTER SIXTEEN

"Hey!" Sophia yelled.

At first, she didn't think it would be enough to stop the Chupacabra from charging. The beast seemed to have forgotten about her, his attention owned by the kitten. However, just before he was about to launch himself forward, he glared over his shoulder—murder written in his soulless eyes.

"Yeah, you, Ugly." Sophia insulted him, buying another few moments as she hid her hand behind her back. The light spilling around her fingers would be noticed by the mutt.

Whereas before, Ugly had been ruled by instinct and possibly logic, it all seemed to disappear when the kitten showed up. He turned to face her directly, wanting a feast one way or another.

By the glint in his eyes, Ugly was done playing games and going straight for the kill. In a flash, he bounded forward, straight at Sophia, moving so fast he nearly blurred in the air.

His speed was incredible, and by the time Sophia raised her hand into the air, he was only a few feet away. She kept her hand fisted and whipped her head to the side. The last thing she saw before she firmly pressed her eyelids closed was the Chupacabra's snout inches from her hand as she opened her fingers, spraying out a hot white light.

CHAPTER SEVENTEEN

The howl that cut through the moist air was all around Sophia. It made her head feel like it had been split in two. She literally felt like her ears would burst from the assault.

The Chupacabra's shriek was one of instant suffering and mind-numbing pain. Sophia couldn't help but feel sorry for the beast as the force of the light spilling from her hand knocked her to the ground. She hit her head on a tree stump but didn't dare to open her eyes. Instead, she shielded her head with her arm, and kept her other one out stick straight, pointed in the direction where Ugly had been.

A crack punctuated the howl when it ended, but the sound of the monster continued to echo in Sophia's head. She felt it always would. For all eternity, she'd hear the Chupacabra's protest of pain in the back of her mind. Gradually, after a loud sound of something like thunder, the noises of the forests started to return. Little crickets, birds tweeting. The breeze rustling the branches overhead.

Sophia didn't know how long she lay on the ground, her face covered, and her hand in the air, but when the light beam spell had worn off, she dared to open her eyes. Peeking through her fingers, she noticed the forest was shadowy once more, and nothing was radiating from her hand—although it felt burned like she'd touched a hot stove briefly.

Sophia willed her eyes to adjust. At first, she thought it was night based on the darkness around her. Then she realized the darkness was the Chupacabra. The large dog was suspended in the air, where he'd been frozen as he leaped for Sophia. She saw how close she had been to getting mauled.

It was strange to see the animal paralyzed in mid-jump, his eyes full of hostility. Sophia couldn't make out what had happened or if the light beam spell had worked. She noticed that his form wasn't solid anymore.

He was...

"Dust," she whispered in astonishment as she spied the little flakes of dirt slowly start to fall off the animal, like a crumbling rock wall.

Her brow furrowed with confusion and also sadness that she'd had to do this to the creature. With a fondness for life that Sophia hadn't expected, she raised a hand, about to brush it over the dog's face just as a gust of wind swept passed her. With it, the wind took the Chupacabra, sending the dust and dirt and ash that made him up into the air, past the row of trees and away, into the forest where he would become a part of it once more.

CHAPTER EIGHTEEN

Sophia wasn't sure how long she stood there watching the ash travel on the breeze, blowing around like smoke through the forest until it all dissipated and disappeared. She felt mesmerized by the sight before her, but she also reasoned she was taking a moment to pay her respects to the Chupacabra.

Again she was reminded that things weren't black and white in this world. There wasn't just evil and good. All of them were mixed together, and erasing evil sometimes felt like it also blotted out goodness. One couldn't exist without the other. Just like for every good dragon that hatched, there was an evil one.

Although she knew that ridding Sherwood Forest of the Chupacabra had to happen, it still filled her with sorrow to know she had extinguished it from the Earth forever. All living creatures deserved respect, although some had to be ended since reason wasn't a part of their cognition.

Sophia was pulled from her quiet reverie by a creaking sound. She whipped her head up, recalling where she was and, more importantly, where Lunis was. Speeding over to the large tree, Sophia looked up and nearly burst out laughing. She pressed her lips together and bit her tongue to stop herself.

So, the disguising spell appears to have worn off, Lunis said, not amused by his current predicament.

"It appears," she mused, squinting to determine where the blue dragon began and the tree ended. When he had been in kitten form, he had looked so small sitting on the moss-covered branches of the tree. Without any warning, the disguise spell had come off, and now Lunis was tangled inside the tree full of knobby branches. His neck was looped around a set of limbs that went up and outward before deciding to dip back down again. His legs and body were pinned between larger branches that were easily the size of small trees themselves. The only part that was free was his tail, which was looped around sections at the back, trying to stabilize him.

Any bright ideas on ways of getting me down? he asked, embarrassment evident in his tone. Asking for help wasn't something dragons were good at, even those who were a part of the new generation.

"Besides calling a lumberjack?" Sophia teased, unable to help herself. She consoled herself with the notion he wouldn't pass up the opportunity to tease her if the roles had been reversed.

I was actually hoping not to damage the tree, or I'd already be down by now, Lunis told her dryly.

Sophia nodded, appreciating his noble heart. She knew he could shake and thrash his spike covered head into the branches, making them crumble to the ground and freeing him. But the tree was old and had a presence they both respected.

"What about a compartment spell?" Sophia offered, thinking of the magic that allowed dragons to fit into small spaces.

He shook his head. *My magic is a bit too depleted for that. I used up a great deal, trying not to get eaten earlier and protect you.*

"I appreciate that," she said, thinking. "Mine is too, or I'd shrink you back down and then get you out that way."

And you're out of food, he guessed.

Sophia nodded, feeling around in her pockets just in case and to her disappointment, finding an empty candy bar wrapper.

She chewed on her lip, thinking. She had enough magic to portal to the Gullington. There she could refill her reserves and then return.

It wasn't ideal, and leaving Lunis would hurt her heart, but they needed a solution, and they still hadn't done what they'd come to Sherwood Forest to do—gather all the mushrooms.

On the heel of these thoughts, Sophia noticed activity around the green forest. At first, she thought it was the twig and leaf-like people returning. That was true, but there was something else.

Color.

All around them, blossoming in various places were a wide variety of the most striking colors, adding magic to the green of the forest.

CHAPTER NINETEEN

Steam rose from the forest ground as turquoise and pink blossoms unfurled from plants. Fruit appeared on the trees all around them, dropping into place like it was suddenly springtime. With a popping sound, various vegetables and herbs sprouted from stalks, vines or bushes. Within a few minutes, the whole forest became a plethora of lush foods that filled the air with many enticing aromas.

As the steam spiraled, the forest floor became visible. Sophia spied mushrooms rise up from the moss-covered ground, and squashes of every color appeared, making a path fit for a Brownie to cross.

Sophia's stomach rumbled as she peered up at Lunis wide-eyed. "I think I've got the food covered, and my reserves will be full really soon."

Do you think it's safe to eat? Lunis asked from his place in the tree now full of apples.

Sophia reached over and pulled a small cucumber from a vine and sniffed. "I think so, but there's only one way to tell."

Famous last words, he muttered.

"Well, I don't have much choice, now do I?"

He pursed his lips and nodded, not appearing very comfortable, cramped as he was by the various branches. With the shiny red apples swinging around him, he was in an even tighter position than before.

Sophia pulled the small knife Subner had made for her from her pocket and used it to cut the end of the cucumber. It was perfectly ripe, having fully grown only minutes before. The freshness hit Sophia's nose, making her smile. Unable to hold off any longer, she took a bite of the cucumber, the pure flavor more than enough to satisfy her taste. It didn't need anything, not salt or sauce.

Well? Lunis asked, having watched as she devoured the vegetable.

"I don't think I'm going to die," she said between bites, pulling a few red cabbage leaves from the ground and ungracefully stuffing them in her mouth. They, too, were delicious, all by themselves. Their crunch was perfect and their freshness divine.

Well, that's a relief, Lunis muttered. *You dying would ruin just about everything.*

He reached out as far as he could and swallowed an apple hanging from the closest branch whole. *Hey, that's pretty good for an apple.*

"Everything here is incredible," Sophia said, using her knife to cut off a cluster of plump cherry tomatoes. The smell of the vine was earthy and contrasted with the sweetness nicely when she popped a small tomato into her mouth.

Yeah, but I don't usually eat fruit, Lunis stated.

"But you do eat nachos and Cheetos and whatnot," she argued between bites.

That's different, he said. *Those are carbs and good for my overall morale. Fruits and vegetables are usually the opposite of good for me. They make me want to cry.* He was on his third apple. *If fruits tasted like these all the time, I could get used to this.*

Sophia nodded. "I might not even mind this stuff in desserts." She paused, thinking for a moment. "No, wait. There's a time to eat a salad, and then there's a time for chocolate pie. Let's not get too far ahead of ourselves."

Lunis giggled. *I agree. Where is the chocolate tree, anyway?*

She shrugged. There was so much forest all around them. They could literally eat their way through it for hours. "I'm not sure, but I'm guessing this is one of Mama Jamba's marvels."

It was under attack by the Chupacabra, making it impossible to thrive, Lunis added.

"But now..." Sophia rose up on her tiptoes, trying to reach a large fruit she didn't recognize. It was round and tannish in color with things that sort of resembled spikes but didn't look too sharp.

You know what that is, don't you? Lunis asked, his voice tentative.

She paused, giving him a cautious glare. "Why? And no."

It's a durian fruit, he answered. *I was totally falling in love with this place until I spied that. If you touch that, I'm going to have to torch your hands to get the smell off.*

Sophia peeled away from the large fruit. "Is it the stuff we saw cats sniffing on YouTube that was making them gag?"

He nodded. Exactly. *If it's bad enough to make cats, who lick their own behinds, gag, I would stay clear of the stuff.*

"Why would Mama Jamba create food that smelled so awful?" Sophia asked.

She was probably having a bad day, Lunis suggested. *Like when she said she stubbed her toe and created Death Valley in California.*

Sophia laughed. "Yeah, funny that the hottest place on Earth is a result of Mama Jamba trying to find her way to the bathroom at night."

Yeah, so steer clear of the durian fruit, Lunis said.

"I'm full actually," Sophia related, feeling quite satisfied after nibbling on the various fruits and vegetables.

Then help a dragon out, Lunis demanded, wiggling to try and reach another apple, but unable to get to it.

Sophia pointed at the massive dragon, and he shrunk down at once to the kitten form, looking adorable once more. He blinked at her with his oversized eyes, and she nearly exclaimed from the cuteness but decided it would be better if she refrained. Dragons didn't like asking for help, but even more than that, they loathed being considered cute. Puppies were cute. Kittens were adorable. Hedgehogs were delightful. Dragons were supposed to be majestic.

The kitten climbed down headfirst, but since his front was so much heavier than the rest of him, he tumbled in the middle of the trunk. The blue and green kitten landed on his back, his paws hanging over his back legs, so he was sitting similar to a person.

Lunis glanced up at Sophia with a challenging expression. *Don't say a word.*

She held in the laugh. "I wasn't going to."

You were, he admonished, trying to roll over on his feet, his over-sized kitten belly making it difficult.

"I might have been tempted to say something about how cats don't always land on their feet," she dared to tease.

I could really use some meat, after all, Lunis declared, trying again and finally rolling over to his paws.

"Is that your way of threatening to eat me again?" Sophia asked. "You know, my demise will be your own."

He shook his head. *No. I won't kill you. Just snack on an arm or something. You don't really need two, do you?*

"I guess not," she pretended to answer. "You don't really need Disney Plus anymore, do you?"

He lowered his chin, a scowl making his cute kitten face appear suddenly different. *You wouldn't...*

"I might cancel all the cable channels if you eat one of my arms," she sang.

He shook his head. *Fine. You can keep them for now. Will you change me back now?*

"Into what?" Sophia asked. "A nice dragon? A complimentary dragon? A thoughtful dragon?"

A man-eating one, he said, glaring at her.

Sophia shook her head. "Here, I thought we were done with the threats."

You know you'd never want that, Lunis remarked, lifting his paw and appearing about to lick it. Totally mortified, he pulled it away. *Seriously, change me now before I have the urge to chase my tail.*

Sophia nodded, flicking her wrist at him as she stood back to make room for the large dragon. Like the pumpkins that had materialized, the dragon blossomed into his full form on the forest floor.

He glanced himself over, checking he had all his claws and limbs. When he was finished, the dragon shook himself like a dog after a bath. *That feels much better.*

"So you don't like being a cat, I take it?" Sophia asked, watching as fog or whatever it was curled across the forest, making it appear even more mysterious.

I'm a dragon, he told her. *Being anything but that is unacceptable.*

She nodded with understanding. "But it worked, and we got rid of the Chupacabra."

He agreed, indicating something in the distance. *I suspect the residents of Sherwood Forest are most grateful and coming to show it.*

CHAPTER TWENTY

arching toward them from multiple directions were the leaf and twig creatures. They were spilling out of holes in the ground and trees, with bright, hopeful expressions on their faces as they looked at the cornucopia of fruits and vegetables still sprouting.

For Sophia, it felt like a *Wizard of Oz* moment when the Munchkin people filed out of their homes and began singing and dancing, rejoicing the Wicked Witch was dead. In this case, the twig and leaf people were undoubtedly excited to have the Chupacabra gone and their forest back.

The creatures, made of parts of the forest with their bodies covered in leaves or twigs, weren't humming or singing, but their happiness was apparent in the way they moved. How long had the evil mutt terrorized their home, making it so no fruits or vegetables grew? It didn't matter, Sophia reasoned. The forest was back to normal now, and for her purposes, that meant she could complete the reason she came to Sherwood Forest.

However, as she looked around at the space, she was automatically overwhelmed. There were literally mushrooms everywhere. They were growing from the sides of trees, up high. Down low, they covered parts of the forest floor like rugs. Long mushrooms sprouted from clumps of dirt buried in holes in the trees. Fat mushrooms created homes for twig people who were peeking out, trying to ensure the rabid dog wasn't going to return. There had to be thousands of mushrooms and getting all of them would take quite some time.

Not if we enlist some help, Lunis stated, having read Sophia's thoughts.

She blinked at them. "Do you mean these guys?" Sweeping her hand in the direction of the little people.

We did return their forest to normal, he reasoned.

Sophia nodded but didn't feel especially happy. "I don't like the idea of taking all of the mushrooms, though. I mean, they use them for shelter, and over foraging can't be good."

You said Mama Jamba told you to get all of the mushrooms, Lunis argued.

Sophia pursed her lips and thought for a moment. "Yes, but I'm making an executive decision. For one, gathering all of them will take time we don't have. And secondly, I don't think it's wise to ever go into any forest or area or whatever and take all of something. That's how we run out of resources. That's how we come into disputes. We're supposed to do things in sustainable ways."

Like plant two trees for each one you chop down, sort of thing, Lunis offered.

"Exactly," Sophia said, her hands on her hips.

Hey, you do you, boo. You do you, he sang. *You're the one answering to Mama Jamba.*

"Well, that's my call then," Sophia decided. "If it's not enough, then I'll suffer the repercussions."

I wonder what that woman is like when she's mad, Lunis said with a whistle. *I mean, if she creates Death Valley for stubbing her toe, imagine what she'll do to you for not following orders.*

Sophia shrugged this off. "It's just a risk I'll have to take."

She didn't want to admit the idea of disappointing Mama Jamba was overwhelming. Mother Nature was the sweetest person she'd ever met, but those were the types you didn't want to let down. They were the ones whose anger would be quiet and understated, and what they didn't say would scar her soul. She gulped. "It's fine. This will work. I'll make it work."

They both knew Sophia was mostly saying that to make herself feel better.

Now you need to enlist some help. Lunis indicated the twig and leaf people who were marching around, gathering up bits of food in baskets made from nutshells and other various things from the forest. *Or are you too good for that too?*

She rolled her eyes at him and crouched so she was closer to the ground. "Hey," Sophia began, getting the attention of many of the twig-creatures close by. "I was hoping you'd help me. I need one of every type of mushroom that you have here. I'm not sure if you are willing, but I was hoping that you might consider it since this is your domain."

The creatures with soft brown eyes and quizzical expression regarded her like she was an alien.

Sophia sighed, realizing she was going to have to do the foraging herself. She wasn't sure how she'd be able to tell if and when she'd gotten one of all the different varieties. She worried this would cause her to over forage, the one thing she was trying to avoid. With a defeated breath, Sophia summoned a wicker basket that would hopefully be deep enough to carry all she needed.

The brown basket wasn't sitting on the moss-covered stone for more than a few seconds when all the twig and leaf creatures in sight took off. They didn't flee as Sophia had feared they would. Instead, she realized they were moving to gather and bring things to her, depositing them into the basket she'd summoned.

The forest creatures were helping her. They had needed a place to put all the mushrooms. They moved efficiently, making quick work of something that would have taken Sophia and Lunis hours.

When the basket was full to the brim, Sophia knew they'd filled it with one of every type of mushroom in Sherwood Forest.

She smiled as they went back to gathering their own food, moving slower now, with less urgency. Sophia picked up the basket, not wanting to leave this enchanted forest, but grateful she'd been successful.

"Thank you for your help," she said to the forest as she opened a portal for her and Lunis.

The leaf and twig creatures didn't say a word back as she started for the portal to the Gullington, but Sophia somehow felt their gratitude for what she and Lunis had done, and it was as beautiful as the plant life all around them.

CHAPTER TWENTY-ONE

Sophia should have been surprised to find Ainsley with her ear pressed to the stone floor of the Castle when she entered, the basket of mushrooms in tow. However, her short time at the Gullington had conditioned any sense of surprise out of her. At this point, she thought she'd be more astonished to find the housekeeper holding a mop or actually cleaning.

Beside Ainsley, who was wearing a pale blue gown made of the finest satin, was Trin, who gave Sophia a questioning expression as she stood next to the elf.

"Well, don't be afraid," Ainsley encouraged. "Pop down here already."

"Not afraid," Trin argued, irritation on her face. "It's just that due to my cyborg technology, I have excellent hearing and don't need to put my ear to the floor to hear something down there."

Ainsley lifted up onto her knees and sat back. She appeared so strange in her elegant dress, on the floor—well, as strange as anything the eccentric shapeshifter did. Shaking her head of loose, red curls, arranged perfectly over her shoulders, she smiled politely. "It's not about hearing anything, really. If you want to find out if the Castle is asleep, then you have to feel for it. The floors vibrate when it snores, but only slightly and usually most in this spot."

"Why do I want to know if the Castle is sleeping?" Trin questioned, giving Sophia an expression that said, "What in the hell have you gotten me into?"

Sophia still stood by her decision to make the cyborg the housekeeper to replace Ainsley at the Castle. It would take some adjusting, but if anyone could fit in there, it was Trin. Filling Ainsley's shoes, when she left, wouldn't be easy. It had been Sophia's goal not to find someone to replace Ainsley, but rather to add their own flair to the place. Once Trin was comfortable, Sophia thought the cyborg would be fantastic.

"You need to know when the Castle sleeps to prepare for the aftermath that will ensue when it wakes up," Ainsley explained, looking around the entryway, an undeniable fondness on her face. "When it wakes up in roughly an hour or seventy-two, it's usually full of energy which equates to mischief."

Since getting her memories back, Ainsley spoke in a more refined way. However, there was still the old Ains with her typical playfulness lurking beneath the surface. Sophia knew that's who she was at her core.

"Mischief?" Trin questioned, worry in her tone.

"Oh yes," Ainsley answered, with a laugh. "This one time, it moved all the dining furniture. We spent a fortnight eating in the armchairs in the sitting rooms until we found the table."

Trin scowled. "That sounds awful."

Ainsley nodded. "Until we realized the Castle had put the dining furniture on the balcony."

Trin's brow furrowed. "I didn't know there was a balcony. I didn't see one from the Expanse when I walked around the Castle."

"There's not one anymore," Ainsley explained. "We ate alfresco for a little over a week before the weather turned cold, and the Castle deleted the balcony and moved the furniture back into the dining hall."

"So, when the Castle wakes up, I should be prepared for the unexpected, then?" Trin asked.

Ainsley shrugged. "Hard to say. Sometimes nothing changes. Sometimes it renovates itself. Usually, there's a rearranging of things. Evan always ends up with a surprise or two. Now settle down here, and I'll show you how to tell if the Castle is sleeping."

"If the Castle is Quiet, can't we just go and see if he's sleeping?" Trin questioned.

Sophia glanced over her shoulder, looking at the stained-glass window of the angel on the front door of the Castle. Through the colored glass, she could see the gnome working on the Expanse. She'd passed him when she'd entered through the Barrier.

"It doesn't work that way," Ainsley told her. "You've got to get over this idea that Quiet is the Castle."

"But he is," Trin argued.

"No, the Castle is Quiet," Ainsley said with conviction.

Trin rubbed her temple with her cyborg's hand. "I think we're talking semantics at this point."

Ainsley sighed. "I get that this is difficult to wrap your mind around, but you will in time. The magic that makes Quiet the Gullington is some of the strongest I've ever witnessed. It's complicated."

"I'm starting to sense that." Trin looked up at the rafters high above, appearing overwhelmed.

"Think of it this way, the Castle is like Quiet's heart," Ainsley began. "The Pond is his lungs. The Expanse is his brain. The Gullington is his body. Just as your heart isn't you, it is part of you, the Castle isn't Quiet—it's part of him."

"Oh," Trin said, understanding dawning on her face. "That makes sense, actually."

Ainsley nodded. "Of course, it does."

"So, in a way, my job is to care for Quiet's heart," Trin mused, her gaze falling to the floor.

"Your job is to care for the heart of the Gullington," Ainsley corrected. "If you keep looking to the gnome to understand this place, then you'll remain confused. He doesn't like it much that we know he's the one in charge of everything here, hence the reason he kept it a secret until you poisoned him."

Trin blushed with embarrassment, several gears making screeching sounds on her chest. "Yeah, I was hoping we'd forget about that."

Ainsley laughed, a high-pitched sound. "Fat chance. I dare say it's the reason you got this job. Few would be so bold." The elf nodded proudly. "I think you'll do just fine here because you can't be pushed around. If you could, then you would never be successful at the Gullington. The guys have tough skin and tease incessantly, Hiker is demanding and unreasonable, and Mama Jamba is always leaving crumbs behind even when she's not eating. It's quite perplexing." Ainsley's gaze connected with Sophia. "Then you've got S. Beaufont here."

Sophia was surprised when Ainsley pointed at her. "Me? What did I do?"

"You ensure that things are always in flux," Ainsley answered at once before turning her attention back to Trin. "Do you know we sat around this place not doing a damn thing for the better part of two centuries? Then S. Beaufont turns up, and she's full of surprises. For one, she was a woman. You should have seen them guy's faces. It was like they hadn't seen a female all their life. Then she started sneaking off on missions, making Hiker madder than hell. She went and found Mama Jamba and brought her back, and things have never been the same ever since. I hope they never are." Ainsley winked at Sophia. "Keep the men on their toes when I'm gone, would you?"

Sophia nodded, feeling that familiar pang of sorrow at the thought of Ainsley leaving the Gullington.

The shapeshifter settled back down on the ground, putting her ear to the stone. "Now, come on down here and tell me if you can feel the snoring, Trin. It's very subtle, but I think you'll get the idea."

The cyborg did what she was told, kneeling down and pressing the side of her face to the cold floor. A moment later, her face lit up with a smile. "I feel it. That's so cool."

Ainsley sat back, looking around. "Yes, it's nice. If you want to find what the Castle did with your suitcase of stuff, now is the time. I, for one, need to find my flute. Apparently, the Castle doesn't like it when I play it, but the stuffy old building can just deal."

Sophia couldn't help but laugh, considering the mischievous and playful ways of the Castle. She looked forward to it waking and seeing how it would renovate itself after its nap.

CHAPTER TWENTY-TWO

S peaking of napping, Mama Jamba was sleeping when Sophia entered Hiker's office to find the old woman snoring loudly on the old Chesterfield sofa.

Sophia twitched her mouth to the side, giving Hiker an uncertain expression. From behind his large desk, his eyes drifted to the basket of mushrooms.

"I see you've been busy," he said, his eyes fluttering with annoyance. "My riders going foraging for mushrooms seems like a waste, but…"

What he wasn't saying was that arguing with Mama Jamba on the subject would have been futile. It was a strange task for a dragonrider trained for battle, but Sophia had realized there was no job too big or small for the Dragon Elite. Hell, she was prepared to scrub toilets if that's what she needed to do to protect the dragons and the world at large. She didn't see how it could, but Sophia also knew not to underestimate things, or she'd find herself sporting a toilet brush.

"We rid Sherwood Forest of a Chupacabra if that makes you feel any better about how I spent my time," Sophia related.

Hiker considered this for a moment before nodding. "Marginally, it does. What was a Chupacabra doing there?"

"Lost dog, I'm guessing," Sophia suggested.

Hiker arched an eyebrow, his gaze drifting to Mama Jamba. "Something tells me that woman was behind it."

Sophia glanced at the old woman, sleeping peacefully and sounding like she was about to start vibrating the Castle with her snoring. "Well, I have what she asked for, but…" She held up the basket of mushrooms.

"She's not asleep," Hiker told her.

Sophia shook her head. "Of course she is. Why else would she be snoring and all?"

"Because I asked her a very direct question she didn't feel like answering," he answered.

Sophia laughed. "So, faking sleep was the way to get out of it."

Hiker pursed his lips. "I'd prefer that over some other things Mama has done to avoid helping me. She disappeared for the better part of a century once when I asked her how to avoid another Bubonic Plague outbreak in major cities. Apparently, the answer was, 'Figure it out yourself.'"

Sophia knew the leader of the Dragon Elite was exaggerating. Mama Jamba had gone into hiding a few times, the most recent occasion when Sophia'd had to track her down inside the center of the planet.

"I guess you did figure it out then," Sophia guessed, remembering her history.

Hiker combed his hands through his long blond hair and nodded. "That's what the Dragon Elite do. We figure things out and help the planet to avoid disasters." He snapped his fingers in Mama Jamba's direction, making a sharp, crisp sound. "Mama! Go ahead and quit the act. I won't pester you anymore for information that would cost you little effort to pass along to me."

At once, the old woman with Dallas hair sat up, looking quite alert. "Well, I'm glad we've come to an agreement on the matter." She apprised Sophia with a scrutinizing expression. "You didn't get all of the mushrooms like I asked."

Sophia held her chin up firmly. "No, I didn't. Instead, the twig and leaf people gathered one of each at my request."

Mama Jamba considered this. "I'm sure the Celcidas were most grateful for your help with the Chupacabra."

"The Celcidas," Sophia repeated, vaulting the term for the leaf and twig people away in her memory.

"Yes," Mama Jamba affirmed. "Lovely race. Very peaceful and great little helpers."

"Are you the one responsible for putting a Chupacabra there?" Hiker asked, accusation in his tone.

Mama Jamba pursed her lips. "Son, why would I do that?"

"To create an extra bit of complication for Sophia," he answered. "She obviously couldn't just go to Sherwood Forest to gather mushrooms. That would be too simple."

The old woman brushed lint off her velour tracksuit. "Son, despite the fact that you think I go out of my way to make things difficult for you and the Dragon Elite, I try and do exactly the opposite. I needed a place for the mushrooms to grow for the tracking spell for the demon dragons. Sherwood Forest was an ideal location. It just so happened to have a Chupacabra invading it. I figured it was a win-win situation. Have Sophia rid the forest of the little guy and also make it a place for the mushrooms to grow."

Sophia laughed. "That little guy nearly ate Lunis as a snack."

Mama Jamba nodded. "Disguising him as a kitten was a very clever approach. The guys would have tried to slice the thing in half and probably died in the process."

Hiker looked between Sophia and Mama Jamba in confusion. "Wait, you disguised your dragon as a kitten? That's highly dangerous. You could have really created problems for him."

Sophia knew he was right, but shrugged. "As it was, he might need counseling to deal with the emotional pain. I caught him purring, but he totally lied about it."

Casting an annoyed glare at Mama Jamba, Hiker said, "What do you mean, the guys would have died in the process?"

"I said, probably," Mama Jamba corrected. "And it's true. They use brute force, whereas Sophia employs strategy. I don't know many who would have used a kitten to fight a Chupacabra."

"Not anyone sane," Hiker admitted.

"Hey, it worked," Sophia argued.

"That it did," Mama Jamba interrupted. "However, why is it that you only got one of each mushroom when you were instructed to get all of them?"

Sophia set the basket down on the coffee table in front of Mother Nature. "Because it felt wrong to take all of them."

Hiker growled with annoyance. "We don't make decisions based on how things feel."

Mama Jamba's eyes cut over to him, her chin down. "You don't, son."

"The Dragon Elite don't," he argued.

Sophia cleared her throat. "Feelings are a part of who I am. I contend they can be vital for my decision making."

"Really? Well, they seem to have vitally misdirected you," Hiker stated. "You didn't do what Mama asked you to, and now we've lost time, and we're that much farther from being able to track down the demon dragons."

"Depleting the forest of every single mushroom was wrong," Sophia told him with conviction. "It wasn't right to take such an unsustainable approach for our purposes. We're important, but not more so than others we are supposed to share resources and this planet with. If we just took everything, then we'd become the problem. We'd be the ones that others would need to protect mortals from instead of us being the ones who protect them."

"Sophia, sometimes your self-righteous attitude goes too far," Hiker complained, anger flaring on his face.

Heat made Sophia's head tense with a sudden headache. She felt both frustrated and embarrassed. She was certain that what she'd done was the right thing, but arguing it with Hiker was making her angry in a way she rarely felt.

"Where's the line, sir?" Sophia asked, throwing her arm wide. "Do the rules apply to everyone else and not us because we think we're in charge? How are we supposed to garner trust with a 'Do as I say and not as I do' mentality?"

Hiker narrowed his eyes at her before spinning to look at Mama Jamba. "You thought she was ready for a leadership role. Now look at what you've done. We've empowered a holier than thou, pious pain in the ass."

"Son, I didn't force you to promote Sophia," Mama Jamba began. "I suggested it, but this was your decision. May I advise the mark of a good leader is standing by their decisions rather than blaming others when they think that things have gone wrong?"

"Fine, then I take responsibility for making the child a leader," he grumbled.

Sophia narrowed her eyes at the Viking but decided it best to ignore him. "I stand by my decision not to wipe out all the mushrooms in Sherwood Forest."

"Admitting when you make a mistake is a virtue, Sophia," Hiker said, his voice rising.

"I didn't make a mistake." Sophia matched his volume, her fists by her side.

He sighed dramatically, stomping back over to his desk. "Well, now what are we going to do to track down the demon dragons, Mama?"

Calmly, Mother Nature leaned forward and picked up a single mushroom from the top of the stack. "I'm going to make the potion like I planned. It will take some time."

Both Hiker and Sophia whipped around to face the old woman.

"What?" Hiker asked, shocked. "You don't have all the mushrooms."

She held up the one in her hand, studying it. "No, and I didn't really need them."

"But you told Sophia to get all of them," he continued, confused.

"I did," Mama Jamba said. "She used her own judgment to do what she thought was best."

"She defied Mother Nature," he argued.

"She listened to her heart," she disagreed. "Just imagine how hard it was for her to do that knowing that one of the most powerful entities alive told her to do one thing, and she didn't follow those instructions." Smiling proudly, Mama looked at Sophia. "The mark of a good leader is following what they think is right when those more powerful than them advise them otherwise. Always listen to your moral compass, Sophia. It will never steer you wrong. Your feelings calibrate it. Listen to those too."

Hiker pressed both his hands to the sides of his head in a vice grip. "So you didn't want Sophia to actually get all of the mushrooms, then?"

"Of course not," Mama Jamba scoffed. "That would have depleted the forest and left many animals without. What an awful thing to do."

"Are you always trying to test us?" Hiker asked, irritation heavy in his voice.

"Empower you," Mama Jamba corrected. "I'm trying to help you to become the best versions of yourself."

"Being straight would do that," he stated.

She shook her head. "That's coddling, son. I might be your mama, but I'm not about enabling my children. If I tell you everything you need to know and exactly how to do things, then you never have the opportunity to figure things out on your own. One day, I might not be here to help you, and you've got to know how to trust your own instinct and find your own way."

"What?" Hiker questioned at once, worry in his tone. "What do you mean you might not be here one day? Are you running off again?"

Mama Jamba began humming as she sorted through the basket of mushrooms, ignoring the question entirely.

"Mama?" Hiker demanded.

"Oh, son, I don't know the future," she said, her focus still on the mushrooms. "I don't have any plans of leaving the Gullington, but you never know where the winds will blow you."

"The thing is, you actually do since you control them," Hiker reminded her.

Mama Jamba batted her eyes at him. "That's true. Now, I better go get started on this spell. Please remember that although this might lead you to the demon dragons, there are no guarantees."

Hiker nodded. "Yes, we can't force them to return. I remember your warning from before."

"Very good, son." Mama Jamba picked up the basket to leave the study. Over her shoulder, she sang, "I think that's a fine idea, son."

Hiker blinked at her. "What is?"

"That thought you just had," she answered as she trotted out of the office.

Sophia was just about to follow the old woman out when Hiker cleared his throat loudly, a gesture obviously meant to pause her.

"Yes, sir?" she said, turning to face him.

"I'm sorry," he muttered, barely audible.

Sophia didn't say a word, merely pressed her lips together.

"I realize that you and I have two very different styles," he went on. "That's one reason I thought you'd make a good leader. I get that doubting you isn't helpful, but you are new in this role. Mama doesn't make it easy by saying one thing and then expecting another. Anyway, my point is, you did well with this mission."

Sophia decided rubbing it in that she was right was probably ill-advised. She just nodded and said, "What would you have me do next, sir?"

"Go and check on the potion for Ainsley," he ordered. "There isn't much else to do until Mama creates her spell, and I know the elf is anxious to return to the elfin council."

Sophia knew she didn't imagine the regret in Hiker's voice. She kept her gaze low and nodded, realizing that as hard as it was for her to let Ainsley go, it was going to be a million times harder for him.

CHAPTER TWENTY-THREE

Sophia half-expected for Rudolf to materialize beside her when she strode down Roya Lane. The king of the fae always seemed to be hanging out on the magical road, conducting some sort of business. She hadn't heard from him about their new business venture regarding the healing elixir. He was apparently taking care of most of the details, working with Bep—the potions expert. Ruling over a kingdom had to be demanding, Sophia had reasoned.

Keeping her head down, Sophia hurried to Rose Apothecary to see the potions expert. She had expected the healing elixir would have been ready already, but then again, it was a pretty complex potion that hadn't been tried before with these ingredients. Sophia felt strange to be giving the first dose to Ainsley. It worried her it might not be right and could have complications, but the elf knew the risks and was adamant about taking it when it was ready.

The door to Rose Apothecary chimed when Sophia entered the shop, marking her arrival.

"We're closed," Bep barked as soon as Sophia stepped through. "Come back in a week."

Sophia blinked at the potions expert who was hunched over a cauldron in the middle of the shop. There were ingredients everywhere, and a strange, sweet odor wafted through the usually orderly shop.

"It's me," Sophia called, striding over to the magician, careful to step over the many things strewn across the wooden floor.

"It's me isn't a way of introducing yourself," Bep corrected, stirring the cauldron. Sweat was beading on her forehead from the heat rising up from the flames below the pot. "And, we're closed."

"For a week?" Sophia checked over her shoulder at the door. There wasn't a "Closed" sign on the front. It hadn't been locked.

"Until I say so," Bep stated. "Maybe a week. Maybe longer. Depends."

"On?" Sophia asked.

"We're closed," Bep said, leaning down so low her head nearly disappeared inside the cauldron.

"You mentioned that," Sophia agreed, striding over. "How is the healing potion coming along?"

"How do you know about that?" Bep asked, whipping her head up and spying Sophia with surprise. "Oh, it's you."

"Who did you think it was?" Sophia demanded.

"A customer," Bep answered.

"That's how you treat customers?" Sophia laughed.

"When we're closed, and I tell them so clearly."

"Again, why are you closed?" Sophia wanted to know. "Not in the business of making money?"

"I used to be, and then I took on this project for you, and it's taken all my attention. The store has to remain closed until I get this right," Bep explained, returning her attention to the cauldron. "It's a very tricky and demanding potion. I need more of the dragon eggshells. I told you that."

Sophia shook her head. "No, you didn't."

Bep picked up a pinch of purple powder from a bowl and tossed it into the cauldron, making it hiss with complaint. "I told that flamboyant man you work with. He said he'd bring by some in a few days, and that was several days ago." She looked up suddenly. "He can't tell time, can he? Probably can't count either. Fae have no bearings."

"Probably can't count or tell time," Sophia admitted. "But that's not like Rudolf. He's unpredictable, but he is dependable. He said he'd be in charge of delivering the dragon eggshells. I gave him all that we had, and he was keeping them safe for us."

Bep raised an eyebrow. "You can't trust a fae. He swindled you. Took all the dragon shell eggs and sold them on the dark market."

Sophia shook her head. "Rudolf wouldn't do that."

"That's exactly what a fae does," Bep argued. "I bet you he told you that you'd be business partners. He came to you with the idea, and said he'd handle all the details if you'd provide him with the dragon eggshells."

Sophia chewed on her lip, not wanting to admit that Bep was correct. "I'm sure he's busy and hasn't had a chance to deliver you more ingredients."

Bep shook her head, taking a step backward. "Well, we've got another batch that's no good. I can't make any more until I get those eggshells."

Twisting her mouth to the side, Sophia thought. "I think I can scrounge up some pieces from the Cave and Nest at the Gullington. They won't be large sections like you had before, but enough to work with until I can find the ones I gave to Rudolf."

"You won't find that shifty fae," Bep told her. "He ran off with your dragon eggshells. But yes, that will work."

Sophia's chest ached. She refused to believe King Rudolf Sweetwater had deceived her. He was many things. Insulting. Ridiculous. Ditzy. Annoying. However, Sophia knew at her core he was trustworthy. He had more money than anyone she knew. There was no reason for him to double-cross her.

How do you think he made so much money? Lunis said in her head, having witnessed everything she'd seen and heard at the shop through scrying.

Sophia sighed. *He got his money through the Las Vegas Strip.*

Right, Lunis chirped. *And you think that someone who profits off of gambling and general debauchery in a place nicknamed Sin City is worthy of your trust and wouldn't deceive you?*

He's helped me many times, Sophia argued. *Liv says he's saved her butt several times. Why would he do something like this?*

I don't know, Soph, but you've got to track him down. I can check into gathering up the bits of dragon eggshells in the corners of the Nest, but it won't be much, and I don't suspect that any more eggs will be hatching soon.

Sophia nodded, realizing that Bep was watching her, and didn't know she was having a conversation with her dragon in her head. *Okay, have one of the guys deliver the dragon eggshells to Bep. I'll find Rudolf, and if he has double-crossed me, then the Captains are going to grow up fatherless.*

Then they might have a fighting chance of being half normal, Lunis teased.

Sophia shook her head. The Captains were the first halflings in history, being both mortal and fae. She wanted to believe that having Rudolf as their father would make them even more legendary. However, she was starting to doubt her judgments. Maybe she didn't know the king of the fae at all. If that was true, what else had she misjudged?

CHAPTER TWENTY-FOUR

Where before Sophia had cut around Roya Lane, not wanting to be noticed, now she marched boldly in the direction of the Fantastical Armory, her head held high. She shoved past gnomes blocking the avenue and elves panhandling for money, not in the mood for their antics. She was plainly madder than hell.

As soon as she'd left Rose Apothecary, Sophia had used her phone to track down Liv. Thanks to the location sharing app, she knew her sister was hanging out at the Fantastical Armory at the end of Roya Lane.

If anyone could help her track down Rudolf, then it was Liv. Hopefully, she had room in her schedule. Otherwise, she wouldn't have her sister to pull her off the fae when she rearranged his face. She was having a hard time believing what Bep said about him double-crossing her, and yet, there was little other explanation.

Sophia swung the door open with more force than she intended when she entered Subner's weapon shop. Liv, Subner, and Papa Creola all tensed at the sound of the intrusion.

With an angry glare on her face, Sophia stood in the doorway, trying to quell the fire building in her.

"Soph?" Liv asked, hurrying over. "What's going on?"

Of course, her sister could read the frustration on her face.

Before Sophia could open her mouth to explain, Papa Creola drew in a breath like he was smelling the air. "She believes she's been deceived."

The way he phrased that gave Sophia pause. She tilted her head to the side. "Haven't I, Papa Creola?"

He raised both his eyebrows and shook his head. "Deception is a subjective state. You are the only one who can tell whether it's happened to you."

Sophia narrowed her eyes at the elfin hippie. She should have expected such a nonhelpful answer. Returning her gaze to Liv, she cleared her throat. "It's Rudolf. I have reason to believe he's skipped town with my dragon eggshells."

Liv's mouth popped open. She appeared about to say something and then shook her head. "He wouldn't do that."

"That's what I thought," Sophia agreed. "I'm having a hard time trying to come up with another explanation. He was supposed to give them to my potions expert and he hasn't. I tried calling him, and his phone goes straight to voicemail."

Liv nodded. "That's because he doesn't understand that his phone has to be charged regularly. It's always dying. He thinks just sending it positive thoughts works to fuel it." Pulling her phone out of her pocket, Liv began scrolling through her contacts. "I always call his wife, Serena's phone if I really need to get ahold of him."

"Meaning that you want a headache," Subner said dryly from the other side of the shop.

"Pretty much," Liv said, nodding, holding the phone up to her ear. After a moment, her face brightened. "Hey, Serena. Is Rudolf around there?"

She paused, listening.

"You haven't seen him," she stated after a bit. Then she groaned. "But you had LASIK this morning and haven't seen anything...Right. And the triplets? Who is watching them?"

Liv lowered her chin, annoyance on her face. "You realize they can't watch each other."

Sophia could hear the mortal on the other side of the line.

"Because they aren't old enough," Liv argued and then shook her head. "Yes, please call the nanny and have her come over. Now, do you know where your husband could be? When was the last time you saw him?"

Liv appeared to really be restraining herself after listening to Serena's response. "Yes, of course, I meant before the surgery." Another pause. "That long ago?"

She mouthed, "A few days" to Sophia.

She slumped, realizing that Rudolf could really be anywhere.

"He said he was going to get you some hallucinogenic cookies," Liv repeated tentatively. "Yeah, I think I know where he was headed. Thanks, Serena. Please get someone to watch the Captains." She listened. "Actually, I think the babies being really quiet is more of a cause for concern than if you could hear them."

A worried expression covered Liv's face but was quickly replaced with relief. "Oh, good. I'm glad to hear the staff says the babies are quiet because they aren't there. Get some rest and good luck with the eyes."

She paused. "Yes, I'll tell Rudolf to bring you some Jolly Ranchers when we find him. Of course, you want green apple. Like there's any other flavor."

Liv shut off the phone right away, and sensing Sophia's concern she managed a smile. "Apparently, the nanny picked up the triplets before Serena's surgery, but she forgot because that was yesterday, and she doesn't always remember things between sleeps."

"Makes sense," Sophia muttered. "So he went to Crying Cat Bakery, did he?"

"That's the last place that Serena knew he was going to," Liv answered.

Sophia swung around and made for the door. "Well, then let's go track down that fae. He better work on a healing elixir because that might be the only way to save himself when I get a hold of him."

CHAPTER TWENTY-FIVE

"I just don't think it's funny," Cat said when Liv and Sophia entered the magical bakery.

Lee sighed, running her hands through her short hair. "I don't think you get the joke."

"That's the thing. I don't think it's a joke," Cat retorted in her thick French accent.

Lee glanced at the sisters and nodded. "Good. You all can tell Cat how funny I am."

"She's hilarious," Liv stated blankly. "We've got a question."

"I do too," Lee cut her off. "I've decided to try a new type of assassination."

Sophia coughed abruptly, giving the assassin baker a pointed expression.

"I-I mean, another type of business venture," Lee corrected. "That definitely isn't meant to kill people."

Sophia covered her face, wondering how she got mixed up with these types. She was half grateful she did because they were entertaining and made her seem normal. Then she wondered if she was actually the crazy one to have friends like this. "You're practicing this new assassination style on your wife? Is that right?" Sophia asked.

"Well, it's obviously not working so no harm, no win," Lee answered, changing the usual phrase of "No harm, no foul." The baker assassin smiled sweetly at her wife. "I try all my killer moves on this woman. She's invincible, though. I try and drop an anvil on her head, and it tumbles to the side and misses her. The woman has more lives than a lynx."

"More than nine, huh?" Liv asked.

"Can you stop trying to kill people with anvils?" Sophia complained. "It's very Wile E. Coyote and the last time I checked, you're not a cartoon. Oh, and by the way, can you also stop trying to kill people?"

"You would be luckier telling her to kill people," Cat said, striding over to a table. "Tell her to do something, and she does the opposite. 'Pick up your clothes, Lee,' and guess what? Nothing happens. 'Kill that guy over there, dear.' Guess what happens? He lives. Lee is great at playing the opposite game."

"He was a paying customer," Lee argued, putting her hands on her hips.

"He came into the shop before I'd had my coffee," Cat stated.

"It was five o'clock in the afternoon," Lee said.

"And I had just woken up...without coffee," Cat said like that should have been obvious.

"Anyway." Lee focused on the sisters. "I'm thinking of a more subtle art of ass...ridding the world of people."

Sophia sighed. "It doesn't matter how you phrase it."

"Okay, cool," Lee said victoriously. "We're going to be open about this now. I like being candid."

"That's not what I meant," Sophia disagreed.

"Anyway, I was thinking of killing people through laughter," Lee went on. "Many people tell me that I'm so funny it hurts."

"Who says that?" Cat asked, combing through bits and bobs scattered across a table.

"People," Lee answered. "Anyway, I've heard I'm deadly funny."

"I think you heard things wrong." Cat continued to sort through various objects, getting Liv's attention.

"What's all that?" the Warrior for the House of Fourteen asked.

"Not stolen merchandise," Cat answered at once and started to whistle inconspicuously.

Liv sighed. "When you say, 'not stolen merchandise,' do you mean the opposite?"

"Yes, I mean bought items," Cat stated.

Sophia shook her head at her sister. "I've found it better to just not ask questions. Pretend you have seen nothing."

"Oh, the old, 'don't ask the question unless you're prepared for the answer' approach," Liv grumbled. "Yes, I had a boyfriend who went by that mentality. Real stand-up guy. By that, I mean, he kept his head in the sand all the time."

"Exactly," Sophia explained. Liv knew the bakers because she knew everyone as a Warrior for the House of Fourteen, but she wasn't quite as familiar with Lee and Cat. "Just pretend for the next few moments they aren't giving you clues to all the illegal things they run."

"Here I thought we'd never find common ground," Lee said with affection. "Anyway, let me try some deadly jokes on you."

"I don't want to die," Liv declared.

"No worries," Cat said. "I think she'll have a better chance of killing people with bad jokes than with laughter."

"I think you need to get back to sorting through the stuff you pinched off the back of that truck, dear," Lee told her wife over her shoulder.

Sophia put her fingers in her ears. "I'll act like I didn't hear that."

"Hear what?" Liv asked, playing along.

"Okay, so here's a joke," Lee started, clearing her throat. "What's the key to comedy?"

Sophia glanced at her sister, expecting her to answer. Liv just returned the expression.

"Hey, so what's the key to comedy?" Lee repeated.

"What?" Sophia asked.

A beat later, Lee chirped, "Timing."

Sophia's eyes darted to the side. "Um, I think you missed the punch line there."

Lee burst out laughing, slapping her leg. "That's the point. Get it? Timing. And I missed the timing?"

"The joke needs work," Liv said carefully. "Get it right, and it will kill."

"Right now, it's killing me," Cat complained darkly, continuing to sort through packaged items and humming.

Sophia shook her head. "Although this is great fun, we were hoping you could help us. Have you seen Rudolf Sweetwater?"

"Rudolf?" Lee scratched her head.

Liv rolled her eyes. "Yeah, the braindead guy who is in charge of an entire race of people. Deadly attractive and also fatally annoying."

Lee combed her fingers over her chin. "Not ringing a bell. Does he have a nose ring?"

Sophia's nose flared with frustration. "The guy I sent you to the Great Library with."

Lee continued to think. "Red hair and I wanted to murder him?"

"You're thinking of me, darling," Cat told her.

"Of course I am," Lee said. "Oh, I remember now. The guy who is dumber than a sack of flour."

"Yes!" Liv exclaimed like they were playing charades, and Lee had finally gotten the clue.

"Oh, him!" Lee sang. "Yeah, I expected him a bit ago and he never showed. He was supposed to bring me some illegal demon blood I was going to use in a cake."

Sophia closed her eyes. "Please refrain from providing those details. When was that? Do you have any other information?"

Lee thought. "Honestly, I was drunk and I thought I heard some yelling out here. A voice that sounded like Rudolf, but when I checked, there were just signs of a struggle and no sign of the fae, so it was probably nothing."

"Signs of a struggle?" Liv asked.

Lee waved her off. "Nothing of importance. It's just that I found a chunk of blond hair in the alleyway. Probably just some cool date planned by a thoughtful lover."

"This hair?" Liv asked. "You don't by chance have it?"

Sophia shook her head. "Come on, like she'd keep that—"

"Of course I do," Lee interrupted. "I was going to put it in a souffle."

"Remind me never to eat here," Liv muttered to her sister.

Sophia nodded as Lee pulled a clump of hair from her pocket.

"You kept it in your pants pocket?" Sophia wondered why she was surprised by this.

Lee blanched at her. "It's good luck."

Liv shook her head. "You have weird friends, Soph…"

"Well, your friend might have double-crossed me," Sophia argued.

Her sister was already busy doing a spell on the short patch of blond hair. All the blood drained from Liv's face when she faced Sophia. "Ru didn't double-cross you, Soph. That's his hair. I think he was abducted."

CHAPTER TWENTY-SIX

The spell Liv had used didn't tell them anything except that the clump of hair belonged to Rudolf. Lee had said there were signs of a struggle in the alleyway. They were jumping to conclusions, thinking he'd been abducted. Although Rudolf did many strange and unexplainable things, he would never, ever willingly lose his own hair. He prided himself on his shiny locks of blond.

Even more unlike the fae was to let his friends down. He was many things, but strangely enough, he was reliable. If he said he was bringing something to Lee, then he would do it. If he was supposed to deliver the dragon eggshells to Bep, then he would have done that, unless something was preventing him.

Sophia's heart, which had been constricted with anger moments prior, was suddenly aching. She didn't understand why someone would go after the fae, but the longer she thought about it, the more sense it made. He had his fair share of enemies, having been around for longer than most people she knew of. His flippant attitude and airheaded ways ensured that most went away from an interaction with him irritated and offended. Also, as the king of the fae, he was a powerful and rich man. So it went to reason there were a ton of giants, gnomes, magicians and elves who might want him for various reasons.

"I just hope he's okay," Sophia said to Liv as they exited the shop.

Liv took a tentative bite of a chocolate cake donut and paused as she chewed, as though waiting to see if she'd keel over dead from poison. "He's Rudolf. He's more resilient than a *turritopsis nutriculas*."

"Oh, no," Sophia groaned. "You've been poisoned and have lost the ability to talk."

"Jellyfish," Liv said, taking another bite. "That's what the *turritopsis nutriculas* is, but more specifically it's an immortal jellyfish. Once they reach adulthood, they revert their bodies back to that of their younger selves and do it all over again. Pretty impressive, although the little shits ruined my honeymoon last year."

"I thought a bunch of deranged elves or pirates did that," Sophia asked, wondering how their conversation had derailed and then reminded herself she was talking to Liv, and that was par for the course.

"The pirates made it more exciting," Liv explained. "The jellyfish made it so I couldn't escape the ship by diving into the water, which was annoying."

"Most people don't prefer such excitement on their honeymoon," Sophia related.

"Most people are boring," Liv retorted.

"I'm not arguing with that." Sophia watched as her sister finished the donut. She must have given her a strange expression because Liv flashed her an embarrassed grin.

"No, I'm not really hungry, thinking about Rudolf being in danger," she explained, wiping her hands on her pants. "I had to force that down. I wouldn't have eaten this if I didn't need to ensure my magical reserves were good for whatever was coming next."

Sophia nodded, wishing she'd thought ahead the same way. Liv was practical, even in the face of emotions. She was good at compartmentalizing—something Sophia needed to learn.

"Yes, about what's to come next," Sophia said, chewing on her lip.

"We need information." Liv watched as a shifty bunch of gnomes walked around them, giving the sisters a wide berth. "I'm going to go and see Mortimer at the Official Brownie Headquarters. His Brownies might have seen something. If not, it's at least worth having him keep some eyes out. If Rudolf is in the presence of mortals, he'll know about it."

"You think that's possible?" Sophia asked, not having considered mortals. "I mean, Rudolf is pretty powerful, and a mortal abducting him would be difficult."

Liv shrugged. "Remember never to discount your potential suspects, especially at the beginning of an investigation. Rudolf is powerful but doesn't demonstrate it often. He's also trusting to a fault and prone to seeing the good in things that aren't there."

Sophia felt the pang of hurt again at the idea the optimistic fae had been abducted by someone. "Okay, and I'll go and see Mae Ling at the Fairy Godmother College. She might have a lead for us."

"We have the weirdest informants," Liv related. "But I'm glad for them."

"I agree," Sophia said. "I'll give you a call if I find out anything."

"Same," Liv stated, heading in the direction of the plain brick wall where the Official Headquarters for the Brownies was located. "And Soph..."

She paused to regard her sister, whose usual light expression had faded away. "Yeah?"

"Don't worry," Liv told her, hope in her voice. "Rudolf will be fine. For as many imbecile things as he's said, he isn't dumb, and he's a totally unlikely hero. I've been in battle with him enough to know he always rises to the occasion, somehow, someway."

Sophia smiled, having needed to hear that. "I know you're right." She stood there for a long moment, studying her sister, emotions brewing to the surface on her face. It appeared Liv's rogue emotions might have escaped from their locked compartment, if for just for a moment. Rudolf was one of her best friends, despite the fact she pretended she couldn't stand him. She was the godmother to his children. He had walked her down the aisle. No matter how stoic she pretended to be, Rudolf in danger had to be affecting the Warrior for the House of Fourteen.

"And Liv," Sophia said after a moment.

"Yeah?"

"Also, you don't worry," Sophia stated. "We're going to get Rudolf back. No matter what."

CHAPTER TWENTY-SEVEN

Sophia took a bite of the macaroon that opened the portal to Happily Ever After College, grateful for the nourishment. She also looked forward to visiting the college, where the weather was always pleasant, and the grounds were safe.

She felt like she had jinxed herself with that thought after stepping through the portal. Something raced at her from across the grassy lawn of the college. Sophia didn't have a chance to make out exactly what it was. She just saw horns barreling in her direction and threw up her defenses immediately.

Lifting her hand, she created an invisible dome shield around her. A large creature, the size of a horse, rammed into the shield before falling backward, shaking its head as it continued to stalk around her, obviously not deterred.

Being safe for the moment, Sophia took a moment to study the creature, which she'd never seen before. It was a magical creature, no doubt. The large animal was stalking back and forth, it's head down, heavy breaths cycling through its nostrils and looked quite angry with her. Even still, it was beautiful, resembling a stag with its large rack of horns on its head.

However, very different than a stag, the creature had white and navy blue fur, but not in a design like Sophia had ever seen before. Instead, its long white hair was marked with spirals of blue, like it had been spray painted. Down its back was longer, spikey blue hair that ran all the way down its tail, which resembled a cat's, long and curled at the tip. If it wasn't for the hostile expression in its eyes, Sophia would have thought the animal was exquisitely breathtaking. As it were, the creature looked to be plotting ways to murder her.

"Calm down, Okapi," Mae Ling said, hurrying over from the side, where Sophia hadn't even realized she'd been stationed next to a group of students. "She means you no harm, nor us or the lands."

Instantly, as if put under a spell, the creature shook its head and stepped away from Sophia's shield, appearing suddenly pleasant.

"You're safe," Mae Ling stated, turning her attention to Sophia. "Impressive reflexes."

Several yards away, the girls were starting to whisper, pointing in Sophia's direction.

"Did you see that?" one of the students asked another.

"She's a dragonrider," another mentioned.

"She fights in battles," a third commented.

All of them were regarding Sophia like she was the strange creature with antlers.

"What is that?" Sophia asked, daring to take her shield down as the magical animal began to graze on the soft green grass.

"That," Mae Ling began, drawing out the word, "is the very rare and incredible dahalo. Bermuda Laurens has kindly loaned us some of her animals for teaching purposes." She swept her hand at the grounds behind where the students were standing and Sophia noticed more magical creatures.

Although she wasn't familiar with the dahalo, she did recognize the animals grazing behind the girls. Anyone would have recognized the three white unicorns busy trimming the grass and seemingly unaware of the crowd of magicians around them.

Beside them, also nestled in the grass, were little creatures that looked much like hedgehogs, but Sophia knew they were of the magical variety. The little spiked creatures popped and disappeared and reappeared in various places as though playing a strange game of hide and seek.

"What are those?" Sophia asked, striding over to where the brown hedgehog creatures were stationed in the grass. There were roughly half a dozen, although it was hard to count them since they kept disappearing.

"Those are sonics," Mae Ling explained. "They are fiercely loyal creatures which are also full of good luck."

She knelt and picked up one of the animals, offering it to Sophia to hold. They were pretty much the cutest things Sophia had ever seen, making her want to protect it with her life. She took it, cuddling the creature to her chest.

"That sense of protectiveness you're feeling over the sonic is its defense mechanism," Mae Ling explained. "Those who lay eyes on them find their cuteness to be so irresistible they will do anything to guard the animal against harm. For that reason, they usually bond to one person and are quite protective of them, offering their person unwavering loyalty and luck."

"They are so very cute," Sophia said as the small animal nuzzled against her.

"They are," Mae Ling said matter-of-factly. "But you are already bonded to one magical creature who, by the way, I'd like to share with the class at some point. Would you be willing to bring your Lunis to the college the next time you visit?"

Sophia nodded. "Sure. I'm certain he will enjoy the attention."

Mae Ling frowned slightly. "Yes, you don't have a typical dragon, do you? Most wouldn't appreciate the attention."

"Lunis does," Sophia stated. "He's a diva like that."

"Well, our purposes would be for studying the creature," Mae Ling explained. "We learn about all magical animals here at fairy godmother college because they play a pivotal role in creating love and goodness in the world."

Sophia couldn't argue with that. "Yes, unicorns are supposed to promote peace and love, right?"

"That's correct," Mae Ling affirmed. "They also represent purity and healing. Although they are quite rare, much like the dahalo, this herd actually calls the grounds of Happily Ever After college home. They have been with us since the very beginning."

"Wow," Sophia whispered in awe as she watched the creatures with glistening white coats and long silky manes. The horns on the top of their heads appeared like porcelain, catching the sunlight streaming down.

"And the dahalo?" Sophia asked.

"Oh, they are very protective as well, like the sonics," Mae Ling explained. "As you can see, the creatures are fiercely territorial."

"Yes, that one nearly bowled me over." Sophia pointed to the majestic creature who seemed quite docile now as it grazed alongside the unicorns.

"You spooked it when you stepped through the portal," Mae Ling imparted. "You handled the situation correctly, using a defensive measure rather than an attack which would have resulted in an injury to you, Okapi, or both of you."

Sophia nodded, glad she hadn't pulled her sword and made the situation worse.

"The dahalo bring fertility to the lands they graze upon," Mae Ling informed her. "They also bring fertility to any in their presence. For that reason, they are revered for their abilities to promote new generations and bring children into the world."

Sophia smiled, amazed that magical creatures could have such positive effects on the world at large. "I see why you study them, then."

"Yes and speaking of which…" Mae Ling looked toward the sky. She turned her attention to the students who were quiet, listening to their exchange. "It's time for lunch, ladies. You may take a break now and return after your refreshments."

The women nodded, filing for the school building in the distance. When they had all left, Mae Ling gave Sophia a studious expression. "Now, you came here to ask me something."

Sophia was so enthralled by learning about the magical creatures, she's nearly forgotten the horrible reason that had brought her to

Happily Ever After College. She swallowed, laying the sonic back down in the grass next to the others. It disappeared at once and then reappeared a few yards away.

"Yes, it's about King Rudolf Sweetwater," Sophia began, feeling guilty for having a good time when Rudolf was out there somewhere, maybe abused and imprisoned.

"I don't know where he is," Mae Ling said in a heavy voice.

Sophia deflated. "Oh, well, it was worth a shot, asking anyway."

"I can tell you of someone who does," Mae Ling continued.

"Really?" Sophia asked, hope blossoming in her chest.

She was certain that Mae Ling would mention Mortimer or Father Time or maybe even Mama Jamba. What she imparted though, was not what Sophia expected.

"The person who knows where King Rudolfus Sweetwater will be is the one responsible for having him abducted," Mae Ling began.

Sophia tensed, listening intently. "Yes?"

"This person didn't do it, but they know who did," Mae Ling continued. "They know why he was abducted, which will tell you where to find him."

Sophia could hardly take the suspense much longer. "Who is it, Mae Ling?"

"It's a Councilor for the House of Fourteen," the fairy godmother said, a rare bit of anger flaring in her voice.

"What?" Sophia exclaimed. This was not what she was expecting. Clark, her brother, was a Councilor for the House of Fourteen. Hester DeVries, the renowned healer, was a Councilor. Liv's sister-in-law, Raina Ludwig was a Councilor. She knew all of them, had been raised with them and thought they could be trusted. Then she remembered the others, the ones who always filled her with unease.

Her mouth popped open.

"Who is it?" Sophia asked, expecting Mae Ling to say Bianca Mantovani.

Like reading her thoughts, Mae Ling shook her head. "It is the Councilor for the House of Fourteen who goes by Lorenzo Rosario. He's the reason that King Rudolfus Sweetwater is missing."

CHAPTER TWENTY-EIGHT

"I've never liked that man," Liv said when Sophia told her the news about Lorenzo Rosario.

The sisters were strolling the gardens in the House of Fourteen, constantly checking over their shoulders to ensure they weren't being overheard by someone. The House of Fourteen wasn't a safe place with traitors in their midst. That had been the case for decades, ever since their parents were murdered for trying to reveal the real history about mortals' inability to see magic.

However, Liv had thought that things were better now the Sinclairs had been gotten rid of. To their disappointment, it appeared there were still those who couldn't be trusted in the House of Fourteen, people who were dangerous and had ulterior agendas.

Sophia hadn't thought communicating what she'd learned from Mae Ling over the phone was a good idea. If Lorenzo was double-crossing the House, there could be magical taps on the phones. A council meeting was to start soon, meaning that Liv had to be at the House.

"Why would Lorenzo want Rudolf abducted?" Sophia asked, staring at the large fountain in the middle of the gardens. A demonic mermaid apparently lived in the water. Liv had warned her never to go near it, but after seeing the magical animals at Happily Ever After, Sophia was curious about the creature. She quelled the curiosity, though and worked to focus on the conversation at hand.

"It's hard to say," Liv mumbled, off in thought. "He and Bianca haven't liked mortals in the House of Fourteen for a while. They were supporters of the Sinclairs, but I don't know how Rudolf would be connected to their long term goals of returning things to the way they were."

Sophia shook her head. "It's so ridiculous that after everything, there are still those who don't want to share this world with mortals."

"They are seen as lesser by many snotty magicians, giving the rest of us a bad name," Liv admitted.

"But it shouldn't be about magic," Sophia argued. "Mortals hold the objectivity to our world precisely because they don't have magic that can either cook a man's dinner or cook the man."

Liv smiled. "I get it. You get it. Those who are corrupted by magic, don't. Anyway, yes, finding out the agenda behind abducting Rudolf is key."

"Doing it without drawing attention to ourselves is important too."

Liv laughed suddenly. "Maybe Lorenzo has a few extra hundred brain cells he wanted to get rid of."

Sophia didn't laugh. "Aww, the poor guy might be abused right now. Hurt and lonely."

"He might also think he's in an Escape room, and it's all a funny joke," Liv teased.

Sophia felt something move around in her pocket. Stiffening, she reached in, wondering what she'd find. To her relief, she found a small sonic. Pulling it out of her pocket, she held it up in her palm. He must have snuck into her cloak when she wasn't paying attention. The sonics' ability to pop between locations made them excellent at hiding away and sneaking into places.

"Oh, my gosh," Liv said, gushing. "That's the cutest thing I've ever seen."

Sophia nodded. "It's a sonic."

"Looks like a hedgehog," Liv imparted.

"Well, I think they are similar, but this one is magical."

She laid the creature down on a topiary, hoping it would be okay there until she could return it to Happily Ever After College.

"Hedgehogs," Liv began, shaking her head. "Why don't you just share the hedge?"

The little creature sniffed and winked at her.

"No," Liv said from the corner of her mouth as if answering for the creature.

Sophia laughed. "These are good luck if you want to keep this guy."

Liv shook her head. "Plato would eat it for lunch."

Sophia nodded. "Yeah, Lunis probably would too."

"Then we'd have bad luck," Liv added.

"I don't need that with a global dragon crisis and Rudolf missing."

"So how are we going to handle this Lorenzo situation?" Liv asked. "I'm thinking either we spear him with my sword or yours."

"I don't think that will work."

"Okay, then. How about both?" Liv suggested.

"No, I think we have to play this carefully," Sophia said. "If we call Lorenzo out on this, then we will get farther away from the truth. He'll start to cover things up, and we'll lose our lead. Not only that, but getting a House member out of their position is difficult—"

"Tell me about it," Liv groaned. "I had to kill the Sinclairs to get them out."

"Exactly," Sophia said. "So instead, we find a way to get information out of Lorenzo secretly. We play the game. We don't let anyone know that we're onto him. We play this as stealthily as possible."

Liv nodded. "I like that approach. It's careful and smart and gives us a chance to kill Lorenzo without him seeing it coming."

"We won't be killing the flea eating jerk yet," Sophia stated. "First, we need all the information out of him."

"Yes, and dead men can't talk," Liv related.

"So we scare him into admitting all he knows," Sophia continued. "Then we figure it out from there. We have to play this strategically."

"I like this plan," Liv said. "It's a bit conservative. Do I get to at least give Lorenzo a black eye at some point?"

Sophia nodded. "One hundred percent. When the time is right."

"Okay," Liv agreed. "This is smart because Lorenzo and Bianca and Haro have ruled the voting and allowed another shady family into the House of Fourteen, throwing everything off balance. If I tried to storm in now, exposing Lorenzo, things wouldn't go in my favor."

Sophia groaned. "So, the Sinclairs have finally been replaced then?"

Liv nodded. "Unfortunately, by a family who has deep pockets and lots of questionable agendas."

"Why is everything always political?" Sophia asked.

"Because those with power like to take advantage," Liv answered.

Sophia hung her head, feeling a sudden pang of hopelessness.

Liv wrapped her arm around her shoulder and hugged her in close. "Don't worry. There's another part of that. Those who want the best for the world know how to steal the power." She cinched her in tightly. "That's us. We are the ones who are going to save the world. We may not crave power, but we know how to get it because it saves the world. Don't worry. The Beaufonts will always persevere."

Sophia smiled. "You're right. *Familia est Sempiternum.*"

CHAPTER TWENTY-NINE

After concocting an idea for how to get the information out of Lorenzo, Sophia decided to return to the Gullington to prepare. She needed to rest up and touch base with Hiker. This would also give Liv an opportunity to get some things in motion. Getting Lorenzo out of the House of Fourteen was key but doing that was tricky since Councilors rarely left the place—preferring the security of the magical building.

So to find out why Rudolf was abducted, you're going to abduct someone? Lunis questioned as the pair sat on the crags overlooking the Pond. Sophia was dangling her feet over the side while Lunis did pretty much the same thing, sitting almost like a human.

"Yeah, tit for tat sort of thing," she answered.

I'm good at kidnappings, Lunis bragged.

She gave him a skeptical expression. "How do you know that?"

It just seems like something that I'd be naturally good at.

Sophia shook her head. "Sorry, I have to leave you behind for this one. Lorenzo can't know it's us, and dragon wings beating are pretty noticeable."

I don't have to fly, he argued. *I could tiptoe and just be the muscle.*

She laughed. "You are definitely the muscle. I think I have to do this one with Liv."

He sighed dramatically. *Oh, Liv, the bane of my existence.*

"She's not either," Sophia said, turning to face Lunis. "You guys get along famously."

He looked down his nose at her. *She hasn't once called me by my real name. Every time I see her, she makes a pun. The last time she said something like, 'I didn't realize you took up smoking, Kyle,' when smoke billowed from my nostrils.*

Sophia giggled. "I contend that you two are pretty much the same. You are the king of bad puns."

That's false, he argued. *I'm the laird of good puns.*

"You'd rather be a laird than a king?" Sophia questioned.

Yes, I'm noble like that, he said smugly.

"And so modest too."

I guess I'll stay here and change dragon diapers while you go off and live the glamourous life, he said grumpily.

"Yeah, so glamourous," she replied. "I've got to risk my life to abduct a two-faced jerk who is behind something to do with Rudolf."

Maybe there's a war building between magicians and fae again that we don't know about, Lunis reasoned.

"When was there one before?"

Ages ago, he answered. *It doesn't get talked about much in the history books because it was pretty embarrassing for both sides. Magicians prepared for this huge war, sticking all their resources into it, pretty much going bankrupt as a race. The fae got distracted by something shiny or whatever and forgot to show up. They apparently all went on a booze cruise on some huge ship. When they got back, the magicians were bored and broke, and both sides forgot what they were fighting about.*

"I'm glad that gets glossed over in the history books," Sophia related.

That's the thing about wars though, Lunis began, slipping into his sage-like tone. *What starts them is usually forgotten about during the actual battle. By the end, the various sides forget what started the whole thing. It becomes about winning rather than being right.*

Sophia nodded. "That makes sense. There's too much ego in war."

Which is why the Dragon Elite have such an important mission, he concluded. *It's our job to erase those issues and get disputing parties to compromise, avoiding violence and other acts of war.*

Sophia pursed her lips, suddenly feeling heavy. It was like that lately. Back and forth between lightness and then once reminded of their current problems, back to feeling weighed down. "That's exactly why we have to take back our roles and get the world to respect us as adjudicators."

I sense that's going to get a lot harder before it gets easier, Lunis said.

"Why is that?" Sophia asked, not liking his rare pessimistic attitude.

Because something has Hiker in a foul mood and I'm guessing it's global news related to the demon dragons.

"Really?" Sophia asked, tilting her head to the side. "How do you know that?"

Because he's standing right behind us, glaring in our direction, Lunis told her.

Sophia turned to find her dragon was correct. Standing on the steps of the Castle was the large Viking, his arms crossed, and a frustrated expression on his face.

CHAPTER THIRTY

"I don't see how Nevin Gooseman and his gang of blind followers can blame this on us or the demon dragons," Sophia reasoned watching as Hiker thundered across his office, pacing with his hands balled up in his hair.

In the background, a small television broadcast the news about earthquakes that were rocking the United States.

Hiker paused, glaring out the window. "They can spin it all sorts of ways."

Sophia didn't reply but instead turned her focus to the television as Nevin Gooseman started to speak.

"It's about balance," the politician began, standing in front of the White House. "These demon dragons have thrown that off completely. Before they began hatching, we never suffered from so many natural disasters. The earthquakes are just the start. Tsunamis will be next. The tropical storms building in the Atlantic will soon rock the east coast. Our nation is under attack, and it's because of those beasts. The Dragon Elite want you to bow to their command, but I assure you that you will lose your liberties in the process. They say they have Mother Nature on their side, but if that was true, then we wouldn't be facing such dangers on this planet. It appears they don't have Mother Nature on their side as much as they are holding her hostage. Where is she, I ask you?"

The man looked straight at the camera, with heat in his eyes. "Hiker Wallace, the supposed leader of the Dragon Elite, if you truly have Mother Nature, then prove it. I challenge you to show us she's on your side. If you don't and these natural disasters continue, then we will have no choice but to conclude that you and your evil dragons don't work for her, but rather against her. Maybe our efforts need to be in saving Mother Nature from the very people who have tricked us into believing they are working for her. If that was the case, then I don't think we'd be facing so many global issues. We never had these kinds of issues when the Dragon Elite were in hiding —a story that also doesn't add up. Tell us the truth, Mr. Wallace. Show us the truth."

At the conclusion of this, the crowd in the distance cheered. The camera panned out to show the spectators, many of them holding signs that read: "Free Mother Nature."

"Oh dear me," Mama Jamba said from her perch on the Chesterfield. She was looking into a small mirror on the coffee table and putting pink foam curlers in her hair.

"This is serious." Sophia understood why Hiker was so upset. Nevin Gooseman had planned this attack very carefully, and it had the potential to ruin the Dragon Elite for good. It was all about perception and right then, he was making everyone see things the way he painted them.

"It's beyond serious," Hiker affirmed. "We can't ignore this any longer. Mama, I'm going to need your help."

The old woman scrunched up her brow, rolling her bluish silver hair onto the curler. "You know I can't do that, son."

He sighed. "You can, but you won't."

She indicated her hair. "Do I look like I'm in a position to be seen by the public?"

"Take out the curlers," he ordered. "I'll call a press conference."

She shook her head. "I don't do press conferences, you know that. It's not my responsibility to make the world believe in me. Actually, it would only make things worse if the world saw me. Papa Creola and I made that decision a long time ago."

"Why?" he growled.

Mama Jamba stood, her height not changing dramatically. She was just a bit shorter than Sophia and rounder, of course. "Do I look like one of the most powerful entities in the world?"

"Well, no, but appearances are deceiving," Hiker reasoned.

"I know that," Mama Jamba replied. "You know that. However, the world judges everyone based on appearance. If I came out to the public, it could have far-reaching effects. People might not believe I am Mother Nature. They might lose faith in this planet, thinking someone so unassuming created the Earth. Believe me, son, it is better for everyone if I stay hidden and inconspicuous."

He clenched his hair again, his frustration palpable. "But you choose to look like that. You could be bigger than a mountain with vines for hair and totally god-like."

Mama Jamba sighed, taking a seat again and curling her feet up under her. "That really is exhausting. It's a waste of energy. I spent the first couple of centuries on this planet like that, and it really didn't suit me. I like my current appearance."

"It's just for a small press release," Hiker argued. "Then you can change back."

"No, son!" Mama Jamba exclaimed. "I've made up my mind. You'll just have to handle this yourself. I trust there's an option that you haven't considered."

"I just don't understand why you won't help," Hiker continued, undeterred. Sophia had never seen him like this. "The world needs you right now. They are scared and turning their backs on the very organization meant to help them."

"The world needs you right now, son," Mama Jamba imparted, her tone softer. "Gods shouldn't have to show themselves to help their followers believe. Faith has never been about seeing. Only a false god would put themselves on display. I firmly believe I'd lose followers by showing myself. Besides, I have many enemies, and making an appearance could be deadly for me."

Sophia thought that made sense. However, she knew how frustrating this was for Hiker. He believed Mama Jamba could fix this for them, but that wasn't going to happen. As she often did, she was relying on her children to fix their own problems. Their problems had never been so large. Nevin Gooseman had called Hiker out and made allegations about Mama Jamba. Not showing her was potentially devastating for the Dragon Elite's reputation.

"Well, I have to do something," Hiker muttered, glancing at the television, which was still showing protesters holding up signs that read: "Free Mother Nature."

"Why are there so many natural disasters happening right now?" Sophia asked, getting Mama Jamba's attention.

She smiled sweetly at her. "Because…"

Hiker growled, turning his back on them and staring out the window.

"Because there's so much global unease?" Sophia guessed.

"See, you all don't need me feeding you the answers," Mama Jamba said proudly. "You already know the truth. You just have to trust yourself."

Sophia nodded. Again that made sense. Mama Jamba taught them how to think for themselves. If she explained everything, they'd think the way she wanted them to instead of relying on their own thoughts. "So the storms and earthquakes are a result of mortals not trusting the Dragon Elite and causing so many protests. In essence, the more they fight us, the worst things will get?"

"Then Nevin Gooseman will point his finger at us," Hiker stated bitterly, his hands clasped behind his back.

"We just have to refute what he's saying," Sophia declared with confidence.

"No," Hiker said.

"We have to say something," Sophia argued. "We have to make a statement."

Hiker sighed. "When you argue with an idiot, those watching can't tell which is which. I refuse to stoop to his level and give attention to these ridiculous claims. We are the Dragon Elite. We're the reason that world wars have been avoided. The ones that did occur were during the times the dragons couldn't be seen by mortals."

"Well, thankfully, they can't see the demon dragons right now." Sophia sighed.

"And neither can we since we don't know where to look," Hiker said, turning to face Mama Jamba, who had gone back to doing her hair. "How are you coming along with that spell to track the demon dragons down? We need to find them, but right now they aren't showing on the Elite Globe and searching the planet is an inefficient use of our time and energy."

"It isn't ready," she answered.

"I figured as much," he said irritably. "How much longer?"

She shrugged, rolling her hair. "Hard to say."

Hiker, having expected such an answer, nodded.

"So you're not going to address Nevin Gooseman's allegations?" Sophia dared to ask. "You're not going to explain that Mama Jamba isn't our prisoner or that we're not responsible for the natural disasters?"

Hiker shook his head. "No, we're not. Much like Mama, we're going to hold strong, and when mortals believe in us again, it will be based on faith. She refuses to show herself to prove she's powerful, and I do too."

The old woman smiled wide. "That's it, son. Try and convince them, and you'll have to always persuade to get their favor. Allow them to find their way to you, and they will always return. Real leaders don't have to demand loyalty. They earn it by virtue of being strong and true."

Hiker drew in a breath. "I know you're right. I'll send the others out to assist where we can with relief efforts connected to these natural disasters. And you, Sophia—"

The leader of the Dragon Elite was interrupted by Sophia's phone buzzing in her pocket. She ignored it, but Mama Jamba didn't.

"You're going to want to get that, dear," she said, pointing to Sophia's pocket. "Hiker, Sophia will need to go on a side mission. It's of supreme importance."

He sighed. "Should I ask what it involves?"

Sophia checked her phone. It was a message from Liv. Everything was in place. She glanced up. "I've got to go abduct a Councilor for the House of Fourteen."

Hiker pursed his lips and nodded. "That seems about right. Don't get caught and try to not sully our already tarnished reputation."

CHAPTER THIRTY-ONE

Getting Lorenzo Rosario out of the House of Fourteen had proven a bit more difficult than Liv had envisioned, but it was necessary. Only Royals could enter the House of Fourteen for the most part, so if Lorenzo was abducted there, the list of suspects would be narrowed down quite a bit.

The Councilor's fear for his own safety and cowardly ways was definitely one of the reasons he didn't leave the sanctuary of the House of Fourteen. A man like Lorenzo had his share of enemies, ready to pounce on him when he finally ventured out. For that reason, he was more on guard than most as he hurried down the streets of Los Angeles.

"So, what exactly did you have to do?" Sophia asked Liv as they lurked in the shadows of an alleyway located along the route that Lorenzo was about to take.

The homeless man digging through the dumpster on the other side of the road didn't pay them much notice. This was because they appeared much like him wearing torn up clothes and dirty faces. Sophia had used a disguising spell to make both herself and Liv appear like older homeless women. Her hair was coarse and gray, and heavy wrinkles lined her face. Liv had decided she wanted to be an old man with stringy brown hair and a crooked nose. There was no way Lorenzo would recognize them, as long as Sophia kept the spell up, which would be a challenge if anything else drained her magic. Liv had promised to use her own reserves for anything they should need.

"I destroyed all of his medications," Liv said with a dry laugh. "After doing a bit of investigating, I found out that Lorenzo stocks up on his medications once a year from a specialty pharmacy here in the valley. He had to go in person to get it since the magicians who run the operation have strict controls on the substances, thanks to laws passed down from the House of Fourteen."

"I like the irony," Sophia said, laughing too. "But, you had to destroy his supply then?"

Liv nodded. "Yeah, damn House of Fourteen is going to hell apparently. Long overdue for maintenance. A stupid leaky roof is causing all sorts of problems."

Sophia gave her sister an impressed look. "Messing with the House is pretty difficult. I didn't think it could be magicked."

"Yeah, well, I know a lynx and normal rules of the House of Fourteen don't really apply to him," Liv explained. "So poor Lorenzo happened to go into his room to find his year's supply of medication all ruined."

Checking the darkened alleyway, Sophia listened carefully. Someone was coming.

"Are you ready?" she asked over her shoulder at Liv.

She balled up a fist and wrapped her other dirty hand around it, a vengeful expression on her face. "Yes. One hundred percent. Can't wait to give that traitor a black eye."

Sophia gave her sister a cautious expression. "First, we get the information. Then you can give him a memento."

CHAPTER THIRTY-TWO

Right on cue, Sophia stumbled out, cutting Lorenzo Rosario off as he made to cross down the darkened street. The magical pharmacy that was his destination was just up ahead on the right, but he'd never make it there. Not before they closed, although the sisters had no plans of killing the Councilor for the House of Fourteen. As Liv had said, keep your enemies close and don't kill them unless you have to. Sophia was hoping they wouldn't have to. Having the blood of a Royal on their hands wasn't ideal and could lead to all sorts of other problems.

"Watch where you're going," Lorenzo complained when Sophia knocked into him.

Not only did she not heed his warning, but she used her fast reflexes to sweep his legs out from underneath him.

He fell on his back immediately, his head hitting the concrete hard. Before he could defend himself, Liv pointed her finger at him from the shadow, binding his hands with invisible ropes and putting a disarming spell on him.

Through a muffled cry, he tried to resist, but the fear in his eyes told Sophia he knew he'd been outmaneuvered.

She shook her head at the magician, who sported a black goatee and clicked her tongue. "Today obviously isn't your day."

Grabbing his hands, she waited for Liv to take his legs. The sisters lifted the incapacitated man up and carried him awkwardly into the dark alleyway where they'd already set the stage for the next steps.

"Can I have his shoes when you're done with him?" the homeless man digging through the dumpster called.

Liv nodded. "Sure thing, buddy. Looks like you could use some new threads too."

Sophia glanced down at the embroidered silk robe Lorenzo was wearing. It was of the finest quality and would look strange on the bum, but it was probably enhanced with magical properties to keep him extra warm in cold temperatures and cool when it was hot. The garment would be ideal for someone who had to sleep on the streets.

"Thanks," the homeless man said, waving from beside the dumpster. "That would be much appreciated."

"Who says homeless people don't have manners?" Liv asked, walking backward and holding Lorenzo's legs as they carried the larger man. His eyes were wide with fear, and no doubt he thought they were taking him away to kill him. That fear would work in their favor. They needed him to believe his life was in danger. That would ensure he talked.

CHAPTER THIRTY-THREE

To most, the alleyway appeared ordinary with puddles of murky water and trashcans. However, to the two magicians who had staged it, the space was full of secrets. For starters, it wasn't an open space that led to a dead-end brick wall. The wall that divided the space in half was invisible up until Liv nodded toward it.

Suddenly a new wall appeared at her back with a single metal door. Picking up her foot, Liv kicked the unlocked door open, showing the interrogation room they had set up for Lorenzo's stay with them.

"We upgraded you to a suite because we heard you were a man who enjoyed the finer things in life," Liv said, her voice scratchy and not sounding like her. Sophia worried her sense of humor might give her away.

The interrogation room was small and cramped and mostly dark beside a single light hanging overhead, casting the place in a yellow glow. Sitting in the middle of the musty space was a metal chair with restraints.

"As you can see," Liv went on as they worked to put the bound man into the chair, "there are great views, and we've paid extra attention to all details."

Lorenzo wasn't struggling as they placed him into the chair, binding him to the back, thanks to the spell Liv had put on him. Once he was in place, the sisters stepped back in unison, looking their handy work over. The magician appeared quite uncomfortable pinned in the seat, restrained in several places, and paralyzed from the neck down so he couldn't use a spell against them. Once they removed the magical gag, he could mutter an incantation, but it wouldn't work since they were the only ones who could perform spells in the interrogation room at that moment.

"I think you can take off the disguises," Liv said, winking at Sophia.

She nodded and waved her hand in her sister's direction. Instead of going back to her normal appearance with long blonde hair and a sassy expression, Liv took on a different look. Although she was always gorgeous, she was extra beautiful with her straight brown hair and bright blue eyes. Large turquoise wings flitted a bit, and anyone would recognize her as a male fae.

Sophia also changed her appearance, making herself into a female fae with purple wings.

"Oh, that's much better," Liv said, checking her appearance over. "Being a mortal was gross." She snapped her fingers at Lorenzo, and his mouth popped open at once.

He moved his tongue around and realized the gagging spell had come off, and he could talk. Sophia recognized the form his mouth was taking and knew he was trying a spell. The disappointment that fell over his face made her rejoice. He now knew his magic was useless.

They'd thought of everything.

Liv clapped her hands together, chuckling. "Okay. Let's get down to business and have you start talking before I rearrange your face."

CHAPTER THIRTY-FOUR

"What do you fae want?" Lorenzo demanded, his voice raw and full of hostility.

"Want?" Liv asked. "What makes you think we want anything? Maybe we just brought you here for fun."

"This isn't fun," Lorenzo complained, struggling with his binds to no effect.

Liv wagged her finger. "I can't help it if you're not making the best of this situation. It's all about perspective."

"It is a crime of the highest to abduct a Councilor for the House of Fourteen," Lorenzo said, not trying to break the binds after realizing it wouldn't work.

"That offense is major," Liv stated. "But not bigger than abducting the king of the fae. I believe that crime is punishable by death."

Lorenzo's eyes widened. "I don't know anything about that."

Liv gave Sophia an annoyed expression. "Can I give him a black eye now?"

Sophia shook her head minutely. "Save that for right before we kill him."

The protest that escaped Lorenzo's mouth echoed off the stone walls of the interrogation room.

Liv nodded obediently, ignoring the sounds of fear now blubbering from the coward's mouth. "Cool. Oh, and I can't forget the shoes for the nice guy across the way."

She waved her hand and the fine leather boots disappeared from Lorenzo's feet, to reappear by the door.

"Stop it!" Lorenzo yelled.

"Start talking," Liv encouraged, stepping in close to the Councilor.

"I don't know anything," he answered at once.

"Oh, man," Liv said, shaking her head. "You're a bad man and a bad liar. Those are the worst and always make me want to stomp my feet."

Lorenzo realized what Liv was going to do a moment too late. The howl of pain when her boot came down hard on his exposed foot made Sophia roll her eyes. This guy was weaker than she realized, having spent the majority of his life sitting on the bench, looking down on Warriors and ordering them to risk their lives while he stayed safe. Sophia knew Liv was enjoying this more than she would have if this was just a random guy who had information about Rudolf. This was payback for all the times Lorenzo had belittled Liv, ordering her to do things he himself was too weak to do.

"I-I don't know what you want me to tell you," Lorenzo stuttered, drool coming down his chin.

"Let's start with why someone would abduct our king," Sophia said, narrowing her eyes at the despicable man before them.

"How should I know?" he spat.

Sophia could tell Liv was really restraining herself from punching Lorenzo in the face.

"Oh, I almost forgot we also promised the gentleman a new robe," Liv sang, twirling her hand.

The elegant silk robe disappeared from around Lorenzo, exposing him in his white undershirt and pants. His shoulders scrunched up with tension as if being exposed was far worse than being physically hurt.

"No, that robe has been in my family for generations!" he yelled.

Liv shrugged. "Sounds like it's time to part ways with it."

"You can't give it to a crummy mortal," Lorenzo complained.

Liv toggled her head back and forth. "Thing about it is, we totally can. See, you're fully restrained, unable to do magic, and no one can hear you scream."

"Who are you?" Lorenzo demanded, narrowing his eyes at Liv. "You aren't normal fae to do magic like this."

Sophia worked to keep the expression of worry off her face. Lorenzo was right. The spells they were using were incredibly powerful and complex. No normal fae could do them. If they weren't careful, he could track their spells if he knew where to look. Registered magicians were tracked by the council. However, if he continued to believe they were fae, he wouldn't know to look.

Liv leaned in close. "I'm your worst nightmare. When someone abducted our king, a force like nothing you've ever seen was unleashed. Underestimate the fae, and we will show you why we've survived so much longer than magicians."

He spat in her face, shaking his head. "You've survived because you're weak little twats that suck up resources and are useless."

Liv peeled back, wiping her face. "Is that why you had our king abducted?"

Lorenzo swallowed. "The reasons have nothing to do with the fae."

In a flash, Liv reached out and wrapped her hand around Lorenzo's jaw, making him tense all over. His face turned red. "Why did you have King Rudolf abducted?"

"I didn't," Lorenzo protested, fear in his eyes now. "It was Nevin Gooseman."

Of all the things Sophia had expected Lorenzo to say, that wasn't one of them. "What?" she asked in disbelief.

Lorenzo's eyes slid to look at her as he tried to nod, but Liv's grasp was making it difficult. "It's true. It wasn't me. I told him Rudolf could help him. That's the only way I'm involved."

"Why?" Liv demanded, her hand tightening over his windpipe. "Help him with what?"

"He needs to get into the Great Library," Lorenzo stated. "It's closed just now, but I knew Rudolf could get him in."

Liv pulled her hand off the man, disgusted at having to touch him any longer. "Keep talking, or I'll be breaking more of your toes." She indicated his foot.

He nodded, seeming to have resigned and decided to be compliant. "Nevin needs to figure out how the Dragon Elite hid the evil dragons. They've camouflaged them somehow. The spell will be in the Great Library. I told him that much and that Rudolf could help him get in there."

"He wants to expose the dragons why?" Sophia asked, her chest vibrating with anger.

"Why wouldn't he?" Lorenzo retorted. "Those beasts are destroying our world. They need to be eliminated from this planet."

Now it was Sophia who was having trouble restraining herself. Liv must have spied it because she gave her a look of warning.

"What else do you know?" Liv asked, raising her boot over Lorenzo's other foot.

He shook his head rapidly. "That's it. I promise. That's all I know."

Liv narrowed her eyes, but she must have determined that Lorenzo was telling the truth. Still, she wasn't going to reward him for good behavior.

She slammed her boot down hard on his other foot, which was immediately followed by the sound of cracking and a piercing scream.

She backed away, giving Sophia a curt nod. "You know, I shouldn't have all the fun. Remember that parting gift I wanted to give this guy? That honor is all yours."

Sophia didn't think she could punch a man she'd known all her life. Then she remembered the comment he made about getting rid of her dragons and his part in Rudolf being abducted and so much more.

Without a moment of hesitation, she pulled back her fist and slammed it straight into Lorenzo's eye before striding for the door where Liv was waiting for her, holding the fancy boots and robe.

"Nice," Liv offered, opening the door to the makeshift interrogation room. "Well, enjoy your stay. We hope we've made you as uncomfortable as possible. You'll be here for the rest of the night until this little paradise disappears at sunrise. Then you'll be free to go, although you might want to call a cab. I think walking is going to be a bit uncomfortable."

"You can't leave me here!" Lorenzo yelled, his voice vibrating.

"The alternative is that we kill you," Liv offered.

"No!" he screamed. "So help me God, I will find out who you are and when I do, I'll have a Warrior murder you."

Liv sighed. "Yes, because fighting your own battles is beneath you."

"I'm a Councilor for the House of Fourteen!" Lorenzo bellowed. "I don't have to stoop to such things. I will have you taken down. Watch your back, fae!"

Liv laughed. "I'm not afraid of your Warriors, coward. Send them after us. We will be waiting."

With that, Liv strode out the door, Sophia on her heels, her pulse beating loudly in her head.

CHAPTER THIRTY-FIVE

S ophia's knuckles only hurt for a few seconds after she launched her fist at Lorenzo's face. Her chest, however, swelled with satisfaction. Those who thought punishing enemies didn't work hadn't had the satisfaction of punching them in the face. Revenge could be sweet if it wasn't taken too far.

The sisters ducked into a burger joint after Sophia took off their disguises. It was time to replenish their reserves, especially after the extraordinary amount of magic they'd both used.

Liv slumped after they slid into opposite sides of a booth. "I bet the food here is good."

"Why is that?" Sophia asked, feeling the sticky floor under her boots.

Liv sniffed the air. "They don't change the grease in the fryer. Also, I spied pixies running the kitchen in the back when we entered, and everyone knows they are excellent cooks."

"I actually didn't know that," Sophia said.

"Well, you do now." Liv drummed her hands impatiently on the counter.

A gnome waddled in their direction with an ordering pad and pen.

At the sight of Liv, he rolled his eyes. "Are you here to try and shut us down again?"

Liv's eyes scrunched up with confusion. "Shut you down? Oh, wait! I have been here before. I thought that was a dream. Are you still smuggling in illegal spices that spell customers to think your food is better than it is?"

"What do you think?" the gnome asked, crossing his short arms over his chest.

"Oh, good, we're playing the guessing game instead of you answering my questions directly."

The gnome sighed. "No, when you nearly destroyed the kitchen with your spell work and scared all our customers away, we straightened up. I hired pixies to run the back, and business has been better."

Liv scratched her head. "Sounds like I really ruined your day."

He nodded. "More like my year, but we've recovered."

"You've learned your lesson."

"You really don't remember that?" Sophia asked.

Her sister shrugged. "Sounds like a regular old Tuesday afternoon. After a while, it starts to run together. I shut down restaurants like this a dozen at a time."

"Such a delightful magician," the gnome said dryly. "We're all so grateful for what you do, Warrior Beaufont."

Liv smiled sweetly, batting her eyes at the gnome. "Then I suspect today's meal is on the house, huh?"

His lips drew together when he blew out a breath. "You're just not satisfied unless you're ruining my business."

"I'll pay," Sophia said, her stomach rumbling with hunger.

The gnome shook his head. "No, it's fine. A Warrior and a dragonrider's money isn't good here, but do leave some food for other customers."

Liv nodded. "Of course. We'll take a couple of cheeseburgers and some fries."

"That's all?" the gnome asked his head to the side and a skeptical expression on his face.

"And some jalapeno poppers..." Liv said uncertainly, testing the boundaries.

"And?" the gnome questioned.

"Onion rings," Liv stated tentatively.

"Fine, and I'll bring out some fried pickles too," the gnome said, trotting off.

"Who says that gnomes are stingy, unreasonable people?" Liv said proudly.

"I believe that's what you said when you destroyed my kitchen," the gnome called over his shoulder.

"Oh, and a pitcher of beer too!" Liv yelled to him as he disappeared through the back.

Sophia laughed. "You really have a reputation, don't you?"

Liv nodded proudly. "Shorty straightened up, and now he's running a viable operation that contributes to the community and doesn't deceive. I'm like a strict parent. The kids might loathe me now, but later, they will thank me for making them better."

Sophia was about to respond when a basket of fried pickles appeared on the table, followed by a pitcher of ice-cold beer and two mugs. "Wow, talk about service."

Liv's eyes widened with delight. "Yeah, a perk of eating at a magical establishment." She glanced around, missing something. "Do you think it's too much to ask for some ranch dressing?"

A second later and a bowl of ranch appeared next to the fried pickles. "Nice!" Liv exclaimed, taking a few napkins from the dispenser next to the wall.

"Do you think that vat of ranch dressing will be enough?" Sophia asked, gawking at the large bowl filled to the brim.

"It will tide me over until the fries come," Liv said. "You'll have to order your own." She winked, obviously joking and moved the bowl to the middle to share.

"So, Nevin Gooseman," Sophia said in a low voice, careful to not be overheard, although there wasn't anyone close by. Most of the customers were in the front or playing pool in the side room.

Liv popped a fried pickle covered in ranch dressing into her mouth. "Yeah, I actually didn't see that one coming. I hadn't expected this to be about the Dragon Elite."

Sophia sighed, filling their mugs with beer. "I should have expected this. Everything is about the dragons right now. We are to blame for all that is wrong in the world."

"No," Liv argued. "You're powerful, and that scares dumb politicians who want to run the show their way, which probably means immorally. Those who want to take advantage of the system, don't want people like me policing magic or people like you settling disputes. Too bad for them the Beaufonts do what they like and aren't deterred."

"So Ru." Sophia kept her voice down as the jalapeno poppers and onion rings appeared on the table. "We know who took him but not where they have him."

"I can try and see if Mortimer has a lead on Nevin Gooseman's whereabouts, but he's a magician, so I'm doubtful," Liv said, digging into the onion rings.

"Yeah, and I've actually looked into that man's location, thinking that we could negotiate, although Hiker was against the idea."

"And?" Liv asked.

Sophia scowled, shaking her head. "He's well hidden."

"I'd expect no less from a corrupt politician who wants to dominate the mortal world." Liv grabbed a jalapeno popper but dropped it. "Wow, those are hot."

"Well, we know where he's headed," Sophia told her.

"Yeah, so how about I station myself at the Great Library and wait for the pansy to show up," Liv offered. "Plato is hanging out there anyway, trying to fill the role of the librarian, so it's a good spot for me."

"What about your warrior cases?" Sophia inquired.

"They can wait," Liv responded. "I'm overdue for a vacation, and what better place than Zanzibar?"

"Thanks, that would be great." Sophia took an onion ring. "Do you think Rudolf will really lead Nevin and his goonies to the Great Library?"

"I don't see what choice he has," Liv replied. "It does prove how desperate this politician is to take you all down. He just can't let well enough alone. It isn't enough to discredit the Dragon Elite and ruin your reputation. He won't stop until he's taken out the evil dragons."

Sophia reflexively chewed and swallowed, not even tasting the food. The current conversation had made her lose her appetite. "He truly believes the demon dragons are going to ruin the world. I don't know where he got that information, but I'm going to have to stop him."

"I'll help in any way I can," Liv offered. "However, we'll have to play this carefully so that Lorenzo doesn't figure out we're the ones who abducted him. He can make my life hell if he wants to, and he usually does want to. If he finds out that I broke his toes, he'll be even more motivated than usual."

"Don't worry," Sophia offered. "We'll play it carefully. He won't know, and we're in the perfect position to keep an eye on him."

"Yeah, I suspect he was helping Nevin because his end game is to have control over the mortals."

Sophia nodded. "So team up with a magician who wants to rule them and take down the Dragon Elite, and the pair can run the world."

"Seems that was their plan," Liv agreed.

"Too bad I'm going to ruin things for them the same way you shut this place down for breaking the law," Sophia remarked.

Liv smiled widely. "That's my girl. Give them hell and make them sorry they ever dared to cross you. They might thank you for it one day. Either way, the world will be better for it."

CHAPTER THIRTY-SIX

On the way out of the bar and grill, Sophia noticed a few strange things but reasoned she might have had too much to eat or too many beers. Maybe the gnome was still spelling his food after all, she reasoned.

Sophia rubbed her eyes, doubting her vision as she passed the third set of magicians who appeared blurry. She hadn't really slept much, having made finding Rudolf a priority, but not sleeping was pretty normal for her.

As she strode to a place where she could open a portal, Sophia dismissed the whole thing, assuming it was just a result of the darkening streets. She passed a few mortals, and they appeared normal. Realizing she'd need to take a nap straight away, Sophia opened a portal to the Gullington. Just as she was about to step through, she noticed another strange figure. This time it was an elf. Much like the magicians, the person was blurry on the edges, like they were a digital image that was slowly being erased.

Sophia stepped through the portal, thinking she was finally losing her mind. Once she was through and staring at the Barrier, Sophia knew the problem wasn't a lack of sleep.

The look on Lunis' face as she entered the Gullington told her there was something very wrong. The thoughts streaming through his head explained briefly what had happened. Sophia could hardly believe that in such a short period of time, the world had further gone to hell.

The Dragon Elite could *not* catch a break.

CHAPTER THIRTY-SEVEN

"How could this happen?" Sophia asked Hiker. She'd flown Lunis to the Castle and slid off his back at the stairs, then run straight up to the leader of the Dragon Elite's office.

He shook his head. "I don't know. We don't know much about the affliction."

"But it affects only magicians and elves?" Sophia asked.

She hadn't been seeing things when she'd walked through the streets of Los Angeles. The magicians and elves she'd seen going blurry were suffering from a strange illness affecting the races. It was erasing them until they potentially disappeared. The illness was so new that the effects were unclear. What they did know was that those who caught it lost their magical powers and they blurred, but that was all that was known.

"So far, the only cases have been of magicians and elves," Hiker explained, picking up a newspaper and glancing it over. "It started a few days ago apparently and has since spread rapidly."

He thrust the newspaper at her. She read the headline, and her mouth popped open with disgust. *"Are the Dragon Elite Responsible for the magical illness?"*

"What?" Sophia asked, repulsed.

"Read it," Hiker encouraged.

Sophia scanned the article, not surprised to see Nevin Gooseman mentioned several times. He was cited as stating that his team of scientists believed the disease was related to the dragons who were responsible for spreading it. He further stated that correlation evidence proved the onset happened when dragons started circulating through the populations, and the hardest hit cities were the ones most frequented by the dragons.

"This is ludicrous," Sophia nearly yelled.

Hiker nodded gravely. "I know."

"There's no proof," Sophia went on. "Can't we reference the past when dragons were in and around the population, and no one got sick?"

Hiker gave her an uncertain expression. "There's not a lot of documentation on that. Much of it was erased when the House of Fourteen, known as the House of Seven then, rewrote history. Besides, people are afraid. It was bad enough when mortals were fearful of dragons, thinking they were all evil. Now our own race, as well as elves, are afraid of us, all because of some speculation from Nevin Gooseman."

Sophia slapped the newspaper down on Hiker's desk. "He's behind this. I just know it."

Hiker nodded. "I suspect you're right. I believe he'd go to great lengths to take us down, but poisoning his own race is a bit much."

"Oh, that man knows no boundaries," Sophia said bitterly and then related what she'd learned about King Rudolf.

Hiker's expression turned even more sour. "Abducting a king. All so he can uncover the demon dragons. He has to be stopped."

"If we go after him, then we just look like the savages he's been trying to make us out to be," Sophia reasoned.

"That's the thing he wants," Hiker stated. "He wants us to retaliate and defend ourselves, making us look guilty. We're running out of options. I might have to cave and make a statement."

"Liv is stationed at the Great Library," Sophia explained. "When Nevin Gooseman shows up there with Rudolf, we can cut him off."

Hiker nodded, looking heavy. "That's something, but we need to find out how to discredit him. That's how he's attacked us. If we make him irrelevant, then he'll lose his credibility."

"We have to fix this illness affecting magicians and elves," Sophia said. "Whether it's a setup or not, we can't allow others to suffer. They are being used as pawns."

"I realize that," Hiker agreed. "We need an expert who can also back us up. Someone the world trusts and can state that dragons can't spread illness like this."

Sophia thought for a moment. "I think I know just the person. Maybe she can help us to find a cure."

Hiker didn't ask any questions, apparently trusting Sophia's strategy on this. "I also need you to go to the House of Fourteen and quell their concerns. We can't have them turning on us right now. We've got to hold a strong front, but I sense they are being persuaded by the propaganda that Nevin Gooseman is shoving down everyone's throat."

"I can do that." Sophia knew she wasn't going to get that nap she so desperately needed.

She made for the door and saw Mama Jamba wasn't in her usual spot. She paused, finding that odd.

"She's working on the tracking spell," Hiker said, having read the confusion on Sophia's face.

"Oh, that's good," she stated, continuing toward the door.

"Oh, and Sophia?" Hiker said, making her pause.

"Yes, sir?"

"Going to the House of Fourteen is important," he began. "Finding this expert to support us is crucial, and a cure is imperative. However, if you don't get some rest, you'll be worthless to anyone, including the Dragon Elite. Before you set off again, get some sleep."

"But, sir—"

"That's an order, Sophia."

She nodded, noticing the concern in his light eyes. "Yes, sir. Of course."

CHAPTER THIRTY-EIGHT

Sophia thought it would be impossible for her to sleep, knowing that some strange affliction was robbing her race and elves of their magical abilities and making them blur like they were graphic images and not real people. However, once her head hit the pillow, she was sucked into a dreamless sleep and not released for ten solid hours.

She awoke with a start, her heart beating wildly like she'd just run a long distance. After a quick shower she hurried onto the Expanse, hardly chewing the bagel Ainsley forced into her hands on her way out.

Sophia wasn't surprised to see her dragon majestically standing on the grassy hill beside the Barrier, dutifully waiting for her. His blue scales reflected the morning sunshine, and his eyes sparkled with curiosity.

Off to the circus, then? he asked coyly.

"Ya, da ja wanna gow?" Her mouth was full of sticky, thick bread that glued her jaws shut.

I don't speak bagel, but I'll interpret that as "Do I want to go?" he said, sounding amused.

Sophia nodded, stuffing the rest of the bagel into her mouth and chewing rapidly.

Then the answer is yes, Lunis replied, kneeling and extending his wing for Sophia so she could climb onto his back.

She wiped the crumbs off her hands and climbed into the saddle. It hadn't been long since they'd flown together, the last time being on the way back from Sherwood Forest, however, going a day without her dragon was too much. Flying was more natural for Sophia than walking, it seemed. She didn't just enjoy the rush of air and the high vantage point from the sky, she craved it like it fed her soul.

In a few graceful movements, Lunis took off, striding for the Barrier and launching into the sky once through.

Without a need to talk to communicate, Sophia created a portal to the magical circus where she'd last seen Bermuda Laurens and her menagerie of strange and amazing animals. As the premier expert on magical creatures, Bermuda Laurens was respected across all the races. If anyone could discredit the claim that dragons couldn't spread this strange new disease, it would be the giantess. However, Bermuda Laurens wasn't known for being helpful or getting involved in other's affairs. Trying to convince her to help might be difficult.

Sophia hoped her intuition on this wasn't correct, and the magical creature expert would be willing to help. If not, then she'd need a new plan before heading to the House of Fourteen, where the council would no doubt be in crisis mode and potentially prepared to distance from the Dragon Elite for the rest of time.

CHAPTER THIRTY-NINE

I f Sophia doubted whether the world at large was affected by Nevin Gooseman's allegations, the short ride to the circus confirmed her fears. From the sky, she and Lunis witnessed people on the ground glare up at them in fear. Many ran for shelter. Some gave them challenging expressions that seemed to say, "Stay away, dragon."

Before, the world had been fearful of the demon dragons. Somehow Nevin Gooseman had taken it a step further, making mortals and magical races despise and fearful of all dragons. It was all wrong, and it had to be stopped.

It hadn't been that long ago that when Sophia and Lunis flew over cities, people looked up at them and cheered, excited and mystified to see an ancient dragon and rider soaring through the skies. The Dragon Elite had been revered for bringing down Thad Reinhart—a well-known tycoon responsible for enslaving mortals and polluting the planet. They had also been commended for defeating Mika Lenna, the CEO of the Saverus Corporation, which they'd exposed for abducting magicians and turning them into cyborgs.

The world had quickly forgotten these successes and now feared the very organization meant to protect them—the Dragon Elite. The irony wasn't lost on Sophia.

What do you call a hippie's wife? Lunis asked randomly.

Sophia furrowed her brow, pulling her gaze up from the ground. *Say what?*

It's a pretty straight forward question, he stated. *What do you call a hippie's wife?*

It's a random question, is what it is.

Look, Soph. Stop worrying about those judgey mortals and magicians. You can't change the way those rambling waffle jackers on the ground think, Lunis said calmly.

Can I change the way you call people names, though?

That's unlikely, he told her. *I'm trying to clean up my language so I'm going to start calling meanie people pita eaters or Lunchables.*

I don't really see the insult there, Sophia replied with a laugh. *I didn't know your language was a problem.*

Oh yeah, I curse like a pirate when you're not around.

I think the phrase is that you curse like a sailor.

No, he argued. *I'm constantly talking about Bell's booty and rolling my Rs when I growl.*

I had no idea...

And I happen to enjoy Lunchables and pitas, so it goes to reason that I plan on snacking on these people I'm name-calling. Lunis sounded rather amused.

I didn't know that you liked Lunchables, Sophia remarked. *It would take like a few hundred to fill you up.*

Of course, I like them, he said, sounding insulted. *They are great for when I'm on the go.*

Why is it that you often sound like a soccer mom?

Because I'm practical and sporty, he answered. *I draw the line at wearing sneakers with a dress. That's just bad taste, Karen.*

There are so many things to question about what you've just said.

Anywho, as I was saying—

Lunchables are really high in sodium, Sophia interrupted.

Thanks, doc, but I think I'll be all right.

Because you're a dragon and protected by the chi of your ancestors? Sophia asked.

Because I work out, he corrected.

Okay, before the conversation totally got derailed by your sudden relation to soccer moms, I think you were about to say something sagely. What was it?

I'll tell you, Lunis began. *First, remind me later that I need to stop by a TJ Max.*

A laugh burst out of Sophia's mouth. She hadn't expected Lunis to say that or any of this. That's why he was the best.

Why do you need to stop by that store? Sophia asked. *Is it to get shoes that match your dress so you don't make the same bad life decisions as Karen?*

He shook his head, which she spied from his back. *No, I'm getting those at Target. Anyway, TJ Max has a really cool* As Seen on TV *section. I really want to get one of those veggie slicers that turns zucchini into pasta.*

Because?

Because then I can have low-carb spaghetti, duh.

So, you don't care about your sodium intake, but you're watching carbs?

If you were up on the trends, you'd know that no one is eating carbs right now, Lunis stated, sounding very smug. *Carbs are out. Keto is in.*

So sorry, Sophia said. *I've been busy trying to cure Ainsley and find the abducted king of the fae and cure magicians of a mysterious illness.*

Excuses, Lunis retorted.

Okay, well, as soon as I get a break, I'll attend a Pampered Chef party with you, she joked.

He scoffed. *Again, you're so out of touch. Pampered Chef parties are like totally 2015. I bet you're still listening to* Call Me Maybe *and wearing floral prints.*

Did you just reference a Carly Rae Jepsen song?

Hey, I just met you, and this is crazy, Lunis began to sing. *But here's my number, so call me, maybe.*

What is happening, Sophia asked in disbelief.

I'm taking your mind off your troubles, Lunis said, a smile in his voice.

She grinned. *Yes, you are. Thank you.*

Soph, we're going to fix the world. They will see us for the heroes that we are again. But it will take time and strategy. In the meantime, don't let those cracker jacks get you down. Let the Karens of the world think what they want until we have the proof to show them how wrong they are. Then they will be worshipping us and begging for our help once again.

Sophia nodded. *Good advice. When did Karens get to be poked fun at so much? I feel sorry for them.*

It's just a phase and will pass, Lunis told her. *Next year it will be Olivia's. Everyone will be like, don't pull another Olivia. Or man, that girl is a real Olivia.*

Sophia shook her head. *She doesn't go by that name,* she said, referring to her sister.

Huh, Lunis asked. *What do you mean?*

Liv, she answered. *She doesn't go by Olivia.*

Liv who? he asked. *I don't know who you mean.*

My sister, she said blankly.

Oh, is that her name, he teased. *I thought she was a Karen.*

Sophia laughed.

Okay, back to my question, he continued. *What do you call a hippie's wife?*

I don't know, she answered. *Sunbeam? Echo? Starla?*

Mississippi, he said with a laugh.

Oh wow, that's really bad.

If you think that one was bad, check this one out. Lunis cleared his throat like he was a comedian standing on stage about to do his routine. *Why did the can crusher quit his job?*

Why?

Because it was soda pressing, he said with a laugh

Sophia groaned. *You and Lee should do a lunch date to exchange material. You both have jokes that kill.*

I hate Russian dolls, Lunis interrupted as they approached the big top at the back of the circus where Bermuda Laurens was stationed with her magical creatures.

Oh yeah? Sophia asked. *Why do you hate Russian dolls?*

Because they are so full of themselves, he explained, laughing at his joke again.

And here I thought the jokes couldn't get any worse, she said.

I'll be here all week, Lunis assured her, coming in for a landing. *Be sure to tip your waitress, and try the veal.*

CHAPTER FORTY

L unis had made Sophia feel much better, taking her mind off of the Lunchables on the ground that were casting repulsed stares at them.

She was so lightened she didn't pay any notice to the circus performers strolling the grounds who gave them a wide berth when they landed in front of the big top. Sophia knew the giantess didn't like unexpected interruptions, but there was no way to give the magical creatures expert a heads up she was arriving.

The last time she'd been inside the big top full of exotic animals, she'd spooked Venice, the winged lion, causing all sorts of problems. For that reason, Sophia poked her head through the flaps as quietly as possible.

She should have been surprised to see a large blindfolded snake staring at her when she looked into the tent, but at this point, her threshold for such things was pretty low.

Standing beside the snake, which was the size of an anaconda but was not one, since it was in the magical circus, was none other than Bermuda Laurens. The pair, both being oversized, made each other look normal. Just a girl and her blindfolded snake, Sophia thought with a silent laugh.

"Um, hello," Sophia whispered, gaining Bermuda's attention.

"Hello," Bermuda said, not taking her eyes off the large snake. "Come on in, and yes, you can bring Lunis in here."

"Oh, thanks." Sophia pulled back the flap of the tent all the way to make room for Lunis to enter beside her. He ducked under the low hanging part of the tent and slid into the space that was full of strange creatures, many making curious sounds.

"How did you know I had Lunis with me?" Sophia asked, trying to keep her focus on the giantess, although many strange sights around the big top were vying for her attention.

"Beside the fact that I could smell him?" Bermuda asked.

Sophia sniffed the air. "I've told him to bathe regularly, but that's about as likely as him eating carbs, apparently."

The giantess shook her head, still studying the large snake. "No, dragons have a very distinct smell. Also, Johnathon told me that you'd be visiting." She indicated a centaur standing in a golden ring at the back of the tent.

The big top had seven golden rings, and in the center of each was a magical creature, all of them different from the last time that Sophia visited.

"Oh, and centaurs can see the future, isn't that right?" Sophia asked.

Bermuda shook her head, giving Sophia her usual "you understand very little" expression. "They don't think of it that way. For them, there is no future or past. Time isn't linear. They see the fabric of time woven together in a different way than the rest of us."

Sophia wanted to argue that this was a game of semantics, but that wasn't going to gain her any favors with the grumpy giantess. Instead, she cast her gaze at the back, smiling at the half horse, half man. His blond hair was braided down his back, and he had an expression of pure superiority plastered across his face.

"It's pretty incredible that you have a centaur in the show," Sophia said, keeping her voice down in case this offended Jonathon. Centaurs were notorious for being separate from society and not cooperating with other magical races.

"Jonathon understands that we're in a vulnerable time globally," Bermuda informed her, stepping away from the blindfolded snake. "He agreed to help me in the name of promoting education. Mortals are starting to disrespect the power of magical creatures. They went from not seeing them, to taking them for granted or thinking they are freaks. I'm running this show as a way of trying to fix the problems that have arisen."

Sophia nodded. "Yes, that's actually why I'm here."

"I know why you're here," Bermuda said at once.

"Oh." Sophia gave Lunis an uncertain expression. He was appraising the creatures in the tent. "Is that because Jonathon told you?"

Bermuda shook her head. "No, it's because I have a brain and know that you're in trouble. People fear dragons. Nevin Gooseman has created many problems for you and the Dragon Elite. It is those problems which are spreading across the globe, making mortals distrustful of all magical creatures."

"So you can help me, then?" Sophia asked, grateful that this might go more smoothly than she thought.

"I'm not sure that I can." Bermuda stroked the snake affectionately. Like a cuddly puppy, it pressed back into her palm, seeming to enjoy the attention.

"But you're an expert on magical creatures," Sophia argued. "I was hoping you could supply a statement to the public, informing them that dragons aren't responsible for spreading this ailment to magicians and elves."

Bermuda sighed, returning her gaze to Sophia once more. "I'm afraid that me being an expert in magical creatures right now is about like being a computer technician during the Renaissance. There just isn't much interest or need."

"Of course there is," Sophia argued.

The giantess gave her a look of regret. "I'm glad you think so. I, of course, feel valuable. Currently, magical creatures are being disregarded, and so is anyone connected to them."

"Well, what can we do?" Sophia asked, suddenly feeling desperate.

"We fight ignorance with facts," Bermuda stated. "Nevin Gooseman is appealing to scare tactics. He supports nothing with information, but rather uses fear and emotion. That's hard to combat, but it isn't impossible."

"So how do we prove that dragons don't spread this disease?"

"We discover where it came from," Bermuda answered. "More importantly, you find the cure. Then not only will you clear the Dragon Elite's name, but you'll also be heroes."

Of course, that had been part of the plan but getting there would take time.

Apparently reading the disappointment on her face, Bermuda gave Sophia a rare sympathetic expression. "I can offer my educated opinion on this matter to the House of Fourteen. The mortal world may not think much of me right at the moment, but I haven't lost my credibility with the magicians."

Sophia brightened suddenly. "Really? That would be great. I'm headed there next."

Bermuda nodded like she expected this. She snapped her fingers, and a rolled-up piece of paper appeared in her hands. "You can show this to the council. It states that, to the best of my knowledge, dragons aren't responsible for distortion."

"Oh, is that what they are calling it?" Sophia asked, stepping forward cautiously to take the paper, but also trying to keep her distance from the large snake hovering overhead, swaying and flicking its tongue in her direction.

"Yes," Bermuda stated. "Dragons have the ability for healing and peace. Although I can't say without a doubt they aren't the cause of distortion, it is highly unlikely."

"I wish mortals were listening to you," Sophia muttered bitterly. "They don't associate us with peace at all. They want the demon dragons gone."

"They are afraid of that which they don't understand," Bermuda explained. "Hence the reason for my show here. Education is the only way to truly create peace in this world."

Sophia nodded. "We have hidden the demon dragons from

mortals, but I'm not certain how long that will last. We need to track them down and then, I don't know. Maybe we can change them or something."

Bermuda scowled at her. "Why would you want to do that?"

"Because if we don't do something, mortals will hunt them."

"Then that will be the mortal's problem," Bermuda said matter-of-factly. "You can't change a demon into an angel or the other way around. They are meant to be what they are for a reason. I've heard you speak of balance before, so this isn't new information to you. Don't abandon your logic in search of a quick solution or to avoid conflict."

Sophia suddenly felt very small. Yes, she was standing in front of a giantess and a large snake, but mostly because of the way in which Bermuda was lecturing her like she was a child. "You're right. I just worry about the demon dragons out there. They were hatched into a world that doesn't understand or appreciate them."

"The world has never been an understanding place," Bermuda observed. "It didn't just start, but rather is a long-standing problem. I'm not certain it will ever truly appreciate magic. Before mortals couldn't see magic, and I believed that was a problem brought on because they were once fearful of it. Now they can see magic once more, and they are once more afraid of that which confuses them. Your job is not to hide it. Your job is similar to mine. You are to educate. Show mortals that ignoring evil isn't the way. A wise man once said, 'Evil gives color to the good in the world. If not for it then the world would be full of gray.'"

Sophia smiled to herself. "I like that. And it's true. Teaching that will take time."

"I don't disagree there," Bermuda told her.

They were quiet for a moment as Sophia thought, and the giantess went back to petting her snake. Lunis had ambled off to investigate the centaur named Jonathon. The pair appeared to be having a pleasant conversation.

"The snake..." Sophia started. "Why is it blindfolded?"

"Basilisk," Bermuda corrected. "Now that you know what it is, the answer to your question should be clear."

Sophia nodded and took a step backward. "If it didn't have its eyes covered, then it would turn us to stone if we looked at it directly, wouldn't it?"

"That's correct," Bermuda stated.

"So the basilisk, it doesn't mind wearing the blindfold?" Sophia asked.

"If you turned everyone around you to stone, what kind of life would that be for you?" Bermuda countered.

Sophia thought for a moment. "It would be quite lonely."

"Of course it would be," Bermuda agreed at once. "No, Bae prefers to sacrifice his sight for a life of companionship." She stroked the basilisk's head.

"That makes sense," Sophia said, her eyes darting around the tent. Beside where Lunis and Jonathon were talking, there was a large wolf that had a shimmering coat and horns on its head.

On the other side of it was a golem, Sophia recognized. She was going to ask if Bae's blindfold had slipped and turned the creature that appeared like a fat man to stone but figured that was bad taste. There was also a smallish rhinoceros that had moss and flowers growing from its chin and back. Most of the creatures weren't those Sophia was familiar with. While her curiosity was piqued, she decided that now wasn't the time for a magical creatures lesson.

"You have another question for me," Bermuda stated, rather than asked.

Sophia nodded, chewing on her lip as she pulled her attention off the strange magical creatures at Bermuda's back. "Distortion. What do you know about it? Besides that it isn't caused by dragons?"

The giantess thought for a moment. "I think it has a magitech origin."

"Like it's caused by a signal or something?" Sophia remembered that something similar had been broadcast to make it so mortals couldn't see magic. Liv brought down the signal, and that was part of the cure.

"Possibly," Bermuda replied.

"So it's been manufactured," Sophia said bitterly. "All to make the Dragon Elite look bad."

"Someone really doesn't want you ruling world affairs," Bermuda observed.

"So, I need to find the source and take it out," Sophia said, mostly to herself.

"Maybe, but that might take some time," Bermuda explained. "To me, finding the cause of something is one approach, but it won't fix those already affected. I would focus on using your efforts to find a cure. Then you can save your people and the elves and be seen as what you are—a hero."

Sophia drew in a breath. "I want to do that, more than anything. It makes me sad to think of my race losing their powers and disappearing."

Bermuda nodded solemnly. "It is a very sad disease."

"I just don't even know where to start with finding a cure," Sophia said.

The giantess thrust her finger into the air. "But one must exist."

"How do you know?" Sophia asked.

"Because if my hunch is correct, then it was created by the very person who has the most to gain by discrediting the Dragon Elite," Bermuda said.

"Nevin Gooseman," Sophia related. "I only wish I could prove that."

"I hope you do," Bermuda stated. "However, he *is* a magician, and so far, he is unaffected by distortion."

"That means he has the antidote or a vaccine or some way to keep it from affecting him," Sophia reasoned, suddenly feeling hopeful.

"That's my thought," Bermuda agreed. "Now, I don't know any more than that, but I did meet a healer on my travels who could be of help. They don't practice in Western medicine and work through unorthodox ways, so their cure would be different than whatever Nevin Gooseman is using."

"Worth a shot," Sophia remarked.

Bermuda agreed with a nod. "Getting to Rumi will be very difficult, though."

Sophia narrowed her gaze. "Did you say Rumi? Like the ancient poet?"

"That's the one."

"But he's dead."

The giantess frowned. "Since when did someone being dead prevent them from acting in the living world?"

Sophia's eyes widened with astonishment. She didn't even know how to reply.

"Rumi is more alive than most thanks to the words he left behind," Bermuda told her. "You see, the legacy we leave behind can make us immortal, and that is truer for no one more than that great poet."

"Okay, although I get what you're saying," Sophia began slowly. "I'm not sure how the ghost of a man or his legacy can create a cure."

Bermuda shrugged. "I don't either, but if anyone can, it will be Rumi. Like I said, his approach is nontraditional. It is based on feelings and words, but as a magician who speaks spells, I think you know the power of words."

Sophia nodded. "That's true. How do I find Rumi?"

"You will need to travel to his tomb in Konya, Turkey," Bermuda explained. "Since he was a philosopher of love, take two who you love dearly with you. That is the only way I know for someone to enter his tomb."

Sophia scratched her head. "Two who I love? Will something happen to them?" she asked, thinking of the ones she'd take, it was obvious when she thought of the words of Rumi and the feelings his poems inspired.

"The ones we love are always at risk," Bermuda stated. "That's why we can never take them for granted because nothing is guaranteed."

Suddenly, Sophia felt a huge foreboding hanging over her. She sensed she'd have to put her loved ones at risk in order to find the cure for distortion, and that wasn't something she took lightly. Solutions involved risks and Sophia knew the ones she loved would want to be a part of the solution. That was one of the very reasons she adored them so completely.

CHAPTER FORTY-ONE

Sophia was grateful for Bermuda Laurens's help but couldn't shake the foreboding feeling of having the requirement of bringing two people she loved along with her. It felt like she was going to have to put them at risk. However, there were no rewards without that.

On the way to the House of Fourteen, Sophia's heart broke over and over again at the sight of magicians and elves blurring in the distance. She and Lunis made the decision he'd return to the Gullington to avoid getting any more unnecessary attention.

Even though Lunis encouraged her not to worry what the jack-fruits of the world thought, they both knew it was hard to entirely dismiss it. Especially having to watch people suffering and knowing they believed dragons were responsible for it.

Sophia entered the House of Fourteen, for the first time not feeling welcome there. It wasn't that anyone in the entryway denied her entrance. There was no one there to do that. The Councilors and Warriors would be in the Chamber of the Tree. However, the House of Fourteen was very much like the Castle and changed itself depending on many different factors.

When Liv was fighting the war to enable mortals to see magic, the

House changed often. It was common knowledge among the Royals the old structure changed depending on who was in it and what was happening in the magical world. When Sophia entered, the walls of the entryway were black, and the area dark like all the lights had burned out.

Smoke swirled along the floor, and Sophia had the feeling she was entering a Halloween haunted house. The floorboards groaned when she took a step, as though protesting her entrance.

Sophia reasoned the dark appearance of the place was a result of what magicians were going through globally. It also could very well be because the Dragon Elite were presently seen as enemies.

Clutching the rolled-up document Bermuda Laurens had given her, Sophia started for the Chamber of the Tree. When she entered through the Door of Reflection, she felt even more unwelcome than before. Even those who usually regarded her with kind expressions gave her skeptical glares.

Sophia tried to shrug it off as she made her way to the center of the room, all eyes on her. The space had fallen silent.

"You dare to enter our sanctuary," Bianca Mantovani hissed.

Sophia's eyes darted to Lorenzo Rosario beside her, and she had the urge to rejoice. Around one of his eyes was a purple and greenish bruise. It did little to cover the rude glare on his face. Beside Bianca was a face Sophia didn't recognize—Marty Martinez, according to Liv. They were the new family who had bought their way into the House of Fourteen and secured a position on the council.

She glanced around the Chamber of the Tree, not seeing the Warrior paired with Marty. The new Councilor, Marty Martinez was an older man with gray and black hair and a full beard, his eyes untrusting, and a strange smirk on his face.

"Yes, I dare," Sophia said with confidence, looking at Clark, who had an unreadable expression. "You will remember the House of Fourteen was once my home."

"What if you brought distortion into our home?" Lorenzo demanded, tilting his face to the side, fully showing his black eye.

"What happened to you?" Sophia dared to ask, curious about what his answer would be.

"None of your business," he fired back.

"Well, I am in the business of settling disputes, so I thought it might be my business," she stated, smiling sweetly at him, making the scowl on his face deepen.

"I don't think Sophia could spread distortion," Hester DeVries said, although her usual warmth was absent.

"I think," Haro Takahashi began carefully, "that we don't really know enough about the disease to make any conclusions."

"Dragons aren't responsible for spreading it," Sophia told them, her voice clear and strong.

"Of course, that's what you'd say," Bianca said with a sigh.

"It's true," Sophia insisted. "But you don't have to believe me." She held up the rolled document. "Bermuda Laurens, the expert on magical creatures, has provided her expertise on the matter."

Haro flicked his wrist, and the paper flew from Sophia's hand up to his own. He unrolled it and glanced over the page. "She says she doesn't believe distortion to be connected to dragons."

"So she isn't sure," Lorenzo said, sounding satisfied.

"She isn't one to state facts unless she knows them to be one-hundred-percent true," Sophia argued.

Haro handed the paper down the table, and each of the Councilors glanced at it.

"She states that it is incredibly unlikely," Clark said after reading the page. "And as you said yourself, Haro, we don't know much about distortion. We don't even have any evidence linking dragons to it."

"No, just a deranged man with an agenda." It was actually Raina Ludwig who made this observation. Sophia was glad for it because she didn't want to be the one to bring up Nevin Gooseman, not with Lorenzo there and possibly suspicious about who abducted him.

"The Dragon Elite do firmly believe that Nevin Gooseman and others in power in the mortal government are behind this," Sophia declared.

Bianca sighed like she was bored. "It's convenient to discredit those who oppose you, Ms. Beaufont."

"That's not what we're doing," Sophia argued. "He's made false accusations. This is going too far."

"Where is Hiker Wallace in all this?" Marty Martinez asked, his voice high pitched.

"He is leading the Dragon Elite," Sophia answered.

"He was asked to show evidence of Mother Nature's support," Lorenzo observed. "Where is she? If she really is allied with the Dragon Elite, then why doesn't he present her?"

"Because she isn't a trophy we put on display." Sophia's chest was rattling with anger now. "She is the most powerful entity in the world and will not show herself just because a two-bit politician demands it. If you think she should, then you misunderstand how this world works. Those in power do not bow to the whims of the weak."

A small smile flicked to Clark's mouth. "Well put."

Bianca shook her head. "Keep the nepotism to yourself. We are trying to have an objective meeting."

"I think when you're attending to matters, that's highly unlikely," Clark fired, uncharacteristically engaging in conflict with a Councilor. He normally tried to avoid such things.

Sophia liked this change and thought Clark was picking up Liv's normal role in her absence.

"That's quite enough, Councilors," Haro said authoritatively. "Now, Sophia, how does the Dragon Elite plan to fix this global issue with distortion?"

"The way I figure it, the problem isn't ours to fix," Sophia answered with confidence. "This falls under your jurisdiction since it involves magical races."

A flash of hatred spread across Lorenzo's face. "How insulting. You bring sickness to us and—"

"We are not responsible for this." Sophia cut Lorenzo off. "We, as the Dragon Elite, will not turn our backs on the House of Fourteen or the elves. That's how it is supposed to be. We are supposed to support each other, not create divisions when others make slanderous rumors."

"That is how it should be," Hester said, looking down the bench at the others, giving Lorenzo in particular a pointed expression.

"Therefore, I've already determined where I can search for a cure," Sophia explained. "I will be devoting my efforts to finding it so that we can help those affected. Then we will need to find out where distortion came from and eradicate the source."

Raina nodded, offering a supportive smile. "That's most generous of you to devote your time and energy to this. We are most grateful."

"I'm happy to do it," Sophia said proudly. "But once this is under control, I will hope the House of Fourteen will show the Dragon Elite the same loyalty and allegiance we've given you. Your reputation has come under scrutiny quite recently, and instead of shutting you out, when your own were being abducted by Saverus corporation, we assisted you."

Clark nodded. "It's true. I think this is a good reminder that we are stronger together. If we allow the politics of the mortal world to tear us apart, then our extinction will be imminent. The mortal world is much larger than our own, and it would take very little for them to tear us down if we don't stand together."

CHAPTER FORTY-TWO

"One hundred percent," Wilder said to Sophia as they strode down the corridor of the Castle.

The old building had changed a lot since her last time there, but not like the House of Fourteen. There were more windows, and the hallways were larger, which was impressive since they had already been pretty wide.

"Are you sure?" Sophia asked, noticing there were arrows on the stone floor indicating the direction they should go, although she wasn't sure why. "I'm not sure what we're going to face at Rumi's tomb, but I don't think we're going to be lavished with hearts and kisses."

"Of course, I'm going to go." Wilder paused at the next junction and raised an eyebrow at the strange new look of the hallway. "For one, it's a crucial mission. We have to find a cure for this distortion. And secondly, you asked me, and I'll do anything for you."

Sophia smiled at him, that familiar feeling of butterflies making her feel weightless and heavy at the same time. It was strange and amazing to her that someone could fill her with so much emotion.

"Thank you," she finally said after a moment, having trouble finding her voice.

"You're always welcome," Wilder replied, his dimples surfacing when he smiled down at her. He leaned in closer, a kiss no doubt about to follow, but they were interrupted by the hallway widening even more.

Sophia's head jerked up. "What do you think is going on here?"

Wilder laughed. "I think it's connected to Trin's new role as a housekeeper and the approaching date of Ainsley leaving. The Castle seems to be making room for the changes to come."

Sophia nodded. "That makes sense." She pointed to the arrow on the stone floor. It was pointing in the opposite direction. "And these arrows?"

"Maybe the Castle wants us to go the other way now," Wilder suggested. "We were just strolling and talking, but now we have a mission, and it wants us to embark on it, quite possibly."

"Yeah, and who knows what will happen if we go the wrong way down a one-way road," Sophia joked.

He flashed her a wide grin, a devilish light in his eyes. "You know, I like that you wouldn't flip out if we went the wrong way down a one-way road."

"That's what you like about me?"

Wilder nodded. "Yes, people who freak out over small stuff or even major stuff are the worst."

"Well, as they say, 'Don't sweat the small stuff and it's all small stuff.'"

"Is that a Rumi quote?" Wilder asked, putting his arm around her shoulder and steering her the other way.

Sophia shook her head. "No, he said much more profound stuff than that. Things like, 'Let yourself be silently drawn by the strange pull of what you really love. It will not lead you astray.'"

"I like that," he replied, a playful expression on his face. "See, and that's exactly why I'll follow you on this mission, or anywhere you go."

Blushing, Sophia lowered her chin. "You and your lines."

"They aren't lines," he argued. "They are inspired words. You bring them out of me."

"Well, although I love the things you say to me, you might want to get them out now because I believe that Lunis will barf if he hears you sweet-talking me."

Wilder picked up her hand and pressed it to his lips. "Don't worry, I won't make your dragon sick on this mission. I will make him roll his eyes a few times."

Sophia lifted up on her tiptoes and kissed the man before her. "He's going to do that regardless."

CHAPTER FORTY-THREE

The Mevlâna Museum in Konya, Turkey, was an impressive sight. The place where Jalal ad-Din Muhammad Rumi was entombed was a large building with a series of domes, but the most interesting part was a turquoise mausoleum and small mosque in the back. It reminded Sophia of the Castle with its turrets and spires but done in a different architectural fashion.

Can you spot me for the admission fees? Lunis asked, standing on one side of Sophia. *I'm all tapped out.*

She laughed. "I don't think that will be a problem."

"So how does this work?" Wilder asked, studying the outside of the buildings with his trademark discerning expression.

Lunis rolled his eyes. *It's a museum. There are artifacts and things inside. You aren't to run or cause general tomfoolery. Instead, you have to pretend to look at the objects and read the little placards beside them. You will be bored, Scotsman.*

"There's the first of many eye rolls I will earn," Wilder fired back.

"I think that we just have to state our intent once we find Rumi's tomb inside," Sophia said, ignoring her dragon and Wilder's usual banter.

What I don't get, Sophia, is if you were supposed to bring two who you love, why did you bring this guy? Lunis indicated with his head in Wilder's direction.

The dragonrider glared down at Sophia. "Your dragon has the maturity of a schoolkid."

"You should hear his jokes," Sophia replied, then pointed at the mausoleum. "My research says that's where we'll find Rumi's tomb."

Oh, that reminds me, Lunis began as they made for the turquoise structure. *Do you know why there are gates around cemeteries?*

"Why?" Wilder asked, appearing sincerely interested.

Because people are dying to get in! Lunis cheered.

Wilder laughed loudly, earning a punishing look from Sophia.

"We're about to enter a holy building," she said flatly. "Will you two behave and show some respect?"

Yeah, Wilder, Lunis said, looking down his nose at him. *Tuck in your shirt and show a little decorum, would you?*

He bowed slightly in Sophia's direction, twirling his hand in front of him. "My apologies, my lady."

Lunis rolled his eyes and muttered, *Suck-up.*

CHAPTER FORTY-FOUR

Sophia was surprised to find Rumi's mausoleum empty, but she didn't know why. She guessed it had many visitors every day—worshippers who came to show their respect to the ancient poet. However, for whatever reason, the large and elaborately decorated space was empty.

If the outside of the Mevlâna Museum was impressive, the inside of the mausoleum was extraordinary with its many bright colors and artwork. The tomb itself was unlike anything Sophia had seen. Rumi had been entombed in the thirteenth century, so it went to reason that burial practices were different then.

An archway covered in tiles stood behind the tomb, which was more like a metal tent than a casket. It had folds on the corners and sat behind a metal gate.

The flow of the lights made the walls dazzle with gold and filled the air with a gentle warmth.

A hush fell over her companions, and their playful behavior and banter fell away at once. An expression of respect filled Wilder's face, and Lunis also seemed to have a quiet moment of reverie.

At the gate, Sophia paused, the two she brought because of her affection for them at her back. Bowing her head and operating purely out of instinct, Sophia opened her mouth, her words flowing out of her.

"Dear Jalal ad-Din Muhammad Rumi, poet, scholar, and theologian, we seek your help to find a cure that will heal our people of a serious illness. Whatever you require of us in exchange for this cure, we are ready to do. Your will directs us from this moment forward."

Sophia lowered her chin as her words ended. She had felt like something was speaking through her, which was an odd experience for her. At the conclusion of her words, nothing happened. Worried she was missing something, she glanced back at Lunis and then Wilder. Both offered her tentative expressions.

Opening her mouth about to ask for their advice, she was cut off by a strange sawing sound. Lunis' eyes widened as Wilder's narrowed with interest.

Sophia spun around to find the tomb of Rumi shifting back to reveal an opening in the stone floor. A set of stairs led down into the darkness. The intricately decorated gate in front of them swung open, and the intent was clear: they were being invited into the mysterious darkness where challenges no doubt lay.

CHAPTER FORTY-FIVE

Once Sophia was right in front of the opening in the floor, she spied words carved into the stone, no doubt those of Rumi's.

She read the words aloud like they were instructions. *"This is love: to fly toward a secret sky, to cause a hundred veils to fall each moment. First, to let go of life. Finally, to take a step without feet."*

The darkness cloaked the three as they descended. Similar to the Castle, the entrance to the staircase widened when Lunis entered, making room for him. It was obvious to Sophia that this place was full of powerful magic. She had always suspected that Rumi was a magician, but now she knew it for a fact. She also knew what Bermuda had meant about him not really being dead. Somehow, she could feel him, like he was inviting them into his home, and setting a place for them at the dining table.

Sophia suddenly felt blind once she'd descended three steps. She reached out, trying to create a light orb, but nothing happened.

"Magic doesn't work here," Wilder said, his hand protectively touching her arm, as though trying to ensure she was still there.

Sophia's connection to Lunis told her he was directly at her back.

"Yeah, I know," she said, thinking. "How are we to see?"

Maybe it's a test of fate, Lunis reasoned. *We have to go down the staircase blindly.*

"Okay, I can do that," Sophia said, edging her foot forward to find the lip of the step. Carefully and with Wilder holding onto her, she took the next step. Together the three progressed down several steps in total silence.

It seemed that a staircase such as this, under an ancient tomb, would go on for quite some time. So Sophia was surprised when she didn't find another step. Instead, the stone floor seemed to go on for a bit.

She paused. "I think we're there, but I still can't see anything."

"I don't understand," Wilder said. "Are we supposed to do the tasks blindly, like showing blind faith?"

Shush, Lunis encouraged at their backs. *Listen.*

Sophia didn't know what he meant until she held her breath and closed her eyes, although that changed nothing. It was just more blackness.

A moment later, she heard what he was talking about. There was a whisper in the distance. No, it was all around her. Or was it just in her head? She couldn't tell. For a long moment, she concentrated on the low voice, urging it to get louder so she could make out the words. Sophia thought it might be a different language at first, but as she let out a calming breath, she made out the message, recognizing Rumi's words from her studies.

"If light is in your heart, you will find your way home," the voice said.

Sophia's eyes sprang open, but there was still only blackness all around her. She repeated the message she'd heard in her mind.

Wilder tapped her elbow three times, and the gesture seemed to say, "I heard that too."

"What does that mean though?" Sophia asked. "How do we have light in our heart?"

"By home, I think it means 'our way to Rumi,'" Wilder imparted.

Think of the love you have for me, Lunis said, slipping into his sage-like tone.

"Or me," Wilder whispered, a laugh in his voice.

"Yeah," Sophia said, thinking of the way Wilder made her heart feel alive, and how Lunis filled her soul with tenderness. How loving them made her a better person. They enriched her life in a way she'd never thought possible. Even in the pitch darkness, she could see Wilder's smile in her mind. She could feel Lunis' heat. She was alight in brand new ways. Her path felt clear.

Sophia strode forward, Wilder holding onto her, Lunis on their heels. She was worried she'd fall off a cliff or ram hard into something. When the urge struck her, she turned, knowing it was the right path to take. That happened twice more before she halted suddenly, Wilder nearly running into her, Lunis nearly ramming into him.

"What is it?" Wilder whispered in her ear.

"We're here," she said but didn't know why or where the words came from.

It was still completely dark. She felt Wilder tense.

Then the voice in Sophia's head echoed again, quieter this time. She let out a breath and focused on it. After a moment, it became clear.

"Don't you know yet? It is your light that lights the worlds." They were unmistakably the words of Rumi.

Sophia gasped, suddenly startled by how the poetry struck her.

"That's true," Wilder said beside her. "You light up the world. My world."

His words made her certain he'd heard the same thing as her.

And you light up mine, Lunis said, his tone sincere and not marked by his usual teasing quality.

Sophia felt so loved suddenly, she was breathless. Her heart seemed like it would overflow. Just as she thought it would burst, flames in torches on the wall illuminated where they hung.

She gasped in surprise. There wasn't too much to see, just two stone walls and an entrance to an unseen place. The walls were taller than Lunis, and above them there didn't appear to be a ceiling, only unending darkness.

Engraved on the wall to the right was the phrase, "Each moment contains a hundred messages from God."

On the wall to the left were different words from Rumi that read: *Remember, the entrance to the sanctuary is inside you.*

"What do you make of that?" Sophia asked.

"Should we try entering?" Wilder offered.

In answer, Sophia took a step forward, daring to enter the strange structure. As soon as she was even with the stone walls, she shot into the ground and flew up so fast, her heart felt as though it went into her throat.

A scream escaped her mouth and she halted abruptly to find herself alone on a pedestal. She looked down in awe and realized where they were and the horrors the ones she loved were about to face.

CHAPTER FORTY-SIX

High above on her pedestal, Sophia gazed down at the labyrinth, a huge maze that went on for hundreds of yards. She could see there were two ways out, but they weren't escapes. Rather they led to two very dangerous villains—ones she knew the ones she loved had to face. That was the way. She knew it, and it terrified her.

Looking up at her with horror in their eyes were Lunis and Wilder. Daring to look over the edge of the pedestal, Sophia gazed down at them, making both their faces relax in relief.

"I'm okay," Sophia called, her voice echoing down to them several stories below. It was good that she wasn't afraid of heights, or the situation would have been much more terrifying.

"You're trapped," Wilder stated.

She nodded. "I think there's only one way to get me out."

I fly up there and get you, Lunis told her.

"I don't think you can," she said, fueled by instinct.

He unfolded his wings and tried to flap them, but regret filled his expression. *You're right.*

"What do you see?" Wilder asked.

She stood up and gazed around, wishing that Lunis could scry her and see what she saw, but their magic didn't seem to work. "It's a labyrinth," she said, calling down to them. "I think that you, Wild, have to go to the right. You, Lun, need to go to the left."

"Why do you think that?" Wilder asked.

She gulped. "Because it's based on what you need to fight."

Lunis lowered his chin. *Which is?*

"A minotaur for you," she began. "And a warrior for Wild."

"First, we have to find our way through the maze," Wilder guessed.

She nodded. "I can help you."

"Actually, you can't," Wilder called up to her.

She opened her mouth to reply, but nothing came out. Her voice was gone. Her lips moved, but her words were silent. Then she heard what Wilder and Lunis must have heard, and it gave her chills.

"Let silence be the art you practice."

CHAPTER FORTY-SEVEN

Sophia couldn't help the ones she loved. Worse than that, she was in the perfect position to advise them. From up high, she could tell them exactly how to navigate the maze. And yet, she had no voice to talk. She had to watch, powerless to help as the two she loved with all her heart, stumbled around a very complicated labyrinth to find themselves face to face with deadly villains. Then the real challenge would begin for Sophia. She'd have to stand by and be forced to watch as they battled.

That was going to break her heart over and over again. She would always rather fight for the ones she loved than watch them do it.

In her silence, Sophia heard the voice of Rumi again. It said: "You have to keep breaking your heart until it opens."

Sophia gulped and nodded. She leaned over the side of the pedestal and gave the two on the stone floor meaningful expressions. They understood the direction in her eyes.

With his shoulders back, Wilder set off for the entrance to the maze to the right. Lunis gazed up at her a moment longer with regret before starting forward. Their telepathic connection had been severed while they were here. That had happened a few times, and it always made both their hearts ache. Lunis and Wilder had to manage through the maze on their own. They had to face the dangers ahead without her help. Sophia had to watch, only lending the prayers in her heart to keep them safe.

CHAPTER FORTY-EIGHT

Wilder wasn't sure whether he'd rather be entering the maze and facing a dangerous warrior in the tomb of Rumi with no magic, or be Sophia, having to watch from up high, powerless to help. He decided he'd rather be the one moving than standing still, fighting rather than the one having to remain idle and watch. It would be very difficult for Sophia—especially since she preferred the action.

It was no wonder to Wilder she had to bring two she loved to Rumi's tomb. That was what made it all the more difficult. Watching those you loved face dangers was like experiencing a nightmare and unable to wake from it.

The maze was so complex that Wilder was quickly lost. All the walls and corners and openings looked exactly the same. There was no way to know which way to go, and no clues that pointed toward the end or which way he'd gone.

Wilder doubled back several times, meeting dead ends again and again. He was certain he'd gone down the wrong paths several times, but there were so many junctions he quickly lost track. If he had use of his magic, then he could have done a tracking spell or left a trail to know which way he'd been. As it was, he didn't have any bread crumbs.

However, he did have his sword, the clothes on his back, and a flask of water. Since the sword would definitely be needed and a dragonrider never wasted water, Wilder decided to pull his shirt off, leaving him bare-chested.

He began tearing the material into pieces he could drop behind him, showing him paths he'd taken and crossed off as options.

With relief, he found after a short bit the pieces of clothing didn't disappear, which had been a concern. This place was protected by strong magic and was full of mystery. It appeared it was designed so that those in it couldn't cheat to reach the end. Sophia couldn't help them. They didn't have magic, and Lunis couldn't fly.

Wilder had always regarded Rumi as a peaceful person, but what he hadn't realized was the poet must have been incredibly crafty to have such a place under his tomb.

Having finally made some progress, Wilder glanced up to where Sophia was perched on the pedestal. No matter where he was in the maze, he could see her and her him. It seemed right to him that Sophia would be put on a pedestal. He knew that for him, she'd always been on a pedestal—ever since that first moment when he laid eyes on her when she entered the Castle, rocking all of their worlds.

Wilder had never been the romantic type. He'd never cared much about anything but Simi and his family. Then Sophia came along, and he didn't know how his heart could have expanded so much. She had quickly become his life. His purpose. The thoughts connected to his reason. Some said that love made you crazy, but for Wilder, it had done the opposite. Never before had he thought so clearly. Sophia made what was important clear. Everything that wasn't connected to love was pointless.

The voice of Rumi that Wilder heard in his head suddenly spoke, and he paused. *"I once had a thousand desires. But in my one desire to know you, all else melted away."*

Wilder held his hand to his bare chest, feeling tenderness in his heart. Nothing was truer for him than those words. It described Sophia and his love for her perfectly.

He saw the worry on her face as she stared down at him. Her gaze constantly drifted between him and something to his right. That had to be where he was headed to, to meet and no doubt fight this warrior.

Her head jerked to the side, and Wilder guessed she was watching Lunis on the far side of the maze. Wilder's ears picked up on a scratching noise coming from where Lunis would be, and he wondered how the dragon was faring. Suddenly he was highly aware of how alone the three of them were. They had started together and quickly been separated, all so they could find a cure to heal the world. The irony wasn't lost on him.

The voice of Rumi greeted Wilder's ears once more. "Do not feel lonely, the entire universe is inside you."

He nodded to himself, remembering they were never truly alone. That had been something Wilder had to remind himself of during the many years locked inside the Gullington. He had gotten used to it easier than most, having always been a loner. Meditating with Mahkah had helped Wilder to remember they were all connected. Now he had Sophia, loneliness was an affliction because he never wanted to be separated from her for long.

Wilder turned a corner to find another dead end. He spun around, intending to double back. However, the way he'd come was blocked. He was trapped.

Turning in a circle, he tried to figure out what he was missing. How had he gotten locked inside the maze? More importantly, how was he going to find his way out?

He looked up at Sophia, wishing she could help him. Wishing he could find a path to her.

Then he heard the voice of Rumi in his head once more, and he knew what to do. The words echoed in his soul long after they faded away, giving Wilder hope. Over and over, he heard, "Go find yourself first so you can also find me."

It was so easy, and yet, that was how life always worked—easy solutions to complex problems.

Withdrawing his sword, the dragonrider looked at the wide blade, seeing his own image in its reflection. He felt confident when he stared at his face. He felt at home. Wilder, more than ever, knew himself. His two centuries on this planet had taught him many things but falling in love with Sophia had made him find his heart, helping him to find himself.

Staring at his image, he found himself smiling. To himself, for all to hear, Wilder repeated words he knew weren't his own, but rather belonged to the ancient poet, "Life is the soul's light."

Even though his gaze stayed on his image in the sword, Wilder still saw the stone wall in front of him shimmer and disappear. Unhurried, he brought his gaze up to find himself face to face with a formidable force.

CHAPTER FORTY-NINE

Dragons had excellent senses of direction. They didn't need maps or compasses to tell which way to go. With that being said, Lunis was lost within seconds of being in the labyrinth.

The place was no doubt created to increase confusion and make the most rational thinker lose their mind.

He had never thought he'd be stripped of his ability to fly for a task. Being separated from Sophia was definitely draining to his spirit, but that was something they'd dealt with before. The most astonishing thing was he didn't have his connection to the collective consciousness of the chi of the dragon. He'd always had that, even from the beginning. At that moment, he wasn't even sure how it would help him. It wasn't like the dragons had ever been inside the tomb of Rumi.

The poet's words sifted across Lunis' mind, reminding him he wasn't alone in the labyrinth. "When setting out on a journey, do not seek advice from those who have never left home."

Touché, he stated, realizing the philosopher was in his head.

Lunis hung his head when he came to another dead end and realized that navigating through the confusing maze wasn't going to be easy. The walls were just high enough for him not to be able to see over. Sophia, on her place high up on the pedestal, could offer him little information on where to go. He noticed her pointing several times, but the directions weren't really clear to him.

It must have been incredibly challenging for her to be stuck up there and powerless to help. That was something she wasn't good at—being powerless.

Sophia represented strength and goodness and reason. She was so much more than the first female dragonrider. She was the Dragon Elite's salvation, and in being that, he believed her to be the world's protector. Few would ever know that this small woman was the reason the planet continued to spin on its axis, and its enemies didn't win out even with all their advantages.

When Lunis found himself back to the beginning of the labyrinth once again, he had to admit his strategy had to adapt. Entering the maze, he veered off to the left. This time, he used his claws to scratch at the stone, marking the paths he'd taken and crossed off as not options.

This made Sophia happy. She flashed him a smile, and the expression lightened his heart. A smile from Sophia had always been enough to bring joy to him even at his darkest moments.

Rumi's words traversed across his mind just then, obviously brought on by his thoughts: "Everything that is made beautiful and fair and lovely is made for the eye of one who sees."

Well put, the blue dragon said, continuing on, finding the labyrinth even more complicated as he progressed.

What's the key to this? Lunis said, muttering to himself.

Again, he heard Rumi's words in his mind: "What you seek is seeking you."

Yeah, that's not confusing, he teased, wondering how that sage advice would get him through the maze. Lunis knew he needed to get to the other side, where he'd meet a minotaur. The inevitable fight didn't scare him. Nothing scared a dragon—nothing except losing their rider.

He looked up and gave Sophia a meaningful expression—wanting to find his way to her whatever it took.

Okay, minotaur, I'm seeking you, Lunis said to himself. *Come and seek me.* That's when the wall in front of him shimmered and disappeared. Standing dangerously close was an angry beast, with murder in its eyes.

CHAPTER FIFTY

Being trapped some ten stories up on the pedestal was excruciatingly frustrating for Sophia. She paced across the five feet of space on the surface of the pedestal, many times nearly losing her balance and tumbling over the side. Her focus was solely on what Wilder and Lunis were doing on the ground below.

Not having a voice to help Wilder and Lunis was painful. Watching them take the wrong path over and over again was beyond maddening. The joy she felt when they figured out a strategy for negotiating the maze was nearly overwhelming. Wilder had torn up his clothes, leaving them behind like bread crumbs. Lunis had scratched at the floor and walls, helping him to determine the path.

Still, Sophia felt she'd been perched up high for ages, and she'd never be reunited with her dragon and Wilder.

As if responding to her thoughts, Rumi's words echoed in her head: "Goodbyes are only for those who love with their eyes. Because for those who love with heart and soul, there is no such thing as separation."

She nodded, appreciating the message that made her feel marginally better. Then Sophia spied the enemies that Wilder and Lunis would have to face, and grief fell on her once more. The warrior at the end of Wilder's maze was unlike any she'd ever seen.

He reminded her of a prince from Persia with his style of armor and the red sash wrapped around his waist. His arms were covered in tattoos, and in both his hands he held two large curved swords. With a brooding look, he waited stoically for Wilder to reach him. Although Sophia knew Wilder was strong and fast and one of the most competent fighters on the planet, she instinctively knew that facing this warrior would be incredibly dangerous, especially because Wilder couldn't rely on magic.

Her heart ached at the thought of having to watch Wilder battle this foe, potentially getting hurt, or taking a fatal blow.

Rumi's words came to her yet again: "Don't grieve. Anything you lose comes round in another form."

That didn't make her feel that much better, so she turned her attention to the minotaur that Lunis was quickly approaching. It was a formidable opponent to the large dragon.

Its horns were huge, and whereas Lunis stood on four clawed feet, the half-man, half-bull stood upright and would be the same size as the dragon—or at least, he would once Lunis reached him.

Sophia guessed that if Lunis couldn't fly, he also didn't have fire magic. That meant that similar to Wilder, he'd have to rely on his power and speed to fight the minotaur. He'd have to fight in close quarters with his claws and his teeth. There would be wounds. This would be a dangerous...no, deadly fight. That much was clear.

Sophia didn't know how she was going to watch Wilder and Lunis fight these enemies, but she knew she had to. She only wished there was something she could do to help them.

Once more, Rumi spoke in her mind, offering her words of wisdom: "Love is the bridge between you and everything."

CHAPTER FIFTY-ONE

Not much scared Wilder. It wasn't that he'd seen it all in his two hundred years on Earth. Quite the opposite. Much of his life had been spent at the Gullington, idly waiting for the world to open back up to the Dragon Elite. Before that, he'd battled many an enemy. Men and beasts didn't differ much. They had teeth and weapons and strength and prowess, and there was always a way to defeat them. Always.

What he was staring at the end of the maze was a man unlike any he'd ever set eyes on. He was full of magic, that much was clear. It rebounded off the warrior, like smoke from flames. Gold dust wrapped around the armored warrior and Wilder suddenly felt very foolish, having ripped up his own armored shirt to get through the maze.

The sword in the dragonrider's hands also seemed ineffective in comparison to the two curved large blades the man wielded. Wilder's connection with weapons always told him about them when he was in their presence. He could see every battle they'd been in and also feel the death and destruction they'd brought during their fights.

It wasn't a pleasant gift to have, but it was an incredibly helpful one. Right then, his skill told him these blades were forged for a prince who was cursed to never die until killed by the swords he held presently. They were stained red from the many who had tried to conquer him.

What Wilder didn't know was why the prince was cursed or why he appeared angrier than any enemy he'd ever set eyes on. As his shoulder-length black hair swayed from a sudden breeze, Wilder felt the heat that rose up in the warrior just before he dropped into a low lunge, holding his weapons of destruction behind his back. They appeared like wings for a moment, but this was no angel. This was an evil man who was suffering, and it was up to Wilder to rid him of his misery.

"It's time to put an end to your evil soul," Wilder said, holding his blade in front of him and taking up a fighting stance as he measured the apparition who was both real and fake. That which the mind saw was real enough to kill.

The prince didn't speak, but Rumi did: "Actually, your soul and mine are the same. We appear and disappear with each other."

Wilder didn't know what that meant, but he didn't have a moment to deliberate on it as the prince disappeared and then reappeared directly at Wilder's back. He swung around, his sword clanging against the prince's who hit him with a force that nearly toppled him off his feet.

Not only that, but the evil prince was fast, swinging the double blades and making Wilder have to move quicker than he'd had to do in quite some time. He had never battled anyone like this that was so powerful when he was lacking his usual powers. Usually he could rely on the chi of the dragon to aid him, offering him enhanced strength and speed. He didn't have that advantage this time, and Wilder feared it would be the death of him.

CHAPTER FIFTY-TWO

Having fire magic would have made the fight against the minotaur quick and painless. That wasn't an option for Lunis. Rumi had ensured these fights would be brutal and difficult and boil Lunis down to his core, only allowing him the strength of his muscles and the sharpness of his claws and teeth.

It wasn't going to be a fair fight, though, since the minotaur clearly had magic. That much was clear as the beast held out its hands, and a giant hammer appeared out of nowhere. It was covered in strange gold dust that no doubt enhanced it.

Oh, this got interesting, Lunis said, having learned from Sophia that one didn't lose their humor in battle. It didn't distract but rather kept you grounded.

The minotaur opened its mouth and roared, making the floor shake under Lunis.

I get it, Percy, Lunis joked. *You're angry. Someone put a ring in your nose and made you incredibly angry. We've all got problems.*

The minotaur obviously didn't get the jokes. It lowered its horned head, a flash of hostility glinting in its eyes.

Lunis suddenly became aware of how large the creature was. He, as the largest dragon at the Gullington, didn't know what it felt like to be small. His connection to the moon made it so he could grow rapidly. There was no moon or magic to rely on right then. Instead, Lunis was facing a monster that had all the advantages while he'd been stripped of his own.

Rumi apparently didn't agree with the fleeting moment of self-loathing as his word drifted across Lunis' consciousness. "Stop acting so small. You are the universe in ecstatic motion."

Lunis lifted his chin, offering Percy his own murderous glare. He opened his mouth and roared so loudly that not just the floor shook, but also the walls and the pedestal where Sophia stood. At that moment, the blue dragon found strength he didn't know he had, having to rely on his power and strength and nothing else for the first time ever.

CHAPTER FIFTY-THREE

Fear vibrated in Sophia's chest. Whipping her head back and forth, she wished she could see both Wilder and Lunis at the same time, but they were at opposite ends of the giant labyrinth. Everything was happening so fast.

When she watched Wilder, she couldn't see what was happening with Lunis. When she shifted her focus to her dragon, she was certain she was missing something critical happening to Wilder.

The stress of it made Sophia want to close her eyes and block out her current reality and the fact she couldn't do anything to help. She knew she couldn't do that, though. Sophia's job was to watch, powerless, and lend her support through love. To have faith that the two she believed in most would succeed—even if every advantage was awarded to their opponents.

You can do this, Sophia thought with conviction as the warrior with the two swords covered in dried blood swung around, doing a dance.

His two large blades spiraled around him, taking over the space he shared with Wilder. With few options to avoid being impaled, Wilder ducked as the swords swung over his head. Then he was forced to leap into the air as the warrior dropped to the stone floor, bringing the blades low.

Sophia knew that Wilder could move fast. He was the fastest fighter she'd ever met. Right then, he couldn't rely on the chi of the dragon to assist him, and the fear of having to keep up with the swift attacks was evident on his face.

A roar from the opposite end of the labyrinth stole Sophia's attention, and she whipped around to face Lunis. The giant minotaur slammed his hammer down on the stone tiles, making the floor crack under Lunis' feet. He rolled to the side, narrowly avoiding getting attacked by the hammer.

The assault to the floor chimed like a bell going off in Sophia's head. Worse than the excruciatingly loud noise was the hammer hitting the stone made the maze room quake, violently shaking the pedestal where she stood. It threw her off balance and over the side of the stone structure.

She caught the lip of the pedestal with one hand, the other slipping off. Her legs kicked, and Sophia bit her tongue, thinking this was her end. Falling from that height would end her. She knew it. Sophia couldn't rely on the chi of the dragon to heal her.

However, she wasn't going to go out like that, not today. Not when the ones she loved were facing greater dangers.

Reaching up, she grabbed the lip of the pedestal with her other hand. The stone was unforgiving to her fingers, biting into her skin, but she didn't care. She'd bloody her hands if it meant getting back up the surface of the pedestal.

With a grunt and brute force, Sophia lifted herself up, swinging her leg over the side of the narrow structure. The movement wasn't graceful, and it required so much strength that when she was back on the pedestal, she rolled over on her back and had to catch her breath—looking up at the blackness above her that seemed to go on forever.

In the distance, she could hear the sounds of the fights ensuing on her behalf. When her breath had returned, Sophia pushed up to a standing position to continue to watch as those she loved fought for their lives.

CHAPTER FIFTY-FOUR

Sweat poured down Wilder's face. His heart felt like it would beat out of his chest. He had never exerted himself this much in a battle. The devastating part of it all was he was on the defense. He hadn't even gotten a chance to attack the prince.

So many times, the stained blades came close to piercing Wilder and ending him. He had always been the hopeful type. Optimism was something that came easily to him. Right then, straining to survive these attacks, Wilder believed these moments were his last. There was no way to survive the prince, let alone kill him with his own swords. Wilder didn't even know how he'd get them away from him. Like every good warrior, the prince used the swords like they were an extension of him. They moved fluidly from his hands, slicing close by Wilder's face, making a whistling sound.

When one gave him a haircut, coming entirely too close to the top of his head, Wilder realized the current strategy wasn't going to work. He was a step behind each move and never in a position to plan his own attack.

I'm going to have to be bold and take a risk to beat this villain, he thought with renewed vengeance. *And winning was going to happen,* Wilder decided.

This was for Sophia. It was to save magicians and elves. It was to save the Dragon Elite. There was nothing more important for Wilder. He'd left his family behind long ago. The Dragon Elite was his family. His race was. And Sophia.

Feeling a fire ignite in his belly, Wilder let out a roar and ran the opposite direction from the prince, appearing to be fleeing from the fight. He darted back into the maze, grateful he left the trail marking his path.

The prince sprang after him immediately, hot on his heels but thankfully not running as fast, weighed down by carrying double swords.

CHAPTER FIFTY-FIVE

As long as Percy the minotaur had the giant hammer, Lunis didn't think there would be any defeating him. The weapon made it impossible to even get close for an attack. All the beast had to do was slam it on the floor, and it shook the dragon off balance and rattled his teeth so hard he thought they'd fall out of his mouth.

Lunis had caught sight of Sophia nearly falling from the pedestal, and that had almost cost him his life. He knew he couldn't get to her and yet, watching her struggle seared his soul. Percy, of course, had taken that opportunity to his advantage with another slam of his evil hammer.

Why don't you put that down and fight fair? Lunis growled.

The monster opened his cavernous mouth and roared, spit flying.

Worried he'd slam the hammer down again, sending Sophia to her death, Lunis decided it was time to be bold. He hadn't been able to get an attack in on Percy, struggling to just maintain safety as the beast thundered around like an angry construction worker.

In pure bull fashion, Percy lowered his head down, horns pointed in Lunis' direction, and charged. There wasn't much room to avoid the assault, and Lunis didn't like that style anymore anyways. It was time to fight.

186

He lowered his own horned head and braced himself for the attack. There was no avoiding what would happen next. Lunis just hoped he survived it.

CHAPTER FIFTY-SIX

It felt like Sophia was the one in the battles. Her pulse was racing so fast, and her breath was shallow. She didn't know what Wilder was doing. It wasn't like him to run from a fight. Maybe he'd decided there was no defeating the warrior. She wouldn't blame him. Repeatedly, Sophia was forced to watch as the sword grazed by Wilder, nearly cutting him several times.

A gasp flew from Sophia's mouth as tears ached in her throat. Seeing the person she loved nearly take a fatal blow was breaking her heart over and over again.

If they retreated now, then maybe the pedestal would lower her to the floor, and they could sprint back up the staircase and abandon the mission. It wasn't ideal but dying for the cure also wasn't an option. For as much as she believed in Wilder, right then she really didn't know how he could defeat this warrior.

The enemy was just too fast, too strong, and full of magical force.

Trying to keep her focus on Wilder fleeing through the maze, Sophia watched, holding her breath. Then her attention was yanked away when she caught sight of the minotaur charging at Lunis. Unlike before, he didn't dart out of the way. Instead, he lowered his horned head and appeared to brace himself.

Sophia hiccupped on her breath as the two connected. The minotaur's horns entangled in Lunis' immediately, making a screeching sound. The pair pressed into each other, trying to force the other one back.

It reminded Sophia of two bucks or moose fighting in the wild, their antlers hooked together.

Lunis jerked his head to the side with a force to impress. However, it didn't appear to do much to throw the minotaur off his feet. The beast was doing a remarkable job of maintaining his position.

A roar flew from Lunis' mouth that was full of his anger and pain —making Sophia's heart break further. She couldn't take this any longer. Tears streamed down her cheeks, blurring her vision.

She almost didn't see it when Lunis picked up one of his front feet and threw it into the side of the minotaur, knocking him loose and into an adjacent wall. The hammer was sent sliding in the opposite direction.

Sophia nearly jumped up from excitement but stayed firmly planted on the narrow surface of the pedestal. Her victorious reaction would have been premature, though because the beast immediately recovered from the loss, using magic to increase his size. Before he'd been the same height as Lunis, but after a brief moment, he swelled, and towered over the blue dragon.

CHAPTER FIFTY-SEVEN

Wilder pushed himself to run faster than he ever had without using the chi of the dragon. He knew if Simi was there, she'd tell him to employ strategy over strength. That was the only option he had left facing a prince who was stronger, faster, and all around better than him. Simi appreciated that Sophia always used strategy rather than brute force. Wilder hadn't yet told Sophia that his dragon adored her, and that was saying a lot because she'd only ever cared for him.

I have to tell Sophia this, he thought.

Wilder sprinted around a corner and then another, following the strips of clothes he'd left behind. Soon he had lost the prince, putting some space between them. It wouldn't last. He was certain the magical prince knew how to navigate the maze.

Wilder didn't need much time. Less was more, actually. What he needed was an advantage, and right then, the best one would be the element of surprise.

When he was around a corner, Wilder threw his back up against a wall and held his sword at the ready. He was careful to keep his breathing slow to not give his position away. Straining to listen, he waited until the approaching footsteps grew louder.

He tightened his grip on his sword and let out a breath. When the prince raced around the corner, Wilder swung his sword straight into the warrior's chest. It clanged first against the swords on either side of the prince, before pushing through and slamming into his armor.

As Wilder suspected, having seen the battles connected with the prince's swords, his weapon wouldn't pierce the warrior. The only thing that would was the enemy's. However, the attack had been successful to a degree, and the prince flew backward, slamming into the stone wall behind him.

One of his swords slipped from his grip and slid across the floor, landing in the far corner. Wilder's gaze darted to it, and he considered racing after the weapon—his only salvation in this fight. His moment of hesitation cost him greatly, giving the prince the chance to leap forward, thrusting the other sword into Wilder's ribs, slicing through his bare skin and producing the worst pain Wilder had ever experienced.

CHAPTER FIFTY-EIGHT

"No!" Sophia tried to scream, but no sound came out of her mouth.

She hadn't thought it was real, seeing Wilder get stabbed. Then she saw the blood around the warrior's sword. She witnessed the pain and disbelief on Wilder's face. There was no disbelieving what had happened.

For a moment, Sophia considered how she could climb down from the pedestal, but the way it was designed, there was no way to do it safely. Rumi had thought of everything.

From her place perched up high, Sophia watched as the warrior added insult to injury, pressing the sword even harder into Wilder's midsection, forcing a scream from his mouth.

With a satisfied expression, the villain stepped back, narrowing his eyes. Wilder stumbled backward, his hands on the hilt of his enemy's sword protruding from his side.

Sophia gagged on her tears as she watched the man she loved yank the blade from his body. She couldn't understand what he was doing. He knew it would cause him to bleed out. The effort and pain it must have caused was unfathomable to her.

More surprising was the triumphant expression on Wilder's face as he held his adversary's weapon. Even as blood gushed from his wound, he seemed to have a sweet surrender. A chill ran down Sophia's back. She didn't know what was coming next, she knew someone was about to die.

CHAPTER FIFTY-NINE

The fight hadn't been fair before, and now it was even more uneven, with the minotaur hovering above Lunis.

The blue dragon looked on the bright side. At least he'd gotten the hammer away from Percy. However, that did little to lift Lunis' spirits as he glared up at the beast. Few creatures were bigger than Lunis. He'd never taken that fact for granted, but right then, he felt sorry for many of the animals he'd battled and squashed easily due to his size.

Before, there hadn't been a lot of room at the end of the labyrinth for the two large creatures. Now there was even less.

You're one of those types who hogs the armrest on planes, aren't you? Lunis dared to ask the beast.

In reply, the minotaur narrowed his beady eyes as if he were offended by being considered a bad neighbor on a plane.

Percy's hands were huge, easily the size of a car tire. When he reached down for Lunis with his greedy fingers, there was little way of avoiding his grasp. Lunis darted to the side, but the minotaur expected this and slammed his other fist into Lunis' side, launching him until he connected with the stone wall.

The pain of the assault was all encompassing. It stole the blue dragon's breath. The adrenaline of the moment wasn't enough to distract him from the pain as he hit the wall so hard it cracked.

Lunis needed to get up. That much was clear as the minotaur thundered over to where he was lying in a heap, but his body wasn't listening to the commands from his brain. He was moving too slowly and soon, the beast was towering over him once more.

Barely able to move his back legs, Lunis realized that something was wrong. He was pinned. His wing was wedged into the crack in the stone. Pulling at it, he growled from the searing pain. The only way to escape the next attack would be to yank it free but doing so haphazardly would result in injury. That much was clear, but Lunis had no other options.

If he stayed pinned, Percy would make quick work of him, and an injured wing would be the least of his problems. Making an impromptu decision, Lunis yanked his wing from the crack in the wall, the sharp stone ripping at his wing, and tearing it in several places.

The minotaur apparently didn't expect this, though, and Lunis had a moment of surprise as he rolled free from his spot, tumbling on his side until he was on the far side of the arca.

The pain was mind-numbing. Looking down, Lunis saw why. His right wing was ripped badly in several places, the bones were broken, and blood gushed from many wounds.

CHAPTER SIXTY

Sophia didn't know if her heart could break any more. First Wilder and now Lunis. They were both hurt badly. Watching the minotaur toss Lunis around like he was a tiny animal was bizarre and wrong and infuriating. She didn't think she could take it anymore.

Her dragon was injured. Not that he could fly right then anyway, but he had to be in incredible pain. If they had their connection, she'd feel his agony, and that would be something. She wanted to share in his pain and let him know he wasn't alone. They weren't connected, and there was little she could do to reassure Lunis, cowering in the corner.

The minotaur appeared invigorated by the fact he'd gotten a few successful blows on the dragon. His dark eyes sparkled with delight before he lowered his large horns again. This was it. It was the mino- taur's finishing move. He knew Lunis was hurt, and he faced off with him again. This time when their horns locked, he'd have the weight and size advantage, taking control and slamming Lunis into the stone wall. Then he'd be done. With Lunis gone from this world, Sophia wouldn't survive long either.

She didn't jump down from her perch, because then she'd kill herself and Lunis in the process. Instead, the dragonrider forced herself to watch as the minotaur charged at the blue dragon.

Sophia held her breath, firmly believing she was about to watch Lunis' death. She knew that Wilder was hurt on the other side of the maze, but she couldn't pull her gaze away as the minotaur burst across the space with incredible speed.

Lunis wasn't lowering himself to challenge the minotaur. Sophia couldn't understand what he was doing. Was he giving up, she wondered in a panic. Things were desperate. This was the worst possible situation they'd ever been in. She couldn't understand him surrendering.

He didn't move from his position against the wall. The minotaur was nearly on him, about to puncture him with his sharp horns. Dragonhide was strong, but it wouldn't be able to withstand an assault from minotaur horns. Not with the force that was fueling them as the beast charged.

Sophia held her breath, her eyes unblinking. When the minotaur was about to connect with Lunis, the dragon moved. In a flash, like he was fueled by magic once more, Lunis shot to the side, rolling over his broken wing as the minotaur charged.

It all happened so fast the monster didn't have a chance to slow or change direction. Its horns, meant for Lunis, slammed into the wall, piercing into the stone, and the creature was stuck. The force of the assault made the thick stone buckle down on the beast. As large as it was, it couldn't withstand the weight and crumpled as the avalanche of stone rained down on it, pounding it flat.

Lunis stepped forward, his eyes narrowed on his enemy's limp body. His tail swished before he turned, putting his focus on Sophia, a hopeful expression once more on his face.

CHAPTER SIXTY-ONE

The stab wound was spilling blood. Painful wasn't the word for it. Never had Wilder experienced anything so burning hot. He staggered back, holding the prince's sword, willing himself not to pass out.

His enemy wasn't underestimating him. The prince realized his mistake, stabbing him and leaving the sword for Wilder to retrieve. Now the prince was weaponless, and Wilder held the one thing that could end him.

They both knew it wouldn't take much to also take Wilder down. He was badly injured, and a well-placed attack to his midsection would take him out.

The evil prince darted forward, throwing a kick at Wilder's side, aiming for the bloody wound. Instantly, Wilder jumped back, sucking in his chest to keep himself free of the attack. The effort made him scream with pain.

A smile flickered across the prince's mouth. He was enjoying this.

That filled Wilder with an incredible desire to stamp out this evil. It was unfair to allow such a despicable force to exist when innocent magicians and elves were suffering around the world.

Wilder was going to get that cure. He was going to save his people. He was going to make Sophia proud.

Darting forward, Wilder whipped the sword from side to side, finally taking offensive measures against the prince. For a moment, he thought his connection to Simi, and the chi of the dragon was back. He was moving quickly again, his motions blurring. Then he realized it was his motivation spurring him on, giving him speed, and making him a deadly force.

The fear that sprang to the prince's eyes was all the encouragement that Wilder needed.

As the prince avoided his own sword slicing through the air, he was being forced back toward a dead end. When his back was up against a wall, Wilder pulled back the blade covered in his own blood and plunged it into the prince's chest. He wasn't one to kill an unarmed man, but the stakes had changed.

The prince screamed out as the sword passed through his heart. Blood welled up from the wound as Wilder twisted the blade, ensuring the assault would be deadly, although he knew all that had to happen was for the prince to be stabbed with his own weapon.

Narrowing his eyes, Wilder pulled his hands off the hilt and immediately cradled his side and his own injury. Wilder took a step back and watched as the prince slid down the stone wall, a hollowness in his eyes as his head drifted to the side, and he took his last breath.

Wilder lowered his head, showing his respect at the demise of his enemy. The reign of the evil prince was over. He had been a worthy opponent, but in the end, love won out.

CHAPTER SIXTY-TWO

Relief flooded Sophia's being as she watched Wilder defeat the warrior. She knew he was injured. Lunis too, but they were alive. All she had to do was get them home to the Gullington, and Quiet would heal them. It might take time, but as long as they survived, that was all that mattered.

She was worried for them, having to traverse their way back out of the maze in their injured states, although neither would give up nor complain. She was still stranded at the top of the pedestal.

For a moment, she panicked, thinking there would be more challenges—more enemies to defeat. Lunis and Wilder were strong, but they wouldn't be able to fight much more.

On the heel of her worries, the stone walls of the labyrinth sank into the floor, disappearing. Lunis and Wilder stood in an open space, a hundred yards dividing them from each other and Sophia; their path was clear.

Both bounded in her direction, moving as fast as their injuries would allow them too.

Sophia expected the pedestal would lower or her magic would return, that she'd be offered some way down. However, her circumstances didn't change.

She blinked as a tiny light appeared in front of her. It grew larger until a figure sprang from it. A man appeared, wearing beautiful robes, a long white beard, and a turban on his head. The kind look in his eyes was full of unconditional love, and she knew without a doubt who hovered in the air before her.

"Rumi," Sophia mouthed, no sound coming out. Something catching in her throat. All of the stress and emotion had her on the verge of tears.

He bowed his head, his hands in front of him in prayer position. "Sophia Beaufont. You are very loved and loving. Such has been proven."

Her eyes watered as her gaze darted to the two on the floor, looking up at her, seeing the figure of Rumi before her. Wilder appeared close to passing out, and Lunis was bleeding badly. She needed to get them home.

Rumi followed her line of sight before saying, "The wound is the place where the light enters you."

She nodded, believing he was saying they would be okay. After watching what they went through, she wondered if she would be. If possible, she loved them more than ever.

"I've come for a cure," she began, swallowing down the tender pain in her throat.

"And you have earned it," Rumi stated in a deep voice, holding out his hand. In it, a small round bottle filled with thick red liquid appeared. It didn't seem large enough to cure all those sick with distortion. "You will know of someone who can replicate this."

Sophia nodded and held out her own hand. She knew exactly who he was referring to. The potion floated across and landed in her palm.

"The world..." Sophia began, realizing she should maximize her time with Rumi and get as much as possible out of it. "It's in a bad place. I don't know if I can fix it."

He nodded, a smile in his eyes. "Yesterday I was clever, so I wanted to change the world. Today I am wise, so I am changing myself."

She vaulted these words away. Fatigue was making it hard to think. Her gaze floated back down to the pieces of her heart on the floor, staring up at her. "How do I get to them?" Although she realized she was in the presence of a man thought to be dead for centuries, she needed to be reconnected with those she loved.

He smiled with understanding. "Lovers don't finally meet somewhere. They're in each other all along."

Sophia tilted her head to the side, getting a little fed up with the riddles. Rumi must have sensed this because he continued, offering more advice.

"Your heart knows the way. Run in that direction."

She could hardly believe it when automatically, Sophia took a step forward. She expected to fall straight down, but instead, a golden stone formed under her feet. Below it, another step formed. Carefully, she stepped down, the staircase slowly illuminating as she progressed, taking each one carefully until she was on the floor once more, reunited with her heart.

Lunis and Wilder ran to her, but Sophia paused, not wanting to hurt them with her embrace. They didn't care because Wilder wrapped her in his arms, and Lunis folded his uninjured wing around the pair of them, pressing them in tightly to him. The three stayed like this until their breaths returned to normal, and their hearts were mended once more.

CHAPTER SIXTY-THREE

Once Sophia had ensured that Wilder and Lunis were safe and as comfortable as possible at the Gullington, she set back out, knowing time was of the essence. If Hiker was relieved she'd been successful, it was overshadowed by the fact she'd brought back one of his dragonriders shirtless and covered in blood.

He took charge of Wilder at once, an expression of concern on his face like she'd never seen him wear before. Sophia reasoned they'd spent many years together and had to be quite close.

Sophia wasn't even sure that Hiker heard her when she told him she had the antidote and needed to get it replicated. He nodded, helping Wilder to his room where he could recover.

The fatigue that would soon take her out didn't even register for Sophia as she stepped onto Roya Lane with the antidote to distortion and Baba Yaga's grimoire.

It still felt strange to visit the magical lane and not run into King Rudolf. He was always striding down the streets, making a scene. Sophia had messaged Liv briefly to check in and tell her of her progress with the antidote. Her sister was proud she'd been success-ful, but had nothing to report about the Great Library. There'd been no signs of Rudolf or Nevin Gooseman or his men.

That was good news because Sophia had been too busy to jump in and take the evil politician out. Hopefully, the timing would work out, because she really wanted to be there when Nevin Gooseman showed up. It was time they met in person, and she got to the bottom of his agenda. She also looked forward to whatever Liv would do to him for abducting Rudolf. Sophia was fiercely protective of those she loved. The only one who was possibly more so was the Warrior for the House of Fourteen.

Sophia wasn't exactly sure why she'd had the urge to bring Baba Yaga's grimoire with her, but something that Rumi had said sparked the idea. She was operating based on instinct, and it seemed to be serving her well.

The door chimed when Sophia entered Rose Apothecary. Again she found Bep, the potions expert, hovering over a cauldron, hard at work on the healing potion. The dragon eggshells had been delivered to her, or what they could scrounge up since no one knew where the stock Rudolf had was located. It would have to do until he was rescued, and hopefully it was enough to get the cure for Ainsley.

"Hi," Sophia said, pushing her hair out of her face and realizing she needed a shower...and a nap...and a burger.

"You look awful," Bep said, glancing up at her.

Sophia nodded. "Thanks. I went on a once-in-a-lifetime vacation. Never again."

Bep offered her an amused expression. "Clever pun."

"I have good teachers on the subject," Sophia replied, pulling the small vial from her pocket. "I have another job for you."

The woman sighed. "Because creating a healing potion isn't enough?"

"Well, this distortion business is pretty critical," Sophia explained.

The store owner cocked an eyebrow at her. "Yes, and although I was hoping the healing potion would be a cure-all for that too, I don't think it will work. It's just too broad, and this distortion disease is very complicated."

"That was my guess too," Sophia said, handing the antidote over.

"This is the cure for distortion, but I need you to replicate it. Do you think you can do that?"

Bep pulled the cork off the small bottle and sniffed, her eyes widening. "Indeed, it is. Where did you get this?"

"You wouldn't believe me if I told you," Sophia said dryly.

The potions expert nodded. "You doubt me."

"No, at this point, I doubt my sanity."

"I could replicate this, but not without some help," Bep told her. "It's very complicated."

"I figured as much." Sophia pulled Baba Yaga's grimoire from her cloak. "How about if you had a bit of direction."

The woman's eyes widened with shock. "That's not..."

"It is," Sophia affirmed. "I've been charged with protecting it. If I leave it with you, you've got to promise that you'll keep it safe."

"Baba Yaga's grimoire," Bep said in disbelief. "I will guard it with my life. In the wrong hands, this is a very dangerous book."

"Exactly," Sophia agreed. "So, you can replicate the cure?"

"I believe so," Bep answered. "But it will take some time."

"The healing elixir is important, but I need you to devote your attention to this right now," Sophia told her. "I don't know what's going on globally with those who have distortion, but we have to help them."

"I agree," Bep said. "And that works, because the healing elixir needs to rest for a bit."

Sophia let out a long breath. "Good, I'm glad it's all going to work out."

"It always works out," Bep stated with confidence. "It just sometimes takes some time to get there."

Sophia nodded, appreciating the sage advice.

"Before you go," Bep began, striding for a shelf. She picked up a small bottle of purple liquid. "Take this if you want to recover from your travels quickly. I don't mean to be rude, but the bags under your eyes are a bit concerning."

Grateful she could avoid resting and get right to the next task demanding her attention, Sophia smiled and took the potion. She pulled off the lid and downed it in one swallow. It was thick and sweet and instantly made her feel better.

"Oh, you look as fresh as ever." Bep gave her a proud smile.

"Thank you," Sophia said, feeling her eyes widen, and her mind sharpen like she'd had a full night's rest and a big meal.

"You never need to thank me," Bep replied. "Just be yourself and keep doing what you're doing."

CHAPTER SIXTY-FOUR

Excited to see how Lunis and Wilder were doing, Sophia hurried back to the Gullington, grateful that Bep had supplied her with a replenishing potion. Not only did she feel better, but the potions expert also said she looked even more beautiful than usual.

Hurrying through the Barrier, Sophia paused at the sight of the Expanse. It wasn't Lunis and Wilder lounging on the grass that surprised her. It was that around them were all the adult dragons: Simi, Bell, Tala, and Coral. Next to them was everyone else from the Castle: Hiker, Mama Jamba, Trin, Ainsley, Evan, Mahkah, and Quiet.

They all appeared to be waiting, their gazes directed at her as they stood shoulder to shoulder. Even more perplexing was the guys had their shirts tucked in, and if Sophia wasn't mistaken, Hiker appeared to have combed his hair.

Cautiously, Sophia approached the group, aware they were all regarding her with sneaky grins.

"What's going on?" she asked and hadn't entirely finished the question when the singing began.

"*Happy birthday to you,*" they began in unison, out of tune. "*Happy birthday to you. Happy birthday, dear Sophia. Happy birthday to you.*"

Her hands flew to her mouth, and she nearly choked on her

surprise. In her haste to find Rumi and the cure and rescue Rudolf, Sophia had completely forgotten it was her birthday.

"Oh angels above!" she exclaimed as her eyes fell on Lunis, who was lying on his stomach, his injured wing covered. Beside him, against his side was Wilder, who also appeared to be bandaged. They both were bright-eyed, with wide grins on their faces. "It's my birthday! How did you all know?"

Mama Jamba pursed her lips. "How did I know? Come on, dear. I know when everyone's birthday is."

"What she doesn't know," Evan began, "is how old you are."

Sophia nodded with understanding. Technically she didn't know how old she was either. It was complicated thanks to the chi of the dragon and being with Lunis since he hatched.

"She's a unique case," Mama Jamba stated. "Her dragon made her age rapidly and matured her, but age is a relative thing. Just ask Papa Creola about it. He'll tell you that age isn't just a number."

"No, it's a word," Evan joked.

"Happy birthday, Sophia," Wilder said, trying to push up from her dragon to a standing position but struggling from the effort.

"Stay where you are," she commanded, rushing over and throwing her arms around his shoulders, squeezing him as tightly as she thought was safe. "How are you?"

"I'm fine," he answered with a smile. "I'll make a full recovery and not even have a cool scar to show for bragging rights."

This filled her heart with relief. "And you, Lun?" She glanced up at her dragon.

He grinned at her. *Same as Wild. No cool scar, but at least I've got a fun story.* He glanced up at Bell. *Have you defeated a giant minotaur?*

The elder pursed her mouth at him. *That's the third time you've asked me that and the answer is still no.*

Well, I did and have the battle scar and T-shirt to prove it, Lunis joked.

"We have gifts for you," Mama Jamba said, ushering the others to the side to show a table that was set up on the Expanse with beautifully wrapped presents and filled with scrumptious foods, all of Sophia's favorites. At first glance, she noticed queso and chips and salsa, chicken tenders and ranch dressing, sliders stacked up high, French fries, and southwest eggrolls.

"Wow, you all did this...for me," Sophia said, suddenly breathless.

"I thought it was a bit much too." Evan gave her a wink.

Ainsley picked up a gift bag and thrust it into Sophia's hands. "Me first."

Smiling, Sophia's hands shook as she reached into the bag and pulled out a familiar garment. "Are these my jeans?"

The elf nodded. "Yes, you're welcome. I thought I'd give them back to you for your birthday."

"Thanks," Sophia said.

"And from me," Evan stated, handing her a box that wasn't wrapped. "It's a useless box." On the front, there was a switch and slit in the lid.

Sophia flipped the switch, and the box opened. A finger popped up and closed the button, making it automatically shut again. "Wow, I've never wanted something like this, and I'm sure it's going straight into the trash."

"You're very welcome," Evan said proudly.

Mahkah stepped forward, handing Sophia a small wrapped present. "This is to ensure you have pleasant dreams."

Sophia pulled the lid off the present and found a beautiful turquoise dream catcher. "Thank you. How very thoughtful of you."

"You're very welcome," the quiet dragonrider told her softly.

Appearing out of place and embarrassed, Trin pointed to the Castle. "Quiet and I made some renovations to your room. I hope you don't mind. We outfitted it with some new magitech that will make your life easier and hopefully more comfortable."

"That's amazing," Sophia gushed, smiling at the cyborg and then the gnome.

"I made you these," Mama Jamba said, holding out her cupped hand for Sophia. She put her palm under Mother Nature's and felt something light drop onto her skin.

When Mama Jamba pulled her hand away, in Sophia's palm were shiny hoop earrings.

"These are beautiful." Sophia was overwhelmed by how shiny they were.

"They are," Mama Jamba agreed. "If they work, then one day, their sparkle will save your life."

Sophia's eyes widened, and she went to put them on immediately. "Thank you."

"I'm starving," Evan declared. "Can we cut the cake already?"

"No." Ainsley picked up plates and began handing them around. "Let's eat before things get cold."

Sophia was too overwhelmed to even think about eating, although the food all looked amazing. The three-tiered chocolate cake covered in ganache frosting appeared mouthwatering.

The others moved off to the table, loading up on food. Sophia watched for a moment, her heart feeling full.

"I didn't get you anything," Hiker said quietly at her shoulder.

She glanced up and grinned. "That's fine. You combed your hair, and that's enough."

He reflexively put his hands to his hair. "You noticed. Figured I could clean up a bit for the festivities."

His gaze fell on Ainsley, who was telling Evan not to double-dip. "I do have something for you, though, but it's not material. It's advice."

She turned, giving him her full attention. "I can always use that."

"That's one thing I appreciate about you," he began. "You're always open to information. That's important for a leader."

"Thank you, sir."

He cleared his throat, pinning his hands behind his back. "Sophia, you have the power to save the world. I see that in you and think you probably will a few times over. However, the key to a good leader is to raise up others who can help. You can't do everything, always. Sometimes you've got to learn to delegate."

She nodded, thinking of her experience at Rumi's tomb and having to stand by and watch as Lunis and Wilder fought. "You're right. I need to know when to fight and when to let others do so."

"Good, I'm glad you agree," Hiker said. "Because if you run yourself into the ground trying to do everything, then we all suffer."

Without another word, Hiker strode off to the table, leaving Sophia alone. Noticing Wilder trying to get up, she hurried back over to him. "Would you stay put already?"

He grinned at her, holding out his arm. She nestled down on the ground into his side as he pulled her in close. The pair leaned back on Lunis, enjoying his warmth.

"I'm glad you two are doing better," she said, feeling such fondness for them. "You're both amazing."

"You're the amazing one, Soph," Wilder said, kissing her forehead. "For your birthday, I made you a Spotify playlist. I'll send it to you later. I hope you enjoy it."

She smiled up at him. "That's perfect. I know I'll love it."

I know it will make me barf, Lunis declared.

"What did you get for her?" Wilder asked, glancing up at the dragon.

The best gift ever, he replied proudly. *The one that keeps you young and healthy—humor.*

"Oh, I can't wait for this one," Sophia said, already laughing.

My new thesaurus is terrible, Lunis began. *Not only that, but it's also terrible.*

Wilder groaned, but Sophia laughed, feeling suddenly giddy.

She glanced at the festivities, enjoying watching her friends eat and laugh and celebrate, although the world was a crazy place outside the Gullington. Much like Hiker advised, they'd learned when to fight and when to rest.

This was a rare opportunity where they needed to relax and recharge. Tomorrow, they'd return to saving the world, but if they didn't take this time for each other, and for themselves, they couldn't save anything or anyone.

I got fired from my job at the bank today, Lunis continued.

"Oh, really?" Sophia asked. "Why is that?"

An old lady came in and asked me to check her balance, so I pushed her over, he said with a sly grin.

"I didn't think they could get any worse." Wilder groaned, although he had a wide grin plastered across his face.

"They can always get worse," Sophia said, leaning her head on her dragon's belly and threading her fingers through Wilder's.

Last one, Lunis promised.

"Oh, good," Wilder teased.

Well, last one for now, Lunis corrected. *What's green and has wheels?*

Sophia thought for a moment. "What?"

Grass, the dragon replied. *I lied about the wheels.*

Feeling free and happy, Sophia laughed, grateful for the love in her life and the ones who made it so she wanted to make the world a better place. This was the planet where those she loved lived after all, and they deserved the very best. She'd ensure they had it.

CHAPTER SIXTY-FIVE

The poisoned food slid through the slot at the bottom of the door at its usual time. Rudolf's stomach rumbled with a fierce hunger that was hard to ignore, but he wasn't going to eat the food. Not this time.

It had been three days since his last meal. That was when he figured out that the idle-minded lard spunk-bubble handlers had been lacing his food with a common drug used to strip magical creatures of their magic.

As soon as he had been abducted, King Rudolfus Sweetwater tried to escape using his powers, but his kidnappers had something that disabled him. Magitech, he suspected.

Thankfully, it didn't work for long, and they must have known. Turning off a fae's magic isn't an easy feat, and as soon as Rudolf figured out what was happening, he started overcoming the obstacles.

Then he lost his magical powers once more. And again, just as his magic started to return, it diminished until it was gone entirely. Rudolf couldn't figure out what was happening. He was the smartest person he knew, which was saying a lot because he knew an accountant, and this situation stumped him.

That's when he realized they had been spiking his food and not with the normal roofie Rudolf preferred on a Saturday night. The kidnappers were up to no good and wanted Rudolf for more than just his good looks and rock-hard abs, so they were poisoning his food, blocking his magic.

That wouldn't do.

Rudolf had to escape. He missed the Captains and longed for Serena, his wife. His kingdom would need him. Also, he really needed a proper shave. He was starting to feel like a magician with the stubble on his cheeks and unkempt hair. The king of the fae shuddered at the idea of even remotely resembling a homely magician. Or even worse, a dirty hippie. What if the facial hair caused him to become a vegan? Was there anything worse in the world, he wondered to himself. Maybe having to stand in lines or pay taxes.

Picking up the plate of poisoned food, Rudolf went over to the toilet in the corner. The few dozen times he'd been abducted and imprisoned, he'd stayed in horrible accommodations. This was no exception. The room was windowless with only a bed, a toilet, and a slot in the door for food to be delivered. Even worse was that the bed covers were covered in plaid.

He shook his head at the atrocity. Abduct a man. Strip him of his powers. Interrogate him for hours. For the love of all that was holy, do not expect him to sleep in a bed made from T-shirt material that looked like something a lumberjack would wear to a funeral. What was wrong with these people?

Obviously, there were many things wrong with these kidnappers besides their bad taste and lack of hospitality. At first, Rudolf thought this was a fun game Serena had set up for his birthday. Alas, when she didn't show up or have him chained to the bed, he concluded it was a bona fide abduction.

Rudolf waited for talks of a ransom. He'd expected to have the kidnappers take videos of the king of the fae suffering in his cell, unable to sleep for fear of lying on the plaid bedding. His people would pay any amount to get him back. The magicians, who were notorious for being poor, would low ball and only ask for a few hundred million. That would be chump change for the fae and handed over without batting an eye.

However, there was no ransom request as far as Rudolf could tell. Instead, for hours each day, his kidnappers asked him the same question over and over again. A ridiculous question that the king of the fae refused to answer. Where was the Great Library?

Of all the reasons to abduct him, this seemed like the worst. It was just a building with a bunch of books. Okay, all the books in all the world. There weren't even any slot machines in the place. Or a bar, or strippers. Not that Rudolf knew of anyway.

Yes, Rudolf could take them to the Great Library—a place hidden to most. Since he had once been the Fierce, one of the protectors of the Great Library, it was easier for him to find it. But the Great Library had been further hidden due to losing its last librarian. It was now even more difficult to find, but thanks to Rudolf's association with Plato, he knew where to look. It appeared someone knew that.

Rudolf wasn't talking, though. He didn't know why these unimaginable lorry plonkers wanted to get into the Great Library, but the reasons couldn't be good. There was a lot of valuable knowledge inside that place, and it was protected for a reason. With no librarian, if Rudolf led them to the Great Library, they could have access to everything, and the potential dangers were endless.

No, Rudolf wasn't talking.

What he was going to do was escape this dilapidated place and do what was most important, get really wasted. Then he'd kiss his children and slap his wife's butt.

Scraping the poisoned food into the toilet, as he'd done for the last three days, Rudolf grimaced before flushing it, making his captors think he'd eaten. At his kingdom, he wasn't responsible for doing dishes. Hell, he didn't even have to chew his food if he didn't want to. He had people for that. Scraping food off a plate was a new low for him. Rudolf reasoned it was humbling. After several hundred years on this planet, it was good to keep himself humbled.

As he'd been doing, Rudolf opened the slot and slid the plate back through, launching it down the long hallway. From what he could tell, there were several guards stationed on the floor. He wasn't in a basement, as he suspected since he spied light a few times through the slot. The guards wore really lousy shoes. Rudolf shivered with disgust, remembering spying the shoes when he'd looked through the slot. Sneakers, the low lives wore rubber-soled sneakers like they were blind and didn't care if they burned out other people's eyes. Some people just didn't care how they looked.

Rudolf glanced down at his dirty tunic and slacks, grateful when he felt his magic pool inside of him. The three day fast had worked. His magical powers were back. He considered using it right then to change his clothes, but that might deplete his reserves and then he'd still be stuck.

Shaking his head, he decided he'd escape his kidnappers, then change and make for the closest bar. Priorities.

Although Rudolf's magical powers had returned, they weren't at full steam yet. For one, the poison was still in his system. Also, much like magicians, fae's powers were somewhat replenished by food and water. Not being able to eat had inhibited his strength. This was the reason the fawning wank trailers had used food as the delivery device for the poison. Rudolf had upped his water intake, which wasn't poisoned, and that appeared to be enough to give him back his magic.

Holding out his hand, Rudolf tried to open a portal. He was crestfallen to find there were barriers in place that prevented portal magic. Whoever his captors were, they were of the magical variety.

Rudolf had gotten a brief glimpse of the men who grabbed him and remembered how ugly they were, so they were probably magicians.

Unfortunately, it would be a bit longer before a martini could grace Rudolf's lips. He'd have to sneak out of his cell and through the house full of atrocious artwork from the Renaissance period. Magicians always had the worst taste. They refused to admit that baroque artwork was superior. The good news for Rudolf was he should have enough magic to accomplish the task since, on even a bad day, he was more powerful than a slew of magicians.

Pressing his ear to the door, the fae listened, ensuring it was quiet in the hallway. When he confirmed there was no one on the other side, he pointed his finger at the door, unlocking it.

Letting out a long breath, Rudolf turned the doorknob, excited to be escaping his cell and getting his freedom back.

CHAPTER SIXTY-SIX

Rudolf had been right. His captors were gross magicians. Now that he was outside his cell, he could sense them. Their magic was a different brand than fae, giants, elves, or gnomes. It felt dirtier, more corrupt.

Rudolf also knew that the bad-taste-magicians had taken him based on the modern design of the hallway. It was like Frank Lloyd-Wright had thrown up all over the place. The king of the fae shuddered, wondering if he could take much more abuse to his eyes.

In a room up ahead, Rudolf heard voices. Using a camouflaging spell, Rudolf decided to blend into the narrow hallway. He suspected it would kill his soul a little to take on the appearance of the clean lines and black and white photography on the walls, but it was his only option for going unnoticed as he made his escape. He didn't have enough magic to use an invisibility spell.

Once he confirmed that he'd blended and taken on the appearance of whatever was around him, like a chameleon, Rudolf set off down the hallway. Ahead were two doorways on either side. Beyond, there was an open bank of windows that led to an open grassy yard. That would be his escape route.

As he neared the first doorway, Rudolf tensed, recognizing the person's voice who was talking. He'd heard it on the news recently. Liv had demanded he flip the channel from cartoons so she could watch. She really was the most boring person in the world, always subscribing to world news and talking about things like sanctions on magic and laws. Still, she was kind of fun at times, so he kept her around. She'd literally do anything to help him, and loyalty was something that meant a lot to the fae.

The man's voice though—he was the politician who had been campaigning against the Dragon Elite, Nevin Gooseman.

Rudolf narrowed his eyes, sudden anger making him scowl. He shook his head, worried about the frown lines such a thing would cause. *How dare this man give me wrinkles,* Rudolf thought bitterly.

Pressing in close to the wall next to the doorway, Rudolf listened to the politician who was talking to someone else in the room.

"Well, if the fae won't talk, then he's useless to us," Nevin Gooseman stated with no flamboyance.

Magicians really were the worst. How did they not bore themselves to death on a daily basis?

"I was hoping we could get the location of the Great Library out of him by now," another man said.

"He has until tomorrow to start talking," Nevin Gooseman said.

"If he doesn't?" the other guy asked.

"Get rid of him," Nevin Gooseman answered. "But make it fast and clean and ensure that his body can't be found. He is the king of the fae, after all."

"Yes, sir," the man affirmed.

"What is your plan if he starts talking?" a third man asked.

"If he takes us to the Great Library," Nevin Gooseman began, "then we will storm the place with our magitech military. I suspect security will still be a problem. Besides, I'm going to do the mortal world a favor and destroy the place. It really isn't fair that magicians keep a copy of every book ever written and don't allow anyone but a few to have access to it."

Rudolf couldn't believe what he was hearing. This guy was a magician but held so much power because he chose to rule over mortals.

He'd been trying to sabotage the Dragon Elite for months. Now he was going after the Great Library—a place that needed to be protected since it was full of so much knowledge. Secrets that in the wrong hands would be deadly to the planet.

"And the information you hope to find in the Great Library?" one of the men asked.

"It's key to uncovering the spell hiding the evil dragons," Nevin Gooseman replied. "Once we can see them, our magitech military forces can shoot them down, killing them for good and making the world a better place."

Rudolf's head was suddenly hot with anger. He couldn't believe this guy.

Although Rudolf wanted to escape the nightmare of bad design where he was being held prisoner, it suddenly occurred to him he couldn't. He had to play this right if he was going to help his friend, Sophia Beaufont. He knew from her sister, Liv, she'd been struggling to combat what Nevin Gooseman was doing to the Dragon Elite.

If Rudolf escaped, there would be no evidence to indict Nevin Gooseman and his cronies. That's what the Dragon Elite needed to discredit him and earn back the great reputation they deserved. If Rudolf left, Nevin Gooseman would just find another way to go after the Dragon Elite. No, he had to stay and find evidence to bring the politician down and help Sophia and Liv to fight this guy.

Which meant Rudolf needed a way to communicate with Liv. That would be his next objective. Then he'd find the evidence that would help the Dragon Elite. Then he'd have a bottle of prosecco. Maybe two...definitely two, he decided.

Turning for his prison cell, the fae tiptoed across the hall. He couldn't believe he was about to willingly lock himself back up for his friends. They were worth it, though, and he'd do anything to help them.

CHAPTER SIXTY-SEVEN

Evan tapped his fingers on the table, his impatience palpable. Under the dining room table, Sophia could hear Wilder's shoe also drumming. Even the usually calm Mahkah kept glancing at the kitchen door, as though expecting to make it open suddenly. Quiet, however, appeared serene, his napkin pressed into the collar of his shirt and his fork and knife in hand.

Hiker blew out a breath, finally breaking the silence. "Okay, how much longer is it going to take?" he bellowed in the direction of the kitchen.

"Things take time, son," Mama Jamba informed him, creating what appeared to be a ball of wax at her usual place at the table. "When you understand that, you become more at peace with the process."

The leader of the Dragon Elite sighed dramatically. "Oh, good, a lecture. When I'm starving. Great idea, Mama. This should be fun."

"You aren't anywhere close to starvation," Ainsley remarked, striding from the kitchen, and to everyone's disappointment, carrying nothing. She was wearing a long pink gown full of ruffles and a devilish expression.

"What's the holdup?" Hiker demanded.

Ainsley took a chair at the table and shrugged. "The Castle and

Trin are trying to figure things out. It's sort of a lesson in trust, and both appear to be struggling."

"Can't she just slice up some bread, meat, and cheese and save the trust exercises for later?" Evan groaned.

"She could," Ainsley reasoned. "It's better if they work this out now while I'm here to supervise."

"Can't you do something about this, Quiet?" Hiker asked the gnome who was looking down at his plate as if expecting the food to magically appear.

He mumbled something, banging the fork and knife in his hands on the table a few times.

"You're quite right," Mama Jamba agreed, continuing to mold the ball in her hands. "You do things your way, and the rest of us will just adapt."

"I shouldn't have to adapt in my own Castle," Hiker muttered, looking back over his shoulder.

"Actually, son, you should have to adapt wherever you are," Mama Jamba imparted, breaking the well-formed ball in two.

"What are you doing?" Evan asked, leaning over to get a closer look at what Mother Nature was up to.

"I'm sitting listening to a grown man complain that his belly is empty," she answered.

"Me too." Evan pointed to the wax in Mama Jamba's hands, which she was now molding into snake-like objects. "But, I was referring to the project you've brought to the table."

"It's the spell to find the demon dragons," Mama Jamba explained, looking up at Sophia. "It needs some more time."

She nodded at once, always curious about the strange magic Mother Nature used. It rarely made sense to her.

"Oh, of course, it is." Evan laughed. "So you mold a statue, and it points to where the demon dragons are hiding out. Is that right?"

Mama Jamba glanced up, giving him an annoyed expression. "Don't be ridiculous, dear Evan. That would be a very haphazard approach. When the spell is done, it will just highlight the demon dragons on the Elite globe for a bit of time."

"Yeah, dear Evan," Wilder mocked. "Why are you so ridiculous?"

"Because the hunger has gone to my brain," he complained, holding his stomach.

"Oh, so you've been hungry for a very long, long time, then?" Wilder asked.

Evan turned his attention to Hiker. "Sir, can I have permission to pull out my phone and order us some food? I'll get you fish and chips from that place you like."

"No," Ainsley answered at once. "We are going to show confidence in Trin and the Castle that they can work through their differences. You all can just suck it up and wait."

"Their differences?" Sophia asked, letting the question hang in the air.

Ainsley nodded, seeming to understand what she was asking. "Trin wants to do everything manually. The Castle wants her to rely on it to provide based on her thoughts and the requirements you have. When Trin finally acquiesces, the Castle doesn't deliver what she was expecting, and then she gets angry, making her requests muddled. So far, they've managed to produce an overcooked duck and under ripened carrots."

"I'll eat it at this point," Evan said, looking over his shoulder as the door swung open.

The cyborg was carrying a large bowl of split pea soup that looked rather appetizing.

"That smells nice," Ainsley said, smiling at the housekeeper in training.

Trin nodded, the movement marked by a mechanical sound. "Thank you. But it's cold."

"There is a stove back there," Evan pointed out.

Ainsley shook her head. "Cold soup sounds lovely."

"Is there any bread?" Hiker asked, raising an eyebrow at the bowl as Trin slid it onto the table in front of him.

"There is, sir." Trin had an embarrassed expression on her face. "Unfortunately, it is of the sweet variety with currants and chocolate throughout."

"I'll take some of that," Mama Jamba chirped.

"Oh good," Trin said with relief. "Because I wasn't able to make your pancakes. I'm very sorry."

Mama Jamba waved her off. "We adapt. That's what we do."

The cyborg retreated back in the direction of the kitchen, the hydraulics in her legs marking each step.

"I don't understand why Quiet can't just go back there, and the two of them talk this out," Evan stated, watching with disappointment as Hiker spooned soup into his bowl.

"That's not how it works," Ainsley said flatly. "You don't go to the Elfin Council when you have a leak in your house. That's like calling a doctor for a hangnail. You just have to work it out on your own."

"Duh, Evan," Wilder said, condescendingly. "Don't you understand how this magical Castle run by the unassuming groundskeeper no one can understand works?"

"I can understand him just fine," Ainsley argued.

"Me too!" Mama Jamba cheered.

"I have on occasion," Sophia admitted.

"So he speaks to the women, then," Hiker observed, eyeing the cold soup with mild interest before taking a bite and grimacing at the cold temperature.

"Or maybe it's the women who know how to listen properly," Ainsley stated in her new, refined tone.

"Huh?" Evan asked. "What'd you say?"

She reached out and slapped his arm, making him startle. "Get your elbows off the table and sit up straight."

Quiet mumbled something, dug into his own soup happily.

"Well, I can try," Ainsley argued in reply to whatever he said.

Mama Jamba gave Quiet a pointed stare. "Monkeys can be taught to do all sorts of things."

Evan sat back in his seat, crossing his arms. "Do I always have to be the butt of the jokes?"

Sophia smiled across the table at him. "You don't. But you offer us entertainment, so what's wrong with that?"

"Everyone has their part to play in this place," Ainsley added.

"Sophia is the smart one, Wilder is the handsome one, Mahkah is calm and you, Evan are the comic relief. I might actually miss you a tiny bit when I'm gone."

He blinked at her in surprise. "Wow, I have to admit I'm happy to hear that."

The elf smiled at him fondly. "Then, I'll just get an untrained lap dog that makes a mess and barks incessantly, and the feelings will be gone."

CHAPTER SIXTY-EIGHT

Liv Beaufont hadn't had a day off in years, and that wasn't about to change. Even though she was lounging beside the turquoise waters of Zanzibar, it still didn't count as a vacation day.

Sitting on the steps of a shack perched on a set of rocks off the coast, Liv tinkered with a digital clock that had a particularly stubborn problem to fix that she couldn't figure out. Her role as a Warrior for the House of Fourteen didn't give her a lot of free time to fix electronics like she used to before taking back her magic and reentering the world she'd once known.

However, since she was on a stakeout for her sister, Liv figured she could spend the time fixing electronics for John. Before setting off to guard the Great Library, Liv had loaded up on a bunch of broken items from the repair shop and was now occupying her time fixing them and portaling them back to John.

"Have you tried turning it off and back on?" Plato suggested beside her on the rickety steps to the Great Library.

She rolled her eyes at the lynx. "Thanks, but your years in tech support won't help here."

He shrugged, staring off before saying, "You know, I've got security measures up again. I'll know if Rudolf gets close."

"Are you trying to get rid of me?" she fired back immediately.

"No...maybe."

Liv lowered her chin and scowled at her familiar.

"No, I just wanted to offer you the opportunity to go home and see Stefan if you wanted," Plato said, his voice uncharacteristically sympathetic.

She nodded. He had sensed she missed her husband. More than that, since the lynx was pretty much in her head full time. "I appreciate that, but I need to be here in case things shake down fast. I promised Sophia."

"You're worried about the fae," Plato added.

"No!" Liv exclaimed, too fast—her eyes sliding to the right. "Maybe a little bit. I get he's managed for all these centuries somehow. What if he can't bumble his way through this one? What if he's hurt? Shouldn't he have led them to the Great Library by now?"

"Of everyone, I have the least amount of confidence in that man," Plato began. "With that being said, I'm not worried. The gods or angels or whoever reigns over this place seem to always be looking out for him."

Liv messed with the wires inside the digital clock and shook her head at Plato. "Don't pretend like you don't know who is in charge of this place, and you haven't met and had tea."

"They don't drink tea," he informed her.

"Nectar of the gods or whatever," Liv said with a laugh.

"So when are you and Stefan having kids?" Plato asked coyly.

She knew he was trying to get her mind off her troubles and worries. It was sweet, but if she told him that, then he'd bite her.

"When are you getting married, Plato?" she queried him in reply. "There's that sweet neighborhood cat that keeps coming around from the village. I think she likes you." Liv nodded in the direction of the huts on the shore.

"What do you think you'll name your baby?" he questioned right back.

"Billy," she answered at once. "Can I be your best woman at the ceremony?"

"What if it's a girl?" he asked.

"Still Billy," Liv declared. "Where will you and kitty honeymoon, you think?"

"What if you have twins?" Plato questioned.

"Billy and Billy," Liv replied. "Do you think she'll take your last name? Wait, do you have a last name?"

"Yes." He sounded offended. "It's Plato."

"What's your first name?" she asked, surprised.

"Do you want me to throw your baby shower?"

"Do you want me to throw a shower for your wedding? Can I make the toast at the ceremony? Can we get a DJ?" Liv asked in quick succession.

"No, no, and no," he quipped. "The wedding is off."

Liv snapped her fingers. "Darn it. I already bought my dress."

"It won't fit anyway when you're as big as a house and pregnant," Plato imparted.

"You know, you're a real pal, No-First-Name Plato."

"You know I'm always here for you. Got to go." With that, the lynx disappeared.

Liv laughed and shook her head and saw the digital clock lighting up. Thinking she finally fixed it, she turned it over to find something she hadn't expected.

"What the hell!" Liv exclaimed. "Rudolf, what are you doing in there?"

CHAPTER SIXTY-NINE

Staring back at Liv from the screen of the digital clock was none other than King Rudolf Sweetwater, the very man she was looking for.

"It's cramped in here," Rudolf said, shaking his head, which was the only thing Liv could see. It appeared to be floating inside the device.

"You're inside of a clock," she stated.

"Oh, that would be why I keep seeing numbers all around me," he remarked. "It's two-thirty, by the way."

"Thanks," Liv said. "Now tell me why you're inside of a digital clock, where you are, other pertinent information, and if we have time whether you're all right."

"I'm not okay." Rudolf let out a sigh.

Liv's heart dropped, as worry coursed through her. "Have they hurt you? Starved you? What's happening? Do you need me to come and break you out?"

"Liv, it's worse than you would have ever guessed," Rudolf began. "Do you know what they serve my food on? Metal plates. It's like we're camping or something." He shivered with disgust. "When I asked if they had something more palatable to look at like Wedgewood or Haviland china, they grunted at me and told me to eat up."

Liv sighed. "So they are feeding you, then? That's something, at least."

He shook his head. "They are, but I'm not eating it."

"Ru, if you're turning up your nose to the food because it's not caviar and truffles, then you better hope they kill you before I do."

He smiled at her. "You're so thoughtful. I appreciate you want to put me out of my misery. I'm not eating because although the pork and beans they serve me *is* atrocious, it's also drugged to take away my magical powers."

It suddenly made sense. Liv had wondered how Rudolf had managed to magically appear on the surface of the digital clock if he were being held hostage. Of course, his captors would find a way to block his magical powers so he didn't escape, and somehow he'd managed to figure this out and get around it. This man surprised her more than anyone. He couldn't so much as cross the street by himself but could navigate and persevere in the face of extreme and complex dangers.

"So you've been starving yourself," she said, thinking.

"Yes, and then I was able to use my magical powers to scry you via a device," Rudolf explained. "I knew you'd have one around you because you always do since you're a nerd who will never ever get a date and die alone."

"I'm married," Liv reminded him. "Once again, you walked me down the aisle. Remember that?"

"Not in the slightest," Rudolf answered at once.

"Anyway, if you have your magical powers, can you break out of there?" Liv asked.

"I can, but I won't," he replied. "You see, I found out who had me abducted and why."

She nodded at once. "Yes, Nevin Gooseman. He wants you to lead him to the Great Library. That's where I am now."

"Oh," Rudolf said, drawing the word out. "You stole my thunder on that."

"Tell me where you are, and I'll come and get you." Liv tried to sound encouraging.

Rudolf glanced around in his surroundings. "It's awful, Liv. The cell where they have me is bad enough, but I broke out of here, and you won't even believe what Nevin Gooseman has in his house."

Liv bolted to a standing position, holding the digital clock between her hands. "Does he have caged animals? Other prisoners? Dragons?"

Rudolf blinked at her. "Not that I'm aware of. No, but this is serious."

"What is it?" Liv questioned, her pulse suddenly beating in her head.

"I think, when I escaped, I spied something incredibly disturbing in his living room," Rudolf said in a whisper, looking over his shoulder.

"What?" she demanded, the suspense almost too much.

"A Jackson Pollock painting," he said.

Liv rolled her eyes and blew out a breath. "You're ridiculous."

"I am?" he asked, offended. "I'm not the one who tries to pass off splatters of paint as artwork." He glanced over his shoulder as though he heard something. "Liv, this guy scares me. I haven't been able to sleep properly since I got here."

"Because of fear of what they'll do to you?" she asked.

He shook his head. "Because they expect me to sleep on flannel sheets. You know my body requires a high thread count."

"I know that your body is about to have a few new broken bones," Liv said dryly.

"Worse than that." Rudolf continued to check over his shoulder. "I don't have long, because they are going to put me in a coffin tomorrow if I don't start cooperating, and I don't mean in a good way."

"Is being in a coffin ever in a good way?" Liv had to laugh.

"Serena and I have this fun game where she likes to pretend that I'm dead," he offered. "It's really cute. She says I look sweet when she shuts me in the coffin."

"You two, a love story for the ages."

He nodded, not catching the joke. "Anyway, I hadn't been giving them any information about the Great Library because I thought whatever reason they wanted it for would only lead to bad stuff."

"Yes, they want information on how to uncover the demon dragons," Liv explained.

He sighed. "You're really ruining all of my reveals for this convo, but whatever. Anyway, I've run out of time and heard them say they were going to off me tomorrow if I didn't talk."

"Then get out of there," Liv urged, her heart pounding again.

He shook his head. "No, I'm going to tell them how to get to the Great Library, which they plan to raid and then flatten."

"Great idea," Liv said. "Do you want to tell them where the Gullington is while you're at it? Maybe give them a way to get into the House of Fourteen? My home address?"

"No one would want to go into your place," Rudolf answered. "Plato watches your guests in the bathroom. Stefan leaves demon blood everywhere. You can't shut a cabinet to save your life. Clark doesn't let anyone do anything and demands a coaster be used at all times. Total fun ruiner."

"I don't disagree there," Liv chuckled.

"Anyway, my idea is that I slowly lead them to the Great Library, but stall a bit," Rudolf explained. "You see, you need evidence that Nevin Gooseman is corrupt. If I get a bit more time here, I think I can unearth that and help Sophia bring him down."

Liv smiled wide. "That's genius! Good work, Ru. There's also a strange disease circulating amongst magicians that I think Nevin Gooseman might be behind."

He pursed his lips and sighed. "Oh, Liv. Your race's ugliness isn't a disease, nor do I think it can be cured."

She rolled her eyes. "New disease. It's called distortion and hit right after you were abducted. It makes magicians and elves blur until they fully disappear. It's happened to a few already."

"Oh," he said with a laugh. "Sounds like it might do you all some favors."

"Ru, this is serious."

"Of course," he said, his laughter fading at once. "Anyway, I'll dig up some information—as much as I can. In the interim, I'll buy some time by asking for maps and telling them that finding the Great Library is really difficult and takes planning."

"Good," Liv chirped. "That will give us a chance to prepare. You say Nevin Gooseman plans on storming this place?"

"Yeah, apparently he has a magitech army."

"That doesn't surprise me," Liv replied darkly.

"I'll start sending over information as I find it so that you and the Dragon Elite know what you're up against," Rudolf told her. "Then, when we're ready, I'll lead them to you."

Liv smiled, feeling victorious. "Thanks, Rudolf. You really came through on this one."

"I haven't yet, but I plan on it."

Although he annoyed her to no end, there were few as good as King Rudolf Sweetwater and Liv was grateful to call him her friend.

"Okay, I've got to go," Rudolf said in a rush. "I'm going to conserve my magical powers until I can sneak out of here and find some food. Where should I look in this abstract and modern art freak show of a house for something to eat?"

"You could try the kitchen," Liv suggested.

He shook his head. "I don't know this foreign word you use. I'll just hunt around until I find something. I'll let my nose lead the way."

She grinned, grateful that Rudolf was okay and hadn't changed a bit. "Good luck, Ru."

CHAPTER SEVENTY

"You called for me, sir," Sophia said, standing at Hiker Wallace's door. She'd been trying to organize the new walk-in closet Quiet had added to her bedroom for her birthday when Trin came to tell her Hiker wanted to see her in his office.

The cyborg had also helped with the renovation by adding magitech that made the clothes rotate on a rack like one would find at a dry cleaning shop. All Sophia had to do was stand under a spotlight at the front of the closet and think about what kind of clothes she wanted, and the intuitive beam picked up on what she needed. Then the system rotated until it created the right outfit and pulled it from the racks.

"Yeah, come in." Hiker waved her in, cutting his eyes over to Mama Jamba—a deliberate expression on his face.

"If you want me to leave, son, then that's all you have to say," the old woman chimed, leaning over the Elite globe.

"I need you to leave," he told her.

"Well, I'm busy working on this tracking spell," she replied, winking at Sophia.

He sighed. "Fine. It's not like it matters. There's no privacy from you anyway."

234

"No, there's not," Mama Jamba sang. "Still, I'm sure you like to imagine that there is at times and that I don't know about that one habit you have."

"What hab—never mind." He cut himself off.

Sophia strode farther into the office, wondering what this was about. She was between cases, waiting on Bep to finish replicating the cure for distortion and then finishing the healing elixir for Ainsley. Liv was at the Great Library, and there hadn't been any word about Rudolf from her. Mama Jamba was still working on the tracking spell for demon dragons.

That meant there was little for Sophia to do, which left her time to organize her closet and train with Lunis on the Expanse. She was grateful for the break, but it also made her antsy, knowing magicians were suffering from distortion, and her friend Rudolf was being held captive. For her birthday, Hiker had given her advice, telling her to know when to fight and when to rest and delegate. This was one of those times when she apparently needed to rest and prepare for the next mission.

On the heel of her thoughts, Hiker said, "I have something I need you to do."

Sophia's eyes widened with excitement. "Really? A mission? Something to do with adjudication?"

He scratched his chin, uncertainty bouncing around in his eyes. "Sure, we can call it a goodwill mission."

Mama Jamba snickered to herself. "Call it what you want, but I know the truth."

He cast an angry look in her direction. "If you have to be here, can you at least pretend like you're not so that I forget you're eavesdropping?"

"I can try," she sang.

Sophia returned her gaze to the leader of the Dragon Elite. "Lunis took some of the dragonettes on a flight up north for a training mission, but once he returns, we can set off for this mission."

Hiker shook his head. "You won't need Lunis for this."

"Oh," Sophia said, surprised.

He cleared his throat, obviously uncomfortable. "This will involve you going to Roya Lane."

Sophia's brow scrunched up. This was a different request for Hiker to make. "Really? To go to see Papa Creola? Subner? Visit the Brownie's Official Headquarters?"

He shook his head. "No, there's a seamstress on Roya Lane. The very best. I need them to make something."

Sophia had met an interesting seamstress in Montana when she had to have a dress made to meet Saint Valentine. That dress had magical properties, so she was curious who this one was and what made them so special.

"It's called the Silk Armor," Hiker explained.

"Ooh." Sophia realized Hiker needed armor made. That would be a good use of her idle time. "Is the armor for you, sir?"

"What?" he asked, confusion springing to his face. "Um, no. Not me. It's not really armor. I mean, it is, but...well, I need the seamstress, Jeremy Bearimy to make a dress."

"Did you say dress?" Sophia asked, thinking she might have misheard.

Mama Jamba laughed. "He also said, Jeremy Bearimy."

"That's his name," Hiker scolded, giving Mother Nature a punishing look.

"It's also a time theory named by Papa Creola," she replied, still laughing.

Sophia scratched her head. "I know you all get it, but I'm not following you."

"Jeremy Bearimy is the name of a great seamstress who creates the strongest, finest armor," Mama Jamba explained. "He was named for a theory that explains how time moves in the afterlife in relation to Earth."

"Afterlife?" Sophia asked, feeling like she was falling down a rabbit hole.

Mama Jamba waved her off. "Don't get bogged down in details."

"Usually the wait to get in with Jeremy Bearimy takes ages," Hiker continued, letting out a long breath. "However, he owes me a favor, and I think he'll put my order to the front of his jobs."

"Favor?" Sophia was suddenly intrigued.

"I saved him from a mob of angry villagers once."

"Like ones with pitchforks and fire torches?" Sophia questioned.

He nodded. "Exactly. People are afraid of that which they don't understand."

Tilting her head to the side, Sophia gave him a cautious expression. "Why would these angry villagers be afraid of Jeremy Bearimy?"

He shook his head dismissively. "I need you to pay him a visit and ask him to make a dress."

"For whom?" Sophia asked, wondering if he meant her.

"Not me," Mama Jamba imparted.

"For me?" she questioned.

Hiker's gaze fell on a piece of paper on his desk. "It's for Ainsley. I want to give her something when she leaves here. Something that reflects her style and is timeless, much like her. As a delegate for the Elfin Council, she doesn't have a safe job and—"

"You want something that is armored and protects her," Sophia interjected, guessing what Hiker was having a hard time getting out.

He nodded. "Yes, and I trust Jeremy Bearimy will be able to make something that is both elegant and protective. I know he can."

"You want me to order this for you because..." Sophia trailed away.

Hiker picked up the piece of paper. "Because I can't very well order a dress myself. Asking the men, well, that would only lead to teasing. I figured you wouldn't mind the opportunity to get out since you're in between jobs."

"And you're a woman," Mama Jamba added. "You'll know how to advise Jeremey Bearimy to ensure the dress is just right."

Sophia nodded. "I'm happy to help, sir."

"Good," he chirped and handed over the piece of paper. "These are Ainsley's measurements as well as some ideas on the style and design based on what I know she likes to wear."

Sophia expected just a few bits of information, but Hiker had filled the paper with details.

"I'll take off right now, sir."

She turned for the door, excited to meet this Jeremy Bearimy and be useful. When she was at the threshold to his office, Hiker said, "Oh, and Sophia."

Halting, she looked over her shoulder.

"Please don't say anything to anyone about this."

Sophia nodded, winking at Mama Jamba before heading out of the office.

CHAPTER SEVENTY-ONE

Although Sophia had spent a lot of time on Roya Lane, she didn't remember seeing a shop called the Silk Armor. That wasn't too surprising, though, since there were tons of stores nestled together, and some of their signs got crammed together or hidden from view. Also, there were some shops that only opened on full moons or lunar eclipses or at midnight. Then there were places like the Brownies Official Headquarters that had an invisible entrance because only those invited could enter. Roya Lane was diverse, and it would take several lifetimes to explore all its nooks and crannies.

Sophia decided to turn down one of the many unmarked alleyways to see if she could find the Silk Armor. This part of Roya Lane was filled with many specialty shops, making Sophia hopeful she was getting close. There was a hat store that catered to gnomes, who had irregularly shaped heads. A shop for big and tall, which obviously sold giant clothing. Then there was a shoe cobbler who guaranteed that their work "would solve all foot ailments."

After tracing up and down the alleyway, Sophia hadn't spied the Silk Armor. She was about to give up when she noticed a figure hiding behind a light pole. Since they were much larger than the narrow pole, they were doing a very poor job of lurking.

Tilting her head to the side, Sophia recognized the figure. "Lee, what are you doing?"

The baker assassin's eyes widened. "Shush, I don't want anyone to see me here."

"Then you might want to try a better hiding place," Sophia said with a laugh. "Or a shrinking spell."

Lee shook her head. "The person I have a hit out on doesn't have very good vision, so I'm fine, but you calling me out isn't helpful."

Sophia looked around, searching for the person who would go on to live a very long life. "Who are you after?"

"You don't know her," Lee said, glancing around. "Just some potions expert who blew me off when I asked for them to help me out."

Sophia rolled her eyes. "You mean Bep?"

The baker assassin sighed. "Lucky guess. Probably a different Bep."

"I don't think so," Sophia disagreed. "She is working on projects for me. Important ones that will cure the magicians who have caught distortion. Also, another one that will provide a healing elixir that will help my friend and possibly many others."

"Yeah, but I need an ointment for my rash," Lee argued.

"Fine, when Bep completes the healing elixir, I'll give you some."

"So I shouldn't kill her?" she asked, quite seriously.

Sophia shook her head. "Please don't."

"Well, you should pay her a visit, because she seemed to be having trouble with whatever she was working on," Lee informed her.

Sophia stuck her hands on her hips. "Was it because you were intimidating her to try and work on your ointment?"

"Come on! Would I do that? I was trying to persuade her with my good humor."

"By good humor, do you mean those jokes that are intended to kill?" Sophia asked.

"It's amazing how a small tweak can really change the intent of a joke," Lee mused. "I just have to scale them back if I want to endear someone to me instead of killing them with laughter."

Blinking at her, Sophia shook her head. "I sometimes wonder if you and I live in the same world. It definitely seems we share two very different realities."

"Yeah, speaking of grandfathers—"

"We weren't talking about grandfathers," Sophia interrupted.

"Exactly," Lee said, nodding along. "My grandfather has the heart of a lion."

"That's nice," Sophia replied absentmindedly, looking around for the Silk Armor.

"Incidentally," Lee continued, "he also has a lifetime ban from the National zoo."

"Oh...dear..." Sophia groaned.

"You get it?" Lee asked, laughing loudly.

"Yeah," she mumbled.

"Oh good. Then it's like a communist joke." Lee's eyes were dazzling with excitement.

"Please don't," Sophia begged, knowing what was coming next.

"You know because a communist joke isn't funny unless everyone gets it!" Lee exclaimed, followed by more laughter.

"You and my dragon would get along famously," Sophia muttered.

A disappointed expression fell over Lee's face. "Oh, you still going on about dragons, thinking they are real. You're really out of touch."

"I'm a dragonrider for the Elite."

"I'm your fairy godmother." Lee held up her hand like she was holding a magical wand. "Where would you like me to transport you?"

"No, you're not," Sophia corrected. "She's much shorter than you and has black hair. If you could tell me where the Silk Armor is, that would be great."

"I can, but it won't do you any good," Lee told her. "Jeremy Bearimy is booked solid for the next century."

"I have an in." Sophia pulled the piece of paper Hiker had given her from her cloak.

Lee lowered her chin and regarded Sophia with an edge of hostility. "Why is it that you get all these special favors? With Bep and now with Jeremey Bearimy? I've been trying to get him to make me armor for ages."

"For your assassin business?" Sophia asked.

"No, for oven mitts," Lee answered. "But that's a really good idea. I never considered wearing armor on one of my jobs."

"You didn't..." Sophia shook her head. "Never mind. Anyway, where is this seamstress shop?"

"Well, it's a good thing you ran into me," Lee said.

"I caught you trying to hide behind a skinny lamp pole."

"Are you calling me fat?" Lee asked, offended.

"A broomstick would have a hard time hiding behind that lamp pole," Sophia retorted.

Lee smiled broadly. "So, you're calling me skinny, then."

"In my head, I'm calling you all sorts of things," Sophia replied.

"Same." Lee pointed down the alleyway. "Anyway, the Silk Armor recently changed the way you can find it since Jeremy Bearimy got so busy. His shop is like the friend request settings on Facebook. You can only find it if you're friends of a friend."

For a half-beat, Sophia closed her eyes, wondering if she was hallucinating or this was just a really bad joke the universe was playing on her. "I don't understand."

"Well, on Facebook, if you want to friend me, I have it set so only friends of friends can," Lee explained. "So you'd have to know Slick Rick or Murder Mike."

"They sound like lovely people," Sophia said.

Lee shook her head. "They are in prison, but I'll introduce them to you if you want. Anyway, the shop is two doors down on the right."

Just as the assassin baker said this, a door illuminated on a blank brick wall that hadn't been there seconds before. A sign materialized that read Silk Armor.

"Oh, great!" Sophia exclaimed, grateful she had run into Lee, although similar to an interaction with Rudolf, she felt a bit off balance suddenly.

"Good luck with getting your first training bra made," Lee said, waving as Sophia started for the shop.

Sophia was going to argue but decided that there wasn't any point. The assassin baker obviously lived in her own world and Sophia sort of envied her for it.

CHAPTER SEVENTY-TWO

Sophia entered the Silk Armor shop and was immediately put on guard. She yanked Inexorabilis from its sheath, adrenaline and fear coursing through her as she stared into the beady eyes of a giant tarantula.

The beast reeled back on its back legs, and kicked its hairy front legs in her direction, its fangs snapping.

Sophia froze and so did the monster. They regarded each other with tentative stares, waiting for one of them to attack.

Even though she expected the biggest spider she'd ever set eyes on to attack her, it seemed to be calculating something in its head. Its eyes darted to her and then to Inexorabilis in her grasp, and the fear in his eyes morphed into curiosity.

That's when she noticed the seamstress shop around the large spider, whose midsection was easily the size of a riding lawnmower.

There were spindles of silk everywhere, all of the same gauzy white color. She put it all together. The angry mob Hiker saved Jeremy Bearimy from. His comment about people being afraid of what they didn't understand. The name of the shop: Silk Armor.

She took a step backward and lowered her sword. "You're Jeremy Bearimy, aren't you?"

"And you are the daughter of Guinevere Beaufont," the tarantula stated.

"You knew my mother?" Sophia asked, sheathing Inexorabilis, not fearful of the huge creature, who most would find menacing. Bitterly she thought, *Wouldn't have hurt, Hiker, to tell me that Jeremy Bearimy was a giant tarantula.* He was probably having a good laugh about right now. Lee, too.

"Of course," Jeremy Bearimy said, scuttling back a few steps, and taking a less defensive stance. "I made her armor. She was the only Warrior for the House of Fourteen I ever worked for, but your mother was a different kind of magician."

Sophia always liked hearing others who knew her mother talk about her. She had only ever heard wonderful things about the woman who died when she was really young. She was parts of Liv and Reese and, Sophia hoped that in her heart, she was part of her.

"Are you here because of her armor?" Jeremey Bearimy asked. "You're not a Warrior for the House of Fourteen, correct?"

"No," Sophia responded. "My sister Liv is. I'm certain my mother probably died in that armor."

The tarantula's old soul eyes turned remorseful. "I'm sorry for your loss. And yes, she wore it all the time. It would have saved her life many times, I suspect." He lifted one of his eight legs and pointed to the sword on her hip. "I remembered seeing that sword when Guinevere visited, which was how I recognized you. And you look just like your mother."

Sophia blushed. "Thank you. That's nice to hear."

"So if you didn't come here to have her armor repaired, then I'm not sure I can help you," Jeremy Bearimy said. "I have orders to complete for the next century or more, at least."

Sophia nodded. "I've heard. But I've been sent to you by my leader, who says you will put him ahead."

Jeremey Bearimy's fangs rubbed against each other, like a nervous habit. "You don't work for the House of Fourteen, you said. I can tell by the way you held your mother's sword and the armor you're wearing that you are a warrior. Who do you work for?"

"Hiker Wallace, the leader of the Dragon Elite."

The tarantula's legs moved fast as it turned around, putting its large body in Sophia's direction. She peeled back slightly.

"Juergen!" the spider yelled. "Get in here! We have an important job to do!"

Sophia smiled, glad the name of her leader evoked so much urgency, in a good way.

The tarantula, for as large as he was, moved with a strange grace, picking up each leg carefully and pivoting back around. "Hiker Wallace. It has been a long time since I heard that name. He was quite right to expect me to put him ahead. I wouldn't be here right now if not for him. I was a nobody then, with no talents and only the ability to evoke fear in those who didn't understand that I had no interest in harming them."

A smile lit up Jeremy Bearimy's eyes. "I'm sure you can relate based on your own reaction during our initial meeting."

"I'm sorry," Sophia said, bowing her head.

He waved her off, brushing one leg. "Don't be. There's something in the collective social consciousness that tells humans of every culture to fear spiders. I think it's because my ancestors ate yours."

Sophia chuckled. "That would do it."

He nodded. "The same is true of your kind and snakes, sharks, and many other deadly creatures. It is more about self-preservation than the prejudice of a species, but I do appreciate the modern culture is more open-minded because I have no interest in harming humans. They are my best customers. Even if they weren't, I wouldn't eat you. I hear you taste awful."

"Good to know," Sophia said with a laugh. "I'll tell my dragon that since he's always threatening to eat me."

"Oh," Jeremy Bearimy said with delight. "You work for Hiker Wallace, so that would make you a rider for the Dragon Elite. How very wonderful. Does he want armor made for you?"

Sophia shook her head, about to hand over the instructions that Hiker had given her but was interrupted by a ruckus from the back room.

Half expecting another giant tarantula to enter from the large archway that led to the back where shelves were lined with supplies, Sophia was surprised by the man who bumbled through, carrying several boxes under his arms. He had a long beard and wide eyes as he tripped over the lip of the rug and dove forward, careful to protect the boxes he was carrying as he rolled over on his head and back, springing up to his feet like he meant it to happen.

"Sorry, sir. Sorry for falling. For dropping the samples," the man said, shaking his head of long hair, trying to get his bearings.

"It's quite okay, Juergen," Jeremy Bearimy said dryly. "And half expected."

The man was vibrating with excitement as he set down the boxes, pulling the lid off the first. It flew from his hands and dropped to the floor. He paused, looked down at his accident, and then to Jeremy Bearimy.

"Just the measuring tape," the tarantula ordered, extending two of his legs in his assistant's direction.

"Actually, what Hiker wants isn't armor," Sophia interjected. "It isn't for me."

One of the spider's eyes swiveled in Sophia's direction. "Go on then."

"Hiker wants you to make an elegant dress that also has the strength of armor," she explained. "It's to protect a delegate for the Elfin Council."

"Oh," he replied, drawing out the word. "I had wondered what had ever happened to the lovely Ainsley Carter."

Sophia nodded. "She shall be returning to her post on the council soon. Hiker wanted a gift for her since she's served the Gullington and the Dragon Elite for all these years."

A sneaky expression crossed the tarantula's face but disappeared as he turned his attention to the assistant named Juergen. "No measurements are necessary, but I want to see samples of our high-quality fabrics for formal wear."

"Yes, Jeremy Bearimy," Juergen replied, popping up to his feet.

After fixing the contents of the box and nearly tripping again, he shuffled from the room.

Sophia extended her hand and offered Hiker's instructions to the seamstress. "He sent her measurements and some ideas for the dress, but he wants me to weigh in on the details."

"Quite right," Jeremy Bearimy said, reading over the instructions. "Hiker Wallace knows many things, but fashion isn't one of them." He laughed deeply. "Low neckline and spaghetti straps. A delegate for the Elfin Council wearing something like that. No, I think we will opt for long sleeves and something much more practical, especially since it is secretly an armored gown."

"As a delegate," Sophia began carefully, feeling strange about the question she was about to ask, especially since she just met this character. "Is Ainsley really in danger, working for the Elfin Council?"

"I don't know of a time she hasn't been," he answered. "I mean, I'm out of touch presently, not having heard anything about the Dragon Elite in some time, but back in the day, yes."

Sophia nodded. "Yes, we've...well, they've been in hiding for a long time. Things are getting back to how they used to be, or rather to a new normal."

Jeremy Bearimy nodded. "Yes, the world is a different place. That's for certain."

The assistant returned, sprinting as though running from a monster, and nearly ran into one of the tarantula's legs. Casually, Jeremy Bearimy picked up his hairy leg just before Juergen could collide with it. He tripped again and dove, sliding on his front with another box in front of him. It was like he'd made the last move to complete a touchdown. He came to a halt at Sophia's feet and looked up at her with a startled expression.

"I-I have samples for you to review," Juergen stuttered.

Sophia knelt to help with the box and assist the man up, but he seemed adamant he could do it on his own, brushing himself off.

"Please excuse my assistant's klutzy nature," Jeremy Bearimy said, sounding amused. "He gets a bit excited."

Sophia smiled at the man. "I think excitement is the key to living a good life."

"I work for Jeremy Bearimy," Juergen said. "How could I not be excited?"

"It's been a few dozen years, and his enthusiasm hasn't waned," Jeremy Bearimy stated.

Sophia nodded to the assistant. "Good for you. Never let it."

"Just hoping that at some point, nimbleness follows," Jeremy Bearimy admitted.

"The samples," Juergen said, offering the box to Sophia, but fumbling in the process of handing them over and dropping the contents on the ground.

Jeremy Bearimy rolled his beady eyes, but Sophia shrugged it off.

"That one was my fault," she said, trying again to help pick up things, but Juergen's hands moved fast to recover everything first. He did have impressive speed. It just seemed he had to learn to control it.

"I like this one for Ainsley." Sophia took a piece of beautiful pale blue silk fabric and held it up to the light. "I think it would look nice with her hair and eyes."

Jeremy Bearimy eyed it and nodded. "Her complexion, I agree. Also, it will look nice done in a professional yet fancy gown."

"So, this is also armor?" Sophia asked, testing the material and finding it very strong.

"Oh, yes," the spider affirmed. "I spin all of the silk here in the shop. It's how I learned what my calling was."

"He's amazing," Juergen said, standing once more and holding the box out for Sophia.

She shook her head, holding up the blue fabric. "I had a chance to review the samples while you were retrieving them. I pick this one."

"Very good," Jeremy Bearimy declared. "I'll get to work on the gown using the specs Hiker sent and notify you when I'll need to do a fitting."

"But it's a surprise for Ainsley," she argued.

He nodded. "Which means you'll have to do the fittings, and we'll adapt based on the differences in your sizes."

"Okay, that sounds good." Sophia handed the fabric to the assistant and backed away. She never thought she'd do a fitting with a giant tarantula seamstress, but that was on the long list of things she never expected in this lifetime.

CHAPTER SEVENTY-THREE

"Go away," Bep ordered when Sophia entered the Rose Apothecary shop, her back to the entrance and her arms really working to stir the huge cauldron in front of her. "I can't take any more of your bad jokes."

Sophia nearly laughed. "Don't worry, I'm not Lee."

Bep glanced over her shoulder and nodded with relief. "Good. That woman nearly made me crazy with her puns. When are people going to realize they aren't funny?"

"Some people and dragons may never." Sophia covered her nose from the astringent smell wafting off the cauldron of maroon liquid.

Bep pulled the large stick from the pot and found it charred and split in places.

"Is that a good thing?" Sophia asked, noticing parts of the stick floating in the cauldron.

"It's a great thing," Bep affirmed.

"So, this is the cure for distortion?" Sophia asked.

"Yes," she answered. "The healing elixir is in the back resting. It will need some time."

"That seems to be the story of my life." Sophia thought of how many balls she had in the air, all of them waiting to come down. "Lee mentioned you seemed upset about something. Is everything okay?"

"It's a complex potion." Bep indicated the cure she was replicating from Rumi. "I'll get it right, but the size of the batch and the intricate nature will require my diligence and at least a few more days."

"I understand," Sophia replied. "If there is something I can do to help, then just let me know."

"I'm glad you said that." Bep chucked the charred stick in the corner and got a fresh one from a stack before going back to stirring. "Although I'm happy to close my shop and lose business to help with such an important task, it would be nice to be compensated for my efforts."

"Of course," Sophia stated at once. "We were always planning on paying you for the healing elixir or offering you a cut, whichever you preferred. As far as the cure for distortion, I'll offer you whatever you think is fair. I'm sorry that I haven't had a chance to discuss it with you. I never dreamed you were working for free."

Bep nodded. "I'm glad to hear we're on the same page because while I work on this, there's something specific I was hoping you could retrieve for me for payment."

"Oh." Sophia prepared herself for what the potions expert wanted. "Do you need me to find something from an ancient temple where I have to fight a giant scorpion or something?"

Bep furrowed her brow at her, which was covered in sweat from being perched over the cauldron. "Heavens no. I want money."

Sophia sighed with relief. "Great news. I can do money. How much do you want?"

The woman shook her head. "It's not really about the amount. It's about the type."

Suddenly the hope that had been blossoming in Sophia's chest dissipated. "Type? What do you mean?"

"Well, the currency is more important to me than an amount, and there's a specific type that I've been after for a long time."

Sophia arched a curious eyebrow at her. "Please do tell."

"Leprechaun gold," Bep said with a wicked grin. "I want you to get me leprechaun gold."

CHAPTER SEVENTY-FOUR

Lunis's laughter was loud and seemingly unending.

"Are you done yet?" Sophia asked, tightening the saddle manually, and checking its tightness.

He nodded but continued to snicker. *Leprechaun gold,* he said, sounding like he was about to choke on tears from his laughter.

"When you get control of yourself, are you going to tell me why you won't stop laughing about this mission for Bep?" she asked, looking out at the Expanse toward the direction they'd need to set off for to reach Ireland, home of the Leprechauns.

Because Leprechaun gold doesn't exist, he stated, still trying to hold back his laughter but doing a horrible job.

"Well, it must exist because Bep wants it and it's legendary."

It's a myth, he corrected, giving her a suddenly serious expression.

She fisted her hands on her hips. "I read the section in Bermuda Laurens's *Magical Creatures* book last night, and she says that just because no one has reportedly recovered Leprechaun gold, there's no reason to believe it doesn't exist. She went on to theorize that someone who had found the gold wouldn't advertise how to obtain it since it's incredibly valuable, so the secrets have been covered up."

If it is so valuable, then how is it traded, and why is there none in circulation? he argued.

Sophia pursed her lips. "I don't have the answers to everything. I just know that we have to give this our best effort. Maybe it is a myth. Maybe we won't find any gold at the end of a rainbow. I promised a very nice woman who has been working nonstop for me that I'd try, and that's what I'm going to do."

Fine, Lunis said as Sophia climbed onto his back. *I'm willing to humor you on this mission.*

"You're glad to get away from the dragonettes," she countered.

He nodded as they set off. *That too. Those little tykes tell the worst jokes.*

Sophia laughed abruptly. "Now you know how it feels."

Lunis scoffed. *I know you're not indirectly referring to me. I tell the very best jokes.*

"Is it opposite day? Because if so, then yes."

Oh! he exclaimed. *I wrote a book on reverse psychology. Whatever you do, don't go and buy it.*

Sophia tried not to laugh as they soared into the air, cutting through the blue skies that rose over the green lands of the Expanse. Within minutes they were through the Barrier and on their way to Ireland, where Leprechauns were thought to still have many nests buried in the emerald green hills, according to *Magical Creatures.*

The book had gone on to postulate that although the lore stated a Leprechaun's gold was found at the end of a rainbow, there had to be a trick to the myth because it would have been found by someone if that was the case.

According to Bermuda Laurens, the little creatures with red hair who wore green suits were very mischievous and misleading, so the "one who ventures to find their gold, must learn how to not fall for their tricks."

"You know what, Lunis," Sophia said, her hair flying back from her face as they picked up speed.

Chicken butt? he answered, sounding quite serious.

"Are you twelve years old?"

Like one, he corrected. *In dragon years, that makes me like one hundred, so I've got you beat still.*

"Your bad jokes got me thinking." She mulled the idea over as she spoke.

Got you thinking about how awesome a comedian I am? he asked.

Sophia decided to switch to telepathic communication as they broke out over the waters of the Irish Sea.

What if the Leprechauns intentionally misled those searching for their gold? Sophia mused.

Like they rumored it was kept at the end of the rainbow, making searchers spend all their efforts hunting for the end of a rainbow, Lunis thought in her head. *I mean, that's not a bad idea because finding the end of the rainbow is nearly impossible to begin with since they are so short-lived in the first place. If the treasure isn't there, then where is it?*

Well, Sophia began, *I bet that rainbows are still a part of the equation because myths usually have remnants of facts.*

Right, Lunis chirped. *It's in constructing them that's key. So maybe the gold is marked by the rainbow, as in its directly below or directly above it.*

At its apex, maybe, Sophia offered.

Maybe, Lunis replied.

Now I get it rains a lot in Ireland, Sophia continued, *but how are we going to ensure we can find a rainbow? Time is an important aspect, and we can't hunt around all day for a random rainbow.*

Looks like we're going to have to manufacture one, Lunis suggested.

Then that begs the question, does the gold show up at every rainbow, and if so, why? Sophia pondered.

I think you're overthinking things, Soph. I think rainbows are a result of certain conditions, yes. They only show up in certain places, and where they show up is like an X on a treasure map. When the conditions are right, they present themselves, and if you know where to look, you'll find the gold of the Leprechaun.

So, Sophia said, sounding triumphant, *it seems you're starting to warm to the idea that Leprechaun gold could exist.*

I think if anyone finds it, it will be us, Lunis answered. *Currently, I'm holding out until I learn more. We could find gold under or above the rain-*

bow. We could also find a pot of fire and damnation. There may be a very good reason that those who find this supposed Leprechaun gold are never around to tell their tales.

Sophia gripped the reins but found herself smiling despite Lunis's words. *Ready to find out what's behind the myth?*

His wings flapped like flags in the wind. *I can't wait.*

CHAPTER SEVENTY-FIVE

When Sophia and her dragon crossed over the border of Ireland, they halted hovering in place.

Below, the hills were somehow brighter in color than where they'd come from in Scotland. They shimmered with a neon green color and sparkled like they'd been dusted with pixie dust.

"What is it about this place?" Sophia asked, finding her voice again now they weren't flying.

It's protected by different energy than Scotland, Lunis explained, slipping easily into his wise tone. *Different clans and groups spread their magic over the lands to guard it, giving it a different appearance. Ireland is unique in its own right.*

Sophia nodded, feeling a fondness for the island not far from her home at the Gullington that was so similar and yet so different.

Below them, the grassy hills met fields of barley and wheat that swayed in the wind. To complete the idyllic experience, in the closest field, attached to a stick was a scarecrow that was keeping the birds at bay.

Do you know why the scarecrow won an award? Lunis asked, changing his tone to a sneaky one.

"Oh my," Sophia said. "Please tell me why?"

Because he was outstanding in his field. Lunis's laughter echoed across the open space.

"Did you just come up with that on the fly?" Sophia asked.

It's a gift, he replied.

"Okay, well, before you tax yourself with any more joke telling, let me work to create a rainbow." Sophia thought for a moment about the right spell for such a thing. She'd created wind and rain and fire but nothing like a rainbow. For a moment, she considered creating a storm and then adding the other elements involved in a rainbow's construction, but she decided it was better to cut corners.

This is going to be a costly use of magic, Lunis told her as she held out her hand before she started the incantation.

She pulled in a breath. "Yes, but I think it's necessary since there are no storms on the horizon, and we don't have all day."

I agree, Lunis stated. *Hopefully, once we have the rainbow then the next parts will be easy and not require too much magic from you.*

Sophia nodded, focusing on creating a rainbow for the first time in her life. The energy pulled out of her hand and projected into the sky before them. Like Lunis had thought, a rainbow didn't just show up in a random place, constructed by different elements. It showed up where it was supposed to, like an X being illuminated on a map.

Sophia knew this to be true because she'd had her hand and energy focused in front of them, but no rainbow appeared there even when she felt her magical reserves plummet, meaning she'd created the spell. At first, she thought she'd failed and depleted her strength in the process.

Then she heard the sounds of tinkling bells behind them and looked over her shoulder to find a glistening and perfect rainbow, vibrant in color and seeming to make music as it arched over the green hills.

CHAPTER SEVENTY-SIX

"It's so beautiful," Sophia observed, taking in the prism of colors. She hadn't seen many rainbows in her life, having not left the House of Fourteen much as a child. Even if she had, the one in front of her would be breathtaking.

To see a rainbow of her own creation made her feel like a goddess. Mother Nature was the one who created rainbows and storms and everything in between. As Mama Jamba often reminded Sophia, her power was in all her children.

Not only did it steal Sophia's breath to see the rainbow she'd created, but from their vantage point, high up in the air, it was even more inspiring.

The rainbow stretched as far as Sophia could see in both directions, the ends disappearing behind rolling hills. Getting to one of those ends would take some time, and the rainbow would no doubt disappear before then.

Sophia imagined treasure hunters speeding for the end of the rainbows, hungry for gold. There was no way anyone could make it on foot or by dragon. On the off chance that a rainbow's end materialized beside someone, would they really see it? That was like standing in the middle of a storm. One doesn't realize where they are because they are in it. It's only once they get some distance do they realize what's all around them.

"See any gold?" Sophia dared to ask Lunis, sensing his skepticism growing.

I see lots of sparkly things that could be mistaken as gold, he observed.

She knew exactly what he meant. From their vantage point, there appeared to be golden dust radiating from the rainbow, sprinkling down on the green grass below. Sophia urged Lunis to move in closer to the rainbow, so they were right underneath it.

The tinkling sound of the bells grew louder as they got closer. When she was directly under the translucent structure, which was like a bridge that reached across the sky, Sophia stuck out her hand, letting the golden dust fall onto her fingertips. She expected it would disappear on her skin like mist. To Sophia's surprise, the specks of golden dust actually gathered in her palm for a moment.

Just when she was about to rejoice that she'd figured it out, the dust spiraled in the air and disappeared.

"Well, that was disappointing," Sophia said with a sigh.

She put her other hand out, observing the same phenomenon. The gold dust pooled like water and then slipped away.

Well, I'll give you this one, Lunis began. *The gold is right, but gathering it appears to be impossible.*

Sophia chewed on her lip, searching the land around them. "That can't be."

Why? the dragon challenged.

"Because all myths have a bit of truth around them," she reasoned. "Every lore was based on something and even if it's not literally true, there's a shred of something that's real."

I don't like to be a Pessimistic Patsy on the subject but—

"Why are you Patsy?" she interrupted, finding herself laughing despite the acute disappointment. "Why not a Patrick or a Pete?"

Fine, we are in Ireland, he stated. *I'll be a Pessimistic Patrick, although as I was saying, I don't mean to be, but I think you're grasping for straws on this one, Soph. You might just want to face that there is no gold at the end of the rainbow.*

"I did face that," she argued. "There isn't any gold at the end of the rainbow, or if there is, I'm not getting to it in time. There definitely is gold raining down from this structure."

Raining down, Lunis said with a chuckle. *Rainbow.*

For some reason, his bad joke made Sophia glance at the green and golden hills underneath them. The gold dust partially obscured the fields below. Then for a moment, Sophia thought it actually made her see something.

Sitting in the middle of the barley field directly under them, surrounded by green hills, was something small and black. And round shaped, like...

"Is that..." Sophia trailed away, squinting at the object below.

Oh, I'm never going to hear the end of this, Lunis said. *Yes, I think that's an empty pot.*

CHAPTER SEVENTY-SEVEN

Hardly able to believe her eyes, Sophia blinked at the small empty black pot sitting in the field of barley directly below the apex of the rainbow. She wouldn't have seen it, but the wind had blown when she was looking in that direction, making the long grains sway, and revealing it.

When the breeze changed direction, it was obscured once more, but Sophia still knew where it was.

"Why is it empty?" Sophia pondered.

Maybe because we're supposed to fill it, Lunis offered.

"Of course!" In her chest, Sophia's heart began to thump with excitement. "The golden dust dissipates if it is gathered by anything but the leprechaun's pot."

That's a theory, he said, the skeptical tone still present.

"Well, let's test it." Sophia encouraged her dragon to dive toward the ground, remembering they were still limited on time. The rainbow wouldn't last for long, and when it was gone, the golden dust would be too...and the black pot used to gather it.

Tucking his head down at a sharp angle, sensing Sophia's concern about the time, Lunis dove for the ground. The fresh air rushed past her, sending her hair back and making her eyes water.

The earth was quickly approaching and the black pot was within view. Sophia's stomach clenched from the sudden drop in altitude, but she swallowed down the feeling, remembering to keep her focus. Time was crucial, which meant they couldn't land and grab the pot. Sophia had to pick it up but doing so would require precision. It would require both rider and dragon to work together in perfect unison.

When Lunis was only a few yards from the ground, he leveled out, keeping his wings still and gliding over the waving barley that seemed to welcome them to the field. Sophia dared to climb out of her saddle and reach over the side of Lunis. She had to pin her boots around the harness to secure herself in place.

The sheaves of barley sped by her outstretched hand as Lunis lowered, his belly nearly grazing the field. Sophia was extended just enough below her dragon. The black pot was coming up, its small cast iron handle extended above it.

Sophia held her breath and reached out her fingers an inch farther. Missing it by even a tiny bit wouldn't do.

One of her boots slipped from its place laced around the harness, and Sophia slid down Lunis a foot, her head in the barley now. She lifted up at once, arching her spine just as they passed over the black pot. She reached out and cinched her fingers around the handle and picked up the surprisingly heavy pot. As Lunis rose into the air, victory rebounded in Sophia's chest.

CHAPTER SEVENTY-EIGHT

Getting back into the saddle with the pot in one hand was no easy feat. Lunis helped by tilting to the opposite side to give Sophia some momentum in the right direction. It helped, but almost too much, and she slid past the saddle and nearly off the other side. It was the heavy pot which felt like it weighed over fifty pounds.

With her free hand, Sophia caught herself as Lunis leveled out, helping her to stay on his back. Not as gracefully as she would have liked, and with the pot banging around and hitting her, Sophia found her way back to the saddle.

Immediately, she steered Lunis back to the rainbow, which was still vibrant with colors. The gold dust continued to rain down, and Sophia held up the pot under the shower, letting it collect into the container.

As Lunis streaked across the bottom of the rainbow, Sophia felt the weight of the pot grow heavier. She wasn't sure if that meant what she thought it did. After a pass, Sophia chanced a glance at the contents. To her surprise and relief, the gold dust had piled up, creating a soft mound inside.

By that point, it would have evaporated from her hand. That had to mean...

"It's working!" Sophia exclaimed.

That's the good news, Lunis said, a catch to his voice.

Extending her hand back out, Sophia kept gathering the golden dust, which was starting to rain down less than before. The rainbow was fading, and she thought that was why Lunis sounded tense.

"What's the bad news, Pessimistic Patrick?"

That we have company and they don't appear happy about you stealing their gold, he answered.

Sophia jerked around to look at the ground, not seeing anything at first. Then she saw them, streaking through the tall barley fields, their eyes murderous and their sharp teeth bared.

Not only was Leprechaun gold real, but so were the mean, little creatures.

CHAPTER SEVENTY-NINE

A tiny fireball streaked by Sophia's head. She nearly didn't duck in time.

Pulling in the pot, she decided they had collected enough gold. Apparently, it was more than enough, according to the angry Leprechauns shooting fireballs at them from the ground.

The little men were as Bermuda Laurens had described. They were a bit bigger than a Brownie, but not as big as a gnome. Like they were attending a Saint Patrick's Day party, each was dressed in a green suit, with a gold buckle and pointy shoes. On their heads of red hair perched green top hats, and covering their pudgy faces were chin beards.

Lunis swerved several times to avoid being hit by the many fireballs now being hurled at them. There had to be a dozen or more Leprechauns on the ground, each launching attack after attack at them.

"Let's get out of here," Sophia encouraged, hunching down low on her dragon.

About that, Lunis stated with a new tension in his voice.

"What?" she asked, perking up to look around. Immediately she saw what he meant. The rainbow wasn't a single arc of a bridge anymore, connecting one part of the land to another. Instead, it had spread out and formed a dome that connected with the ground. The walls of the dome were semitransparent, taking on the appearance of the rainbow, and reflecting streaks of color. It was actually quite beautiful.

What wasn't so nice was the realization they were under this dome.

They were trapped.

CHAPTER EIGHTY

"Well, this just got a bit more complicated," Sophia said, blinking and having trouble seeing clearly with all the lights streaming in through the colors of the rainbow dome. The golden dust had stopped raining down and was now replaced by fireballs flying up from the ground. They streaked by Lunis, who was now doing laps, trying to stay moving.

The fireballs crashed into the walls of the dome, proving it was solid and they couldn't pass through it. When the fireballs connected with the dome, they exploded, sending sparks raining down on them. It wasn't as nice as being sprinkled with gold dust.

Sophia tried to cover her head with both arms, pinning the pot between her legs and ducking as flames rained down on them. The fire didn't affect Lunis, but she was exposed on the top of his back and quickly getting burned in multiple places.

Any bets on whether portals work here? Lunis asked.

Sophia thankfully had enough magic left after creating the rainbow to try a portal. However, she was unsurprised to find that the Leprechaun magic prevented them from portaling when under the dome.

No such luck, Sophia answered.

Well, looks like we're going to have to make a decision, Lunis began. *Fight the little tater tots or give them back their gold.*

I'm not giving them back their gold, Sophia said with conviction. *I haven't taken that much, and it's for a good cause. I'd give them something for it if they'd give me a chance.*

I think they want your life in exchange, he teased, veering around, and avoiding colliding with several fireballs.

We're going to have to fight them, Sophia concluded. *I don't want to hurt them, but it's kill or be killed.*

Do you think creatures with fire magic can be hurt with flames? Lunis wondered.

Only one way to find out, Sophia reasoned, pointing her dragon at the mob of angry Leprechauns, and directing him to cut across them.

As he soared, the dragon opened his mouth and hot fire shot down at the small creatures.

The answer to the question was immediately apparent. The Leprechauns repelled the fire and sent it back in their direction. Lunis had to do some fancy flying to avoid being hit by his own fire—which would have been a huge insult.

So the little redheads can't be burned, Sophia muttered. *Why am I not surprised?*

They can't be burned, which means we should employ the opposite element in our favor, Lunis offered.

Sophia thought for a moment, and then it occurred to her. It was a good idea Lunis had. She only hoped she had enough magic to make it rain.

CHAPTER EIGHTY-ONE

Sophia held her arms out wide, hoping against all hope that this worked. It was hard to hold on with just her legs as Lunis ducked and rolled, trying to avoid being scorched. Several embers had singed Sophia's hair, and the smell of it was strong in her nose.

She knew she'd need both her hands to make a rainstorm, something she'd never really tried to do on this large of a scale.

The fireballs and angry shouts from the ground were growing in intensity.

Anytime you're ready? Lunis urged, nervously.

I'm trying, Sophia stated, pouring all her focus into the task. She clenched her eyes shut and funneled a power usually only the elves had in such strength, as water was their element. However, she was a dragonrider and as such, she could borrow elements from other races. That didn't guarantee it would work. Creating a rain shower was more of a task than a single rainbow.

Sophia was about to admit defeat when she was nearly slung off Lunis as he banked hard to the right to avoid a quick succession of attacks. Then she felt something drop onto her nose. She flinched, worried an ember had fallen on her. She felt it slip down like a tear, rolling over her chin and neck.

Sophia's eyes sprang open to find the dome of the rainbow filled with droplets of water as a spring shower grew in intensity, drenching the Leprechauns below, and making their fireballs extinguish before they came close to Sophia and Lunis.

They held up their little fists and yelled inaudible insults at the pair who had stolen their gold. The best part of the rain shower was that it was making the rainbow fade and with it the dome.

Can't have a rainbow in a storm, Lunis imparted, sounding encouraged by the change of events.

No those come afterward, Sophia said as the dome disappeared completely and a gray sky and clouds replaced it.

Lunis sped forward with Sophia hunched down low. The rain drenched her, soothing the little burns on her skin from the fireballs. She held on tightly to the pot of gold they'd successfully stolen from the Leprechauns and left them far behind in the barley fields of Ireland.

CHAPTER EIGHTY-TWO

Sophia would have reloaded her reserves once Lunis and she got back to the Gullington, but a message from Liv came through saying she had an important update about Rudolf.

With the pot of leprechaun gold disguised to avoid thieves, Sophia stepped through the portal to Roya Lane and hurried to the Mermaid's Tavern, the place Liv had told her to meet her.

She'd never been in the place and immediately knew why upon sitting down at a table with Liv.

"Did you say fifty-year waitlist?" Sophia gawked at her sister.

Liv nodded. "Yeah, on average, it takes about fifty years to get a reservation into this place."

The restaurant was dark and glowing blue. The ceiling was glowing with a blue light that resembled water, making Sophia feeling like she was at the bottom of the ocean. Stone and coral covered much of the floor, and various columns flanked the hung aquarium that filled up most of the wall space. Between the floors, ceiling and aquarium were rivers of lava that gave off steam and bubbled.

The aquarium was unlike anything Sophia had ever seen. It was huge and full of magical sea creatures, like a sea goat, a strange animal with the front half of a goat, and the back half of a fish. It tried to half climb and swim through the clear blue waters in the aquarium.

Similarly, there were sea unicorns that weren't like the mortal version of sea horses, but rather more like actual unicorns with a horn on their head, fins, and a fishtail.

There were also dozens of varieties of strange fish, eels and snakes that were all brightly colored and full of strange magic.

"How did you get us in here?" Sophia asked, flipping through the menu, hungrier than ever after depleting her magic.

Liv gave her an expression over her own menu that said, "How do you think?"

"Is this another place that you nearly closed down?"

"I like to think of it as I helped them to stay in business," Liv said, setting down her menu and leaning back.

"There's no seafood on the menu," Sophia noted, thinking this was odd. Usually, at aquatic-themed restaurants, the menu was full of fish options.

Liv shook her head. "How offended do you think that Zonker fish would be if you were over here eating its cousin? No, there's just meat. Get the dinosaur steak. It's the best."

"What is it made out of?" Sophia asked.

Her sister gave her another incredulous look. "You do get out of the Gullington, right?"

"A bit more than I'd like at times," Sophia admitted. "You're not saying the steaks are actually made out of dinosaurs, are you?"

"Brontosaurus, I believe," Liv answered. "They are really tender."

Sophia shook her head. "I'm not even going to ask how that's possible."

"Well, there was a time travel issue with Papa Creola," Liv explained. "But we fixed all that. Now the Mermaid Tavern has enough in the freezer to last a few hundred years. I mean, one Brontosaurus goes a long way."

"Wait, we're going to have a steak from an extinct animal?" Sophia asked. "That seems wrong."

"They are extinct," Liv reasoned. "I mean, we're just making the best of them. Someone should enjoy their tender meat."

"If time travel was used to bring them back here, then why not bring them here to live?"

"Because it doesn't work that way," Liv told her patiently. "We can't change the events that made them extinct. That's messing with the timeline and a big no-no for Papa Creola. Bringing back the dead dinosaur so that we can cover it in steak sauce, that's A-Okay."

Sophia scratched her head. "Just when I think I understand this place."

"Hey, and if you want to know why dinosaurs are extinct," Liv began, "then you have to ask your Mother Nature. That was all her."

Shrugging, Sophia said, "It was probably a Monday. She says a lot of mistakes in her creations happened on Mondays. She apparently hates them."

"What's a Monday?" Liv asked. "All the days feel the same. For me, they are all Wednesday, halfway through with a long way before any downtime."

Sophia laughed. "Mine are all Thursdays. So close to getting a break…"

"That rarely comes," Liv finished.

"I'm working on that at Hiker's insistence," Sophia related.

"Wow, can you have your boss talk to mine?" Liv asked. "When I mention a break to Papa Creola, he tells me we don't have time for that. When I say he's literally in control of time, he pretends like he can't hear me and starts humming."

Sophia laughed. "Yeah, Mama Jamba influences Hiker a lot the same way. He's chilled out a bit since she came back."

"Then there's your influence," Liv mentioned.

Sophia should have been unsurprised that the waitress was an elf since this was an ocean-themed restaurant, but she was so hungry she wasn't even thinking.

The elf was like many she encountered—of the hippie variety.

"What nourishment does your soul need today?" the elfin woman wearing bangles and a nose ring asked.

"My soul needs you to not talk like that," Liv told her.

If the waitress was offended, she didn't show it. She nodded and put her hands in the prayer position.

"You going for the steak, Soph?" Liv asked.

She nodded in reply. "Yeah, whatever you recommend."

"Good choice," Liv said with satisfaction, turning her attention back to the waitress. "We'll have two dino steaks, medium rare with garlic mashed potatoes and sea salt encrusted green beans. Oh, and a vat of ranch."

The waitress nodded, not having written down a thing.

"When I say a vat, I don't mean those cute little cups that you hatch sea monkeys in," Liv said tersely. "I mean a vat. Like a bath for a lobster."

"I'm feeling you, sister," the waitress replied, her bracelets clanging loudly as she dropped her hands from the prayer position.

Liv pointed at Sophia. "That's my sister. You're a stranger, and as far as I can tell, someone who will never be able to sneak up on anyone with all that jewelry."

"Nothing is a surprise when our intuition guides us," the waitress said.

"Right," Liv replied, drawing the word out, irritation flaring on her face. "Also, we'll take a bottle of Sauvignon Blanc and a baker's dozen of the cheddar biscuits."

"I'm happy to make your request a reality," the waitress intoned before trotting off.

Liv shook her head. "Damn hippies. You'd think working for Papa Creola in his current incarnation as an elf would get me used to it, but I have zero tolerance still."

Sophia laughed and then remembered why they were there. "Rudolf. I want the update."

Liv waved her off. "He's fine. We'll get to that. First, I have to know why you have a pot of leprechaun gold, where'd you get it and also what the hell, that stuff is real!"

CHAPTER EIGHTY-THREE

Sophia's eyes darted to the purse sitting on the table that was actually the pot of gold. "How did you know about that?"

Her sister rolled her eyes. "For starters, you are about as likely to carry around a handbag as I am. They just aren't practical. Secondly, most can't see through glamour, but I'm not most."

Looking around, suddenly nervous, Sophia put her hand protectively on the pot of gold. There weren't many people in the restaurant, although it was booked solid for fifty years. Apparently, that was because the sea creatures didn't like crowds. Sophia still worried she'd gain unnecessary attention. "Do you think it's safe?"

"With you and me sitting beside it?" Liv asked and then laughed. "It could be all the gold in all the world, and it would be perfectly safe. Don't worry, love."

She nodded. "Well, I had to go and fetch it in order to get payment for the cure for distortion."

"Of course you did," Liv said as the waitress returned with a basket of cheddar biscuits and a bottle of chilled white wine. "So, we'll have a cure soon."

"I think so," Sophia replied. "I'm headed there next. Just needed an update from you and to refill my reserves. I made a rainbow and a rain shower."

Liv whistled, looking impressed, and began pouring the wine. "All before noon."

"Yeah, so I can affirm that leprechauns are real, and so is their gold," Sophia stated. "If you ever need some of that treasure, I'll give you tips on how to steal it."

Liv shook her head. "I stay away from the ankle biters. I tend to antagonize those who happen to be shorter than me, which they apparently don't like. But good to know about the gold if that need ever arises."

Taking a bite of the steaming hot cheddar biscuit, Sophia thought she'd faint from the savory flavor. The bread was crispy on the outside, chewy in the middle, and filled with just enough burst of cheddar to excite her taste buds. She was about to exclaim about the flavors when all of the sea creatures suddenly disappeared from the closest aquarium, darting behind rocks and coral, with fearful expressions on their faces.

"What's going on?" Sophia asked.

"The divas have arrived," Liv said dryly, taking a sip of her wine.

Three of the ugliest and scariest creatures Sophia had ever seen swam into view. Sophia knew from reading Bermuda Laurens's *Magical Creatures* that mermaids weren't the beautiful sea people sailors once reported. They were murderous women with long, razor-sharp teeth and withered faces from spending so much time in the ocean, and their hair was stringy and covered in seaweed.

Those in the tank in front of them had gnarly hands and long claws and swam in jerky movements, their eyes were red and they had hungry expressions on their faces.

"Wow, they are something else," Sophia said, watching as they twisted from one side to the other, their necks at strange angles as they stared through the glass at the sisters casually chewing on their biscuits.

"They are something you'll never forget if you have to wrestle with one," Liv said dryly, finishing her glass of wine and immediately refilling it. "The witches don't fight fair. I've got the bite marks to prove it."

"Do you ever have a normal mission?" Sophia asked with a laugh.

"Mission?" Liv questioned. "I fought a mermaid to help out Rudolf because I'm the best friend, and I have the worst ones."

"Speaking of which, tell me all about the king of the fae," Sophia requested. "I'm glad he's okay."

Liv obliged, leaning forward and telling her all about the strange call she'd gotten from Rudolf.

When was she done, Sophia peeled away, shaking her head. "Okay, this is mostly good news. So you'll keep me informed about the information you receive from Rudolf?"

"Of course," Liv answered as the waitress carried over a huge tray that was filled with the largest steaks Sophia had ever seen.

Not only did they look incredibly delicious, but the flavorful aroma wafting off them made her mouth water.

When the hippie had set all the food on the table and retreated once more, Liv gave her sister an encouraging expression. "Don't worry, we're going to get Rudolf back, get evidence on this Never Dumbmen and then take him down."

Sophia cut into her steak, grateful for many reasons. "Then we'll reinstate the Dragon Elite's good name."

CHAPTER EIGHTY-FOUR

The brontosaurus steak was quite possibly one of the best things Sophia had ever eaten, and that was saying a lot. She wondered if that was why those dinosaurs were extinct, but Liv had said it was more complicated. All Sophia knew was she understood why the Mermaid Tavern had such a long waitlist. If she didn't have Liv as an in, then she'd be doing everything she could to ensure she could eat at the restaurant regularly.

When Sophia entered Rose Apothecary, she was surprised not to find the oversized cauldron sitting in the middle of the shop. Instead, there were row upon row of tiny round bottles filled with red liquid like the one Rumi had given her.

"Wow," Sophia said, trying to guess how many antidotes to distortion it was.

"Wow is right," Bep said, striding in from the back, looking exhausted. She slumped into an armchair beside the cash register counter covered with the small bottles. "This wiped me out, but now it's done."

"Thank you," Sophia told her sincerely. "I got what you asked for."

She pulled the glamour off the purse and held up the pot of leprechaun gold.

Bep jumped to her feet, suddenly looking full of energy. "You didn't! That's marvelous. I didn't even know if it was possible or if leprechaun gold existed."

Sophia lowered her chin, having trouble refraining from rolling her eyes. "Why is it that I so often have people assign me tasks they believe to be impossible?"

"Maybe we're testing you," Bep replied, taking the pot of gold and inspecting it.

"Hooray," Sophia said with no real enthusiasm.

Bep glanced up from the pot and smiled. "You know, when I was a young potion maker, they didn't tell me some of the elixirs were supposedly impossible to make. For some reason, that was just left off my curriculum. And guess what?" When Sophia didn't answer, she continued. "I went off and made them. My mentor was shocked when I brought her a bottle of marvel potion and crumb root, all things that are apparently incredibly difficult, if not impossible to make. I reasoned that since I didn't know the restrictions, they didn't really apply to me."

Sophia thought about this and found herself smiling. "I like that. It really is all about the state of mind, isn't it?"

"Indeed," Bep said, returning her attention to the pot of gold. "This is the real stuff."

"Well, it better not be fool's gold," Sophia said with a laugh. "I wouldn't think leprechauns would try and fry me over fake stuff anyway. I do feel bad about taking it from them. They were pretty angry about it."

Bep shook her head. "Don't be. I heard they stole it originally from the giants and have spelled it so heavily and protected it, believing they will try and return and get their resources, but honestly, I don't think the giants give one hoot. They just want to be left alone."

"That sounds like giants," Sophia related.

"Now, where do you want these delivered?" Bep asked, pointing to the cure for distortion.

Sophia thought. "I'll have to do it since you can't ship to the Gullington."

Grateful she'd refilled her reserves, Sophia swept her hand over the many bottles of red liquid, making them all disappear. Moments later they would show up just outside the Barrier at the Gullington. Sophia sent Lunis a quick message, asking him to have the guys pull them into the Castle.

Very soon, magicians and elves would be healed of this awful illness, and the Dragon Elite would be that much closer to clearing their name. Things were finally looking up.

"Now, for the unpleasant news," Bep said, her tone shifting and her chin lowering.

Sophia stiffened. "Because I have to take the good with the bad, right? Are there side effects to the cure?"

"Not that I'm aware of, but that will vary case by case," the potions expert answered. "No, while I was using Baba Yaga's grimoire, I sensed a very strange presence enter my shop. Not wanting to take a chance and having everything that I needed from the spellbook to complete the potion, I locked it up immediately."

Sophia had questions but was interrupted by the chimes of the door opening. Already on guard from Bep's story, she spun around, and was relieved to find Lee striding through the door.

The assassin baker came over with a pleasant smile on her face. "Are you able to help me out with that ointment, Potionmaker?"

Bep pursed her lips. "Are you going to torture me with more of your supposed jokes?"

"Only if you're into that kind of thing," Lee answered with a wink.

"Well, I'm finished with Sophia's potion," she stated. "So I suppose I can."

"The healing elixir," Sophia said in a rush. "Where are we with that?"

"It's resting," Bep answered. "As I said before, that needs to happen. That's actually one of the most important parts of the process. There's time to stir and time not to. We have to know when to relax."

"A common theme in my life right now," Sophia related before turning her attention to Lee. "Do you want the healing potion? Or your own ointment for…what did you say it was? A rash?"

Lee scratched her back and then her leg. "I made the mistake of trying to make a love syrup for Cat out of poison oak. Karma is a witch."

"I don't think that's how the phrase goes," Bep said dryly.

"No," Lee argued. "Seriously, Karma is a little evil witch. That's Cat's sister's name. She put the love syrup in my food, and I've had a stubborn rash ever since."

"The healing potion will take longer than you'll want to wait," Bep told Lee. "Come back tomorrow morning, and I'll have something for you that will bring the rash under control, but hopefully this teaches you not to try and poison your wife."

"If experience has taught me anything," Lee began, "whatever lessons I learn will be erased by the things Cat does to provoke me."

"Aren't they sweet?" Sophia winked at the potions expert.

"Not in the least," she answered. "Anyway, as I was saying, about your spellbook, Sophia. There's a complication to giving it back to you."

Sophia arched an eyebrow at her. "Yes?"

"Well, the moment I take it out of my chest that has protective spells, whatever was trying to steal it will return," Bep explained. "I can't say what it was, but it's powerful and homed on the grimoire. I'm guessing that you Sophia, had a protective quality over the spellbook, and once it wasn't in your presence, it wore off and invited the evil spirits in."

Sophia deflated. "I was assigned as the protector. Darn it."

Bep pursed her lips. "Well, then you really shouldn't have let it out of your possession."

"Thanks," Sophia said dryly. "I was obviously thinking of myself when I asked you to use it to replicate the cure to heal hundreds from distortion."

"You could have stayed with me while I had the book," Bep lectured.

"I do have other obligations," Sophia fired back, growing frustrated.

"I think the whole back story that got us here is null and void," Lee said, being a voice of reason in the conversation. "We've got to figure out how to get the book out of the chest without the evil spirit getting to it. I bet it needs the grimoire to recover or something, and that's why it is hunting for it."

"We?" Sophia questioned.

Lee nodded at once. "Absolutely. Looks like you need some help, and I need something to take my mind off the urge to scratch until Bep has my ointment tomorrow morning. So how are we going to combat this evil spirit and get this spellbook to safety?"

That was a very good question, and one Sophia didn't really have the answer to just yet.

"I'm not sure," Sophia began. "But I know who will, and although they will be madder than hell about this predicament, they'll be obligated to help."

"Why is that?" Lee asked.

Sophia waved her to the door. "Because my boss is their best friend."

CHAPTER EIGHTY-FIVE

"Seriously, you're taking me to meet Father Time?" Lee asked. "That's like almost as cool as meeting Madonna." A moment later, she added, "I'm referring to the singer, not the mother of Jesus, although both are cool, it's just the latter is harder to do."

Sophia cut her eyes at the baker assassin as they strode down Roya Lane. "You offend people easily, don't you?"

Lee thought about this. "Is that why people usually charge off without a word, their faces all red?"

"Might be." Sophia cut around the crowds to get to the far end of Roya Lane where the Fantastical Armory was. She knew it was a risk to take Lee there, but she also knew they needed to get Baba Yaga's grimoire to safety, and having help would be good. Yes, she'd made a mistake, but also not really, since she had managed to get and replicate the cure for distortion. It was all about tradeoffs, and there would always be risks and dangers. They'd left Bep at her shop with the promise they'd return for the spellbook as soon as they had a strategy.

As they strode for the shop run by Father Time's assistant, Lee reached into her pocket and retrieved a sticky honey bun. "Want a bite?" She offered it to Sophia.

"No, thanks," she replied, wondering what the contents of Lee's pockets must look like if she kept such things in there. "I just loaded up on cheddar biscuits."

"Oh, I have an addiction to cheddar cheese," Lee said, longingly. "But it's only mild."

"It just never stops with you," Sophia chuckled, shaking her head.

"A total gift," Lee remarked. "You're welcome."

"When we're in the Fantastical Armory, please try not to touch anything," Sophia instructed. "There will be many temptations for you, I suspect, since it's full of weapons."

"Oh, so not just a clever name then?" Lee winked at her. "Don't worry. I'll keep my hands to myself. To ensure I'm good, how about I tuck my knees into my chest and lean forward?"

Sophia blinked at her, watching as she demolished the honey bun. "Why would you do that?"

"That's just how I roll." Lee laughed loudly. "Am I killing you yet?"

"Slowly," Sophia agreed as they rounded the steps up to the Fantastical Armory.

CHAPTER EIGHTY-SIX

"You were instructed not to let Baba Yaga's grimoire out of your possession. You are forever its keeper until I say otherwise," Papa Creola declared. He didn't appear frustrated, but more like he was trying to play the part as he sat in lotus position on the floor of the Fantastical Amory, his hands resting on his knees.

"No, you said to protect it," Sophia argued, slapping Lee's hands when she went to touch a sword hanging on the wall. "What did I say?"

The baker assassin looked momentarily like a scolded child as she yanked her hand back. Recovering, she said, "I don't remember. I hardly listen when you speak. When anyone does, really."

Shrugging off Lee, she turned her attention back to the hippie. "I had to get the cure for distortion, didn't I?" Sophia asked the father of time. "What else was I supposed to do?"

The questionable look on the elf's face made Sophia narrow her eyes with sudden suspicion.

"You knew I'd have to give the grimoire to Bep to replicate the cure for distortion," she fired. "I didn't even know where that idea came from, but I bet you somehow planted it in my head, Papa Creola. Didn't you?"

He shook his head but smiled slightly. "You give me too much credit. But yes, you really did need to give the potions expert the spellbook to replicate the cure."

"So, you knew it would be in danger then?" Sophia asked.

"But also that you'd trust it to someone as competent as Bep, which shows your judgment is intact, at least," he replied. "I suspected she'd have the good sense to lock up the grimoire once she realized something was after it."

"Thanks," Sophia said dryly, not meaning it. "Bep did sense the evil spirit and locked up the grimoire before it could get to it."

"Which is good because it is an incredibly evil spirit—of the worst type," Papa Creola told her. "A powerful specter that desires a body and will do anything to get one. If that were to happen, well, we'd have worse problems than we already do."

"You mean bigger than magicians and elves losing their magic and blurring until they disappear?" Sophia asked.

"Much bigger," Papa Creola answered. "It's imperative that the specter, once known as Tatiana Chernyy, never succeeds in getting a body."

"I'm guessing the spell to do so is in Baba Yaga's grimoire," Sophia postulated.

"Can I interest you in something?" Subner asked Lee, who was showing a keen curiosity in a set of knives with curved handles.

"She's with me," Sophia cut in.

Lee glanced over her shoulder. "I didn't realize I wasn't allowed to browse, Mom."

"We're not here to shop, especially not you," Sophia scolded.

"But I brought all my pennies and was hoping to spend my allowance," Lee joked.

"She's a bad assassin," Sophia said to Subner. "Don't sell her anything."

"That's my call to make, not yours, Ms. Beaufont," the elf with stringy brown hair said.

"I have so many regrets right now." Sophia glared at the ceiling as if she was talking to the heavens and hoping the angels would take pity on her.

"Like those shoes? They are pretty dull," Lee teased over her shoulder.

"You'll regret those cheddar biscuits. They will be back to visit you," Papa Creola said calmly, his eyes closed.

"When we realize that we control no one but ourselves, we soar instead of struggle," Subner said, pulling a set of knives from the glass case. "You can't stop Lee from purchasing anything."

"I was thinking more about my regrets related to my choice in friends." Sophia understood why Liv drank so much, based on who she worked with and for.

"Let's say it's someone's last day on Earth," Lee began, studying the knives Subner was showing her. "Which one of these beauties do you think they'd like to have as the last thing they see?"

Sophia rolled her eyes. "This can't be real."

"We should always spend all our days like they are our last," Subner intoned in his usual hippie tone. He couldn't help it since this was his current reiteration, and Sophia also knew he and Papa Creola secretly hated it. They were learning to embrace their current reality until they regenerated into something new.

Lee nodded. "I agree. I like to spend every day as if it's my last. Staying in bed and calling for a nurse to bring me more pudding."

Sophia groaned. Papa Creola opened his eyes, finally willing to give her his attention.

"Interesting that you've brought the assassin here," he stated calmly.

"Again, you saw that coming a million miles away," she replied. "Subner is probably selling her the weapon to kill me with."

Papa Creola tilted his head to the side with a skeptical expression. "That would be impossible."

"Why?" she asked at once.

"Because that weapon hasn't been made yet," he replied.

A chill ran down her back. "I'm not sure if I should be grateful for that or deeply concerned. Any chance you'll give me a lead on this weapon and a heads up on the timeline of my death?"

Father Time glared at her with an expression that said, "What do you think?"

"Well, it was worth a try," Sophia mumbled.

Papa Creola shrugged. "You were right to seek my councel to deal with this specter. If you hadn't, which I feared, then Bep would open the chest, and the specter would overwhelm you. It hasn't been sufficiently motivated to take anyone out in a very long time, but it will do whatever it takes to get its hands on the grimoire."

"Hands," Lee said with a laugh.

When no one joined her, she shrugged. "Get it? Because it doesn't really have hands? Not really?"

"It doesn't," Papa Creola imparted. "It does have powers and poltergeist strength, which I dare say are enough to rip Roya Lane in half."

Sophia shook her head. "We can't let that happen."

"No, we can't," Papa Creola agreed. "I've been waiting to trap this monster for a while. Well, I've been waiting for you to get Baba Yaga's grimoire, this distortion business to happen, you to get the antidote from Rumi, and then give it to Bep along with the spellbook to draw out the evil specter."

Sophia lowered her chin. "It's so cute how you work, all without any heads up to us pawns in your game."

He nodded like she was serious. "I agree."

"Do you have a way for us to contain this ghost, Tatiana?" Sophia asked. "Like a proton pack or some other ghostbusting equipment?"

As usual, Papa Creola didn't get the joke. Or maybe he just didn't find it funny. "I can offer you some help, although you'll need two people to do it successfully."

Sophia batted her eyes at him with annoyance before holding out her hand to Lee. "As you saw it coming regarding this situation, probably before I even had consciousness as a fetus, I brought help. None other than the baker assassin who volunteered her services."

"Yes, good call on your part, letting her join you," he agreed, striding over to a counter on the far side of the shop. He retrieved two objects. "Now, containing the specter will be very dangerous, and you'll have to act really fast or it will either get the advantage or flee. Neither of those are options. I need this evil spirit finally gone from this planet."

Adamantly, Sophia nodded. "I'm listening. What do we have to do?"

He held up two hand mirrors. "You've got to get the specter to chase one of you while the other is locked on it with one of the mirrors."

"So one of us should have the grimoire in hand and run like hell," Sophia guessed.

"That one will be you, Sophia," Lee stated. "Rash, remember. Running chafes my legs."

She nodded. "Copy that. Thanks for the reminder about the rash."

"You're welcome. I can show you pictures later," Lee chirped, returning her attention to the knives on display. She pointed to the first one. "Does that one cut through bone?"

"As I was saying," Papa Creola continued, "you need to get some distance from each other, but if the first mirror is locked on the specter, then the second one will do so once you're in place."

"How far from it will I have to be?" Sophia asked.

"Far," Papa Creola answered.

"Stop with all the details already," Sophia remarked. "You're over-whelming me with information."

Father Time sighed, cutting his eyes at Subner. "She is a Beaufont, isn't she?"

"Through and through," Subner said dryly from behind the counter. "They speak the language of sarcasm."

Papa Creola returned his gaze to Sophia. "You'll know when you're far enough away. There will be a sign. But you have to wait until that moment. Too soon before that and it won't work and the specter will overpower and win or escape, which I can't have. Once you're sure you're far enough away, then you'll hold up your mirror and that will trap the specter. As soon as that happens, you'll throw this down." He held up a small perfume bottle. "If you've done everything right, the specter will be sucked into this and trapped forevermore. You can bring it to me, and I'll rid Tatiana from this world once and for all."

"So it is like *Ghost Busters*, then?" Sophia asked. "I mean since there's a containment unit and all."

Papa Creola gave her a confused expression. "I don't know. I'm not familiar with whatever that is."

"You know what I was going to do before I was born, but you're not familiar with one of the most popular movie franchises of the nineteen-eighties?" Sophia questioned.

He handed her the mirrors and the perfume bottle. "To be honest, I slept through the eighties and think I'm better off for it."

CHAPTER EIGHTY-SEVEN

"This will be so much fun!" Lee exclaimed as they made their way back to Rose Apothecary.

Sophia gave the baker assassin an incredulous expression. "We have to release and trap an evil specter who Papa Creola has apparently been after for a while and who sounds incredibly dangerous."

"I know," Lee said, her tone full of excitement. "Much better than the plans I had to hunt down some murderous crabs for a diabolical idea I have for world domination."

Rounding the corner to the potion shop, Sophia shook her head. "You said that out loud."

"So I'm thinking for this mission, I'm Batman and you're Robin," Lee went on.

"I think you need to up your meds," Sophia replied. "I'm the dragonrider who got the case assigned by Father Time. I'm definitely Batman."

"But," Lee argued, drawing the word out. "I'm the one wearing Batman underwear."

"That goes on the long list of things I didn't need you to tell me."

The baker assassin shrugged. "Fine, I'll change my undies before we go, and you can be Robin."

"I don't think that's necessary."

"Do you want details or not?" Lee asked with a serious expression.

"I don't," Sophia answered, rounding the corner into Rose Apothecary. The smell of gardenia and spices was strong in the air. There were always so many interesting aromas in the shop.

Bep glanced up from behind the counter.

"We're ready to face the specter," Sophia said, looking around. "Where are you keeping Baba Yaga's grimoire?"

"It's right there." She pointed to a large black chest that was latched shut sitting on a table in the middle of the shop.

Sophia positioned herself in front of it, one of the mirrors in her hand. She'd given the other one to Lee. "Are you ready?" she asked her.

"What did Batman say to Robin before they got in the Batcar?" Lee asked.

Sophia just glared at her with an expression that said, "I'm ready for the bad punchline."

"Robin, get in the car." Lee howled with laughter.

Bep shook her head. "You'll be taking this one with you, I hope."

"Actually," Sophia began. "She's going to stay here and serve as the anchor. I'm the one who has to run with the grimoire and get the specter to follow me."

"You're leaving her here with me." Bep didn't sound happy about the situation.

"Yep," Lee affirmed. "All I've got to do is hold a stupid hand mirror, so I'll have ample opportunity to test some killer material on you."

"According to Papa Creola, this is going to be very taxing," Sophia warned Lee. "I need you to focus your attention on holding that mirror and tethering its magical energy to the specter."

Lee smirked. "I'm a good multi-tasker. I'll have no problem holding Tatiana and telling deadly jokes."

Bep shook her head as she made for the door. "I'm going to grab lunch. Lock up when you're done trapping the evil spirit and clean up if you make a mess."

"Don't die," she added at the door. "If you do, try and do it outside of the shop. It took me forever to get the bloodstains off the floor last time."

Sophia closed her eyes for a half-beat, wondering if it was too late to start a different profession. Maybe she could be the librarian for the Great Library. Being in a quiet place without so many crazies around her all the time might be nice.

"Baking soda," Lee said, seemingly randomly.

"Huh?" Sophia asked.

"That's how I get blood stains out of things," Lee answered.

She nodded, waving to Bep. "We'll die outside on the streets."

The potions expert smiled and left the shop, leaving Sophia with no choice but to devote her attention to the next phase of the mission, luring the specter out so the chase could begin.

CHAPTER EIGHTY-EIGHT

Sophia's hands shook ever so slightly as she reached for the latch.

"While you're out, can you pick me up some sunflower seeds?" Lee asked, quite seriously. "I've got a craving for something salty."

Grateful for the delay, Sophia rolled her eyes. "I think I'll be a little busy running like hell to put distance between me and the specter."

Lee sighed dramatically. "Fine, fine. But try and hurry. I haven't had a second lunch yet."

"You have my sympathies," Sophia said dryly. "How are you even able to stand there without fainting?"

Nodding, as though she was glad Sophia understood, Lee frowned. "I had a second breakfast later than usual and that helps."

"I had a brontosaurus steak for lunch, and it helped a lot," Sophia related. "I should be able to keep running for a while if necessary, and my magical reserves are full."

"So is your need to stall," Lee observed. "You going to open up this bad boy anytime soon so Tatiana can join us, or do you want to tell me what you had for breakfast first? I'm a good listener."

"When we were in the Fantastical Armory earlier, you said you never listen when people speak," Sophia argued, putting her hands on her hips.

"Did I?" Lee asked. "I don't remember. That was ages ago."

"Ten minutes," Sophia countered.

"Like I said, ages," Lee agreed. "No wonder I'm so hungry." She looked around. "Maybe Bep has a snack."

"Don't eat anything that's in here," Sophia warned. "You have no idea what it is or what it will do."

"Wow, your boy toy must love spending time with you," Lee observed. "Don't touch anything. Don't eat anything. I bet you make him wash his hands after he uses the restroom."

Sophia's eyes reflexively widened. "Remind me never to eat anything from the Crying Cat Bakery ever again. It's people like you that spread a pandemic."

"Oh, you should never eat anything from that place," Lee said, leaning in closer and cupping her mouth. "Between you and me, I think Cat is trying to kill me and poisoning all the food in hopes that I'll consume it."

"It's a wonder that you have stayed in business this long."

"What's a wonder," Lee began, holding up the small intricately decorated silver hand mirror, "is that you've stretched out this nonconversation so long. So are we going to contain a specter already or do you want another killer joke? I've got one about a two-legged cow."

"I'm ready," Sophia said, shaking her head adamantly.

"It's lean beef!" Lee exclaimed, laughing.

Blowing out a long breath, Sophia smirked at her friend before unlocking the latch and opening the chest, releasing Baba Yaga's grimoire and all the energy that rebounded off the spellbook, attracting the worst of the worst.

CHAPTER EIGHTY-NINE

The appearance of Baba Yaga's ancient book was somehow more menacing than before. The grimoire had been created by an evil witch, but it also had helpful spells in it—like how to replicate complex spells. Without that information, Bep wouldn't have been able to copy the cure for distortion. Sophia reminded herself that magic could always be used for good or evil. It just so happened her job often required her to stop those with evil agendas from getting their hands on their objects of desire.

Reaching into the dark chest that was full of other weird artifacts, Sophia pulled the thick leather-bound book from the top.

She pressed the book to her chest and glanced around, expecting the specter to appear instantly.

Glancing at Lee, she gave her a questioning expression.

The baker assassin shrugged. "She might be on the toilet. Give her a minute."

Striding for the shop door, Sophia prepared herself mentally for what she'd have to do next.

"Let's hope her commute time isn't long, though," Lee stated. "I got the tum rums."

"Please make this more about you and your unrelenting hunger,"

Sophia said, glancing over her shoulder toward Roya Lane, which was busy. That would make running from Tatiana more difficult.

Lee looked off longingly. "Oh, I'm glad you care so much about my tum-tum. I could really go for some fry-fry chicky-chick. That's fried chicken." Her eyes widened. "Or some chicky-chicky-parm-parm."

"That's chicken parmesan, I'm guessing?" Sophia asked.

"Have you never seen Parks and Recreation?" Lee asked, appearing offended.

"I save the world for a living," Sophia answered.

Lee scoffed at her. "I kill people and run a shady bakery. You don't see that stopping me from rewatching Leslie Poehler's greatness unfold over and over again. Priorities."

"You really do amaze me," Sophia said, her eyes searching the shop for signs of the specter. The wait was torture.

"Come on, Tat!" Lee boomed, grabbing her stomach like the hunger was killing her.

"I wonder what this evil spirit did when she was alive?" Sophia mused, deciding it was best to keep herself distracted. Lee's humor really did the trick, although she wasn't going to tell her that.

Lee thought for a moment. "I bet she was one of those posh people who spoke with a British accent, even though they were from Cleveland, and drank tea with their pinkies in the air."

Sophia nodded, knowing the type. "On social media, she made vague posts, like 'Man, what happened just sucks. Cheer me up with a pic of your dog.'"

"Those people are the worst," Lee agreed. "Tat probably wore really bright red lipstick and lots of makeup to hide the fact she looks like a troll and went to renaissance conventions, called everyone her best friend, although by definition you can only have one. I bet she bought stuffed animals for adults like they were children and nicknamed literally everyone in her life. She never knew how much money she had, which was usually zero because she couldn't hold down a job, and pretended to be a vegan to impress people. She thought she was better at everything, even though she was the absolute worst."

Sophia raised an eyebrow. "Are you referring to a specific person? That is quite detailed."

"Nope, just some Miranda I dumped in high school because she was cray-cray," Lee replied.

"The truth comes out." Sophia laughed at the assassin baker. "Mirandas are the worst!"

"Yeah, but not as bad as Karens," Lee said impatiently.

"Poor people named Karen and Miranda," Sophia related.

"Poor us for having to deal with them when they stalk me on social media for years and contact all my friends just to see if 'Cat is treating me all right.'"

"So, you're totally over it then?" Sophia asked.

Lee nodded, a smile plastered on her face. "But if I ran into the witch, I'd cut her."

"Murder, you mean?"

Lee gave her an offended look. "Heck no. Putting her out of her misery would be a gift. Miranda gets to suffer through life without me. That's the worst punishment I can think of."

Sophia was about to respond when a white mist rose up from the floor. It started to take the shape of a figure as more mist poured through the hardwood floor between her and Lee.

Tatiana had arrived, and she was chilling.

CHAPTER NINETY

If Tatiana was wearing red lipstick, Sophia wouldn't have known since she was all white. Makeup would have been a big improvement, though. Life or death or both hadn't been kind to the evil spirit. She was hideous and bone-chilling to look at.

Her long white hair flowed out behind her, and the shredded gown she wore did little to cover her emaciated figure. Tatiana's cheeks were sunken, and the place where her eyes had been were hollow sockets. She had definitely been a real Miranda back in her day and had to have done some really awful things to appear so soulless and tortured.

She opened her mouth to reveal a blackness that seemed to go on forever, and a ghoulish sound came out that made a violent shiver run down Sophia's spine. That's when she realized she'd frozen, even though the chase should have been afoot.

Lee still had her wits about her and raised the hand mirror, pointing the reflective side at the specter.

At first, nothing happened, and Sophia worried she'd missed an instruction from Papa Creola. The specter lunged for Sophia, her greedy hands reaching, clawing for the book in her hands.

Still frozen and not sure exactly why, Sophia remained rooted in her spot, not even blinking as the white ghost rushed at her, flying through the chest on the table and the various shelves and objects in the room. When she was a breath away, a beam of purple light shot from the surface of the mirror and wrapped around Tatiana like a bull being lassoed. This yanked her back slightly, but only a few feet.

The specter started forward again but didn't appear to be able to move as fast. She was being restrained by the rope of light, tethering her to the mirror in Lee's hands.

It was good that Sophia hadn't taken off yet, she reasoned because then Tatiana would have pursued before Lee had a chance to hook her.

The assassin baker definitely wouldn't be able to tell jokes while holding onto the mirror. She had the handle in two hands now, and her jaw flexed as her face twisted up with extreme concentration.

The act of holding the specter had to be great to cause this reaction from Lee. Through clenched teeth, she said, "Are you going to run already?"

Like waking from a bad dream, Sophia startled, her eyes widening. "Oh yeah," she hiccupped before spinning around and taking off, sprinting through Roya Lane.

CHAPTER NINETY-ONE

Sophia didn't have to look over her shoulder to determine if Tatiana was rushing after her. She could hear the rush of wind and the specter's howling as she pursued.

If that wasn't enough of an indication that the specter wasn't giving up on getting the grimoire, even though she was tethered to one of the mirrors meant to be her demise, the reactions of those Sophia raced past told her. A group of gnomes jumped out of her path as she passed a pub where they'd been waiting. Elves shrank back into their yoga studios or candle stores at the sight of the specter chasing after Sophia. A set of fairies zipped back and forth across the street, unsure where to go to avoid being caught in the fight.

"Move!" Sophia yelled to them, hoping the simple instructions would clear them from her path.

Her feet were moving as fast as they could, and several times her boots caught the lip of an uneven stone on the cobbled road. She moved her arms, trying to propel herself faster, Baba Yaga's grimoire in one hand and the mirror in the other.

When Sophia passed the Pegasus Correctional Office, she caught sight of Bep, who appeared only mildly interested to see the drag-onrider speeding down the lane and a ghost howling after her. She actually waved, holding up her sandwich as though letting Sophia know she'd successfully secured some lunch.

Grunting from the burst of adrenaline, Sophia swerved around the food cart where Bep must have gotten her sandwich. She had to zig-zag to avoid running into people or objects, and several times she reverted to leaping to get over an obstacle.

However, Tatiana had a clear advantage, passing through objects and people, and not having to choose her path.

Chancing a glance, Sophia noticed that the specter was drawing closer and was only a few yards back. Thankfully the ghost didn't seem to be able to move as fast with the purple string of light attached to her. It was still wrapped around her mid-section, and like a fish on a line being reeled in, it constantly pulled her back slightly.

Still, Tatiana wasn't giving up and appeared to be getting used to the inconvenience. She began swirling in her pursuit, swaying one way and then the other as she continued forward. Her long gown and hair flowed to the opposite side of her as she changed directions. This prevented the string of light from pulling her back and slowing her progress, although she wasn't taking a direct path anymore.

She would catch up with Sophia soon at this rate. Either that or Sophia would run out of street. She could see the end of the lane approach. She was roughly a hundred yards away from where it dead-ended—ironically where the Fantastical Armory was located.

CHAPTER NINETY-TWO

Sophia kept glancing over her shoulder, looking for the mysterious sign Papa Creola had mentioned. Then she'd know when to halt and throw up her own hand mirror, hopefully stopping the specter until she could contain it in the perfume bottle, currently bouncing around inside of the pocket of her cloak.

Besides the new strategy Tatiana had adopted, there didn't appear to be anything different about her. The ghost made a low and long howling sound that seemed to speak of her many troubles. Every now and then, Sophia could have sworn she heard a word like "hate," "pain," or "rage."

How's it going? Lunis said in Sophia's head.

She nearly choked from the sudden interruption.

I'm sort of busy right now, she said, sweat pouring down her forehead and into her eyes.

I can see that, he stated, having scried her current situation.

Then you know right now isn't a good time to talk, she replied.

What I know is that I'm bored, Lunis said. *The others are all off on the dragons, distributing the cure for distortion, so there's no Bell or Simi to annoy, which leaves me without purpose.*

Again, can we chat later? Sophia nearly ran into an elf on a bicycle who didn't appear to know how to stop the thing. *I've got my hands full right now.*

With just a hand mirror and a book? Lunis questioned, not hiding the laughter in his tone. *I think you can hold a lot more than that.*

Haha, Sophia said, not meaning it. The howling behind her growing louder.

I bet you're really curious to know when you'll be able to throw up that mirror to do the next part of this plan.

It had crossed my mind. Any ideas?

I have some theories on the matter, Lunis offered and then was quiet.

Sophia grunted, reminding herself to change her Amazon password so he couldn't use her account anymore.

I heard that, Lunis said rudely. *If you're going to be like that, then I'll just go and lounge on the Expanse and not offer my help. It's a glorious day here—all sunshine and rainbows.*

I loathe rainbows, she spat.

Lunis laughed. *Me too, but seriously, it's a real nice day.*

Sophia's eyes darted up to the gray skies hanging overhead. *I'm jealous. Of that and the fact that you're not being pursued by an evil spirit. If you were, then I'd be happy to distract you with bad jokes.*

Oh, speaking of which, Lee had some good ones. I'll be stealing those.

The dead-end of Roya Lane was just up ahead. It was a single brick wall that had Sophia's gravestone printed across it. She whipped her head over her shoulder and found that Tatiana wasn't any closer or farther away, but still following at the same constant speed.

This theory you have, Sophia questioned. *When do you think I'll have my chance to use the hand mirror and hopefully stop the specter?*

That's the thing, Lunis began. *I don't think you use the hand mirror to stop the old hag.*

You don't? Sophia asked, surprised by this.

No, I think you use it after she's halted, he answered. *If my idea is correct, the first mirror puts a leash on her, and the second one tethers her. Then she gets sucked into the perfume bottle, but only if everything is done correctly. Well, and she doesn't grab and eat you before you've done it.*

Thanks for the sentiment. It really helps, Sophia joked, grateful for

Lunis's humor right then. It was keeping the fear at bay, which had been close to overwhelming her. Then she really would have been done.

The brick wall was only twenty yards away.

Sophia sucked in a breath and held it.

That still doesn't tell me when to use the hand mirror and end this thing, Sophia pointed out.

Sure it does, Lunis replied.

How so? she asked.

You just have to wait.

Wait for what, she questioned.

Until the leash runs out.

Like Lunis had been timing it, his words came at exactly the moment Sophia came to the dead end and turned, throwing her back up against the brick. The specter was still barreling toward her, mouth open and seconds from swallowing Sophia and taking the grimoire.

CHAPTER NINETY-THREE

Pressing as firmly into the brick wall as she could, Sophia considered her options. If the first mirror was a leash and she was waiting for it to run out, then doubling back and trying to duck around the specter wouldn't work.

What if the leash didn't run out and Tatiana got her? Sophia thought, fear close to overwhelming her.

Breathe, Lunis encouraged.

The monster sped for Sophia, reinvigorated by the fact her prey was stuck and just ahead. Her clawed hands reached forward, and she shot straight ahead, no longer zipping back and forth.

Sophia couldn't breathe as she was ordered. She pressed the grimoire into her chest and tensed, wondering if this was it. Papa Creola had said the weapon that would kill her hadn't been forged yet, but he didn't see everything and was sometimes wrong.

I love you, Lunis, she said in her mind, tears creeping up her throat, reminding her she was still alive, if only for a moment.

Don't you 'I love you' to me right now, he said bitterly, the tension finally creeping into his voice.

She could portal, Sophia realized. That would put her and the spellbook in a safe place, but then she wouldn't have trapped the specter. Sophia was fairly confident that the fear was too strong in her right then, and there was zero way she could use her magic, she was so scared. Never before had she'd known panic like this.

It made her chest vibrate and her heart pound. Her teeth chattered.

Don't give up, Lunis said with conviction.

She wanted to believe him, but as the monster closed the distance, Sophia knew it was time to say her final goodbye.

Tell Wilder I love him, she stated. *Goodbye, my best friend, Lunis. I love you forever and always.*

CHAPTER NINETY-FOUR

*N*o, Lunis yelled in her mind, sounding angry.

It hardly registered for Sophia as she looked into the open chasm that was the specter's mouth. The empty sockets of the beast tried to suck her in, and Sophia thought for sure she'd pass out before the ghost swallowed her or whatever she did. These would be her final moments on the planet she loved so dearly and would die to protect, and had failed to.

Don't give up, Lunis stammered with urgency. *This can't be the end.*

Sophia couldn't see how that could be possible as the specter zoomed at her, now only a few yards away.

She pressed her head into the brick wall and tilted it to the side, prepared to throw up a spell if that would help, but not sure of any that would work on an incorporeal being. The normal offensive spells would pass through the ghost, which was why Sophia had asked Papa Creola for help. That seemed like eons ago, and the worst idea since it hadn't worked.

All Sophia could see was the white of the ghost as she flew in closer, her arms outstretched, and her hair and gown billowing behind her.

Biting down hard on her lip, Sophia braced herself for the monster to close the final bit of distance. Just before she did, the specter was suddenly yanked back.

Her howling halted like the breath had been knocked out of her.

If she had eyes to see, Sophia was sure they'd be full of shock. The expression on her face was full of rage as Tatiana realized her leash had run out, and she was only three feet from that which she desired and the one she was hungry to murder.

CHAPTER NINETY-FIVE

The evil spirit tugged against the restraint holding her back. She was so close and just far enough away to keep Sophia safe. For how long, Sophia didn't know.

The purple rope of light was still wrapped around Tatiana's midsection. Peering around the monster, Sophia saw that the beam streaked all the way down Roya Lane, where it began at the reflective surface of Lee's mirror at Rose Apothecary.

Lee, stay strong, Sophia said in her mind, offering encouragement to her friend, who was presently keeping her alive. If the assassin baker faltered even for a second, then Tatiana would shoot forward and complete her mission.

The specter was jerking against her shackle, trying to break it, but it held securely. Her arms clawed through the air, and she twisted her face to one side and then the other, her howls turning into screams.

That was a close one, Lunis said with relief.

You're telling me, she replied. *I'm not out of hot water yet. I've still got to trap her.*

Oh, I was referring to a game of horseshoes I'm playing by myself, Lunis joked, nearly making Sophia laugh out loud.

Thanks for the concern, she shot back.

I told you that you would be okay, he said with sudden tenderness.

But you were concerned, she stated rather than asked.

Always, he replied. *Now it's time to finish this.*

Sophia nodded. Her shaking hands fumbled to push the grimoire behind her back so she could hold the mirror with both hands. If it was anything like Lee's situation, then she'd need both to hold the specter, at least initially.

She pressed her back against the book, using pressure to hold it against the brick wall behind her. At least it was still safe and so was she.

Sophia's hands were sweating so profusely, she nearly dropped the hand mirror. She gasped, seeing a reality where she broke the object, ruining everything.

Thankfully she caught it in time and let out a breath.

The specter, perhaps realizing what was about to happen, lifted her chin and stopped her screaming.

Her hands yanked into her chest as she turned to the side. Sophia thought she was about to retreat, but instead, the evil spirit spoke for the first time. They were the most chilling words that Sophia had ever heard.

CHAPTER NINETY-SIX

The voice of the specter was like a knife sawing through cardboard. It gripped Sophia's soul and seemed to tear it in half.

"I mark you with a devil's curse, forbidding you from ever sleeping peacefully," Tatiana said, her cracked, withered lips making strange movements as she spoke. "Forever and ever, you will know the torture I endure for eternity by keeping me from what I truly deserve."

Sophia would have thought it was just a bold threat meant to intimidate, but then a blast of light shot from the monster's mouth and hit her straight in the chest. The force was unlike anything Sophia had ever experienced. It didn't hurt, but the sensation was far from pleasant. It felt like she'd been shocked by a defibrillator. Only this didn't jump-start her heart, but rather made it stop for a second.

Sophia sucked in a breath, willing her heart to continue beating. The breath was unfulfilling. She was certain this was it, even more so than before. She heard Lunis's voice in her head but couldn't make out his words. Suddenly she was falling through a dark space, and her hands tried to clutch onto a life support as she plummeted to her death.

Just before she hit rock bottom, something woke her from the nightmare.

CHAPTER NINETY-SEVEN

Sophia, Lunis screamed in her mind, bringing her back to reality.

She straightened, realizing she'd been slumping against the wall. The spellbook had slipped from behind her back and landed at her feet. This caught the attention of the specter, but she still couldn't reach it, her leash not allowing her to close the distance.

Wake up, Lunis commanded. *Finish what you came here for.*

B-but, Sophia stuttered, realizing the mirror was still in her grasp. *I've been...*

Yes, you've been cursed, he said, pity in his voice. *We will deal with that later after you survive this. Do what you came here for.*

She nodded in reply and held up the hand mirror.

The specter seemed to expect this and narrowed her empty eye sockets at Sophia. Once more, she howled, but this time just once that spoke of her grief over losing.

For a moment, just like with Lee's mirror, nothing happened. Then a beam of purple light shot out of the reflective surface of the mirror. It instantly magnetized to the specter and wrapped around Tatiana, again and again, like a lasso.

Sophia gripped the handle tightly, thinking it would pop out of her hands if she wasn't careful. Her hands were so slick with sweat she

316

had to concentrate on her grip to keep the handle in place. The energy that ran down her arms from holding the mirror was overwhelming.

On top of that, it was incredibly fatiguing. Sophia couldn't imagine Lee having to maintain this for as long as she had. Holding one's arms straight out for a period of time was taxing enough but doing it when a force was rebounding around them, was quite another.

The tether gripped the specter tighter and tighter, all slack disappearing from the string of light. Sophia didn't know exactly when she should get the perfume bottle but felt powered by instinct. She continued to hold the handle tightly, believing she'd know when it was time.

Just as she stuck her faith in that belief, the specter yanked back a few feet and then forward again several times like a part of a weird tug-a-war. This happened until she was jerked into place and rose high into the air, suspended by the two strings of light.

The tether was complete.

CHAPTER NINETY-EIGHT

The strength it took to hold onto the mirror was so great that Sophia worried she couldn't release one hand to fetch the perfume bottle. However, when the tether was suddenly in place, all the energy rebounding from the hand mirror lessened greatly. It felt as though Sophia was just holding a regular mirror that wasn't connected to a suspended specter.

Still, her arms were fatigued and her legs and body were shaking from exertion.

Drawing in a breath, Sophia dared to take one of her hands off the mirror and slip it into the pocket of her cloak, where she found the small bottle with a silver lid. Using two fingers, she unscrewed the lid and knelt, careful to slide the glass bottle along the pavement without breaking it.

Sophia couldn't quite reach it all the way to the specter, which was hanging like a frozen statue in the air—an expression of horror stuck on her face.

Toeing the bottle, Sophia urged it a few feet forward until it was directly under the white figure.

The hand mirror shook in her grasp and Sophia held it tighter. It vibrated as the monster in the air began to shriek.

Unsure what was happening or if she'd done something wrong, Sophia watched with wide eyes. The specter began spinning in the air, at first slowly, like a ballerina on the top of a jewelry box and then quickly like an out of control ride at a carnival. Tatiana's screams filled the air, overwhelming Roya Lane, and breaking windows. The front display panes of the Fantastical Armory to the side of Sophia burst.

She winced from the explosion, turning her head to avoid getting glass shards on her skin.

Like being sucked down a toilet, the specter continued to spin as she shrunk and sank down into the bottle, like a genie disappearing after granting its wishes. The only wish that had been granted though, was that the specter was gone, and Sophia had survived to witness it.

The purple beam of light disappeared from the hand mirror, and Sophia was released from her job of holding up the object. She dropped her hand like a stone, feeling instant relief.

Striding forward, Sophia knelt and retrieved the perfume bottle, which was now full of a murky white substance. She screwed the cap onto the bottle and shook her head at the object. She couldn't believe that something so small could be full of so much evil. The only thing that mattered was that the specter had been contained and was no longer her problem, although Tatiana might have left Sophia with a new dilemma.

CHAPTER NINETY-NINE

Sophia nearly slammed the perfume bottle containing the specter onto the glass counter of the Fantastical Armory but decided it was probably best to not chance breaking the object and releasing the monster again.

Papa Creola casually glanced up, pulling his attention from a particularly perplexing crossword puzzle question.

"You could have mentioned the part about the leash running out," she said, bitterly.

"I could have," he replied, reaching out and taking the bottle and holding it up to the light.

"That wouldn't be very much fun for you since you feast off the adrenaline and fear I give off when I think I'm about to die, right?" she asked, mock curiosity on her face.

Papa Creola shook his head. "My job is to give you enough information so that you're successful, but not so much that you overthink things."

"I almost forgot to think when I nearly peed on myself," Sophia told him.

Lee entered the shop, rolling out her arm the way a baseball player does after a particularly grueling game. "Speaking of peeing on yourself, I nearly did waiting for this whole thing to wrap up. I should have remembered to take a potty break before we began. Imagine my anxiety when I'm holding a hand mirror that suddenly weighed as much as my wife and my bladder is like, 'Hey, time to empty me.'"

Sophia couldn't help but laugh. "Well, thanks for maintaining focus. If you had slipped up even a tiny bit, I would have been a goner. Especially at the end when the specter was only a few feet from me, at the end of her leash."

"Oh, is that how it worked?" Lee asked, combing her fingers over her chin and looking impressed.

"Well, not that anyone wanted to tell us that before, but yeah." Sophia gave Papa Creola a pointed expression.

"I don't know why you're so angry," he said. He was seriously perplexed why her near-death experience had her on edge. "You were successful and you didn't die."

"I was literally three feet from death," she argued. "Also, I believe that the monster cursed me."

Solemnly, Papa Creola nodded. "Yes, I believe that as well."

"Because you saw it?" Sophia asked.

He shook his head. "I see it about you."

Lee tilted her head to the side, regarding Sophia while squinting one. "She looks tired and a bit flustered, but I don't see anything cursed about her."

"It's marked on her soul," Papa Creola explained.

The assassin baker laughed. "Oh, that's not so bad. My soul was cursed a long time ago." She gave Sophia an encouraging smile. "Don't worry, souls are overrated. I don't think you actually need one. It's like deodorant. You're fine without it."

"You're wrong on both accounts," Papa Creola said before turning his attention to Sophia. "I will work on the method for removing the curse from you, but in the meantime, you'll have to manage."

"What does that mean?" Sophia asked.

"You'll suffer from hallucinations and the inability to sleep," Papa Creola stated matter-of-factly. "When you are able to fall asleep, you'll be plagued by nightmares."

Lee nodded and gave Sophia a commiserate expression. "So you'll pretty much be me."

Sophia shook off her friend's attempts to make light of something that sounded very serious. "Is there something that I can do?"

Papa Creola looked up and to the right, seeing something that none of them could. "You were given something for your birthday that will help, but unfortunately only marginally. It is better than nothing, though."

Sophia thought about the things she had been gifted for her birthday. Mama Jamba had given her a pair of shiny earrings she said would possibly save her life. There were a few other things that could help, but Sophia needed to get back to the Castle and see firsthand. More than anything, she longed to get back after this adventure and hug her dragon and feel Wilder's warmth.

It wasn't lost on Sophia how much she craved the ones she'd grown to love with such fierceness. They were the reasons she wanted to save the world, and they were the comfort she needed once she'd gotten one step closer to making the planet a safer place.

"Good work on containing the specter," Papa Creola complimented her, having glossed over which present would actually help Sophia. She didn't think he was going to provide any more details. That was fine because she was prepared to figure it out herself.

Making for the door, she waved at the father of time as he retreated for the back. "Anytime that you need my help, just call someone else."

"I'll message you when I've had time to look into your curse," he said, a promise in his voice.

"Time!" Lee said with a laugh, slapping her knee and going over to the counter where Subner was hunched, reading a magazine on how to make bongs.

"See you later, Lee," Sophia said, waving to her friend. "Try and stay out of trouble until the next time I see you."

The baker assassin shook her head, glancing over her shoulder at Sophia. "Fat chance of that, but good job on surviving and all. I'd pick you to be on my kickball team."

"Thanks," Sophia said, actually proud of that. She'd never played team sports and hadn't had a normal schooling experience with physical education classes, but always feared that if she had, her height would make it so she was picked last for team sports activities. "Good work to you today. I really couldn't have done it without you."

"That's true," Lee stated. "Don't worry, you'll get my bill."

"Can't wait," Sophia chimed, heading for the door as Lee turned her attention back to the owner and operator of the Fantastical Armory.

"Can I take a look at those Chinese throwing stars?" the baker assassin asked. "I think I could bake something like that into a cake."

CHAPTER ONE HUNDRED

With a new pride for Baba Yaga's spellbook, Sophia slid it into a locked vault she found installed in the wall in her room. It was brand new, not having been there when she left.

After shutting the door to the safe, she glanced up at the ceiling and smiled. "Thanks, Castle. You seem to know what I need before I even do, somehow."

Sophia watched as the flames in the torches on the walls grew brighter and then dimmed, the Castle saying, "You're welcome," in its own way. Like Ainsley and now Trin, Sophia was starting to understand the language of the Castle. She could understand how complicated and confusing it must be for Trin to learn since she'd have to work so closely with the Castle. Sophia still stood by the decision to make the cyborg the housekeeper. She was the right choice and would soon adapt to the strange magic that ran this place.

Thankfully, Sophia hadn't experienced any of the hallucinations Papa Creola said would be a part of the curse from the specter known as Tatiana. She hoped they didn't happen, or he found the cure before they started.

Her eyes slid to her large four-poster bed, and although she was exhausted and it was night at the Gullington, she feared closing her eyes, knowing she'd be plagued by nightmares.

The guys, according to Hiker, were all off, dispersing the cure that Bep had made for distortion. It warmed Sophia's soul to know magicians and elves suffering worldwide would be cured and have their magical powers back.

That also meant there was no one to eat dinner with or take her mind off her new troubles. Sophia's soul might be warmed by the cure she helped to get, but it was also cursed too.

She strode over to the table where her birthday gifts were sitting, not having had the opportunity to really appreciate them since the party.

There was the pair of pants Ainsley gave her back, which had originally belonged to her. That reminded Sophia that soon she'd have to return to the Silk Armor to get the shapeshifter's dress.

Her gaze slid to the walk-in closet Trin and Quiet had built for her. That didn't seem like the thing that would relieve her new affliction.

The silver loop earrings from Mama Jamba were beautiful and sparkly, but she still didn't think they'd be what would help her with this problem. Still, she pulled off the backs of the earrings and put them into her ears. It wouldn't hurt to wear them.

Lunis had offered her a bunch of jokes for her birthday, and that did make her soul feel better, especially when facing real danger. No one made her laugh like her dragon.

Her eyes fell on her phone on the corner of her desk, and Sophia remembered what Wilder had given her—a playlist of songs he'd made on Spotify.

"Castle, please play Haggis," she said, naming the list Wilder had titled based on their running joke about the food served on her first night at the Castle.

The song that started playing was one that Sophia had heard, but not in this form. It was *Teenage Dream*, but sang from a guy's perspective, instead of Katy Perry's.

"I think you're pretty without any make-up on," the singer began, instantly making Sophia smile. Wilder was definitely good for her soul. He was healing. He was like home.

"I think you're funny when you tell the punchline wrong," the singer continued, making Sophia laugh, remembering how many times she'd botched up jokes she'd told Wilder. He always smiled at her in his usual endearing way.

The playlist would make her feel better, but it wasn't what would aid her with this curse.

Hiker had given Sophia advice about knowing when to rest and when to fight. That seemed like rude irony now. She didn't want to close her eyes, fearful of the nightmares she'd have.

Then her eyes slid to the far corner of the table, where Mahkah's birthday gift was partially obscured by the pants Ainsley had returned. The stoic dragonrider had thoughtfully given Sophia a dreamcatcher.

Her fingers were trembling when she reached out for the beautifully constructed dreamcatcher done in turquoise and made of braided leather. Like a spider web, it had a stone suspended in the center. Sophia held it up in the air and let it dangle.

"Of course," she said out loud to herself. It might not work totally, but the gift would hopefully catch most of the bad dreams she'd been cursed with.

She pressed the dreamcatcher to her chest, feeling grateful for her friends, whose thoughtfulness would undoubtedly be her strength and quite possibly save her life.

CHAPTER ONE HUNDRED ONE

"How many more maps do you need?" Nevin Gooseman asked, leaning over King Rudolf Sweetwater, the vein in his forehead pronounced.

Surprisingly, for the fae, it hadn't taken him very long to fluster the politician. Now he just had to stall a little longer until he found more information to help Sophia and Liv take the evil man down.

"Well, these just aren't good enough," Rudolf replied, sweeping his arm at the stack of maps of Tanzania and Zanzibar. He wasn't worried that these guys now knew the approximate location of the Great Library.

Many knew this information and still couldn't find the magical library after months of searching. They didn't know to look for the Fierce, and that was the only way to find the location. They usually gave up, never finding the Great Library. However, there was no Fierce now. Instead, Plato had cloaked the library until Rudolf gave Liv the heads up that they were ready to storm the place.

Before that, Rudolf was stealthily searching for information on the magitech military Nevin Gooseman planned to use to destroy the Great Library—not that it was going to happen. Then Rudolf needed evidence that would discredit the politician and prove he was behind the things he blamed on the Dragon Elite.

The lines around Nevin Gooseman's lips deepened as he frowned. Rudolf considered telling the man but decided he'd save it for later when he was really angry. "What kind of map do you need?"

"It's hard to say," Rudolf began, unrolling a map and studying it. "Something that highlights all the food cart vendors would be good."

"Why?"

"Well, because that's an excellent bit of information that explains how the Great Library has shifted location," Rudolf explained.

"You can tell the location based on where the food vendors are located?" Nevin asked.

"In every city in the world, you can tell tons of stuff based on where food vendors set up shop," Rudolf imparted. "They know the flow of traffic and capitalize on it."

Nevin Gooseman nodded slowly, looking to one of the many men with uptight expressions he kept around all the time. They were the worst and never laughed at Rudolf's jokes. The king of the fae was pretty certain that most of them peed sitting down and lived on large amounts of Metamucil.

"Can we get that information?" Nevin asked one of the suits.

A man with thinning hair and an expression on his face like he'd smelled something bad, nodded. "Yes, sir. I'll have our guys work on that." He pressed his hand to the earbud attached to the side of his head and began speaking in a whisper to the team they had stationed in Zanzibar. Rudolf had already sent them on various tasks, making them count the number of tiles on the old bell tower and measure the refraction of light during different times of day from the square in Stone Town.

Nevin continued to send them on these strange tasks because he was desperate and believed Rudolf was his only chance of finding the Great Library. When the time was right, when he had everything he needed and the sisters were ready, the king would lead the politician to the library where his magitech army would get its ass handed to them.

"Oh!" Rudolf chirped excitedly. "And also I need a map that details the population density, stating how many people live in each area."

"Like a census?" Nevin Gooseman asked, calming a bit. This was a reasonable request. That would not do.

"Yes, but it must be very accurate, down to the exact amount of cats in Stone Town," Rudolf answered.

"Why?" Nevin growled.

"Because cats, similar to the food vendors, give an indication of where the Great Library is."

The old, stuffy magician's nostrils flared. "Why do I get the impression you're sending us on a wild goose chase?"

"Wild cat chase," Rudolf corrected and then shrugged. "I'm telling you what I need to find the Great Library. I mean, if you know of someone else who knows how to track down the location, then by all means, have them help you, but I was the Fierce and know how to find it." He gave them a proud expression, pressing his hand to his chest. "I led Sophia Beaufont to it very quickly."

"How long?" Nevin questioned.

Rudolf teetered his head back and forth, clicking his tongue as he thought. "Oh, I think it took a quick six or eight weeks." He was lying, but Nevin didn't need to know that.

Pushing up off the desk where they'd been going through this for hours, Nevin shook his head. "Why does it have to take so long? All of this strange information you need." He tossed his hand in the direction of the maps lying to the side. "What's with that?"

Rudolf flattened the map in front of him, ironing out the creases and pretending to study it. "There's complex magic that hides the Great Library. It changes places often, and only those who know what to look for can find it. Once you do, then you have access to every book in the world. There's a monumental amount of power in these books."

This made Nevin Gooseman smile wickedly. "Yes, that's what I've heard."

The politician didn't know that Rudolf had overheard his conversation about his plans for the Great Library. He thought that by gaining access to the place, he'd be able to find the way to reverse the spell the Dragon Elite used to hide the evil dragons. After that, the magitech army planned on destroying the Great Library. Nevin thought it was too powerful of a place and didn't like that it was only available for a few chosen magicians.

The politician didn't realize he was proving exactly why most shouldn't know about the Great Library. Knowledge was power, and many abused it. The Dragon Elite always had access to the library, since it was part of their job to protect the planet. A select few magicians had learned of its location. Then there was Rudolf.

"If we get you this information, will you be able to lead me to the Great Library?" Nevin asked, narrowing his eyes at Rudolf.

He drummed his finger on the table, studying the map. "Hard to say. Hard to say."

"Why?" Nevin Gooseman demanded. He really loved that question. It was always, "Why do you refuse to sleep on the bed in your cell?" or "Why do you talk to yourself at night?" or "Why do you smell like rum?"

The answers to those questions were as follows according to Rudolf:

"Because the bed is covered in atrocious plaid sheets that have maybe a thread count of like two-hundred."

"I'm talking to Liv at night because I've got my magic. You don't know that since I refuse to eat your poisoned food."

"I drank all your rum and refilled the bottle with water, but you won't realize that until you have your next uptight party, and I'm long gone."

However, Rudolf never said these things to Nevin Gooseman. Instead, he made up plausible answers. The politician didn't need to know Rudolf was sneaking out of his room at night, using magic and raiding the big metal container that stored food. It was really a cold box, but he decided that it was probably to keep it safe from snakes since they didn't like low temperatures.

Rudolf was able to get his magical reserves up each night, and now his magic was fully back, but Nevin Gooseman had no idea. Actually he had fired one of his many bodyguards, thinking the man with wide shoulders and a flat nose was responsible for eating all of his caviar. Rudolf suspected the brute didn't enjoy finer foods, but he had enjoyed each bite as he sat on the floor next to the metal box while drinking a bottle of champagne.

"It's hard to say how long it will take to find the Great Library," Rudolf began, "because the place moves when it senses someone who isn't supposed to be looking for it is on the hunt. So technically, you're the reason it's taking so long."

Nevin Gooseman seethed with visible anger. "The place shouldn't exist in the first place, and if it does, I should have access to it. Everyone should, but that's fine. I'll remedy that."

"By getting a library card for everyone in the world?" Rudolf asked. Pretending to play dumb was exceptionally difficult for him.

"No," Nevin barked, glaring down at the fae. "Why are you looking at that map upside down?"

More with the "why" questions. This guy just needed to know the answer to everything. Sometimes there was power in not knowing. Ignorance could be bliss. Look at Rudolf. He didn't know the answers to so many questions, and he was the happiest person in the world. He didn't know what the periodic table was or what furniture stores sold it, and he wasn't about to ask around for the answer. The cold box in the food room could remain a mystery for all he cared, and he didn't need to know how magicians looked at themselves in the mirror without falling into a constant depression. Rudolf really didn't understand that last one, but he was fine with never knowing the answer.

He glanced up at Nevin Gooseman and smiled. "How do you know that the map is upside down? Maybe this is the right side up? It's all about perspective."

Nevin looked on the verge of choking Rudolf, which made the king very happy.

"Sir," one of the suits by the door said, trying to get Nevin's attention.

"What?" he asked with a hiss.

"The Dragon Elite has a cure for distortion," the man explained, his voice full of disappointment. "They are disseminating it now."

"What?" Nevin boomed.

That man really loved one-word questions, Rudolf thought, wondering what he'd get drunk on later when the house was quiet, and he could take on his camouflage form and sneak around.

"It's true, sir. I'm sorry," the man who worked for the politician said.

Nevin appeared angry by the realization that thousands of magicians and elves would be saved from an awful disease. "They just won't stop, will they?'

"No, sir," the man replied. "That's how it seems."

"Well, that's fine," Nevin stated, making for the door. "I'll just twist this to our advantage."

At the threshold to the study, Nevin spun around. "Find the Great Library. Do it now, Rudolf."

He left the room in a hurry, his guards watching Rudolf from various places.

The fae smiled to himself, proud the Dragon Elite had been successful. Now he just needed to do his part so they could finally take down the power-hungry politician.

CHAPTER ONE HUNDRED TWO

"You look like hell," Hiker Wallace said when Sophia trudged into his office the next morning. She'd decided to skip breakfast since none of the guys were there, and the leader of the Dragon Elite had taken his meal in his study, fed up with waiting around for food in the dining room.

"Thank you, sir," Sophia said, dragging herself into the office and sliding onto the couch next to Mama Jamba, who was polishing off a plate of pancakes that appeared a bit overdone.

"You got back last night," Hiker said, putting his teacup down. "Did you not sleep?"

"I did but poorly," Sophia told him. "I was cursed by an evil specter who was after Baba Yaga's grimoire, which I loaned to the potion maker on Roya Lane to replicate the cure for distortion that I got from Rumi."

Mama Jamba nodded. "That was going to be my guess."

Hiker frowned at the old woman. "That? That was going to be your shot in the dark for why Sophia has dark bags under her eyes?"

Mama pushed the tray away, farther onto the coffee table. "Honestly, I didn't see the part about it being on Roya Lane coming, but the rest was my best guess."

333

Shaking his head at Mama Jamba, Hiker turned his attention to the television, which was broadcasting coverage of the Dragon Elite distributing the cure for distortion all around the world and healing thousands. "Well, good work on getting the cure. This is exactly what we needed."

A reporter stood in front of a crowd of magicians who were lined up in front of Wilder and Simi. The dragonrider was calmly handing out the small bottles of red liquid, receiving grateful expressions from the sickly looking magicians and elves who were blurring like there was a problem with the television screen. A ping in Sophia's chest reminded her that even if she was exhausted, her heart was still beating and tied tightly to the guy on the screen who was playing the part of a hero with elegance and humility.

Sophia suspected that the dreamcatcher Mahkah had given her had worked to keep most of the nightmares at bay. However, her dreams were still disturbing and had jolted her awake all night, preventing her from getting any real restful sleep.

"So you've been cursed," Hiker said matter-of-factly, returning his gaze to her. "What does it involve?"

Mama Jamba picked up the wax ball she'd been working on before —the spell they'd use to find the demon dragons around the world. She began molding it while giving Sophia an interested expression. "Evil specters can cast some really nasty spells. Did they curse you to not be able to sleep?"

Sophia nodded. "Pretty much. Tatiana Jerkface put a mark on my soul that makes it difficult to fall asleep and gives me nightmares and hallucinations."

Mama Jamba lowered her chin, studying Sophia. "Oh, I see it now. Yes, that's an ugly little mark."

"That won't do," Hiker stated. "We need you rested. We've got missions."

"Thanks for the concern regarding my soul, sir," Sophia muttered.

He sighed. "Of course, I'm worried about your soul, but getting rest is the first priority. Mama, what can you do to fix this?"

"Fix it?" she questioned, raising an eyebrow at Hiker. "Not a thing.

Curses aren't something I can erase. Even if I could, angels prevent me from doing anything with souls."

"Papa Creola is looking into the matter," Sophia informed them. "In the meantime, I just have to manage."

"That's the spirit, dear," Mama Jamba cheered.

"The Castle should be helping, I suspect," Hiker related, his attention back on the television.

"It must," Sophia agreed. "I was able to go to sleep, but not really stay asleep. Mahkah's dreamcatcher also helped."

"Good, then you'll be all right," Hiker said absentmindedly. "What is going on with the Ainsley stuff?"

"It's all in the process," Sophia said, slumping down on the couch and feel like she could fall asleep immediately.

He nodded, not appearing concerned that she looked painfully tired.

"It was cute that you forgot to tell me Jeremy Bearimy was a giant tarantula," Sophia said through a big yawn.

"Did I forget to mention that?" Hiker asked, no remorse in his voice. "Oh, well. I'm sure that was a surprise for you."

"I nearly sliced him with my sword," she informed him.

"That would have been a travesty," Mama Jamba said, pressing the wax flat like pizza dough.

"Yeah, you should really refrain from pulling out your sword when you encounter something different," Hiker said, leaning forward and watching the television screen. "I expect you to show a bit more discretion when sizing up situations."

"I expect you to tell me when you're sending me to a seamstress who happens to be a huge spider," Sophia fired back.

"It slipped my mind." He picked up the remote and turned up the volume as Nevin Gooseman came on the screen, standing smugly behind a podium in front of the White House.

Sophia sat up, wondering what the politician would have to say. Maybe he'd praise the Dragon Elite for finding a cure. Maybe he'd take partial credit for it. Or maybe he'd get off their backs since they'd proven to the world they were there to help heal and not cause problems.

Nevin Gooseman cleared his throat and looked at the camera. "The recent events related to the cure of distortion undoubtedly prove something of incredible significance. The Dragon Elite are responsible for this disease and should be punished."

CHAPTER ONE HUNDRED THREE

"Dude, what is wrong with this guy?" Sophia groaned as noisy chatter broke out from the crowd of reporters gathered in front of Nevin Gooseman.

"Shush," Hiker encouraged, giving Sophia a punishing glare before looking back at the television.

When the noise had settled down, the politician with an unrelenting vendetta against the Dragon Elite continued. "They want to be seen as good Samaritans, as our saviors. The Dragon Elite wants us to thank them for curing the world of this horrendous disease affecting magicians, elves, and who knows who else. I implore you all to not be fooled by them. We cannot allow ourselves to be manipulated."

Nevin Gooseman paused and narrowed his eyes with hostility and shook his head. "I ask you all, great citizens, if someone saves you from a fire, would you praise them if you found out they lit the match that burned your house down? Of course not! How very convenient that our best scientists, doctors, and healers couldn't find a cure for this devastating disease known as distortion. Miraculously, the Dragon Elite, who have been stuck in the dark ages, found a cure and at record speed."

The crowd broke out in a commotion, hushed voices speaking

with urgency. Nevin Gooseman's gaze slid over the reporters before returning to the television camera.

"It seems to me," he continued with a new vehemence in this tone, "that those in the best position to have the cure to this disease are the very people who are responsible for it."

"Oh, I'm going to kill him," Sophia fired, sitting forward as the crowd on the television broke out in even more chatter.

"Not if I do it first," Hiker said through clenched teeth.

"It stands to reason," Nevin Gooseman went on, "that having access to dragons, the very creatures responsible for spreading distortion among our magical communities, would therefore have the resources to create the cure. Or maybe they manufactured this disease and had the cure long before they started infecting their own race. I don't know how the Dragon Elite did this, but I know they are behind the spread of distortion and must not be bowed to in praise for dispersing a cure.

"As a servant to you all, I promise that I will get to the bottom of this. I will unearth the truth. I will ensure the Dragon Elite doesn't take the power they think they deserve and abuse it. If anything, this should prove to our great nation, to our beautiful planet, that the Dragon Elite will go to great lengths to fool you into trusting them. I fear to think what they will do when you blindly turn over that valuable trust. I urge you, intelligent people, not to allow yourself to be fooled. Don't allow them to steal power they don't deserve and will surely abuse."

Nevin Gooseman paused, no doubt for effect before plastering a grave expression on his face. "We are in real trouble. Not only do the Dragon Elite have the power to spread disease, but where is Mother Nature? I asked that Hiker Wallace, their leader, show us proof she lives and that she supports them and he has refused. Yes, he's made statements, but nothing about Mother Nature, and now I dread the very worst."

He shook his head, and lowered his chin, then stepped back from the podium like he was paying his respects at a funeral. "I fear that Mother Nature is dead at the hands of the Dragon Elite."

CHAPTER ONE HUNDRED FOUR

"He did exactly what I expect from a politician," Hiker seethed. "He twisted the events so they worked for his agenda."

The leader of the Dragon Elite had bolted up from his desk at the conclusion of the press conference and begun pacing his office, his boots thundering across the floor.

"He's playing on people's fears." Sophia's anger was fuming as well, waking her up from her tired state.

"Before Nevin Gooseman had this 'Free Mother Nature' campaign going," Hiker began, still stomping. "Now, he's making the world believe that we've killed you."

"That doesn't make any sense," Sophia reasoned. "If Mama Jamba was dead, then what would happen to this planet?"

"It would go to hell quickly," Hiker replied. "There would be natural disasters and disease and chaos."

Sophia pressed back on the couch, nodding slowly. "Which is exactly what's happening globally."

"Yeah, but not because Mama is dead but rather because Nevin Gooseman has created so much turmoil, playing on mortals' fears," Hiker pointed out. "Magicians too. No one will trust us after this."

"You have to make a statement and address this directly," Sophia encouraged, glancing at Mama Jamba, who didn't seem to mind that the topic of the conversation concerned her and rumors she was dead. She continued to mold her ball of wax.

Hiker nodded. "I realize that. I'll tell the public Mama Jamba can't be convinced to come out of hiding by a two-bit politician." He actually grinned. "That will hit Nevin Gooseman below the belt."

"Yeah, and you should say something about the potions expert who created the cure for distortion," Sophia suggested. "Bep will back us up as not having created the cure. If we did, then why would I need her help to replicate it?"

"That's a good idea," Hiker said. He flipped off the television, disgusted by the sight of the angry mortals being interviewed after the press conference. "However, at this point, it's just our word against his, and we're not going to stoop to his level and manipulate the public, which I fear is why we'll lose this."

"We're not going to lose this, sir," Sophia encouraged.

"Well, excuse me for not being convinced of that," Hiker growled. "Nevin Gooseman has the mortals in the palm of his hand. He's convincing the magical communities to not trust us. We're not any closer to finding any information on him. Without that, no matter what we do, we can't win. We heal the world of a disease, and we're seen as enemies. We protect the world, and we're viewed as power-hungry. I just don't know what to do."

"Good thing that I do," a voice on the turned off television said.

Sophia's eyes widened in shock as the head of King Rudolf Sweetwater bobbed around on the blank monitor.

CHAPTER ONE HUNDRED FIVE

"What the hell?" Hiker exclaimed, his eyes bulging.

Sophia jumped to her feet.

Mama Jamba smiled, like the king of the fae's face showing up on a television wasn't bizarre.

"King Rudolf," Sophia said with urgency. "What are you doing?"

"Lying on the floor of my cell in my birthday suit," he replied.

Sophia shook her head. "I mostly meant, what are you doing here on the television screen in the Castle at the Gullington?"

"Oh," he said with a wide smile. "Television screen. That makes sense. It's easier for me to project myself on electronic devices using my magic, but I never know where I'll end up. It sort of depends on where you are."

"Keep the view to just your face," Hiker advised, sitting down in his chair and gazing intently at the king of the fae.

"Oh, but he has a very nice birthday suit," Mama Jamba gushed.

"Why, thank you. I work out." Rudolf winked. "By work out, I mean that I have a lot of se—"

"Anyway, Liv says that you're okay," Sophia interrupted.

He frowned. "That's a relative statement. I have to look at really

341

homely faces all day long, but you are probably used to that, having been raised with ugly magicians, Soph."

She let out a long breath and gave Hiker an encouraging expression that said, "He's here to help us. Don't reach into the television and strangle him."

"What have you learned?" Hiker asked.

"So much," Rudolf began. "There's this really strange patch of land behind Nevin Gooseman's land that is enclosed with a fence and has grass and is lined with shrubs. It's the strangest thing."

"You mean a yard?" Sophia questioned.

Rudolf pressed out his lips and shrugged. "Don't know what it's called. But if that was my property, I'd cover it with concrete and build a casino there."

"Sometimes I regret creating the fae," Mama Jamba remarked casually.

"Sometimes?" Hiker asked, glancing at the old woman.

"Well, they are wonderful to look at," she argued. "But in creating them that way, I made them vain and shallow. No one is perfect."

"Ru," Sophia said, trying to steer the conversation back on track. "What have you learned that pertains to the Dragon Elite?"

"Well," he began. "Nevin isn't happy about you curing distortion."

Hiker groaned. "We know. He just released a statement. It's definitely going to knock us back down."

"I can pee in Nevin's houseplants if that helps," Rudolf offered.

"It doesn't." Hiker gave Sophia a look that said, "How are you friends with this guy?"

"What else?" Sophia urged at the television screen. "Anything linking Nevin Gooseman to bad activity? Anything we can use to bring him down or discredit him?"

"Not yet," Rudolf answered with disappointment. "But don't worry. I'm going to do some more searching tonight after I eat a tube of cookie dough and drink a bottle of rosé."

Mama Jamba clapped her hands excitedly and gave Hiker a wide smile. "That's what we should do tonight!"

"Pass," he replied.

Mama Jamba deflated slightly, then glanced at Sophia. "I'd ask you, but you won't be here."

"Where will she be?" Hiker questioned.

She pointed at the television screen. "Don't be rude, son. You have company."

"There is something that I learned while Nevin was out doing his little press conference," Rudolf continued.

Hiker leaned forward, his chin down. "Go on then."

Sophia braced herself, hoping it wasn't something that killed any more of her brain cells.

"Well, it appears that Nevin has a magitech army he plans on using to destroy the Great Library after getting the information he's after," Rudolf told them.

Sophia nodded. "Yes, Liv told me."

"There's more," Rudolf went on. "Apparently, he learned of the technology that you used to disable the magitech devices when you took down Thad Reinhart's company."

Drawing in a breath, Hiker sat back in his chair, disappointment heavy on his face.

Sophia felt her own regret. They'd been hoping they could rely on that technology to take down the military forces, which would have several advantages with their weapons paired with magic. Alicia, the magitech scientist, had created a small and unassuming device that when used would power down technology like planes, missiles, and other weapons that used magic.

"How is he always one step ahead of us?" Hiker asked, bitterly.

"Well, he's been following you closely since you came back to the waking world," Rudolf said, sounding mature and articulate. "Snooping around, I found he collected every bit of information that covered your takedown of Thad Reinhart and his corporation. Then he further investigated the battle you had with the cyborgs and Saverus. Nevin Gooseman has been planning this for a while. He sees the Dragon Elite as a huge threat, and he has gone to great lengths to ensure the world does too. I suspect he's not going to stop until he's won, or you've put him away for good."

Hiker nodded. "I think you're right. I just don't get his motive."

"He firmly believes the Dragon Elite is too powerful," Rudolf continued. "Strangely enough, I don't think he likes his own race of magicians. His power comes from being worshipped by mortals in this new world where they see magicians as protectors. You, the Dragon Elite, threaten that. Furthermore, those with their own agendas, can't compete when they have to bow to the checks and balances of an organization more powerful than them."

Sophia was stunned to hear the king of the fae speak with such intelligence. She started to wonder if being imprisoned was making him smarter.

Then he followed up his last statement with, "Side note. Mama Jamba, is it possible to erase kale from the planet?"

She thought for a moment and shook her head. "The hippies really like it, so I'm afraid not."

"Apparently boring magicians too," Rudolf complained. "I keep finding it in the cold box in the food room, and it is simply awful."

"Do you mean the refrigerator in the kitchen?" Sophia asked, tilting her head and wondering how Rudolf had gone so many centuries without learning such information.

He shook his head. "I'm going to have to ring off if you're going to start speaking French. That language always makes me think about impressionist painters, and then I get hives." He visibly shivered. "Seriously, Mama Jamba, can we erase Monet, Renoir, and Matisse from the timeline for good?"

She gave him a polite smile. "I'm afraid you'll have to take that up with Papa Creola, dear."

"Will do," Rudolf sang. "Anywho, that's all I've got for now. I'm going to go and eat on Nevin's white couch naked. Seriously, why someone would buy a cream-colored couch when leopard print is always an option, really astounds me."

"Thanks for the information," Sophia told him gratefully. "Please keep us abreast of what else you learn and stay safe."

Rudolf giggled, covering his mouth. "You said 'breast.'"

CHAPTER ONE HUNDRED SIX

"How is that the leader of an entire race?" Hiker asked, shaking his head when the television screen went blank once more, and King Rudolf's face had disappeared.

"The fae aren't smart," Mama Jamba explained. "They thought the statue of David was their leader for a century. It was only when he refused to settle a dispute that a particularly keen fae realized he was made of stone and not just quiet and stoic in nature."

"For the love of the angels," Hiker said, thrusting his fingers into his hair. "We're relying on this fae to help us in our mission to take Nevin Gooseman down?"

"He can be trusted and relied upon," Sophia argued. "I know he seems like an airhead but—"

"Seems?" Hiker interrupted. "I know sheep that are smarter than that man."

"I get it," Sophia agreed. "King Rudolf has a way of surprising. He has always come through for me, and he has strange moments of genius."

"It's true," Mama Jamba added. "He's already come through for you, son. You know now that you can't rely on the device you have to take down the magitech army."

Hiker nodded solemnly. "Yes, but I'm not sure what to do about it."

"Me either," Mama Jamba said. "I think Sophia knows of someone who might have a lead for her." She gave Sophia a pointed expression that at first, she couldn't decipher.

Then it occurred to Sophia and she straightened. "Oh! Right. Yes, Mae Ling. She might be able to help."

"I think so," Mama Jamba said, twirling her hands into her hair and plucking out a single strand. "Like I said, you wouldn't be able to have cookie dough and wine with me tonight, but maybe another time."

Sophia smiled, thinking of how much fun it would be to indulge like that with Mother Nature. "I'd like that."

"What I'd like is for you to take a little nap before you go," Mama Jamba said, slipping into her maternal voice.

Hanging her head, Sophia sighed. "Yeah, easier said than done."

"For some," Mama Jamba said. She held out a grayish-blue strand for Sophia. "Here you go."

"Thank you," Sophia said uncertainly.

"You're very welcome."

Sophia didn't take the piece of hair, but instead looked at Hiker like, "What the hell am I supposed to do with that?"

He shook his head.

"Go on now, dear. Take it." Mama Jamba continued to hold out her single strand of hair. "Tie that around your finger and close your eyes. It should get you to sleep fast and keep the dreams from over-whelming you. That will get you at least caught up on rest. However, I can't really help you out more than that as I really do love my full head of hair."

"Oh, thanks," Sophia exclaimed. "I'll try not to lose the piece of hair." Even as she said it, Sophia realized how ridiculous it sounded, to keep tabs on a tiny strand of hair. Still, she was grateful for the solution, even if it didn't last for long. Holding tight to the strand of hair, Sophia headed for her bedroom, looking forward to getting some proper sleep uninterrupted by nightmares.

CHAPTER ONE HUNDRED SEVEN

As Mae Ling had requested the last time Sophia visited her at the fairy godmother college, she brought Lunis with her on this trip. She knew he'd enjoy the opportunity to get out of the Gullington since none of the other older dragons were there, and the dragonettes were "stressing" him out.

Also, Sophia suspected he'd soak up the attention he'd no doubt be lavished with from the students at Happily Ever After college. The rest of the world might be fearful of dragons, thinking they spread a strange disease, but not fairy godmothers in training. They had Mae Ling and the other faculty imparting their wisdom, full of facts and not based on emotion like the propaganda Nevin Gooseman was offloading on the world.

How do I look? Lunis asked as they stepped through the portal to fairy godmother college.

She shook her head at the dragon. "You look the same as you always do."

He scoffed. *You have pillow creases on your face.*

"Good," she chirped, grateful for the solid bit of rest she'd gotten thanks to Mama Jamba. She had managed to take the piece of grayish-blue hair and set it on her bedside table after the nap and hoped to find it there later. She made a note for Trin and Ainsley, asking them not to dust. She couldn't lose that piece of hair.

Wow, what a beautiful place, Lunis said, gazing around the grassy green lawns of Happily Ever After College like a puppy ready to take off running. The cool breeze wafted through the trees, bringing a floral scent to their noses as songbirds serenaded them overhead.

"It's always the perfect temperature here," Sophia explained. "And always spring."

I'm not going home, he told her seriously.

"That's not an option."

It's cold in Scotland and always rains, he argued.

"You're a dragon," she said. "Get over it."

A series of excited screams echoed from behind them. They both spun around to see a few students rushing over, wide smiles on their faces as they sped in their direction, their hands outstretched.

"A real dragon!" one of the fairy godmothers in training exclaimed.

"He's dreamy!" another said.

"Oh, what a beauty," the third stated, sounding breathless.

They all halted a few yards from the dragon and bowed low.

Sophia nearly rolled her eyes but was secretly grateful to see the proud expression sparkle in her dragon's eyes. He bent his front leg and knelt slightly.

It is a pleasure to make your acquaintance, he said, sounding regal and very un-Lunis-like.

At the students' backs was the rest of the class, who appeared to have been gathered around a herd of unicorns. They were hurrying over, the same as the three girls, Mae Ling with them.

One of the students that had run over first looked at Sophia. "Can we pet him?"

She shrugged. "That's not my call. Dragons aren't pets, and I'm not in charge of him. He makes his own decisions."

The student stepped forward, her hand held tentatively to her chest. "Would it…I mean…is it…do you think…?"

Lunis, in reply to the question she couldn't seem to get out, lowered his head, indicating she could touch him.

She gasped with surprise and carefully laid her dainty hand on the top of his horn-lined head.

"Wow, this is magical," she gushed as the rest of the class arrived, all of them wearing awed expressions at the sight of the blue dragon.

"Thank you for bringing Lunis for the students to see," Mae Ling said, her kind eyes shining brightly.

"You're welcome." Sophia watched as the students eagerly crowded around the dragon, all of them putting their hands on his blue scales, and marveling at the experience.

She backed away and found herself next to Mae Ling.

"He is breathtaking," the fairy godmother said. "What an honor it is to have him here."

"I'm not responsible for any of his bad jokes," Sophia teased, earning a smile from Mae Ling.

"Let's allow Lunis to soak up the much deserved attention while we stroll." Holding up her arm, Mae Ling indicated a grassy path covered with little white flowers.

"Okay," Sophia said, looking back at Lunis. His attention was occupied by the many questions he was getting from the students.

"You have quite a few projects going on." It was a statement rather than a question from Mae Ling.

"Yes, that's true," Sophia affirmed. "Most are in other people's hands presently, but I did come to you to ask for help with a certain one."

Her fairy godmother nodded. "Magitech can be used to fix the world, and it can also be used to destroy it."

As Sophia suspected, Mae Ling was already privy to why she was there, although Sophia usually still needed to ask the question to receive help.

"Yes, and we're a bit stumped with how to combat this military magitech when the time comes," Sophia related. "The options we were relying on are gone, and we can't risk the Great Library being destroyed."

"Quite right," Mae Ling said, heat flaring in her eyes. She was obviously very put off by what Nevin Gooseman was doing. For many, destroying a library was like burning down a forest. Both were made up of trees that changed the world and made it a better place.

"Do you have any ideas to offer me?" Sophia asked, enjoying the fresh air on her face and vibrant, rich colors all around them. Being on the campus of Happily Ever After college was always a healing experience. The place was full of all the good things in the world. It was no wonder it churned out fairy godmothers that brought love to so many.

"I know of the place you need to visit to find the devices that will help you to gain an advantage," Mae Ling answered, striding beside Sophia, her hands behind her back and her long robes kicking out in front of her as she moved.

"That would be really helpful." Sophia was relieved, although she wasn't sure why. Mae Ling was always helpful to her, albeit it was usually full of riddles, much like Mama Jamba and Papa Creola.

Mae Ling paused and held up a finger, giving Sophia a cautious expression. "Before you thank me, please note the journey to get that which you seek will take you far from home, far from the comforts you know, and far from your dragon."

Sophia tensed and her throat constricted. "Lunis? I have to leave Lunis?"

"You should keep him here," Mae Ling said gently. "I can use him to educate the students and having him close will help me to shield you from dangers."

"Shield me?"

"Where you need to go isn't protected in the same ways as Earth," Mae Ling explained.

"Wait, I'm leaving Earth?"

Mae Ling looked out toward the clear blue skies that provided the background to the canopy of green trees overhead. "There's a world out there. You've only seen a fraction of it, and yet you've seen more than most. But yes, to find something to help you to defeat Nevin Gooseman's magitech army, you're going to need something that isn't from this world."

"But leaving Earth…is that safe?" Sophia asked and instantly felt silly.

"Well, you've left before when you went to Oriceran and other dimensions," Mae Ling replied. "There are no doubt risks, but like I said, if you leave Lunis with me, I can tap into his magic and use it to protect you. Not completely, but to a certain extent."

Sophia nodded slowly, trying to wrap her mind around this new information. "Am I going to a different planet? Will I be okay there? Who am I looking for? What do I ask them? Will they speak my language? Will I be able to breathe? Should I wear a suit?"

Mae Ling actually laughed. "Don't worry. It's mostly safe, but no, it's not a different planet. It's a spaceship that's soaring in a galaxy far, far away in a different point in time."

"How am I to get there then?" Sophia's heart was beating fast.

"I've created a special portal on Roya Lane," Mae Ling explained. "You have some time to get there, so you'll be okay. There will be a way back for you. Once you've arrived, you'll be an outsider and they will be leery of you."

"They?" Sophia asked. "Do you mean aliens?"

Mae Ling nodded. "There will be aliens. There will also be humans. There will be those you can later call friends. It all depends on how you are perceived, and that depends on how you react, which is unclear since it's too far for me to see clearly. It is no doubt a risk. I think it's one that is worth the advantages. The final decision on whether you go is completely up to you. I can't make that decision for you. Only you can."

This was way more than Sophia had expected. She thought it would be much simpler, but she was intrigued. Although the fear was present, she also knew exactly what she had to do.

"I'll go," Sophia declared with confidence. "Tell me how to get to this space ship. Please take care of Lunis, although I get he does well, taking care of himself."

Mae Ling nodded, a small smile on her peaceful face. "We all take care of each other, no matter how competent we are. Lunis will be in good hands."

Sophia glanced at her dragon in the distance, being lavished with the attention he deserved. She looked forward to returning and hearing about his adventures. She wondered what stories she'd have to tell him.

"So, where am I going?" Sophia asked, pulling in a tight breath.

"Go to Roya Lane," Mae Ling began. "Next to the Silk Armor, you'll see an unmarked door. It will take you through a portal to a battlecruiser crossing through frontier space off Federation territory. The ship is known as the *Ricky Bobby,* and its crew is good, but they won't take kindly to an outsider unless she proves herself to be true of heart and spirit."

CHAPTER ONE HUNDRED EIGHT

It seemed like a no brainer to Sophia that she should stop by the Silk Armor before setting off on her next adventure, especially since the portal was right beside the seamstress's shop. However, a part of her knew she was stalling. How could she not, she reasoned.

Sophia had gone to other dimensions and technically other planets but going into space onto a mysterious ship was a different story. Especially with Mae Ling's ominous warning about how the crew would be defensive to an outsider on their ship. Sophia would challenge some stranger if she found them randomly in the Gullington. That was her territory, and they'd be an outsider and have the responsibility of explaining how and why they were trespassing.

She gulped, realizing she was about to be that lone trespasser. Sophia was going to this strange place by herself, without Lunis, without Wilder, without anyone but Mae Ling knowing what was happening.

Sophia did have a brief moment where she was granted an opportunity to say goodbye to Lunis. He was so happy, being lavished with attention, she didn't want to worry him by telling him all the details about what she was off to do. Instead, she covered her feelings of fear

SARAH NOFFKE & MICHAEL ANDERLE

the best she could and explained he was going to stay there while she secured what they needed to defeat Nevin Gooseman's army.

Lunis was so distracted with attention that if he picked up on any of her nervousness, it didn't show. Instead, he gave her a fond expression and told her to hurry back as the students hurried over with platters of desserts to hand feed him.

Sophia wasn't worried about her dragon as she stepped onto Roya Lane and stood in front of two doors. One was marked, "Silk Armor" and the other wasn't labeled, but didn't appear like a portal to a battle-cruiser soaring through outer space.

CHAPTER ONE HUNDRED NINE

Sophia was assaulted with a bolt of silk fabric upon entering the shop. She pushed it off her as Juergen dashed back the other way, heading for the back.

"You ungraceful simpleton," Jeremy Bearimy bellowed to his assistant, holding up one of his eight legs like a fist and shaking it in the air. "One of these days, I'm going to teach you how to think first and move afterward."

"Yes, sir," Juergen called from the back, followed by a series of crashing sounds. "I look forward to that."

Sophia had to stop herself from laughing. The pair were perfect for each other. The scary tarantula bossing the grown magician around was unexpected and yet seemed right. She sensed a great competency in Juergen waiting to be discovered. There had to be a reason the great Jeremy Bearimy kept him around when he had his choice of assistants lining up for the chance to work with him.

"Oh, good, you got my message," Jeremy Bearimy said, catching sight of Sophia as he swiveled his eyes in her direction, although his body was facing the other way.

"I didn't actually," she admitted, realizing her phone was still at the

Castle. She'd left it behind, still in a fog of sleep when she awoke from her much needed nap.

He waved her off. "Well, you're here now, and that's what counts. Get over here and stand still."

"You are done with the dress?" she asked, striding in front of the huge spider, suddenly aware of how hairy and strange he was with him breathing down on her, his fangs inches from her face as he worked around her.

"No, not even close, but it's fine," Jeremy Bearimy replied. "I need you to pretend to be Ainsley for a fitting."

"But my measurements…"

"I'll adjust," he told her, using a measuring tape to check her inseam and other parts of her body. Sophia stood frozen. It was a new experience, having a spider measure her. This was almost as weird as going to a different galaxy to invade a battlecruiser to ask them for technology to defeat a magitech army. Almost. She'd have to report back on the differences later.

"So how much longer on the dress?" Sophia asked.

"Not much," Jeremy Bearimy answered. "Although there's much work to be done, I've moved it to the front of the line, so it has my full attention."

The tarantula's legs made a series of clicking sounds as it rotated to the side, calling to the back. "Any time today, Juerg! Did you fall asleep back there!"

"Not at all, sir," the bumbling assistant said, flying into the room carrying a beautiful silk gown and nearly tripping over it. It flew from his arms as he ran into a stack of boxes. He jumped around, grabbing his shins.

Jeremy Bearimy lifted one of his hairy legs and caught the dress as it flew through the air, pulling it down nimbly.

"Here we are," the spider said, handing the garment to Sophia. "Slip this on over your clothes, and I can check a few things. You're smaller than Ainsley and shorter, so you don't need to change. I just need a model to ensure I'm on the right track."

Sophia nodded and slipped the gorgeous dress over her head. She couldn't believe how soft it was. Sophia had felt silk before, but this was of a whole different quality and felt like something made in heaven. It was hard to believe that the softest silk she'd ever felt was also so strong it made the toughest armor. The irony of it was beautiful.

When Sophia had the blue dress on, she instantly felt like a princess—the kind that carried swords and didn't need to be saved. Still, she felt like royalty in the pristine blue dress. Looking into the mirror, she was surprised by her appearance, and the way the silk fabric seemed to make her glow. She actually gasped.

"There we are," Jeremy Bearimy stated proudly. "That's the reaction I'm going for. If it works on you, not being made for you, then it will be perfect for Ainsley."

"It's gorgeous," Sophia told him, feeling breathless.

"It is," Juergen agreed, diving onto the ground and using pins to take up the hem as Jeremy Bearimy eyed the dress.

"Yes, bring up the hem, and then we will cinch in the waist, but only slightly," the spider instructed.

Sophia was surprised by the expert grace the assistant used as he took up the bottom. She would have expected it to take much longer, but Juergen was done quickly, and then Jeremy Bearimy was asking her to take off the dress much too soon. Sophia didn't want to part with it. The dress was of the perfect shade of blue and felt like butter. It wasn't made for her, though, and it would be gifted to Ainsley, as it should be. Sophia thought she could wear that dress every day for the rest of her life and be happy.

"The dress for the great elf will be done very soon," Jeremy Bearimy informed her before she even had a chance to speak. "Stop by here the next time you're on Roya Lane, and I'm sure I'll be done. It won't take me long."

Impressed by how fast and expertly the tarantula worked, Sophia offered him a smile. "Thank you. I'm sure she's going to treasure it always."

He returned the smile and bowed slightly. "I do hope so. It's not every day that I make a dress for someone who is as respected as the shapeshifter."

CHAPTER ONE HUNDRED TEN

I know you're off on a dangerous mission, Lunis said in Sophia's head as she exited the Silk Armor.

She tensed, not having expected to hear from him until she returned and definitely not expecting him to say this.

It's nothing, Lun, she said, trying to downplay the events. She couldn't lie to her dragon, but if she was lying to herself, then she could lie to them both.

Outer space is sort of a big deal, he argued.

I have to do it, she said firmly.

I could go with you.

Sophia shook her head, leaning against the same lamp pole Lee had once tried to hide behind. That felt like a million years ago.

You can't, she stated firmly. *Mae Ling said she has to use your energy to keep me safe.*

So you're still going with the reasoning that you're safe on this mission, then, he countered.

I have to do it, she told him, deciding it was better to change her approach.

You know how much I've always wanted to be a space dragon, he sulked.

Sophia actually laughed in response, making a group of gnomes passing by give her strange expressions. She did look like a loon, randomly laughing by herself.

One day, we'll go to space, and you can satisfy that dream of being a space dragon in this weird fantasy world you've constructed.

Promise? he asked, sounding almost like a teenager bartering for privileges.

I totally promise, Sophia replied. *Right now, I need you here safe, lending your magical energy. I've got to go to this battlecruiser to get something that will help us win the battle against Nevin Gooseman and his magitech army.*

Fine, but I don't like it, Lunis fussed.

I get it, and I'm not saying it's fair, Sophia agreed. *But it's what's got to be done. Besides, I don't think you would fit very easily on a space ship. From what I've seen, the passageways are pretty narrow. If they are going to react to me as an intruder on their ship, imagine the fright you'd give the crew.*

Good point, Lunis said but didn't sound satisfied. *Just promise me one thing, Soph.*

Anything.

Come back in one piece, he ordered.

She nodded, holding her hand to her heart. *I'll be back as soon as I can. Promise.*

CHAPTER ONE HUNDRED ELEVEN

It was actually becoming increasingly difficult for Sophia to leave her heart in one place so she could protect the parts of her world that owned the other parts of her heart. She didn't like having to constantly choose and yet, that's how her life went. Resisting it would do her no good.

More overwhelming than the fear of venturing to a new galaxy was the gratitude that she had a fairy godmother who could help her find resources to defeat Nevin Gooseman's army. The thankfulness she felt for Lunis, and his concern warmed her heart fully. The idea of returning to the Gullington to her friends and a world healed from distortion was enough to carry her through uncharted territory.

Sophia needed all the good emotion she could muster as she was about to step into a world unlike anything she'd ever experienced, and that was saying a lot.

She'd faced multi-headed dragons and magitech dragons and ghosts, and this was her first time to be in space facing...well, she didn't know what she'd find.

Swallowing down the tension building in her throat, Sophia placed her hand on the hilt of her sword and started for the unmarked door next to Silk Armor, preparing to portal farther than she ever had before.

CHAPTER ONE HUNDRED TWELVE

The battlecruiser was cold. Much colder than Roya Lane.

It was also darker, making Sophia's eyes have to work to adjust.

There were strange noises all around her. Engine sounds. Pumping noises. Beeping.

The metal under her feet had holes in it, and air rushed up from below, creating a draft.

Sophia felt the ship vibrating around her like she had been swallowed by a beast and was living in its belly.

Wires snaked overhead and on the floor below. There were many sights to take in, but thankfully, Sophia was alone on the narrow passageway on the ship known as *Ricky Bobby*. She had a moment to adjust before she had to meet strangers and explain to them she wasn't an enemy they needed to chuck into outer space through the trash chute, or however they did things on space ships.

"Hello intruder," a voice echoed overhead from a speaker.

Sophia startled, jerking her head up and looking at the ceiling, which was just like the floor with a grated metal surface and wires. It was like she was in a tunnel, with glowing red and blue lights providing the only illumination.

"Who is there?" Sophia asked, looking from side to side, but not seeing anyone in the open passageway.

"I will ask the same of you," the bodiless voice said, sounding somewhat robotic.

"I'm Sophia," she replied, thinking it was best to be direct. Friendly, without coming off like a pushover. She needed these people's help but didn't want to appear weak. However, she *was* trespassing. Sophia was going to have to play this one carefully.

"Hello Sophia, who trespassed," the voice said, sounding welcoming and reluctant at the same time.

"Who are you?" she dared to ask.

"I am *Ricky Bobby*," the voice replied.

Sophia felt a crease form between her eyes. "The ship I portaled onto is *Ricky Bobby*."

"Portaled, you say," the male voice said, musing on the idea. "That's interesting. I didn't know that was possible."

"Magic makes all sorts of things possible," she replied, looking around and trying to decide what to do next. The question was which way to go. To the right down mysterious hallway number one, or to the left down a similarly mysterious hallway number two? It was a complete toss-up.

"Magic, you say," the voice repeated. "You don't belong in this timeline."

She shook her head. "I'm a visitor seeking help. Maybe you can assist me. I need some technology to help my planet."

"Your planet?" the voice asked.

"Earth," Sophia stated.

"Ohh…" the man said. "I'm sorry…"

"What do you mean you're sorry?" Sophia said, nearly yelling.

"You could stay here if you want."

Now Sophia was angry. "I'm not staying here. Earth is my home. My dragon is there, and my friends and, what do you mean you're sorry?"

"Earth," the voice said and paused. "According to my records, experienced many hardships during your timeline."

"How do you know of my timeline? Or when I'm from?"

"Simple. I conducted a full-body scan," the voice said. "You are a human magician from the year twenty-twenty." His voice trailed away. "Again, I'm sorry..."

"What!" Sophia was yelling now. "What the hell? You're sorry! Why? How do you know anything?"

"I'm from the future," he replied.

"Who are you?" she asked, about to throw a fit.

"I'm *Ricky Bobby*," he replied again.

"I get that, but will you elaborate since that's not making sense," she demanded, trying to keep her cool.

"I'm the AI for this ship, also known as *Ricky Bobby*," he explained. "I run the controls and take care of much of the maintenance. I have access to all of the systems and observe all the day to day operations of the ship."

"You apparently have a database that gives you access to the past history," Sophia muttered.

"Twenty-twenty didn't go so well," *Ricky Bobby* said, sounding regretful.

"According to your history books, which have already been written, but can be rewritten," she argued. "I'm here now, and I'm going to change all that. That's why I need your help or the help of your crew. I need something that stops the war that's coming. I need the Dragon Elite to win and save the planet."

"I'd like to help, Sophia," the AI said. "I really would."

She nodded, feeling like they were finally making progress. "Good, then direct me to your leader so I can get what I came for."

"About that..." *Ricky Bobby* started, tension in his voice. "They aren't here right now."

Sophia dropped her chin, wondering what headache she'd have to endure next. "Fine, then direct me to someone who can help me. I just need some technology that you all apparently have."

"I would," *Ricky Bobby* repeated, his voice trailing away.

"But?"

"But, something else has come up first."

"What?" Sophia asked, feeling like she was close to hyperventilating from all this.

"Me," a woman's voice said at Sophia's back.

She turned to find a futuristic soldier dressed in all black with long blonde hair, glaring at her as she held a gun in her hand, appearing seconds away from firing it and ending Sophia forever.

CHAPTER ONE HUNDRED THIRTEEN

Sophia's instinct was to pull her sword, but instead, she held up her hands, knowing she was the trespasser here. She didn't want to fight these people. She needed their help.

Her hands into the air, Sophia's eyes widened.

"Hi!" she yelped.

Then her face scrunched up with mortification.

Hi?! Really, she thought to herself. That was what she led with, facing a gun pointed at her by a badass looking futuristic soldier on a space ship in a different galaxy, she spurted out a very diplomatic "hi."

"I can explain why I'm here," Sophia said, happy logical words were coming out of her mouth.

The woman, who was both beautiful and looked tough enough to break her into pieces, narrowed her blue eyes. "Is that a sword on your hip? What are you from, the freaking middle ages?"

"Scotland, actually," Sophia answered.

"I'm going to need you to remove that weapon and put it on the floor," the woman said, stilling aiming the gun at Sophia.

"I don't think that's necessary." Sophia tried to sound diplomatic.

Her words caused a new tension in the soldier. She pulled back the hammer on the gun.

"That's too bad," the woman said. "I was hoping to do things the easy way."

CHAPTER ONE HUNDRED FOURTEEN

Sophia was prepared to keep talking it out with this woman, who seemed level-headed, but was just trying to defend her territory. She understood. Sophia would be the same if the situation was reversed, and she was defending her Castle from an outsider.

Before she could offer a reply, something grabbed Sophia's neck and tugged her backward. There was an arm around her throat, and a strong body behind her, cinching her in tightly. The woman lowered her gun, giving the person holding Sophia a pursed expression.

Sophia could have fought the figure holding her, but she was trying to get these people to help her, not get thrown in their brig. So, she did something rare and let the person restrain her. It was a man, she could sense by the size and smell. He wasn't hurting her. Only choking her slightly and pressing her arms down.

"I had this," the woman said, giving the guy a terse expression.

"I know," the man said. "I'm helping."

The woman rolled her eyes. "I don't need your help."

"You're welcome," he joked. "So, what's her story?"

"Well, she doesn't appear to want to fight," the woman observed.

"Her name is Sophia," the AI named *Ricky Bobby* said overhead. "She is from Earth from the year 2020."

"Whoa," the guy said, sounding impressed.

The woman tilted her head to the side. "You're a long way from home. What are you doing here, sweetheart?"

Sophia tried to talk, but the guy's arm was across her windpipe. The gasping noise must have told him she couldn't talk, and he loosened his grip.

"I need your help, and my fairy godmother said you would have the technology to aid me in a battle against someone I think could destroy our planet if not stopped," Sophia gasped out, surprised by the tears that almost spilled at her words. They were true and right, and she realized for the first time ever how important it was they win against Nevin Gooseman.

CHAPTER ONE HUNDRED FIFTEEN

"Did you say fairy godmother?" the woman asked, relaxing slightly.

"Yeah, it's sort of weird, but you have to believe me," Sophia pleaded.

"Oh, I think we can wrap our brains around fairy godmother," the woman joked. "We've got some things that might throw you for a loop, though."

Sophia couldn't see how that was possible since she'd just had a dress fitting done by a giant tarantula, but she was careful not to be too confident. She was in outer space, after all.

"What do you want me to do?" the guy restraining Sophia asked the woman. "Keep her here?"

"*Ricky Bobby*," the woman said, looking up to the ceiling. "Shine a little light on this, would you?"

"From everything I've been able to determine, I think she's telling the truth," the AI stated. "Her heart rate and other vitals remain static when talking. I have no reason to believe she poses any threat to you unless she fears for her life."

"Let her go," the woman ordered, putting her gun in her holster.

She held up her hand when free and said, "Hey, I'm Bailey, and this is Lewis."

Sophia turned to get a glimpse of the guy who had been holding her. He was wearing a suit and had his short brown hair slicked back. He gave her a crooked smile.

"Hey, sorry about restraining you," he said shyly.

"I get it," she replied, rolling her neck back and forth and working out the tension.

"So you are from Earth. Like a long time ago, huh?" Bailey asked.

"Yeah, although I didn't get that I was time traveling," Sophia said. "Mae Ling must have cleared that with Papa Creola or something."

"I have so many questions," Lewis said, checking his watch. "First, I think we have a meeting on the bridge, Bailey."

"I think," she began, "that a time traveler from Earth trumps that bore fest of a meeting." The combat soldier gave Sophia an appreciative look. "You said something about needing our help. What for?"

"I need something that can defend the dragonriders against a magitech army," Sophia explained.

Lewis laughed. "Dragons are real? You're a dragonrider?"

"She has a sword, which I want to play with later," Bailey said and then added, "Carefully. I promise."

Sophia nodded. "Sure. Anyway, I don't know if magitech makes sense to you based on what you call it, but I need technology. Something really advanced that can bring down planes and tanks and missiles that use advanced technology and want to destroy one of our most treasured properties. A place that, if destroyed, will undoubtedly slowly erase humanity. Do you think you have something like that?"

Lewis whistled. "Damn. These are some bad guys you are facing."

Sophia nodded.

"What are they going after?" Lewis asked.

"The Great Library," Sophia answered. "It holds every book ever written."

"Oh, no, they didn't," Lewis said, sounding highly offended.

"Do you think that you can help me?" Sophia asked. She sounded desperate, she realized. "Something that will fight their special army?"

Bailey pursed her lips and nodded. "I don't know what this technology could be, but I know the alien who will, and he will undoubtedly be able to help. Get ready to have your mind blown."

CHAPTER ONE HUNDRED SIXTEEN

To say that Sophia was overwhelmed as she strode through the spaceship flanked by Bailey and Lewis was a severe understatement. The ship was unlike anything she had ever seen. The rush of cool air under her boots was both disconcerting and refreshing. Glowing blue lights ran the length of the corridor, providing illumination but not enough, making the darkness further increase Sophia's anxiety.

"Where are we?" Sophia finally asked, wondering where they were taking her and how far it was. They'd already walked a long distance, but the ship seemed to go on and on.

"Space," Bailey answered at once.

"I think she was hoping for something a bit more specific," Lewis said, a laugh in his voice.

"Outer space." Bailey pointed to a window that looked out of the ship attached to what Sophia thought was an airlock. "Don't open that unless you want to have a really, really bad day. It's cold out there."

Sophia tentatively approached the window, for a moment, fearful she might fall out of it if she wasn't careful. The darkness of space was bright, filled with twinkling stars and planets. She could hardly believe she was standing on a space ship in the middle of a strange galaxy, talking to…well, Bailey and Lewis were humans. But they were from the future.

Oddly, they didn't seem that different from her. Lewis appeared as though he'd stepped out of a portal from Earth wearing a tweed suit with elbow patches and sporting an old watch. Bailey fit the bill as someone from the future in her shiny black catsuit and carrying a gun that Sophia didn't think shot bullets, but that was only a guess.

The importance of stopping Nevin Gooseman from finding the information in the Great Library to destroy the demon dragons and then destroy the Library really hit Sophia then. Papa Creola didn't allow time travel hardly ever, only under extreme circumstances. For Mae Ling to create a portal here, it would have had to be approved by the father of time. Which meant he knew she needed this weapon to combat and hopefully stop Nevin Gooseman and his army.

"Pretty cool, huh?" Bailey asked when Sophia stepped back from the window, overwhelmed.

"To say the least," Sophia replied as they continued walking through the ship.

"To answer your question," *Ricky Bobby* began, his voice echoing overhead. "We are in Precious Galaxy, in the Cacama System, having just left the planet Tueti and are headed to a space station."

"Thanks." Sophia wasn't sure she understood most of what the AI had said.

"You're from Scotland," Bailey said, sounding casual. "Do you live in a Castle?" She laughed like this was a joke.

"Actually, I do," Sophia related a bit sheepishly. "I'm from Los Angeles, but that's not really relevant. It's pretty complicated."

"I can't wait to learn everything," Lewis said excitedly. "We have to have a long conversation over a cup of coffee. You know what coffee is, right? We just got a shipment of beans, and we're taking them to the Precious Galaxy Coffee Company right now. They will be extra fresh."

Sophia nodded. "We have coffee, but I'm not sure how long I can stay."

"Yeah, Lewis," Bailey said dryly. "She has to save the Great Library, remember."

"I remember," he fired back at the girl, winking. "She time traveled, so I just figured that…" He gave Sophia a sudden look of horror. "How are you going to get back?"

She spun to face the way they'd come, although they'd taken so many turns and there were lots of passageways she was lost. "I'm not sure. I'm guessing that I go back to where you found me, and Mae Ling will open another portal. She couldn't leave it open for obvious reasons."

"That's your fairy godmother?" Bailey asked. "Mae Ling?"

"Yeah, she's watching my dragon while I'm here," Sophia said, laughing at how absurd it must sound to the space travelers.

"I want a fairy godmother," Bailey gushed.

"I want a dragon," Lewis added.

"You don't even know how to ride a bike," Bailey countered. "How do you think you'll figure out how to ride a dragon, Sherlock?"

"When do I have a chance to ride a bike around here?" he asked.

"When do you have a chance to ride a dragon?" Bailey teased.

Lewis whipped around to face Sophia. "Is Sherlock Holmes real? I've read all his stories and researched the history, but he seems so incredible, I've always wondered if he was based on an actual person."

"I don't know, actually," Sophia said, tentatively.

"Lewis is sort of obsessed with the detective." Bailey pointed at his clothes. "Hence the inspiration for his suit. He was before his time and definitely dropped into space against his will."

He shrugged. "I like it, but Earth, that's where we are from. How can you not be curious?"

She pursed her lips and shook her head, indicating the floor under their feet. "I'm from here. I'm curious about the fastest way to take down a Trid, and how the Saverus shapeshift and how a Kezzin flosses its teeth."

"Did you say Saverus?" Sophia asked, suddenly concerned. "They shapeshift?"

"Yeah, well, the one we have does, but she's the only one left in existence at this point," Bailey answered. "Why? You heard of them?"

She nodded. "Yeah, I met the guy who is probably responsible for them." Sophia thought of Mika Lena and his bizarre and inhumane organization known as Saverus. He was dead now, but what if the things he created went on to become a species of shapeshifters? Anything was possible and it wasn't really her concern. She was there to get technology and stop her current enemy—Nevin Gooseman.

CHAPTER ONE HUNDRED SEVENTEEN

Sophia was unprepared for so many aspects of the next area they entered. They'd gone from snaking through narrow passageways to entering a huge warehouse type space filled with small and large spacecraft. Everywhere was filled with tons of technology Sophia didn't recognize. Crates were stacked high from floor to ceiling, and music was playing loud overhead. The thing that struck her as most odd was that standing at a workstation and banging his head to the music was a guy wearing a kilt.

How had she traveled through space and time and ended up in a place where people were still wearing the Scottish kilt? Sophia wondered, studying the guy.

He was incredibly attractive with dark hair and piercing blue eyes and a studious expression on his face. One of his eyebrows arched as he studied something in his hands.

The three of them paused a few feet from the guy.

"We've got a treat for you, Pip," Bailey sang, having to talk loudly to be heard over the music.

"Leave it on the table," the guy muttered, all his focus on whatever he was working on.

"I don't know if it will fit," Lewis said with a chuckle.

Sophia thought he was right. Although the workspace was long and wide, it was so crammed with wires and pieces of equipment there wasn't any room for much else.

"Shove something over to make room for my spring rolls," Pip ordered.

Bailey crossed her arms. "We didn't bring you spring rolls."

"Well, then you're dead to me," Pip retorted.

"Too bad, because we really thought you'd like this better than spring rolls," Lewis said with a teasing quality in his voice.

"Unless it's a cake then you don't know me at all. That's the only thing better than spring rolls." Pip's face was scrunched up with concentration.

"It's not cake," Bailey stated.

"I'm busy!" Pip exclaimed. "Can't you two loons see that? Go and play your hopscotch somewhere else. I've got to get this frequency converter fixed, or this bad boy we call a space ship is going down. Is that what you want? Do you want the ship to fall into a black hole?"

"You mean again?" Lewis asked, pretending to sound serious. "I didn't like it the first time we fell into a black hole, so no."

"The ship is not in danger of falling into a black hole if Pip doesn't fix the frequency converter," *Ricky Bobby* informed them matter-of-factly overhead.

"No one asked you for your two cents RB," Pip sang.

"Okay, well, never mind." Lewis sighed disappointedly. "We'll just take the visitor from Earth and the year twenty-twenty elsewhere."

"Wh-What!" Pip yelled, spinning around to face them.

CHAPTER ONE HUNDRED EIGHTEEN

"**D**amn!" Pip spurt out. "She's hauuute!"

He dropped what he was working on and strode over like a hungry wolf. On top of his green and blue kilt, he was wearing a T-shirt that said:

What's the most terrifying word in nuclear physics?

Oops!

Sophia froze as he lowered his chin and appraised her, walking around her in a circle.

"She's a dragonrider," Bailey added proudly.

Pausing in front of her, after making a complete circle, Pip extended a hand. "This might be a bit soon, but will you marry me?"

Lewis laughed loudly. "Maybe a bit soon and premature."

"You're premature," Pip fired at him, not taking his eyes off Sophia.

"Hey," she said, wringing the hand he offered. "Nice to meet you, Pip. I'm Sophia."

He leaned forward and kissed her hand. "She has manners. No one on this ship knows what those are. Just a bunch of barbarians."

"Yet somehow, we manage to save the universe over and over again without all the pleasantries," Bailey said dryly.

"Anyway, Sophia." Pip continued to hold her hand. "About my question. Seriously, what do you say?"

Lewis laughed. "You just met her."

Pip cut his eyes at him briefly. "Just because you never experienced love at first sight, doesn't mean the rest of us can't have a fairytale. Stop trying to rain on my parade and go iron your tie."

Lewis glanced down to check his tie, like it might be suddenly wrinkled.

"Actually, she has a fairy godmother," Bailey explained. "That's how she got here."

This didn't seem to surprise Pip. He nodded. "Yes, to meet her Prince Charming. Anyway, about my proposal? I will make a fine husband, although we can't have children since I'm not a real man. I'm real enough in all the ways that count if you know what I mean?" He winked at her.

Sophia tilted her head to the side. "You're not a real man?"

Pip's hand in hers felt real. It was warm, and his skin was calloused.

"I'm real enough, with the parts that are necessary," he answered.

"He's an AI Geppetto made into a real boy," Bailey supplied.

"What?" Sophia asked, totally perplexed by this new bit of information. Pip looked as real as any man she'd ever seen with the stubble on his chin and his long sideburns. His eyes had depth, and the expression on his face was genuine as he continued to stare at her, making her increasingly uncomfortable. "That's incredible. And Geppetto?"

"That's our engineer mechanic scientist who we think can help you with your request," Lewis explained. "We call him Hatch because his real name is a mouthful. Bailey calls him whatever she feels like at the moment. She likes to come up with little nicknames for all of us cause she thinks it's cute."

"It's adorable," Bailey stated dryly.

"Where is Hatch, anyway?" Lewis asked Pip.

"Probably telling one of the crew members in detail how dumb they are," Pip said, not taking his gaze off of Sophia.

She managed to pull her hand from his, making him frown slightly.

"We'll take it slow if that makes you more comfortable," he told her.

"Hate to break it to you, Kilts, but Sophia can't marry you," Bailey told him. "She's here on a mission. Apparently—"

"Pip, would you turn down that blaring music already! I can't hear myself think!" a voice yelled from behind a set of tall shelves piled high with supplies.

The creature connected to the voice appeared, waddling out from behind the shelves, and Sophia realized just how much weirder things could get.

CHAPTER ONE HUNDRED NINETEEN

A giant, purple, octopus-like alien moved out from behind the shelves, a frustrated look on his face. The large creature's tentacles were busy doing other things, like typing on a keyboard or reaching for something at his back as he stared out at them. His bulbous eyes went wide at the sight of Sophia.

"Well, that's not something you find every day," the strange creature said, puffing out his cheeks.

"I know," Lewis agreed, nodding. "I was surprised to see Bailey up before noon too."

The soldier stuck her tongue out but didn't reply otherwise.

Moving strangely, the large octopus-like creature approached, awe obvious on his face. "I can't believe it. How did you get here?" he asked Sophia.

She stood frozen, speechless.

"True love carried her to me," Pip answered for her.

"A portal set up by her fairy godmother," Bailey corrected. "She's from—"

"Earth," the creature interrupted, supplying the information. "Yes, I can tell." He looked Sophia over. "By your clothes and the make of your weapon, you're from the twenty-first century and a part of a magical race. Not an elf, based on your ears. And not a fae since one wouldn't be smart enough to get here. So you must be a magician."

Bailey elbowed Sophia in the side. "I told you, our resident scientist is pretty smart. If anyone can help you, it will be him."

"You're the scientist?" Sophia asked, finding her voice.

"I get that I don't fit the typical appearance with glasses and a white lab coat, but I assure you I'm competent enough to figure out most complex problems," the creature said.

"Sophia, please meet Dr. A'Din Hatcherik, or Hatch for short," Lewis said formally. "He's of the species of Londil from the planet of Ronin in the Behemoth system located in the Pan galaxy."

Bailey leaned in again. "This will be on the test. I hope you're taking notes."

Hatch looked around at the others. "When were you dimwits going to tell me that an Earthling was on the ship?"

"Hey, Hatch!" Pip said, excitedly.

"What?" he growled, irritation heavy in his tone.

"There's a bona fide Earthy on the ship," he answered.

"I can see that," he spat. "Now, I want to know how. Time travel is strictly forbidden on Earth."

"Remember that bit about her fairy godmother?" Bailey asked, eyeing her nails like they were of sudden interest.

"I remember everything," the Londil replied.

"I sort of have an in with Papa Creola, who you might know as Father Time," Sophia explained.

Hatch nodded, like this made perfect sense. "You would have to."

"She's a dragonrider," Lewis imparted.

"Oh, so you're from twenty-nineteen, then?" Hatch asked, his memory for history remarkable.

"Twenty-twenty, actually," *Ricky Bobby* chimed in.

Hatch's face went slack. "Oh, dear… No wonder you're here."

Sophia twisted her mouth to the side. "Yes, I'm apparently trying to avoid the Earth falling into complete destruction or whatever your history books say happens."

Hatch waved one of his tentacles dismissively. "History is relative and changes all the time based on how the continuum is adapted."

"Or if you're Bailey, then you rewrite history to suit your story," Lewis quipped.

Dismissing this, Hatch went on, "It's sort of like the time theory of Jeremy Bearimy. It doesn't flow in a straight line. Anyway, I won't bore you with theories like that."

Sophia blinked at the scientist like she was on a prank show and waiting for the host to jump out and say this had all been a funny set up. "I'm aware of the theory, and the spider named for it."

Hatch appeared impressed. "Well, don't stick around here or stupid will rub off on you. These numbskulls couldn't supply a theory to save their pathetic lives."

Bailey batted her eyes at Hatch. "Isn't he just the sweetest, most thoughtful Londil in the entire universe?"

"Your Q-ship is ready," he said to her. "Go test the controls and report back with any problems."

"Oh, heck no," Bailey replied. "I'm hanging out with the dragonrider. She said I could play with her sword."

"I didn't actually," Sophia corrected.

"You can play with my sword," Pip said to Sophia, winking at her.

"I'll let you hold my gun," Bailey offered.

"That's okay," Sophia declined. "I'm here because I need a way to combat some pretty major guns and a lot of other dangerous weapons."

"Finally!" Hatch exclaimed, throwing three tentacles into the air. "We're getting to the reason Father Time would allow a dragonrider from twenty-twenty onto *Ricky Bobby*."

"I'm hoping you can help me to combat some pretty major magitech," Sophia said, doubt heavy in her voice.

To her surprise, the grumpy scientist actually smiled. "Not only do I think I can help you, I believe you just gave my meaningless existence true purpose."

CHAPTER ONE HUNDRED TWENTY

"Should we be offended that working for us, supplying technology to save multiple planets, races, and galaxies, hasn't given Hatch purpose before now?" Bailey asked Lewis.

"Completely," he replied.

"Be offended," Hatch said flatly. "That all is good and well as far as projects go, but to actually have the chance to work on magitech, well, that's a whole new level I never thought I'd have the opportunity for."

Bailey held up her hands. "Wait, so if magic is actually real—"

"It is, I assure you," Hatch interrupted.

"Then why don't we have any magic now?" Bailey asked. "Why aren't there magicians and all those other races you mentioned?"

Hatch's eyes slid to the right, his expression saying everything and Sophia felt her hope plummet.

"Apparently, we make ourselves extinct," she muttered.

"Not extinct, but endangered," Hatch corrected, his tone sympathetic.

"Is Earth gone now?" Sophia asked.

"Not gone," Hatch replied. "But a long way away and not someplace we could get to in our lifetime under the current gate structure.

Besides, we don't much care to. Our job is here on Federation Frontier."

"If something did happen to magical races," Lewis began, working out what he was saying as he was saying it. "Sophia changes the history based on your help, won't that change our current lives? Like will magicians all of sudden be all over the galaxy?"

Hatch shook his head. "No, because their Father Time would have considered this and to avoid the grandfather paradox, he sent her to a different, parallel dimension."

Bailey whistled. "Talk about the jetlag you must be experiencing. Time travel, across multiple galaxies and then through into a different dimension."

Sophia blinked, feeling more than overwhelmed. It would be all worth it if she got the technology to help her to fight Nevin Gooseman's army.

"Okay, magic," Pip said, rubbing his hands together. "Let's see it. Make Hatch nice."

Bailey laughed. "I'd pull up a chair to watch that."

Sophia pointed to a barstool over by a workstation, and it disappeared and reappeared next to the soldier.

"Wow!" Bailey cheered. "That's a cool party stunt. What else can you do?"

Sophia shrugged. "Create different elements, like fire and wind. Make myself faster or stronger. Create a shield or cloak myself. It sort of depends on what I need to do."

Pip draped his arm around her shoulder, hugging her in tightly. "We're going to have such a happy life together."

"She's got to return to her home in Scotland," Lewis stated.

"Scotland!" Pip exclaimed, lifting up his kilt. "I'm Scottish."

"You're an AI," Hatch corrected. "Keep that skirt down, would you?"

"It's a kilt," Pip argued. "It's what everyone on Earth wears as the coolest fashion."

"No, no they don't," Sophia said.

"Well, Scotsmen do," he offered.

"Not as much as you'd think," she disagreed.

Bailey hopped up on the stool, making herself comfortable. "Although this is very entertaining, I think we better get to the reason Sophia trespassed on our ship."

Pulling in a breath, Sophia nodded. "Okay, I'll give you the quick version of the story and hope you have a quick solution."

CHAPTER ONE HUNDRED TWENTY-ONE

"Simply fascinating," Hatch said, drumming a tentacle against his lips as he thought.

"So, their planes are powered by magic?" Bailey asked.

"Enhanced," Hatch corrected.

"Not all of them," Sophia explained. "It is only recently that technology and magic have been paired together, and usually it's not a pretty combination. Many of my missions have been to stop power hungry villains who take it too far."

Hatch nodded. "It's a slippery slope. Technology in and of itself is incredibly powerful. So is magic. Put them together, and you can save a planet or destroy it rather quickly."

Sophia sighed. "Yes, a common issue Mama Jamba and the dragonriders are constantly policing."

Hatch's cheeks puffed out suddenly, surprise covering his face. "You know Mama Jamba?"

Sophia laughed. "Well, if by know, you mean that we eat breakfast together and live in the same castle, then yes."

"And she is…?" Bailey asked.

"Mother Nature," Pip snapped at her. "Keep up. My future wife knows all the gods of her world. Our wedding will be amaze!"

"You're not setting foot through that portal when Sophia returns to Earth, Pip," Hatch said, a punishing quality to his voice.

The AI crossed his arms over his chest. "You don't own me!"

"I created you, and I can take you from this world," Hatch fired back.

Pip stomped off like a hormonal teenager. "I can't wait until I can get out of this place! You ruin my life! I wish I'd never been born!"

Hatch shook his head, ignoring the tantrum being thrown by the AI, and turned his attention back to Sophia.

She couldn't help but giggle. "I always thought that AIs were..."

"Dull, mechanical, lacking personality," Bailey supplied. "Me too. Then I came here and learned not to drink the water."

Lewis nodded. "Yeah, we're all mad here."

"It's ship life," Bailey added.

"I don't mean to make this all about me, but—"

"You have the Great Library to save," Hatch supplied. "You're quite right to make this about you."

"Do you think you can help me?" Sophia asked.

"I think that I'm going to need your help to alter tech devices that I've already created," Hatch answered. "Yes, I'm certain I can offer you something. It won't be like what you mentioned before that disabled the magitech you fought in the past."

"Oh." Sophia deflated slightly, wondering if they'd stand a chance against Nevin Gooseman's army if they didn't disable the magitech aspects to the military forces.

Hatch intertwined two of his tentacles, a victorious expression on his face. "It's going to be much more destructive than that!"

CHAPTER ONE HUNDRED TWENTY-TWO

"It's so unassuming." Sophia sat at one of Hatch's many workstations peering at a stainless-steel box with several antennas sticking out of the top. A red button sat under a clear cover, and beside it was a meter that would illuminate when the device was in use.

"The very best things in life are," Hatch offered, bustling around behind the table, doing several different things at once with his tentacles. "People too. Aliens as well."

One of his tentacles was using a screwdriver to open up the back of the box, which Sophia couldn't see. Another was digging around in a box full of tools. A third was typing on a keyboard, and a fourth was scratching the top of his head.

Pip had returned at Hatch's "request," which involved a few choice words and some yelling. He was apparently supposed to be the conduit between Sophia and the device when the time came.

He was sitting next to her, his head on her shoulder, and a pouty expression on his face. "I'm going to miss you so much when you're gone."

Bailey shook her head. "You've known her all of an hour."

"I already like her more than you," he retorted.

She plastered a mock expression of hurt on her face. "I have feelings, you know?"

"I didn't actually," Pip replied, turning his attention back to Sophia. "What's your dragon's name? Tell me all about him. Will he come between us?"

"No, but my boyfriend will," she replied.

Pip shot up, pulling his head off her shoulder. "Sophia! How dare you! Two-timing me with a common ditch digger…"

"He's a dragonrider too, actually," she informed him, laughing.

Lewis nodded commiserating. "Not a lot of options when you live in a Castle, huh?'

"Says the guy who lives on a battlecruiser in the middle of frontier space," Bailey said dryly.

"When you dump Roy Little," Pip cut into the conversation, "do you think he'll cry?"

Since Sophia had zero idea how to respond to that, she was grateful when Hatch snapped the tip of his tentacle in front of them. "Focus. I need Sophia to channel her magical energy into this device. I'm ready to do the conversion and final calibrations. Pip, hold her hand."

"Gladly," the AI said, taking both of Sophia's hands in one of his and then putting his other on top of the stainless-steel box.

"What do I need to do?" Sophia asked, looking at Hatch.

"Just force the energy through Pip and into the device, the same way you'd power technology on Earth," he answered.

Creating magitech wasn't really Sophia's specialty, like Liv's, but she did as she was told, closing her eyes so she stayed focused.

The vibration in her hand and the smell of something burning made her eyes pop open with sudden concern.

Hatch waved her off immediately as she spied Pip appearing to be fried from the inside out. Steam was issuing from his ears, and he was bouncing slightly, his eyes wide like he was in pain.

"He's fine," Hatch assured her. "He just isn't used to funneling magic, and it will take over his systems. The AI will recover quickly and be telling repulsive jokes in no time."

Relieved, Sophia continued to push her magic out, feeling it leave her like she was creating a complex spell.

"Just a little longer," Hatch encouraged.

Sophia felt Pip's hand tighten around hers and immediately felt herself slump as exhaustion took over, the result of draining her reserves. She almost tipped over, but something caught her.

Opening her eyes, she found Bailey standing next to her, a strong smile on her face. "We've got you. Keep going."

Sophia nodded, her eyes fluttering from the sheer act of sending her magic through an AI and into a technical device. It was a strange experience to be on a battlecruiser soaring through space and already thinking of these people as her friends. Since the beginning, she felt at ease with them, like she'd always known them.

That was good because when she passed out, all her weight fell on Bailey and Lewis, who caught her just before she lost consciousness.

CHAPTER ONE HUNDRED TWENTY-THREE

"Do you think I should kiss her to wake her up, like Prince Charming and Sleeping Beauty?" Sophia heard Pip say, although she hadn't opened her eyes yet.

She was trying to assess her internal state, which felt quite shaken. Her anxiety was high, and she felt like her organs were rattling around inside her body.

"I think you should because I want to see her clock you in that pretty face," Bailey said with a laugh.

Pip scoffed. "The love of my life would never. I'm just worried she's locked in a coma."

Sophia tried to shake her head, to tell them she was okay, but her muscles weren't responding to the command from her brain. She had never been depleted quite like this. It must have been a combination of the method of funneling her magic and being in space on a different timeline.

"She'll be fine," Hatch told them. "Sophia just needs to rest, and then her magic will return. I've also put a nutrition patch on her arm, and that will refill her energy. Give her an hour and she'll be back with us."

"Every second away from her is torture," Pip said melodramatically.

Lewis chuckled. "Now you know how I feel about coffee."

CHAPTER ONE HUNDRED TWENTY-FOUR

When Sophia awoke fully, she was lying on the surface of one of the worktables in Hatch's lab. Perched beside her, leaning over her was Pip. She opened her eyes to look into his and startled immediately, bolting upright and knocking her forehead into his.

"Oh, my love!" he exclaimed.

Sophia rolled to the side, clutching her head, which felt like she had rammed it into a metal wall. She tumbled off the side of the table and fell on the floor.

Rolling over on her back, she spied Pip hanging over the side of the table and Hatch giving them both an amused expression.

"That's one way to wake up," Bailey said, striding over and extending a hand to Sophia to help her up.

She took the hand and popped up to her feet, grateful to find her energy had returned, and her magic was restored.

"How long was I out?" Sophia asked, rubbing her head where she banged it into Pip.

"It felt like an eternity," Pip said dramatically.

"About forty-five minutes," Hatch stated matter-of-factly.

"Oh, that was so weird," she related. "I've never passed out like that from depleting my reserves."

"Well, Pip might have figured out how to siphon the energy from you." Hatch scowled at the AI. "So, on top of you funneling your power out, he was also tapping into it."

Pip swung his legs over the side of the table and slid down to his feet. "I was trying to help. I had never felt magic before. It was addictive. Much like you, Sophia."

She ignored him. "Did it at least work? Did all the magic get into the device?"

"Yes," Hatch chirped, sounding excited. "The device is ready to go. I just have to tell you how to use it, so you don't kill yourself."

"Yes, please do!"

Hatch indicated the stainless-steel container with the antennas and buttons that were all put together now. "It's called a CAR because—"

"He's obsessed with cars from Earth," Pip interjected. "He's got a huge collection in the back. Hey, here's a great idea. We can go and make out in his '64 GTO."

"Not unless you want to be disassembled," Hatch threatened. "That's not why it's called that. The acronym is for 'Catch and Race.'"

"That doesn't make any sense, Doc," Bailey said, eating what Sophia thought was maybe a falafel wrap.

He cut his eyes at her. "You don't make sense."

She lifted a can of Coke as if in a toast. "No arguments there."

"Anyway," Hatch continued, returning his attention to Sophia. "The idea of CAR is it will sense any and all magitech in a five-mile radius, so you'd better ensure that you're not using any."

"The Dragon Elite rarely do," she admitted. "Our leader is mostly against technology."

"Remind me not to invite him to my next dinner party," Hatch said dryly.

Pip laughed. "That's cute. You hosting a dinner party. I can just see you wearing a bow tie and apron and having seating assignments."

Lewis grinned. "I'd go to that dinner party."

"I'd get kicked out of it," Bailey added.

"That you would," Hatch replied. "As I was saying, the CAR is going to pick up on all magitech in the vicinity, so don't have any. Not even a phone. Once it's attached, you're going to need to lock onto the devices, whether they be planes, rocket launchers, or helicopters. That's the catch part of the device."

"Then we're going to need to run like hell," Sophia guessed.

Hatch smiled at her. "I'd exchange you for the lot of this bunch of imbeciles. I would have had to draw them a picture and explain it *ad nauseum* for them to get it."

"Do you ever get the impression Hatch doesn't care for us much?" Bailey asked through a bite to Lewis.

He shook his head. "He adores us."

"Yeah, like an infestation of space rats in the lower deck," Hatch grumbled, turning his attention back to Sophia. "So the important part is to get close enough to lock onto this army's magitech. That's when you hit the red button. Then you have roughly a minute to get as far away from them as you can." He indicated with one of his tentacles.

"I want to hit the red button," Pip said longingly, perched next to Sophia, his fingers close to the box.

"Don't," Hatch ordered. "This device only has one charge. That means one chance for Sophia to use it successfully. If you're not locked onto all of the magitech devices when you hit that button, you won't destroy all of them at once."

"Wow," Sophia said, her eyes wide. "It's going to destroy them?"

"Huge explosion," he declared victoriously. "What I've done is quite brilliant—"

"If he does say so himself," Bailey interrupted.

"I do," Hatch said boldly. "It's incredibly genius. The CAR turns magitech against itself. Usually, the magic fuels the technology making it faster, more accurate, exceptionally powerful, so forth and so on. However, the CAR detects the magitech and then ramps up its power until it implodes on itself."

"Wow, that is brilliant," Sophia said, suddenly breathless. Then something occurred to her, making her initial excitement wane.

"There is a problem though," Hatch warned.

"The whole exploding part," Lewis guessed.

The scientist nodded, not offering him a compliment for the accurate guess. "So you need to get close enough to lock onto the magitech."

"That's the catch part," Bailey offered.

"Then you need to get as far from it as possible within that minute after you hit the button," Hatch repeated.

"That's the run part," Bailey added once more.

"Which means, if the army is trying to get to the Great Library, that we need to catch them there, then lure them away," Sophia said.

"That's right," Hatch confirmed. "Or you will take your library down with the magitech army, which will defeat the whole purpose."

Sophia chewed on her lip. "Yeah, this is going to be tricky, but at least we have a tool to use."

Pip chuckled. "She said, 'tool.'"

"You're twelve years old, aren't you?" Bailey asked, quite seriously.

"Twelve and a half," he corrected.

"Well, that's all I can do to help you, Sophia." Hatch puffed out his cheeks, a look of regret briefly crossing his face. "I don't think we'll know if it works, but I wish you the very best. I'm sorry to say, it sounds like you're going to need it."

CHAPTER ONE HUNDRED
TWENTY-FIVE

Sophia was very sad to leave *Ricky Bobby*. She hadn't been on the battlecruiser for very long and yet, she'd quickly felt at home there. Even being greeted by *Ricky Bobby* as an intruder and welcomed by Bailey pointing a gun at her hadn't put a bad taste in her mouth.

The dragonrider knew that the crew of *Ricky Bobby* were only defending their home. She would do the same in their position. Sophia had.

The crew was so much fun and although she didn't want to leave them, knowing she'd never be able to return, they made her miss her friends and her family at the Gullington. She had what they did—a camaraderie worth fighting for. That's what they did, Sophia had learned. They defended the Frontier of Federation space from bullies and madmen and those who wanted to hurt the universe. They were the Dragon Elite, just on a different scale.

Different from when she entered *Ricky Bobby*, all of her new friends walked her back to where she entered. Sophia hoped that a portal would open up, or she didn't know how she'd get back. She had faith in Mae Ling.

"I thought you might want to take this back with you." Lewis handed her a bag of coffee beans that was labeled "Precious Galaxy Coffee Company."

Sophia took it with her free hand, the other one carrying the CAR. "Thanks."

"That's the coffee company that pretty much runs these systems," Lewis explained. "We help by running the beans from Tueti. The CEO helps us out with missions and funding."

"Sounds like a good partnership," Sophia said, taking a whiff of the beans, and getting their rich aroma through the bag.

"Everything is about partnerships," Bailey related, tenderness on her face. "I wish you the best with what you have to do. Glad that we could help, after all."

"We?" Hatch questioned, waddling behind them.

"Hey," Bailey complained. "I brought her to you. Well, after Lewis put her in a headlock, pretty much."

Sophia laughed, having forgotten that part of the meeting. "Yeah, that is a fond memory."

"Hey, you find a girl in a cloak with a sword on your ship, what do you do?" Lewis asked, holding up his hands.

"Ask her to marry you and get your heart broken," Pip whined, kicking at the wall as they halted about where Sophia had entered.

"I'm interested to see what your portals look like." Hatch looked around, his round eyes studying the space.

"Bright," Sophia offered, looking over her shoulder as she faced the group. Holding up the CAR with the coffee beans on top, she smiled. "Thanks for, well, everything."

"Not so fast," Pip said.

Bailey stepped in front of him, holding up a hand. "You don't get to kiss her."

"That really should be her choice," he argued. "That's not what I was going to do. I have my own parting gift."

From the hem at his back, he pulled two T-shirts from his kilt. "I have a company called Pimping Pip's Apparel, where I make graphic T-shirts. Anyway, I thought you and your dragon should have some, although I don't know what size your dragon is. I got you an extra small and him an extra-large."

"That's perfect," Sophia said, smiling at the AI who had instantly become one of her favorite people she'd met on her travels.

He held up the first one that was small. It read:

How do astronomers organize a party?

They planet.

"Oh wow," Hatch groaned. "That's awful."

"Thank you," Pip said blushing. "This one is for your dragon."

On the front, it said:

What did the 30-degree angle say to the 90-degree angle?

You think you're always right.

Sophia giggled. "You and he would get along. Y'all share a similar sense of humor."

"I'm sorry," Hatch related, his lips pursed.

"What is your dragon's name?" Bailey asked.

"Lunis," Sophia said, instantly missing him. Their connection had been severed since she'd been on the battlecruiser.

"He's named after the moon," Hatch said, sounding impressed.

Sophia nodded. "That's right. He gets bigger on the night of a full moon."

"Me too," Pip said with a wink.

Bailey shook her head. "Maybe Sophia could take Pip with her."

"She can't," Hatch stated a warning in his voice. "Not only that but Sophia, I believe this is our first and only meeting. I don't believe you'll be able to return."

She nodded, having suspected that much too. "Yeah, well, thanks to all of you. I think you might have saved my people and a lot more."

"We're all in this together," Hatch offered. "Our world affects yours and yours ours."

Bailey elbowed Lewis. "I think he's going to cry."

"I'm not!" Hatch bellowed. "But it wouldn't kill you all to have a bit of intelligence like Sophia. A strategic mind is a beautiful thing."

Pip tilted his head to the side, looking at Sophia's behind. "So is that as—"

"Your portal appears to be trying to open," *Ricky Bobby* interrupted overhead.

Sophia nodded, her throat tightening. "Good luck to you with everything you've got going on."

Bailey waved her off. "Oh, it's nothing. Just space pirates and ugly aliens that like to smuggle illegal weapons. No one can know that we are behind all the acts of self-sacrifice, making the universe safer. That's the rule. Those pirates and aliens give me a reason to drink."

"Being awake gives you a reason to drink," Lewis teased.

"You give me all the reasons to drink," she retorted.

At Sophia's back, the portal to her world opened, a bright, shimmering light that made them all squint.

"Fascinating," Hatch stammered in awe of the portal.

"I better go," Sophia said, looking at the portal before turning back to the group, her arms full of gifts and her heart full of the love for the strange beings from another world.

"You better," Bailey said, winking at her. "Stay alive and kick those politicians' butts."

"Yeah." Lewis smiled at her. "Keep doing what you're doing. It's a beautiful thing to save the world, even if no one knows you are the one doing it." He gave Bailey beside him a meaningful expression, which she returned.

"Sophia, I'll never forget you." Pip pressed his fingers to his lips and blew her a kiss.

The most surprising was from Hatch, who was offering her a tender expression. "Remember, catch them, get them away from your Great Library, and run like hell. Although I don't suspect we'll know if you're successful or not, the world will. Losing you won't be good for the future."

"Thanks," Sophia said speechless. She took a step backward, knowing it was time to say goodbye to her new friends.

Just as she was about to turn and step through the portal, she paused. "I forgot to ask. You all are the crew for *Ricky Bobby*, but what do you call yourselves? You know, in case I ever want to look you up again?"

Hatch smiled. "We're Ghost Squadron."

CHAPTER ONE HUNDRED
TWENTY-SIX

Sophia felt like she'd been gone from her world for ages when she stepped back through the portal onto Roya Lane. Her heart was heavier than she thought was possible, having to leave behind the crew of Ghost Squadron. She pulled on the strength the encounter had given her. Around the universe, at all points on the timeline, in different dimensions, there were those who were fighting for good. People who would risk everything to save the world they cherished. If Sophia needed another reason to take Nevin Gooseman down, this was it.

Pulling a macaroon from her pocket, Sophia took a bite, although she wasn't as hungry as she thought she'd be after that long without eating and after depleting her magic. She glanced at the nutrition patch Hatch had put on her, and she didn't want to ever take it off as a way to remember the Londil by.

Then she looked down at the CAR, coffee beans, and T-shirts in her arms and realized she had a few ways to remember her new friends. She had the memories, she told herself.

She didn't know what kind of adventures that crew would get up to next, but Sophia knew they'd do it in style. Pip in his kilt, Bailey with her humor, Lewis with his class, Hatch with his brilliance and *Ricky Bobby* with his unwavering attention.

With fondness in her heart, Sophia realized she had her very own *Ricky Bobby*, run by Quiet. Evan, Mahkah, Hiker, Trin, Ainsley, Mama Jamba, and Wilder were her crew. She hoped they spent many rotations, circling the globe, making it a better place together and keeping each other laughing.

CHAPTER ONE HUNDRED TWENTY-SEVEN

You were gone for a whole ten minutes, Lunis accused, sounding disappointed.

Sophia looked between Lunis and Mae Ling with disbelief. "How is that possible? I was passed out for at least forty-five minutes on that battlecruiser, and I had been there for a while before and a while afterward."

Mae Ling's eyes sparkled with mystery. "It's just the way it works, my dear."

The class had been dismissed when Sophia returned, and Lunis appeared sad he wasn't being lavished with attention.

"Well, thanks for opening that portal for me," Sophia said. "Although I'm a bit confounded by the place I went and how it was possible."

Mae Ling seemed to understand her confusion. "Papa Creola recognizes the consequences if the Great Library is destroyed. We all do. Currently, on this planet, there wasn't a means to destroy Nevin Gooseman."

Sophia held up the objects in her hands and indicated the CAR. "I hope we do now."

"It will depend on how you and your team perform," Mae Ling said cautiously. "But I hope so too."

"The portal that you two opened to *Ricky Bobby*…" Sophia trailed away, giving Mae Ling a hopeful expression.

"It's closed now," her fairy godmother answered. "It was a risk to the timeline having it in the first place, but that was one reason I required that you leave Lunis here. That kept you safe and ensured you would return, and not create an anomaly in our history. We are hoping that you change it." Mae Ling gave her a deadly serious expression. "I think you recognize now how important this is."

Sophia sucked in a breath and nodded. "Yes, I get it more than ever."

CHAPTER ONE HUNDRED TWENTY-EIGHT

Technology wasn't King Rudolf Sweetwater's forte. Saying words like forte were. Or drinking games. Or cheating at board games.

Fae didn't really do technology. They hired ugly magicians to set up their security systems and computers and ensure that their appliances brewed their coffee just right, and their toasters didn't burn their hot cross buns.

However, Rudolf was nothing if he wasn't adaptable. This was a man who didn't touch a single woman during the Spanish flu. If that didn't show fortitude, then he didn't know what did. Of course, after it was safe, he pretty much touched every woman he could, but desperate times call for desperation.

Using his camouflaging spell, Rudolf settled down at Nevin Gooseman's computer, knowing that if the politician came into the office at that late hour, he wouldn't spot the fae. He might smell him though since Rudolf had polished off a bottle of bourbon and a box of powdered donuts.

He licked his fingers. It was always the little treats that were the gift that kept giving.

All were asleep in the Gooseman residence. Rudolf's late-night adventures and spying had told him that the security, staff, and family all tucked in around nine o'clock each night, completely bored by their lives. Since no one cared to call on these people and they had zero imagination, they all just sipped their tea and went to bed, preparing themselves for the monotony of tomorrow.

Rudolf stretched, his hands over his head, and cracked his knuckles. Usually, nine o'clock at night was when Serena, his wife, was just waking up from the festivities of the day before. Since they lived and owned the Las Vegas strip, "friends" whose names they never knew were always stopping by. The party didn't peak until around two in the morning and was usually over by the time the Captains were waking up. Fae didn't really need much sleep.

There was actually a century where Rudolf only slept an hour and a half the entire hundred years. He was pretty certain he married someone during that period, although he couldn't find proof of it. He'd just wake up randomly in the present century and yell, "I do! If it makes you feel better, then I'll hitch myself to you!"

Then there was the scar on his left hip he couldn't explain.

He smiled and giggled to himself, the bourbon doing the trick. Maybe it was the powdered donuts. Or both.

"Life is an adventure," he whispered to himself, preparing to hack into Nevin Gooseman's computer. The only problem was, he didn't know how to break into anything but a liquor cabinet or a cookie jar.

"If mortals and magicians can do it, then I can too," he stated, trying to give himself confidence.

He combed his hand over the side of the monitor and winked at the computer. "Hey, baby. Do you come here often?"

The computer screen lit up, showing a password screen.

That wouldn't do. Everything could be seduced. Rudolf had even once seduced a giantess in order to get access to her property. He shivered with disgust, remembering. He could still smell the beet juice under his fingernails.

Directing his attention at the computer, he blew it a kiss and said, "So howwww yooooou doin?"

The password magically filled in and then bypassed the security screen.

Rudolf smiled, sitting back. Life was so easy for him. He didn't understand why magicians complicated everything with trying to understand things when they could rely on charm and good looks.

Then Rudolf remembered that those options weren't available. To them.

Staring at the screen of options, Rudolf was confounded by what to do next. There was a whole slew of documents and data, and he really didn't know where to start.

"What would Liv do?" he asked himself.

Pulling up the search options, Rudolf pecked out the query, "Top secret information."

Nothing came up.

He sighed. "I really thought that would work."

Again he typed up a search, "Bad stuff."

No results.

Drumming his lips in frustration, Rudolf considered giving up. That was the best thing about him. Some people pushed themselves until they were exhausted. They really went the extra mile, stressing themselves out until they succeeded. Not Rudolf Sweetwater. He quit well before that and had no real wrinkles to prove it. At a ripe six-hundred years old, he was one handsome man with few to no accomplishments, no education, and a kingdom of slobs. He had the life.

But this time, he couldn't give up. The Beaufonts were relying on him. The Great Library was at stake. Rudolf wanted to go home and sleep on his satin sheets. He wanted to snuggle his babies and tell his wife to, "Chop chop, bake me a pie, woman." Then Serena would throw an empty vodka bottle at his head, and he'd feel better for being home.

Deciding he was going to give it another go, Rudolf pictured in his mind what he wanted. No, what he needed. Information linking Nevin Gooseman to the conspiracies behind the Dragon Elite.

He held his hands out and directed his magical energy at the screen. At first, nothing happened, and then window after window popped up, showing dozens and dozens of pieces of data, all of them indicting the politician, proving he slandered the Dragon Elite.

CHAPTER ONE HUNDRED
TWENTY-NINE

I *don't think it will fit,* Lunis said dryly, regarding the T-shirt from Pimping Pip's Apparel she brought back from her adventures with the crew of *Ricky Bobby.*

Sophia tried to laugh, but instead, her eyes trailed over the Expanse of the Gullington. "Yeah, I think you're right."

What's wrong? Lunis asked.

She shrugged. "Nothing."

You can't lie to me, he reminded her.

"We both know I'm lying and not even trying, so what?"

You liked them, he said, sounding slightly offended.

"I did. But I like all people. It's just hard to go somewhere and know you can't go back. Sometimes it's easier not to know than never have a chance to return."

That's how I'd feel about Montana, he remarked. *Like if you told me I couldn't go back, I'd be all sad, but as it is, I'm not making any immediate plans of returning. That place is cold, and that's coming from me, a dragon who calls Scotland home.*

Sophia scrunched up her shoulders, feeling a sudden warmth in her chest. "Yeah, that's a good point. And this is home."

Lunis's tail wrapped around her. *Soph, home is where we are. As long as we are together.*

She nodded, feeling a new fondness for her dragon. "Did you enjoy the attention at Happily Ever After college?"

He shrugged. *Sort of, but also not really. I mean, don't get me wrong, it was nice, but it's all based on myth, and although some of it is based on real events, a lot has been blown out of proportion. Dragons are amazing, but at the end of the day, we're as susceptible to dangers as you or any other magical creature. They kept regarding me like I was invincible, and although that's nice, I don't need the false confidence.*

Sophia smiled, leaning back into her dragon. "You know, Lunis, for being a young dragon, you're wise beyond your years."

He lowered his head, pressing it down on hers, but not hard—just letting her know he was there. *The thing is, having the affection of strangers that think you're larger than life isn't as nice as having the depth of affection from someone who knows your flaws and loves you despite them.*

"Or loves you because of them," Sophia countered.

She felt him smile above her. *Thanks, Soph.*

Breaking their special moment as they looked out over the Expanse and Pond in the distance was the buzzing of Sophia's phone. She would have ignored it, but they both knew that was a negligent move with so much going on. She straightened and pulled her phone from her pocket, reading the message from her sister.

Feeling her chest tighten with both excitement and tension, Sophia looked up at her dragon. "It's go time. We're ready to storm the Great Library."

CHAPTER ONE HUNDRED THIRTY

"It's all come down to this," Hiker Wallace said, striding in front of the Dragon Elite, who stood on the Expanse of the Gullington.

"This may not be the end of Nevin Gooseman and his agenda," he continued, his hands pinned behind his back, his chin held up high in the air as the wind pushed his shoulder-length hair back behind him. "This will be the end of this battle. We will see to that."

Mahkah, Evan, Sophia, and Wilder all stood at attention, their dragons stoically at their backs, all of their focus on their leader.

Hiker halted, his eyes pinning each one of them individually. "You all know what you must do, correct?"

"Yes, sir," they answered in unison.

"The timing is crucial," Hiker continued.

"Yes, sir," they said again.

"We've heard the instructions from Sophia about the CAR," Hiker informed them, making everyone nod.

"You will wait for my command," Hiker stated with authority, to which no one objected.

From the steps of the Castle in the distance, Sophia spied Mama Jamba working on her ball of wax, humming as she did so like there was nothing else of interest going on. It was a nice spring day with no cares in the world.

"The two most important objectives are that we protect the Great Library and we get King Rudolf Sweetwater away to safety," the Viking ordered.

"Yes, sir," everyone said again.

"Very good," Hiker said with relief. He picked up the CAR Sophia had given to him, explaining the specifics and directions for using it. They'd sat down like two strategic leaders and mapped out the plan they would follow. It wasn't exact, but the best plans weren't. They allowed for some flexibility, depending on circumstances.

Hiker handed the stainless-steel box to Sophia with a nod of his head. "I trust you to push the button when the time comes."

She nodded. "Yes, sir."

"While in battle, you will follow all orders given to you by your leader Sophia, who will be communicating with you all throughout," he stated and pointed to the earpiece they all shared, using regular technology and no magitech. They'd come a long way since their first battle together.

As Sophia stared at her fellow dragonriders, she looked forward to further progress and to see what other places they progressed toward. Together.

CHAPTER ONE HUNDRED THIRTY-ONE

There was no greater feeling than riding into a battle with her team beside her. Lunis felt the rush too, his heart beating steadily underneath Sophia. She could feel it pounding like it was her own. She felt the heat building in him as he flapped his long wings, soaring over the oceans that stretched around the Great Library.

Of course, the Dragon Elite knew the exact location of the mysterious place due to Plato's help. He'd also communicated it to Rudolf so he could find it when he led Nevin Gooseman's army there. The glamour protecting the Great Library from view had been taken down. That was the only way for this to work. The magitech army needed to see the library. They needed to not believe this was a trap and be on the defensive. Then they could be "caught," and the chase could begin.

Beside Sophia and Lunis was Wilder, riding Simi, her white scales reflecting the evening sunlight that shimmered over the ocean waves. Behind them, riding alongside each other were Mahkah and Tala. Bringing up the rear was the fearless Evan on Coral.

Sophia and Lunis couldn't be seen by the magitech army or anyone but the other Dragon Elite members. The same was true for the guys.

They were cloaked from mortals and magicians alike...at least for now until everything was in place.

"I'm really going to miss this place when it's gone," Plato said, fondly, looking up at the rows and rows of books that went on for miles and miles in the Great Library.

Liv rolled her eyes at the lynx. "It's not going anywhere. The Dragon Elite are going to defend it, and we're going to get Rudolf back."

"True about that first part, but I don't see the harm in a little collateral damage in this fight," the cat replied, squinting from the evening sun streaming through the bank of windows running along the walls of the Great Library.

"Rudolf won't be collateral damage," Liv stated with conviction. "Not on my watch. Especially after the information he dug up on Nevin Gooseman."

"Fine, let the chimp live," Plato said. "It's quite the impressive feat he's made it this long."

Liv nodded, unable to argue with that. "He's really a wonder. How can someone be so unbelievably clueless and at the same time, incredibly competent when the occasion strikes?"

"I think the creator of the fae—Anastasia Crystal—blessed him somehow," Plato imparted.

Liv lowered her chin regarding her familiar through a hooded gaze. "You think..."

He shrugged, starting to stride down the aisle. "I heard a rumor."

She followed alongside him. "That's interesting. I wonder why he got special treatment."

Plato's tail flickered in the air. "Probably nothing to do with anything important like a prophecy about his association to some Royals for the House of Fourteen."

Liv shook her head, not surprised by this information or the fact that Plato knew it. "You mysterious little feline and your vast knowledge."

"As I was saying, I'll miss the Great Library when it's gone, but I was referring to the location," Plato explained.

"You're going to move it then? After this?" Liv glanced around at the huge place filled with every single book ever written. Except for two, which were both in Sophia's possession—*The Complete History of Dragonriders* and Baba Yaga's grimoire. Neither could be replicated, and both were full of incredible magic that in the wrong hands would be very dangerous. "You're going to need a big moving truck and some strong teenage boys. Maybe if you buy them a few pizzas, they'll do it for cheap."

Plato didn't appear amused by this. "I think I can handle it on my own, but I will need help with securing the new librarian."

"I can help with that!" Liv said, excitedly.

He lowered his chin and shook his head. "You do know the rules about being in a library, right?"

She pretended to think for a moment, combing her fingers over her chin. "You're supposed to run through them madly and always reshelve your own books because, as an inexperienced nonlibrarian, you know the best way to do it."

"Get out," he told her bluntly.

Liv glanced over her shoulder, with a mock look of fear. "There's about to be a magitech army out there, and it's really sunny, and I didn't bring my sunglasses or put on my sunscreen."

"In a library," he instructed in his usual dignified tone, "it is customary to speak at a low volume."

"Yeah, but that's like that whole idea of not running with scissors," Liv joked. "It's advice, but not a rule."

"They are both rules," he corrected. "You're not supposed to throw scissors either."

Liv laughed loudly. "Hey, Stefan needed them, and I didn't feel like getting off the couch."

Plato shook his head with a disappointed look. "I will require both

SARAH NOFFKE & MICHAEL ANDERLE

you and your sister's help in recruiting the new librarian I have chosen."

"Does this person know they've been picked yet?"

He lifted an eyebrow and glared at her with a look that said, "What do you think?"

"What if this person won't take the job?" Liv asked, looking around, marveling at the vastness of the Great Library. "I mean, it is a really lonely job."

"You have read a book before, right?"

"Once," she replied quickly.

"For those who read, they are never lonely or bored," Plato told her sagely.

"Yeah!" she said too loudly again. "How does the phrase go..." Liv thought for a moment.

"The quieter you become, the more you can hear," Plato offered, quite seriously.

She shook her head. "No! That's not it."

"Confidence is silent. Insecurities are loud," Plato supplied.

"Nope!" Liv exclaimed. "It's on the tip of my tongue though."

"Oh, I know what it is," Plato said with confidence. "He who knows little knows enough, if he knows how to hold his tongue."

Liv laughed out loud. "I see where you're going with this and it won't work."

He nodded. "Those more powerful than me have tried to make you quiet down and failed."

Her brow scrunched up with confusion. "Who is more powerful than you? Oh, Papa Creola, I guess. But not by much. And yeah, that old man keeps trying to get me to put a lid on it, but I can't be deterred."

"That is both your greatest strength and biggest weakness," Plato observed.

"Oh!" she yelled, her eyes popping with surprise. "Speaking of which, I remember the quote." Liv snapped her fingers as she tried to remember the exact words of the George R. R. Martin phrase. "It goes,

'A reader lives a thousand lives before he dies. The man who never reads lives only once.'"

"Yes, so I dare say that the person I've chosen to be the librarian for the Great Library will not get bored," Plato told her confidently.

Liv sighed dramatically. "Although, I'd argue I've already lived a few hundred lives, and I never have the time to read."

"Try audiobooks," he suggested. "You are the exception, and I think you will live more lives than any reader."

"Oh!" she marveled. "Maybe I'll write my own book one day, full of all my adventures. Do you think people would read it?"

He shrugged. "Only really smart people who can appreciate your sense of humor."

She batted her eyes at him. "Why, thank you, dear Plato."

"Anyway, this librarian will take some convincing, which is why I want you and Sophia to both use your efforts to recruit him," Plato said, slipping back into his business-like tone. "Getting to him will be complicated and somewhat dangerous."

"I'd expect nothing less," she replied with a laugh. "Nothing is worth the end result if I don't have to cross an active volcano and battle a deranged monster to get it. So, where is this future librarian?"

Plato looked out the bank of windows at the ocean that surrounded the Great Library. "I'll give you the information on that at a later date, after the battle today has been won, and the library moved to its new location. It won't be safe to stay here after Nevin Gooseman and his army knows where it is. Even with the complication of needing to find the Fierce to get here, it's not worth the risk to have such unhealthy minds to know about this place. Those who would both want to destroy this place and also believe it should be open to all, understand very little about this world. Knowledge must be valued and protected at all costs."

He looked around at the shelves of books proudly. "The person I've chosen as the new librarian understands that, and when the time is right, I'll call on you and Sophia to find him."

Liv nodded, feeling a rush of sentimentality, brought on by Plato's words. He was right about the Great Library being protected, both in that it should be preserved and also kept secret from the world. In this place, there were spells that, in the wrong hands, could cause serious damage. They could end the world as they knew it. According to Sophia, that might have been the Earth's future, but they were about to change all that.

"I've taken down the protective wards on the Great Library," Plato said, his eyes suddenly distant.

"Making us vulnerable to attack," Liv observed.

"I trust the Dragon Elite won't allow that to happen," Plato imparted.

She nodded, pressing her lips together.

"When the time comes, I plan to move the library, making it vanish from this spot," Plato explained. "I trust those who want it gone, won't stop searching for it, unless they believe it's been destroyed."

"So we're going to fake it so Nevin Gooseman thinks there is no more Great Library," Liv guessed.

"We aren't going to do anything," he said in an authoritative tone. "Yet, it is safer for this place if it is thought to be gone."

"Well, what can I do?" Liv asked. "You know I'm not good at sitting around and doing nothing."

He blinked, drawing in a breath. "Unfortunately, that's exactly what you'll have to do. Pull up a seat and watch because this battle is about to begin."

Liv followed his gaze, finally seeing what he had been looking at for a while, approaching. In the distance, a huge fleet of a magitech army was racing toward them over the ocean.

CHAPTER ONE HUNDRED
THIRTY-TWO

Nevin Gooseman smiled with satisfaction at the sight of the Great Library perched on a set of stones off the coast of Zanzibar. It was a tiny building, but he could sense the magic rebounding off of it and knew it was the real deal.

Rudolf Sweetwater had finally delivered on the location of the Great Library. That was good because he had only one more day before Nevin was going to dispose of him. Too many strange things had been happening at his residence with that fae around.

Nevin knew it was impossible for the king to have his magic since he was eating the spelled food, but his presence was causing problems with his staff, making them misbehave. Someone most recently had gotten a strange white powder on the keyboard to his computer. All the staff had been fired, and Nevin's children scolded.

He couldn't take any chances—not when he was so close to taking the Dragon Elite down. It was all but inevitable.

Nevin leaned on the railing of the roof, where he stood in Stone Town, standing high above the city of Zanzibar on one of the tallest buildings on the coast. It gave him a perfect view of the events that were about to unfold and kept him a safe distance from the action.

In the distance, approaching from the other side of the Great

Library, having come through the portals, was his magitech army. The helicopter that contained the king of the fae was in the lead.

In a matter of a few minutes, Rudolf Sweetwater would be escorted into the Great Library to fetch the book Nevin needed to undo the spell that was cloaking the evil dragons. The fae had been told that if he delivered the book, he'd be allowed to go free.

Technically that was true. Nevin's men would leave Rudolf in the Great Library and fly off with the book in tow. What the dumb fae didn't know was that moments after they were gone, the Great Library and all of its contents, along with Rudolf, would be blown to bits and erased from this world.

It was all going according to plan, Nevin thought with gratitude, rubbing his palms together in satisfaction. This just proved when you did the right thing and rid the world of evil that you were rewarded, Nevin concluded, staring at the magitech army approaching the Great Library. Nothing could stop what would happen next.

CHAPTER ONE HUNDRED THIRTY-THREE

The magitech army was impressive, Sophia had to admit. In the lead was a helicopter that didn't move like one. Its blades rotated with a smoothness, unlike anything Sophia had seen before. The fighter jets behind it were no doubt stocked with too much fire-power. All meant to level the Great Library when the time came. But that time wasn't going to come. Today things were going in the Dragon Elite's favor. Nevin Gooseman had won too many battles up until now sullying the reputation of the dragonriders. Today it ended.

She turned her attention to Wilder hovering next to her, Simi and Lunis barely having to flap their wings to stay afloat.

She gave him a single look and he knew what to do. It would be his job to get King Rudolf to safety. He pressed out his lips, giving her a kiss in the air before speeding off after the helicopter, hoping to cut it off before it got any closer to the Great Library.

Spinning around, Sophia gave the command to Evan and Mahkah who set off at once, their jobs to go after the army. Sophia held onto the CAR before her. As Hiker had advised her on her birthday, there were times to fight and there were times to sit back and let others. Sophia and Lunis would remain cloaked and free from the danger of the battle about to ensue, but their job wasn't easy.

This fight was all about timing, and if they didn't get it exactly right, they stood to lose more than just the Great Library. The dragonriders had never been more at risk than then, when having to race around an army that would inevitably be exploded to pieces, but hopefully only when they were far away.

"What does that button do?" King Rudolf Sweetwater said, pointing to the dashboard of the helicopter and nearly knocking the pilot in the face.

The pilot swatted his hand away. "Stay back there," the man warned, looking over his shoulder where Rudolf sat alone in the back row.

"Can we roll up the window?" Rudolf asked over the intercom, the microphone of the headphones positioned right in front of his mouth.

The magitech helicopter didn't have doors, and the wind rushing through was really messing up Rudolf's hair and making his eyes water.

"Would you be quiet already?" the copilot spat, glancing back at Rudolf.

"Okey, dokey," Rudolf sang, leaning out and looking at the blue waters they were crossing.

Using the magic they didn't know he had, the king of the fae had already unfastened his seat belt. Now he just had to wait for his new ride to show up. It was sort of like waiting for an Uber, although without the app functionality that told him exactly when the driver would arrive.

One would think the fae wouldn't need to take an Uber because he could rely on his portal magic. That person wouldn't understand how scary it was to try portaling after drinking on the Las Vegas strip all night and finding yourself in a prison cell with a guy named Shark. There was an exact science to creating portals and doing it while drunk made for some dangerous mistakes.

"Are we there yet," Rudolf whined, seeing the Great Library in the distance, a few miles away. "I've got to pee."

"Shut up, you idiot!" the pilot yelled.

Rudolf smiled at the raging wagon sniffer. He'd sort of miss him when he was gone. But not his copilot, mange jacker. That guy could go eat a bunch of laundry pods and die for all he cared.

"What the hell is that?" the copilot asked, pointing at the massive dragon and rider who had materialized out of seemingly thin air.

"That's your funeral," Rudolf sang, leaning out of the helicopter and hoping Wilder caught him since he couldn't use portal magic and really didn't want to take a swim.

CHAPTER ONE HUNDRED
THIRTY-FOUR

W ilder was prepared for the attacks the magitech helicopter unleashed. Not wanting to endanger their own, the army behind them didn't fire. That was fine. They'd have their own friends to play with, Wilder thought with a laugh.

Having experience battling magitech, Wilder knew that trying to outpace the missiles locked on him was not a good strategy. It was a waste of energy and took him away from his mission of getting closer to the helicopter. Unfortunately, he couldn't attack it just yet, not with the king of the fae on board.

So the dragonrider put up his hand and threw out a powerful shield that covered him and Simi. It was more than intimidating to race in the direction of the missile flying at him, unflinching. This part was about faith. He had to know that his magic was working, and it would protect him.

When the large missile hit the shield, it exploded but Simi and Wilder didn't feel the effects of it. He could do that maybe one or two more times. After that he'd be out of magic and out of options.

Wilder hoped it didn't come to that. He just had to be swift and get Rudolf before the magitech helicopter fired again. Glancing over his shoulder, he watched as Evan and Mahkah materialized, racing past him. Their fun was about to begin as they took on the giant magitech army behind the helicopter.

Evan didn't love anything more than the rush that accompanied battle. Well, he loved Coral, his purple dragon, more and NO10JO, his cyborg dog. There were no experiences that trumped riding into a fight, though, knowing he was about to hand some bad guys their asses in a rose-scented basket.

He slid his head to the side, winking at Mahkah, who rode the brown dragon known as Tala. For as quiet and unassuming as the old dragonrider was, there were few others that Evan wouldn't want to face in a fight. Actually, the three people that made up that list were in battle with him today and fighting on his side, Wilder, Mahkah, and the scariest of all, the Pink Princess.

Today, Evan had all the advantages in this battle. Coral's element was the ocean, which meant the fight was set in their arena. Releasing the reins to his dragon, he leaned out over the side and flicked his hand in the air, like he was on top of the water and splashing the person in front of him.

Before them were a few cowards, all protected in their magitech fighter jets. Evan could see the pilots, but not the murderous expressions they no doubt wore as the two dragons and their riders raced in their direction.

"Time to play, fella!" Evan cheered, just as three of the jets released attacks in their direction.

He cackled loudly as the missiles chased after them. In front of the missiles, a wall of water rose at Evan's command, making the missiles fall flat and sink into the ocean where they'd detonate safely at the bottom.

Evan gave Mahkah a proud wink. "Ready for the chase to begin?"

He nodded, taking off fast, his black braid streaking behind him as they led the magitech army away from the Great Library, but keep them close enough that Sophia could "catch" them with the CAR.

CHAPTER ONE HUNDRED
THIRTY-FIVE

Her heart pounding in her throat, Sophia watched as the meter rose on the CAR. That was the indication of the magitech registering with the device and being caught.

Watching Wilder have to race toward the helicopter was stressful enough, knowing he had to endure the attacks without retaliating to keep Rudolf safe. To double her stress, Sophia and Lunis had to idly sit by as Evan and Mahkah rode into battle, antagonizing the magitech army.

She knew that both riders were competent and could hold their own in most circumstances, but they'd never faced forces this large and stocked with so much artillery. The army of fighter jets had enough ammunition to blow up the Great Library, which meant if they threw everything they had at the dragonriders posing a threat to them, she didn't think her friends would survive.

"Come on," she urged, watching as the meter slowly ticked upwards. It had about half of the magitech caught, but there were at least a dozen more it needed to capture. Rudolf hadn't been saved yet, which meant there was a stalling game that needed to happen.

The Dragon Elite were trying to ruin everything, but it wasn't going to work, Nevin thought with satisfaction.

Them showing up would actually work in his favor. He wasn't sure how they knew to be at the Great Library but suspected it was of no coincidence. They were the few allowed into the place full of every book on the globe, so they probably had protective wards on the place that told them when there was trespassing.

That was another reason the Great Library had to be destroyed. If it was open to the Dragon Elite, but few others, that was unfair. There was no one more detestable than these magicians who rode beasts and thought that their authority trumped that of major countries and governments.

Nevin knew he'd be stopping the Dragon Elite, but he had no idea he'd have the fortune of doing it that day.

He smiled sadistically, looking out at the battle waging over the ocean. There was no way that three dragonriders and their monsters could defeat his army of magitech. He looked forward to watching them go down. Then he'd flatten their precious Great Library and return to ruling over the mortal world, unobstructed by the Dragon Elite.

CHAPTER ONE HUNDRED THIRTY-SIX

Knowing he couldn't take another attack, already having shielded against two, Wilder pulled down the defensive measure and sped toward the magitech helicopter. It was now or never. The problem with that mentality was it also could mean die now...

He shook off this negative thought and urged Simi to dive low between the helicopter and the ocean. The magitech aircraft was stalled over the waters, having paused to fight the dragonrider. That worked for Wilder but also meant he needed to make his move before they did.

His move obviously confused the pilots and he watched as they leaned forward, trying to figure out where he'd disappeared to. They thought he was trying to get away. Maybe they thought it was a trick because the Asshats released a third missile.

"No!" Wilder yelled, knowing he couldn't put his shield up again. That would ruin the plan and deplete his magic.

There was only one option left as he and Simi soared directly under the helicopter. He caught sight of the blond hair of the king of the fae and hoped the timing worked.

At the same moment that Rudolf Sweetwater jumped from the hovering helicopter, his eyes bright and a smile on his face, Wilder threw his arm in the direction of the missile racing at them. He pulled on the element connected to Simi, harnessing the wind. Shields and water could stop missiles. Unfortunately, wind couldn't. What it could do would hopefully be enough. Wilder hoped the missile would be thrown off course enough, and give them a chance to escape.

Rudolf had ridden many things before. Horses, bulls, even an elf named Mixie. However, he had never ridden a dragon before. What hopefully would come next would make this abduction business worth it. He liked adding new experiences to his memory.

Without any concern for his hair, which was undoubtedly destroyed by the raging wind, Rudolf leaped out of the magitech helicopter when the strapping dragonrider he called Kyle soared underneath. Rudolf refused to call anyone Wilder. That was too cool of a name, and to top it off, the guy had hair that might rival his own, as well as piercing blue eyes that almost hypnotized him. They were almost too much, but he was willing to forgive Kyle if he saved his life.

With an abbreviated goodbye, Rudolf jumped out of the helicopter, making Nerf Graduate and Bastardized Jockey Wanker spin around from the cockpit, shocked that the fae was jumping.

As he free-fell, Rudolf caught sight of the missile speeding in the direction of the dragonrider and his steed. Kyle threw out his hand, and the attack tumbled back in the air like a stone, end over end. It was close. Close enough that if it detonated, they'd be a part of its collateral damage.

Putting himself into position, Rudolf dropped onto the dragon like it wasn't his first time, fastening his arms around Kyle's waist as his manhood absorbed the brunt of the impact. Unable to talk, he coughed from the pain into the dragonrider's shoulder as they soared off just as the missile exploded from the wind attack, propelling them in the opposite direction. Rudolf felt the blast of heat like he was lying on a tanning bed.

Kyle opened a portal in front of them as they soared over the ocean, and soon they were through it and to another, safer land where Rudolf could get drunk on strawberry wine and forget he ever had to look at so much modern art.

CHAPTER ONE HUNDRED THIRTY-SEVEN

One down, Sophia thought, feeling victorious as she watched Rudolf and Wilder disappear through the portal. Now she could "catch" the rest of the magitech devices and finish this fight.

Evan and Mahkah were keeping the army busy, streaking around them as they fired on. However, they couldn't maintain that for long, she knew. By the rush of words in her ear, they were starting to figure that out too.

At first, the communications had been light, full of Evan's banter as he enticed the enemy.

Now they were full of tension as the attacks got closer.

"Just two more," Sophia told them, staring daggers at the CAR, willing it to catch the other two devices she'd counted, for a total of twenty-four.

"Hurry!" Evan yelled, and in the distance, she spied as a missile nearly took off Coral's tail.

The water attacks were apparently losing their stamina and not knocking down the magitech assaults like they had in the beginning.

Her heart lightened as the meter ticked up a notch.

"One more!" Sophia exclaimed, watching as the meter rose one bar. Almost there, she thought.

She glanced up to spot Mahkah throw an attack back at a fighter jet, making it slam into another one.

Blowing out a breath, she marveled at the sheer power that unsuspecting magician had.

However, his attack had cost him the offensive, and now he had two missiles after him. "Get out of there!" Sophia yelled.

He knew she was right and sped away, trying to outrace the attacks.

"Portal, man!" Evan encouraged. "I've got this."

Mahkah didn't appear willing to abandon his team, but with the missiles closing in on him, he had little choice.

The meter rose another notch. "We're there," Sophia exclaimed. "Hitting the button now!"

That was the last thing Mahkah needed to hear. He opened a portal and disappeared. Evan, who needed to get out of there as soon as she pressed the button did so as well.

Sophia held her breath and pushed the red button, knowing she was close enough to watch what happened, but hopefully far enough away to not feel its effects. She looked at the Great Library beside her, seeing Liv and Plato watching from the windows, grateful she could protect the structure, and her friends.

CHAPTER ONE HUNDRED THIRTY-EIGHT

Grinding his fingers into his fist, Nevin nearly yelled. He couldn't believe the dragonrider had gotten away with Rudolf. He shook his head. It didn't matter.

Nevin still knew the book they were looking for. The pilot of the helicopter knew.

He pressed his finger to his ear. "Go on to the Great Library. Get me that book. Now!"

The helicopter that had been hovering in place began to progress toward the Great Library. He might have lost the king of the fae, but Nevin still had what he needed. Soon he'd have the book, and then he'd flatten the place. Everything would work out, even if the obnoxious dragonriders had tried to ruin everything by showing up.

Like the cowards they were, they'd stolen the king of the fae back and then retreated, too scared to face his army. Too bad for them, they didn't know what he had planned for their precious library.

Nevin's frustration turned to laughter as he started his celebration early.

CHAPTER ONE HUNDRED THIRTY-NINE

To Sophia's horror, the magitech helicopter she'd hooked onto with the CAR was speeding toward the Great Library, the rest of the fleet following. They were a fair distance away and wouldn't make it close enough in time, but the helicopter was nearer and could cause problems.

If it exploded by the Great Library, it could damage it. She and Lunis were beside it. They couldn't move. Not until the detonation happened.

Sophia did the only thing she knew. It was her or the Great Library. The choice was easy, even if it broke her heart.

Taking down the cloaking spell, Sophia made herself visible to the magitech helicopter.

The pilot saw her immediately. She knew it because they turned in her direction, away from the Great Library, as she sped away on Lunis. She was careful to maintain the proper distance for the CAR to stay locked on the magitech army, now speeding in her direction too.

Things had gone from good to horrible in seconds. She didn't have anyone to rely on, everyone else having left through the portals. They would believe it was all wrapped up. The army would explode, and then Sophia would join them for a celebration and the press conference where Nevin Gooseman was ruined. What they didn't realize, and what Sophia was coming to terms with, was that she'd be watching them from the heavens—if at all.

CHAPTER ONE HUNDRED FORTY

"We have to help her!" Liv screamed from the Great Library, disbelieving she was watching as a magitech ready to explode within seconds was racing after her little sister.

"We can't," Plato told her. "We have to go. It's time for the Great Library to be moved."

"Plato!" Liv yelled, tears streaming down her face, her heart fracturing. "That's my little sister. That's my world, and she's about to go down to protect this place. It can stay because I would rather it be destroyed than her."

"You don't know what you're saying, Liv," Plato advised. "The death of one isn't worth the greater good!"

"How dare you! She's the best thing that ever happened to me!" Liv fired.

"Sophia knows what she risked being here," Plato said sternly. "This world was scheduled to perish if something happened to the Great Library, and she changed that. She shifted the timeline and changed history. You should be proud."

Liv screamed her anger, all she could feel. "Proud? My little sister is about to die, and all so a bunch of idiots on this globe can go on to destroy each other!"

"Have a little faith," Plato said, looking away from her and out the window.

Liv forced herself to look as her sister raced on the magnificent dragon known as Lunis. Suddenly something bright sparkled off Sophia. It was almost too much for Liv, making her tilt her head to the side. Then she recovered and noticed the evening sunlight was reflecting off Sophia's earrings, and the effect was almost blinding. Even from that distance, it was almost too much for Liv to look at. It was entirely too much for the pilot of the magitech helicopter, causing him to slow and then retreat and giving Sophia and Lunis the chance to get away from their pursuers.

"It's time, Liv," Plato reminded her just as an explosion rocked the foundation of the Great Library, making everything shake around them.

CHAPTER ONE HUNDRED
FORTY-ONE

Sophia could hardly believe it! The earrings Mama Jamba had given her for her birthday had actually saved her life, giving her and Lunis the chance to get away from the magitech helicopter.

She and Lunis raced away, and only felt a fraction of the heat from the blast as the CAR did its job, exploding all the magitech it had caught.

The helicopter. The fighter jets. The army racing toward the Great Library. They all exploded, turning the blue skies above the ocean to orange and red, making it appear that the sunset had happened early on the horizon, and sending sparks of sunlight everywhere.

Sophia shielded her eyes as she looked over her shoulder as Lunis continued to put distance between them and the heat of the explosion. She watched as metal crashed down into the ocean waters, and splashes rose up, followed by steam and more explosions.

When they were at a safe distance, Lunis paused and spun around, knowing Sophia needed this moment to rejoice and to feel grateful for all they'd accomplished.

You did good, her dragon said to her, a thoughtful pride in his voice.

She laid down on him, feeling the CAR under her. "I could never do anything without you."

She felt him smile, as though the gesture had spread across her own lips. *What you don't understand is the sun will rise tomorrow because of you. Solely because you're brave enough to do what most won't. Today you changed history. Tomorrow, who knows what you'll do?*

"I hope to sleep," she said longingly.

Then it sounds like I should take you home, he said, and Sophia opened a portal just as the Great Library disappeared from view. She only caught it briefly as they disappeared, returning to the place she hoped to always call home. And hoped never disappeared.

CHAPTER ONE HUNDRED
FORTY-TWO

"Noo!" Nevin yelled, feeling the floor under him vibrate from the explosions of his magitech army being demolished. He couldn't believe it!

This victory had surely been his. He had all but been able to taste it.

Then everything had shifted. Just when he thought his magitech helicopter would catch the evil dragonrider and his army would level the Great Library, they'd all gone up in flames. Now he was watching from the rooftop as the billion-dollar military force he'd spent years creating was raining down into the ocean.

The Dragon Elite had done this. Now they were going to pay more than ever. He was going to ruin them for good. He knew where the Great Library was, and he would take it down with every gun the United States military had.

Then something weird happened. Something was wrong. The Great Library flickered like it had been an illusion all along, although he knew that was impossible. It did it several times until the building, which wasn't big to begin with, disappeared altogether, vanishing from view. It was gone as if it had been destroyed. That didn't make any sense because his army was also gone, sinking to the bottom of the ocean.

Yet, there was no Great Library. Just a rock where it once sat.

"Sir," a man said at Nevin's back. "There's something you need to see."

"What is it?" Nevin boomed, his hostility at an all-time high.

"It's the national news," the security guard stated. "It's about you. The leader of the Dragon Elite is making a public statement."

Nevin sped off the rooftop to the living area, where he had his security and admin support set up, to find televisions all blaring the same report. Hiker Wallace had finally made an appearance, but there was no Mother Nature next to him.

Instead, he was holding up a piece of paper, a smug look on the dragonrider's face. "Here I have a detailed report taken from Nevin Gooseman's personal computer dating back to two years ago when he manufactured the disease called distortion that infected magicians and elves. This evidence, which the Dragon Elite have turned over to authorities, links Nevin Gooseman not just to the disease of distortion, but to being responsible for it." The leader of the Dragon Elite looked at the camera. "Looks like it's your turn, Nevin, to do some explaining. Try and discredit the Dragon Elite, and we will persevere because we are on the side of good. We are the true protectors of this planet. We are the supreme authority to rule over all. Deal with it."

Nevin yelled so loud that every one of his employees looked at him with fear. He had lost everything. He had been discredited. He had been defeated.

Sadistically he smiled despite the loss. There was no place further down for a man of his status to go. Before, it had been about making the world a better place.

Now it was war. The Dragon Elite was going down. He had nothing left to lose. The dragonriders had taken everything from him already, and they'd pay.

CHAPTER ONE HUNDRED FORTY-THREE

The Great Library had disappeared, but Liv assured Sophia it was fine, and she'd find out more information on it soon. The portal through the Castle would be open soon, once it was in place. Apparently, once the librarian was found. That bit of information was also surrounded by hints from Liv, but Sophia decided after her recent adventures that she could wait to learn the details.

Once she'd returned to the Castle, she'd found the guys ready to embrace her and celebrate, as the world learned the truth about Nevin Gooseman, and the man was totally discredited. With that, the Dragon Elite was getting back their well-earned reputation.

However, there was no time for celebrations because Sophia had gotten word from both Bep and Jeremy Bearimy that the healing elixir and Ainsley's dress were ready. Sophia wasn't off her dragon for more than a few minutes before she was portaling back to Roya Lane.

She returned to find Hiker standing at the Barrier, waiting for her, having heard where and what she'd left for. He was wearing a smart suit, having dressed for his press conference.

"You have it?" he asked, looking at the dress box in her hands, his eyes scanning for the potion.

"It's in my cloak pocket," she explained.

He nodded, but he didn't look relieved by the information.

"Should we do it now?" Sophia asked him, giving him the large box that contained Ainsley's dress from Jeremy Bearimy.

"It's up to Ainsley," he stated, heading for the Castle, not walking with his normal urgency.

"Sir," Sophia began, realizing they hadn't had a chance to discuss Nevin Gooseman or their recent victory.

He glanced at her.

"We did it," she told him with a triumphant smile.

Hiker nodded. "That's what we do. After this, rest up, Sophia because the next battle will be approaching."

"Do they ever stop?" she asked.

"Not in my time, they haven't, but the world is a different place now."

"Why is that?" Sophia asked, curious.

"Because you're in it, and you don't stop," he told her. "I know that you almost died at Zanzibar, although the others don't."

"How?" she asked.

He cut his eyes at her. "Bell was there watching for me."

"Oh." Sophia was happy that if she had died, someone she knew would have been there.

"You could have portaled," he began, but she cut him off.

"That would have ruined the CAR," she argued.

Hiker nodded. "That's what I mean. The world has gone to shit because when things got tough, cowards were the ones fighting. Most would have saved themselves, but you didn't. You stayed. You fought. Even knowing you might have died alone. I was right to make you my second in command." He glanced down at the dress box. "Again, you helped me. Let's hope that now I can help myself."

"She'll be okay," Sophia said. They both knew she was referring to Ainsley.

He pressed his lips together. "She will. I just wonder what will happen in her absence."

CHAPTER ONE HUNDRED FORTY-FOUR

"I don't really feel any different," Ainsley said after drinking the healing elixir Sophia had given her. They stood in the entryway of the Castle, all eyes on the elf.

"I don't think you will," Sophia explained. "I think it's just that you can now leave the Gullington without consequence."

Ainsley nodded. This realization didn't seem to be making her as happy as she had been bragging it would. "Well, then I guess I'll be setting off soon. I just have to gather my things and ensure that Trin is okay and—"

"When you're ready," Hiker interrupted. "No rush."

Ainsley pulled in a long breath. "I think I'll leave first thing tomorrow morning before the sun comes up. I like the idea of being gone before you're all up. Before you can see me off. That way…" Her mouth formed an odd shape like she was having trouble keeping it together. "That way," she began again. "You won't remember me leaving. It will be like I was never here."

"There's no reality where that would happen," Mahkah spoke for all of them.

"It won't be the same without you." Surprisingly, it was Evan who said that.

"Ains," Wilder said, emotion springing to his face. "You were the first person I saw when I came to the Gullington. Do you remember what you said to me when I walked into the Castle?"

"Take off your boots, I just mopped!" she exclaimed.

He laughed. "Then you said it every time I ever walked through the door."

She shook her head. "You think you would have learned after a few decades."

Wilder gave her a sentimental expression. "I did. I just liked being reminded of that first time I walked in here, and everything changed for me. My life changed. My mission became clear."

Ainsley rushed forward and threw her arms around Wilder, holding him tightly before separating and hugging Mahkah and Evan, like they were all the best of friends and didn't bicker on a daily basis. Which was actually true. There were no friends that were closer than the four who had spent more than a century together as the world recovered from its ailments.

"I have something for you, dear," Mama Jamba said when Ainsley pulled away from Evan.

She pushed the red hair out of her face and looked down at the small woman. "Yes, Mama? What is it?"

The old woman held up a small ball of wax. "I lied about working on tracking down the demon dragons. I figured that could wait. Instead, I created a time warp for you with Papa Creola's permission. If you ever want to know how your life would look differently, if things had been different, then you only need to hold this and travel back. It might offer answers. It might offer heartache. After losing so much, I thought it was the one thing you needed."

Ainsley looked to be having trouble swallowing. "Mama, are you sure..."

"Yes, sweet child," Mother Nature answered. "You lost your memory for the better part of a few centuries. You forgot your identity. Now you have to come to terms with that and wonder if you should have regrets. I think the only way for you to know for sure is to look back and see how your life would have been different if you made other choices. Be careful, what you learn might change the way you feel."

Ainsley didn't hesitate before reaching out and taking the ball of wax. "Thank you. I like this because, as you know, I've wondered."

Mama Jamba nodded and hugged Ainsley.

The shapeshifter turned to face Trin, who appeared reluctant about all this. Ainsley smiled at her and then down at Quiet. "You two are going to work things out. I know it, and if you have any questions, well, don't call me. I'll be busy."

"Thanks for all the advice, Ainsley," Trin began, but the elf waved her off.

"Oh, shush you," Ainsley said. "I've left you in the best possible hands, and you're the best possible person for this job."

Kneeling, Ainsley looked directly at Quiet. "You're my best friend, and you know that. So what I want to say to you, I don't have to. Just take care of the rest of them. They surely can't figure out how to do much without us."

Quiet nodded and reached his short arms out, throwing them around Ainsley's shoulders, and held her tightly.

When they separated, Ainsley stood and looked at Sophia, a new tenderness in her eyes.

"None of this would have been possible without you, S. Beaufont," Ainsley began.

"I didn't—"

"You did," she interrupted. "You went into a burning building for me and ran errand after errand and risked everything to set me free. I've never known someone like you. I always hoped I would. I couldn't leave the Gullington unless I knew someone like you was here to protect my family." She looked proudly at Wilder, Evan, Mahkah, and Quiet. "That's what they are. These guys are my family. I get that I'm leaving them and that seems wrong, to leave the ones you love. Only your family understands that sometimes you have to go to find yourself. To find the life you were meant for."

"We understand," Wilder said, taking a spot next to Sophia.

"We want what's best for you," Evan stated, closing the distance.

"Always, Ainsley," Mahkah echoed the sentiment.

She nodded, putting on a brave face. "Well, I better get up to bed. I've got a few centuries worth of stuff to pack."

"Goodnight," they said together as the former housekeeper strode up the grand staircase, brushing by Hiker Wallace, who stood like a statue. He appeared unable to say a word. His eyes didn't leave the stone floor, and he didn't rush after the woman he had once loved and who had lost everything to save him.

CHAPTER ONE HUNDRED
FORTY-FIVE

S ophia didn't know why, but she awoke with a start before the sun
was up. She felt something tugging at her.

The night before, even after the exhaustion of the battle, she'd had
trouble falling asleep, her heart aching that Hiker had just let Ainsley
slip away without a proper goodbye.

Those weren't her troubles, she told herself. Those weren't her
problems. Hiker and Ainsley had to deal with this on their own. The
elf was getting a second chance, and Hiker was proving himself to be
the leader the Dragon Elite had followed for so long, and the world
was ready to believe in once more. Maybe it was better for them to go
their separate ways silently. It hurt Sophia to watch Hiker not say
goodbye. For Ainsley to rush by him, not even glancing at his face.

She pushed her covers off her legs and tiptoed to the dresser,
where she usually had a cup of water. It wasn't there.

Glancing around, and feeling exceptionally thirsty, Sophia
searched her room for water. There was none.

"May I have some water, Castle?" she asked.

Usually, there was a response. A pitcher of water and a glass. Not
this time.

Sighing, Sophia trudged to the door, finding the candlelight in the hallway a bit bright as she walked toward the kitchen to fetch something to drink.

Sophia didn't make it all the way to the stairs before she heard the shuffle of feet and paused. She hid behind a pillar that hadn't been there before but provided the perfect place to spy on the two people in the entryway.

CHAPTER ONE HUNDRED
FORTY-SIX

Ainsley was standing with a single suitcase in her hands, looking down at the floor in front of Hiker Wallace. The dress box was in his hands, looking small, although it was quite large.

"You know I couldn't let you leave without saying goodbye," the Viking began, his voice quiet and full of hesitation.

Sophia didn't so much as breathe as she watched the two, feeling bad about spying on their intimate moment, but needing this. She was praying they let their walls come down.

"We have quite the history, don't we, Mr. Wallace?"

Hiker actually smiled. "You used to call me that. I remember."

"Only when I was cross with you." Ainsley was looking everywhere but at the man before her.

"Are you cross with me now?" Hiker asked.

She shook her head. "I understand. You did what you thought was right back then, putting the Dragon Elite first. I did what I thought was right. Now, we are here, and there is much history behind us."

He nodded. "I can't change it."

Ainsley laughed. "No, apparently, the only one who can change history is a little blonde everyone underestimates and who will surely be the one to save this bloody planet time and time again."

454

Hiker chuckled with her. "You're right about that."

"You know," Ainsley began. "I respect that you made Soph your second in command. That's not something the Hiker Wallace I used to know would have done."

"I'm a man who can change," he said with confidence, also not looking at her. "I hope to prove that."

"To whom?" she asked, and there was a challenge in the question.

"To anyone interested," he answered.

"Oh," she said. There was a fair amount of disappointment in her voice.

Sophia pressed in tightly to the pillar, suddenly not thirsty. She realized the Castle had woken her and made her come out to see this. She squeezed her eyes shut, wishing there was a happy ending for these two.

"I'm sorry that all these years, I've ruined your life," Ainsley said, a joke in her voice, ending the long silence between the two.

Hiker laughed. "It's fine. I think I did a fair bit of under-appreciating you."

"It couldn't have been easy, leading a group who were irrelevant—the Dragon Elite, unseen by mortals."

He nodded. "It wasn't. But you watched me go through it, and you stood by."

"I couldn't really leave," Ainsley argued and then quickly added. "I don't think I would have even if I could."

Hiker brought his chin up and looked at her directly. "I want the best for you, for what it's worth."

"Same to you," Ainsley said, returning his gesture and staring into Hiker's eyes.

They were lost for a moment. Sophia saw it. She wanted to look away. To give them privacy, but she couldn't because she needed this. She needed them to say their peace, so she would know that two people she loved were okay, even if they weren't together.

"I had this made for you." Hiker held the dress box out, and Ainsley dropped the suitcase like she had been waiting for him to hand it over.

A table materialized beside them from the Castle, and neither of them seemed surprised by it.

Hiker laid the box down, and Ainsley lifted the lid off. She stared at the blue dress made from the finest silk in the world.

"It will protect you," he said when her mouth hung open in awe.

"I had it made by Jeremy Bearimy," he went on. "I hope it's elegant enough for your taste."

"It's very nice." Ainsley ran her hand over the fabric. "Thank you."

"I'm glad you like it," Hiker said softly. "I've appreciated your service all these years and—"

"Service," she interrupted, lifting her chin.

"I only mean—" he said in a rush.

"I get what you mean," she said tersely, putting the lid back on the box and tucking it under one arm as she picked up her suitcase. "I better be off. The guys and Soph will be up soon, and I promised they wouldn't have to look at my face again. No goodbyes."

"Ains…you know it's not like that," Hiker said with a raw pain in his voice.

The shapeshifter strode for the door, nodding like she was giving herself a pep talk as she walked out of the Castle. "I know what it's like, Hiker. I'm ready to move on."

At the door to the Castle, Ainsley spun around, looking up fondly at the rafters and the walls and furnishings, tears in her eyes. "Regardless of how it all happened or why, I'm grateful for my years here."

Hiker opened his mouth, seeming to try and speak several times but incapable. Finally, he said, "If you ever want to come back and ruin my life, I would welcome it."

Ainsley seemed grateful for his silly line, laughing suddenly. "I don't think I can go back to being a housekeeper."

He shook his head. "You wouldn't have to be. If you ever want to return, you could be something else. Something more."

"For the Dragon Elite?" she asked, a curious note to her voice.

"No," he declared, a new strength in his voice. "Something you used to be. Someone you used to be to me."

She clenched her lips, holding back emotions. "I have to see what the world out there looks like. It's been out of my grasp for so long."

"You deserve it," he said, his chin held high and with a strength that made Sophia proud in his eyes. "If you ever find yourself missing the Gullington, please know that our doors are always open to you. My door especially."

Ainsley nodded before turning and opening the door to the Castle and walking out into the dawning morning, away from the place she'd called home for so long and was leaving behind.

CHAPTER ONE HUNDRED FORTY-SEVEN

Sophia's heart was simultaneously full and breaking as she made her way back to her room after witnessing Ainsley and Hiker's departure from each other. It felt like two parts of history had been severed before her eyes.

She was grateful the Castle had shown her their goodbye and also remorseful. How could two people who clearly loved each other, let each other go? Ainsley needed to live the life that had been taken from her, and Hiker had the Dragon Elite. She reasoned as she slid into bed, that if things were meant for them, they'd find their way back to each other.

It hurt Sophia's heart, knowing she'd go down to breakfast that morning not to find Ainsley slapping Evan in the back of the head or scolding Wilder for something. She figured it would hurt them too. There was something about that woman that was intrinsically good.

Sophia knew why Hiker had fallen for her. She knew why the Elfin council wanted her back so desperately. She didn't know how the Dragon Elite would move on without her, although Trin was a great replacement in her own way. She'd grow into her role, as they all had to do.

Sophia snuggled into her bed, hoping to catch another hour or two of sleep before she had to awake to another new day full of new adventures. Liv had mentioned something about the new location for the Great Library and finding a librarian. Mama Jamba had promised to track down the demon dragons for them. Then there was the world that believed in the Dragon Elite once more.

There was an ocean of possibilities, and Sophia couldn't wait to wake up to it. She closed her eyes, with a smile on her lips, grateful that for a little while, her planet was safe once more.

SARAH'S AUTHOR NOTES

AUGUST 23, 2020

Thank you so much for reading. Your support of the Liv Beaufont series and this one has been life changing. Thank you! Seriously! Thank you.

Have I mentioned lately that at LMBPN, we have the absolute best readers in the world! It needs repeating. Seriously, it blows me away how supportive you all are. Many of the readers through the various Facebook groups have become my friends. Many have given me great ideas. There are a small, very select few, who do not know boundaries...and sort of creep me out. But that's none of you reading this.

Anyway, more about the awesome, most of you, who I love dearly and keep me writing and a roof over Lydia and my heads. Paul, I'm looking at you right now and all the wonderful ideas you give me. He's going to be the Great Librarian in the next book. What will the sisters have to do to convince him? We shall see...

More about awesome readers: Jurgen, my right hand guy and the guy who this book is dedicated to, asked to become Jeremy Bearimy's bumbling assistant. I offered to make him a wise mage or sage or whatever. He chose bumbling assistant to a tarantula. Who am I to say no?

Some of you who have watched the Good Place will have recognized the name I gave to the seamstress. I love weaving in fun details like that from things I enjoy for you all to find. And I love the idea from the show about how the timeline in the afterlife goes. It's Jeremy Bearimy. That tarantula, by the way, was inspired by a friend I made when out on a nightly walk. He was really friendly and kept following me around. When I posted a video on Instagram of it, someone informed me that he was a mature male tarantula who was looking for a girlfriend. He didn't find one in me that night. And how someone was able to sex a spider and know his dating preferences from a video astounds me…

Bep's Rose Apothecary is a nod to Schitt's Creek. If you haven't watched the show, stop reading this and do so. No, don't stop, actually. Keep reading. Oh, and I had to include the Tom Haverford lines from Parks and Recreation. Leslie Knope is my spirit animal.

One of my favorite parts of writing this book was revisiting the Precious Galaxy series and specifically Ricky Bobby. I woke up the morning I was to write that chapter and was looking for a cool sci-fi location for Sophia to get the tech to defeat the magitech army. Then I was like, why invent something new? I should have Sophia go to RB, the ship I inherited from MA.

And it was so much fun. I was in a different place when I wrote that series. But getting back the voice of those characters was easy. I missed Hatch, Pip, Lewis, Bailey and Ricky Bobby. And I can partially thank Paul for that idea too. He reminded me of that series and all the special qualities of those characters. Thank you!

I'll be in Scotland when this book releases. I hope you all enjoy. I treasure your support and reviews. My job is to entertain you and bring laughter and love to your life. Oh, and I want your tears! And I think after that Ainsley and Hiker scene where he invites her to "come back and ruin his life any day," I've got them! What will happen to that pair? You'll have to come back for the next book to find out!

Much love and peace,
Tiny Ninja

MICHAEL'S AUTHOR NOTES
AUGUST 24, 2020

Before I harass Tiny Ninja™ let me thank you for reading both this book and this whole series! Without fantastic readers like you, I wouldn't get the chance to meet authors like Sarah Noffke, much less harass her.

So, let's get to the fun, shall we?

So TN™ was all 'stop right now and go watch this TV show!' and I'm reading her notes and thinking, *But what about my author notes, Noffke?* I mean, by the time you wrote that comment you had already provided a fair amount of information and engagement in your author notes.

But my author notes aren't even starting on the same page and no where would they get to chat with me! Plus, who wants to go watch TV when there is another book available somewhere? There is author note blocking and then there are proactive efforts to get the fans to ignore the second name on the billing. Huh, backstabbie much Tiny Ninja™?*

Sarah is in no way even <u>remotely</u> like this, but WOW is it fun to ask her this, knowing she is going to respond like WHAT?! and laugh. Maybe it's just me laughing. But at least SOMEONE is laughing.

And don't EVEN get me started with 'why are you in Scotland, Ms. Noffke?' Ahhh, young(er) love, it's so *adorkable*.

If you happen to be in Scotland and notice a young American author the height of a leprechaun walking around with a yellow head of hair, that would be Tiny Ninja™.

(I've probably provided Stephen Campbell (VP of Ops who often puts the books together) a reason to say 'Oh no you didn't, Anderle!' in these notes already.

To which I say, 'Yes I did – and it's so cute you said it that way.')

By the way, I just let Sarah know in one of our SLACK conversations that I was writing a 'fun' set of author notes. I wonder if she will spend two seconds in Scotland thinking about this at all.

Hmmm....

Plus, she needs to deal with author Ramy Vance and his shenanigans before she comes back after me. Because, *priorities*.

I hope you have a fantastic week ahead of you, wherever you are!

Michael Anderle

ACKNOWLEDGMENTS
SARAH NOFFKE

I feel like I'm on the stage at the Oscars, accepting an award when I write my acknowledgments. I stand there, holding this award, my hands shaking and my words racing around in my mind. I'm not an actress for a reason. I'm a writer and talking to people in "real life" is hard. Not to mention a ton of people all at once.

I picture looking out at the audience and being blinded by spotlights and forgetting every word of the speech I memorized just in case I won. The speech would go like this and it's meant for all of you, not the guild. For the fans. The supporters. The people who are the reason I would ever stand on any stage, ever.

Okay, here we go. I clear my throat and smile, looking up at the camera, holding the little golden man. And then I begin:

This was never supposed to happen. I was never meant to publish a book and then another one. And then another. I was supposed to write in private and live a life that Henry David Thoreau called a life of "quiet desperation." I would always hope to share my books, but never bring myself to do it. And you would never read my words. But then, in a crazed moment of brashness, I did share my books and you all liked them. And because of that, I've never been the same. And here I am feeling grateful all just because…

That's why I'm here. Because of you. Thank you to my first readers. The ones who picked up those books that I didn't even outline and you still liked them. You messaged me and maybe you thought it was no big deal, but when your ego is new to the publishing world, it's a big deal.

I can't thank you readers enough. I've found that reading your reviews helps me to start a chapter when I'm stuck or lazy.

I really need to thank someone who has made this all possible and that's my father. I was going to quit. I can't tell you how many times I quit. But when I wasn't making it, he was the one who told me to not throw in the towel. "Give yourself a timeline," he suggested. If I didn't get to my goal by then, I'd quit. And apparently there was magic in that advice, because I'm still doing this. Dad, you're the pragmatic one, but when you believed in me enough to tell me to not quit, I knew I had to follow your advice.

And I thank all my friends who are constantly supporting me with thoughts of love and encouragement. Most don't read my books. I'm sort of self-deprecating, although I'm working on it and will be the first to tell my friends, "My books probably aren't for you." However, every now and then a friend surprises me and says, "I was up all night reading your books." It's always a total shock. But my point is, that even if they didn't read, I still have the best friends ever. Diane, you're my rock. And I love you, even though you will probably not read this.

Thank you to everyone at LMBPN. Those people are like family to me, although I'm not sure if they'll let me sleep on their couch. Well, who am I kidding? They totally will. Big thanks to Steve, Lynne, Mihaela, Kelly, Jen and the entire team. The JIT members are the best.

Huge thank you to the LMBPN Ladies group on Facebook. Micky, you're the best. And that group keeps me sane.

And a giant thank you to the betas for this series. Juergen you are my first reader and friend. Thanks for all the help. And thanks to Martin and Crystal for being some of the best people I know. What would I do without you? A huge thanks to the ARC team. Seriously, if it weren't for you all I might pass out before release day, wondering if anyone will like the book.

And with all my books, my final thank you goes to my lovely muse, Lydia. Oh sweet darling, I write these books for you, but ironically, I couldn't write them without you. You are my inspiration. My sounding board. And the reason that I want to succeed. I love you.

Thank you all! I'm sorry if I forgot anyone. Blame Michael. For no other reason than just because.

BOOKS BY SARAH NOFFKE

Sarah Noffke writes YA and NA science fiction, fantasy, paranormal and urban fantasy. In addition to being an author, she is a mother, podcaster and professor. Noffke holds a Masters of Management and teaches college business/writing courses. Most of her students have no idea that she toils away her hours crafting fictional characters. www.sarahnoffke.com

Check out other work by Sarah author here.

Ghost Squadron:

Formation #1:

Kill the bad guys. Save the Galaxy. All in a hard day's work.

After ten years of wandering the outer rim of the galaxy, Eddie Teach is a man without a purpose. He was one of the toughest pilots in the Federation, but now he's just a regular guy, getting into bar fights and making a difference wherever he can. It's not the same as flying a ship and saving colonies, but it'll have to do.

That is, until General Lance Reynolds tracks Eddie down and offers him a job. There are bad people out there, plotting terrible things, killing innocent people, and destroying entire colonies. **Someone has to stop them.**

Eddie, along with the genetically-enhanced combat pilot Julianna Fregin and her trusty E.I. named Pip, must recruit a diverse team of specialists, both human and alien. They'll need to master their new Q-Ship, one of the most powerful strike ships ever constructed. And finally, they'll have to stop a faceless enemy so powerful, it threatens to destroy the entire Federation.

All in a day's work, right?

Experience this exciting military sci-fi saga and the latest addition to the expanded Kurtherian Gambit Universe. If you're a fan of Mass Effect, Firefly, or Star Wars, you'll love this riveting new space opera.

NOTE: If cursing is a problem, then this might not be for you.

Check out the entire series here.

The Precious Galaxy Series:

Corruption #1

A new evil lurks in the darkness.

After an explosion, the crew of a battlecruiser mysteriously disappears.

Bailey and Lewis, complete strangers, find themselves suddenly onboard the damaged ship. Lewis hasn't worked a case in years, not since the final one broke his spirit and his bank account. The last thing Bailey remembers is preparing to take down a fugitive on Onyx Station.

Mysteries are harder to solve when there's no evidence left behind.

Bailey and Lewis don't know how they got onboard *Ricky Bobby* or why. However, they quickly learn that whatever was responsible for the explosion and disappearance of the crew is still on the ship.

Monsters are real and what this one can do changes everything.

The new team bands together to discover what happened and how to fight the monster lurking in the bottom of the battlecruiser.

Will they find the missing crew? Or will the monster end them all?

The Soul Stone Mage Series:

House of Enchanted #1:

The Kingdom of Virgo has lived in peace for thousands of years...until now.

The humans from Terran have always been real assholes to the witches of Virgo. Now a silent war is brewing, and the timing couldn't be worse. Princess Azure will soon be crowned queen of the Kingdom of Virgo.

In the Dark Forest a powerful potion-maker has been murdered.

Charmsgood was the only wizard who could stop a deadly virus plaguing Virgo. He also knew about the devastation the people from Terran had done to the forest.

Azure must protect her people. Mend the Dark Forest. Create alliances with savage beasts. No biggie, right?

But on coronation day everything changes. Princess Azure isn't who she thought she was and that's a big freaking problem.

Welcome to The Revelations of Oriceran. Check out the entire series here.

The Lucidites Series:

Awoken, #1:

Around the world humans are hallucinating after sleepless nights.

In a sterile, underground institute the forecasters keep reporting the same events.

And in the backwoods of Texas, a sixteen-year-old girl is about to be caught up in a fierce, ethereal battle.

Meet Roya Stark. She drowns every night in her dreams, spends her hours reading classic literature to avoid her family's ridicule, and is prone to premonitions—which are becoming more frequent. And now her dreams are filled with strangers offering to reveal what she has always wanted to know: Who is she? That's the question that haunts her, and she's about to find out. But will Roya live to regret learning the truth?

Stunned, #2
Revived, #3

The Reverians Series:

Defects, #1:

In the happy, clean community of Austin Valley, everything appears to be perfect. Seventeen-year-old Em Fuller, however, fears something is askew. Em is one of the new generation of Dream Travelers. For some reason, the gods have not seen fit to gift all of them with their expected special abilities. Em is a Defect—one of the unfortunate Dream Travelers not gifted with a psychic power. Desperate to do whatever it takes to earn her gift, she endures painful daily injections along with commands from her overbearing, loveless father. One of the few bright spots in her life is the return of a friend she had thought dead—but with his return comes the knowledge of a shocking, unforgivable truth. The society Em thought was protecting her has actually been betraying her, but she has no idea how to break away from its authority without hurting everyone she loves.

Rebels, #2
Warriors, #3

Vagabond Circus Series:

Suspended, #1:

When a stranger joins the cast of Vagabond Circus—a circus that is run by Dream Travelers and features real magic—mysterious events start happening. The once orderly grounds of the circus become riddled with hidden threats. And the ringmaster realizes not only are his circus and its magic at risk, but also his very life.

Vagabond Circus caters to the skeptics. Without skeptics, it would close its doors. This is because Vagabond Circus runs for two reasons and only two reasons: first and foremost to provide the lost and lonely Dream Travelers a place to be illustrious. And secondly, to show the nonbelievers that there's still magic in the world. If they believe, then they care, and if they care, then they don't destroy. They stop the small abuse that day-by-day breaks down humanity's spirit. If Vagabond Circus makes one skeptic believe in magic, then they halt the cycle, just a little bit. They allow a little more love into this world. That's Dr. Dave Raydon's mission. And that's why this ringmaster recruits. That's why he directs. That's why he puts on a show that makes people question their beliefs. He wants the world to believe in magic once again.

Paralyzed, #2
Released, #3

Ren Series:

Ren: The Man Behind the Monster, #1:
Born with the power to control minds, hypnotize others, and read thoughts, Ren Lewis, is certain of one thing: God made a mistake. No one should be born with so much power. A monster awoke in him the same year he received his gifts. At ten years old. A prepubescent boy with the ability to control others might merely abuse his powers, but Ren allowed it to corrupt him. And since he can have and do anything he wants, Ren should be happy. However, his journey teaches him that harboring so much power doesn't bring happiness, it steals it. Once this realization sets in, Ren makes up his mind to do the one thing that can bring his tortured soul some peace. He must kill the monster.

Note This book is NA and has strong language, violence and sexual references.
Ren: God's Little Monster, #2
Ren: The Monster Inside the Monster, #3
Ren: The Monster's Adventure, #3.5
Ren: The Monster's Death

Olento Research Series:

Alpha Wolf, #1:
Twelve men went missing.

Six months later they awake from drug-induced stupors to find themselves locked in a lab.

And on the night of a new moon, eleven of those men, possessed by new—and inhuman—powers, break out of their prison and race through the streets of Los Angeles until they disappear one by one into the night.

Olento Research wants its experiments back. Its CEO, Mika Lenna, will tear every city apart until he has his werewolves imprisoned once again. He didn't undertake a huge risk just to lose his would-be assassins.

However, the Lucidite Institute's main mission is to save the world from injustices. Now, it's Adelaide's job to find these mutated men and protect them and society, and fast. Already around the nation, wolflike men are being spotted. Attacks on innocent women are happening. And then, Adelaide realizes what her next step must be: She has to find the alpha wolf first. Only once she's located him can she stop whoever is behind this experiment to create wild beasts out of human beings.

Lone Wolf, #2
Rabid Wolf, #3
Bad Wolf, #4

BOOKS BY MICHAEL ANDERLE

For a complete list of books by Michael Anderle, please visit:

www.lmbpn.com/ma-books/

CONNECT WITH THE AUTHORS

Connect with Sarah and sign up for her email list here:

http://www.sarahnoffke.com/connect/

You can catch her podcast, LA Chicks, here:

http://lachicks.libsyn.com/

Connect with Michael Anderle and sign up for his email list here:

Website:
http://www.lmbpn.com
Email List:
http://lmbpn.com/email/
Facebook
https://www.facebook.com/LMBPNPublishing

www.ingramcontent.com/pod-product-compliance
Lightning Source LLC
Chambersburg PA
CBHW020228110726
47898CB00004B/1192